ONE GOOD MAN

The Kiss

They had to get it out of the way or today was going to be a bust, which was why Kell had put it out there. Thinking about Jamie's hypnosis to come had got lost in thinking about her mouth. But she was wrong.

Her mouth was not made for eating. It was made for the way she'd used it last night and he was surer than he was about never wanting to eat alligator that she could use it for even more. Those things, all intimately imagined, were giving his body hell.

"I don't think I've ever had anyone tell me that I taste good," she finally replied and, as he glanced over, he saw her face colour with the implications of what she'd just said. "Though I'm sure it had something to do with the JB."

THE MIGHTY QUINNS: TEAGUE

BY
KATE HOFFMANN

Kate Hoffmann has been writing for fifteen years and has published nearly sixty books. When she isn't writing, she is involved in various musical and theatrical activities in her small Wisconsin community. She enjoys sleeping late, drinking coffee and eating bonbons. She lives with her two cats, Tally and Chloe, and her computer, which shall remain nameless.

To Dr Greg B, DVM, for his insights
on equine veterinary medicine.
And for taking such good care of
Chloe and Tally!

Prologue

Queensland, Australia—August 1996

TEAGUE QUINN STRETCHED his arms over his head and closed his eyes against the sun, the warm rays heating the big rock beneath him. The wind rustled in the dry brush. The sounds of the outback were so familiar they were almost like music to him.

He'd managed to escape the house before anyone noticed he was gone, saddling his horse and riding out in a cloud of dust, the shoe box tucked under his arm. When he wasn't working the stock with his father and brothers, he was tending to some other job his mother had conjured out of thin air. He wondered what it might be like to live a normal life, in a grand house in Brisbane, where daily chores didn't exist.

There'd be girls and parties and school and sports—all the things fourteen-year-old boys were supposed to enjoy. Teague sighed. Most boys his age didn't like school, but real classrooms with real teachers, chemistry and biology and physics and math, these were things he'd never experienced.

Instead, Teague was stuck on a cattle station in Queensland, with his parents, his two brothers and a rowdy bunch of jackaroos. Classes took place at the kitchen table, him and his brothers gathered around the radio listening to School of the Air. The closest town, Bilbarra, had a library and a small school, but that was a two-hour drive, much too far to make it practical day to day. Some of the kids on the more profitable stations were sent away to boarding school, but Kerry Creek wasn't exactly swimming in cash. Though the Quinn family wasn't poor, they weren't in the big bickies, either.

Teague heard the sound of hoofbeats and pushed up on his elbows, scanning the approach to the big rock and cursing to himself. Would he ever be able to get away from his brothers, or would they be following him around the rest of his life?

When he didn't see a rider coming from the direction of the homestead, he glanced over his shoulder and watched as a horse galloped full bore from the opposite direction, its rider hunched low in the saddle. Scrambling to his feet, Teague stood on the rock, ready to defend his territory against the interloper.

The boy drew his horse to a stop, the animal breathing heavily. From beneath the brim of a battered stockman's hat, he stared at Teague, a grim expression on his face. He wasn't very big, Teague mused, sizing up his chances if it came down to a fistfight.

But then suddenly, the boy smiled. "Did I scare you?" In one smooth motion, he brushed his hat from his head and a tumble of wavy blond hair revealed not a boy, but a girl. His breath caught in his throat as he stared into her pale blue eyes. Teague swallowed hard. She was the most beautiful girl he'd ever seen.

"I scared the piss out of you, didn't I? You should see your face. You're as pale as a ghost."

Teague scowled, embarrassed that she'd noticed his reaction. "Nick off. I wasn't scared. Why would I be scared of a mite like you? You couldn't knock the skin off a rice pudding."

She slid off her horse. "Oh, yeah. Well, you're so stupid, you couldn't tell your arse from a hole in the ground."

Teague opened his mouth, shocked to hear that kind of language from a girl. But then, he really had no experience talking to girls. With no sisters, he wasn't sure how girls were supposed to talk. On the telly, they always seemed to act so proper and prissy. This girl was acting more like his brothers.

She hitched her hands on her waist and stared up at him. "Well, are you going to give me a hand up or are you going to be mingy about the view?"

Teague studied her for a long moment. There wasn't much to fear from her. She was at least a head shorter than him and a few stone lighter. Though, in a verbal sparring match, she'd probably slice him into dinner for the dingoes. He reluctantly held out his hand and pulled her up beside him.

She scrambled to her feet and took a good look around. A frown wrinkled her brow, then she plopped down and sighed deeply.

"You don't like the view?"

She shook her head. "I thought I might be able to see the ocean."

Teague laughed, but when he saw the hurt in her eyes, he realized the depth of her disappointment. "Sorry," he mumbled as he sat down beside her. "You can't see the ocean from anywhere on this station. Even if you get up to the highest point. It's too far away."

She cursed beneath her breath before turning away from him. "I used to live near the ocean. I could see the water every day. I wish I could see it again."

A long silence grew between them. "That must have been nice," he finally ventured.

"It was better than living out here. Everything is so…dusty. And there are flies everywhere."

"Yeah, but you don't get to ride horses in the city," Teague offered, surprised to find himself defending the outback. "Or keep cattle. Or have a lot of dogs. And you don't see lizards and 'roos like you do here."

"You like animals?" she asked, her disappointment forgotten as suddenly as it had appeared.

Teague nodded. "Last month I found a bird with a broken wing. And I healed it." He pointed to the box beside him. "I'm going to let it go today."

"Can I see?" she asked, bending over the box.

Teague picked the box up, said a silent prayer, then lifted the lid. The sparrow immediately took flight and the girl clapped her hands as it flew into the distance. He felt his cheeks warm. "Maybe it healed itself. It's only a sparrow, but I kept it alive until it could fly again. I find hurt animals all the time and I know how to make them well again." He paused. "I like doing that."

A tiny smile tugged at her lips. "All right, there is one good thing about living on Wallaroo."

Teague swallowed hard, wondering if she'd just paid him a compliment. Then her words sank in. "You live on Wallaroo?" He hadn't even considered the possibility. But now that he thought about it, this was the girl his parents had had been talking about. "You're Hayley Fraser, then."

She seemed surprised he knew her name. "Maybe," she replied.

He'd heard the story by way of eavesdropping. Hayley's parents had been killed in an auto wreck when she wàs eight years old. She'd been moved from foster home to foster home, until her grandfather had finally agreed to take her. According to Teague's mum, old man Fraser hadn't been on speaking terms with his only child since Jake Fraser had run away from home at age eighteen. And now, his poor granddaughter was forced to live with a cold, unfeeling man who'd never wanted her on Wallaroo in the first place.

Teague's mum had insisted that Wallaroo was no place for a troubled young girl to grow up, without any women on the station at all, and with only rowdy men to serve as an example. Yet there was nothing anyone could do for her. Except him, Teague mused.

"You ride pretty good," he said. "Who taught you?"

"I taught myself. It doesn't take much skill. You hop on the horse and hang on."

"You know your granddad and my father are ene-mies. They hate each other."

Hayley blinked as she glanced over at him. "No surprise. Harry hates everyone, including me."

"You call him Harry?"

She shrugged. "That's his name."

Teague felt an odd lurch in his stomach as his eyes met hers. She had the longest eyelashes he'd ever seen. His gaze drifted down to her mouth and suddenly, he found himself wondering what it might be like to kiss such a bold and brave girl.

"It's because of that land right over there," Teague said, pointing toward the horizon. "It belongs to Kerry Creek, but Har—your grandfather thinks it belongs to him. Every few years old man Fraser goes to court and tries to take it back, but he always loses."

"Why does he keep trying?"

"He says that my great-grandfather gave it to his father. It's part of the Quinn homestead, so I don't know why any Quinn would ever give it away. I think your grandfather might be a bit batty."

Hayley turned and looked in the direction that he was pointing, apparently unfazed by his opinion of her grandfather. "Who'd care about that land? There's nothing on it."

"Water," he said, leaning closer and drawing a deep breath. She even smelled good, he mused. He reached up and touched her hair, curious to see if it was as soft as it looked, but Hayley jumped, turning to him with a suspicious expression.

"What are you doing?"

"Nothing!" Teague said. "You had a bug in your hair. I picked it out."

She sighed softly. "I better get home. He'll wonder where I am. I have to get supper ready."

Teague slid off the rock, dropping lightly to his feet. Then he held his hands up and Hayley nimbly jumped down. His hands rested on her waist as Teague took in the details of her face, trying to memorize them all before she disappeared.

Hayley quickly stepped away from him, as if shocked by his touch. "Maybe I'll see you again," she murmured, looking uneasy.

"Maybe. I'm here a lot. I guess if you came out tomorrow night after supper, you might see me."

"Maybe I would." She glanced up at him through thick lashes and smiled hesitantly. Then she gave him a little wave and ran to her horse. Teague held his breath as she hitched her foot in the stirrup and swung her leg over the saddle. "So what's your name?" she asked as she wove the reins through her fingers.

"Teague," he said. "Teague Quinn."

She set her hat on her head, pushing it down low over her eyes. "Nice to meet you, Teague Quinn." With that, Hayley wheeled the horse around and a moment later, she was riding back in the direction from which she'd come.

"Shit," he muttered. Now he knew exactly what his mother had been talking about when she'd insisted that someday he'd meet a girl who would knock him off his feet.

"Hayley Fraser." He liked saying her name. It sounded new and exciting. Someday, he was going to marry that girl.

1

THE DUST FROM the dirt road billowed out behind Teague's Range Rover. He glanced at the speedometer, then decided the suspension could take a bit more abuse. Adding pressure to the accelerator, he fixed his gaze down the rutted road.

He'd finished his rounds and had just landed on the Kerry Creek airstrip when the phone call had come in. Doc Daley was in the midst of a tricky C-section on Lanie Pittman's bulldog at the Bilbarra surgery, and needed him to cover the call. It was only after Teague asked for details that he realized his services might not be welcomed. The request had come from Wallaroo Station.

The Frasers and the Quinns had been at it for as long as he could remember, their feud igniting over a piece of disputed land—land that contained the best water bore on either station.

In the outback, water was as good as gold and it was worth fighting for. Cattle and horses couldn't survive without it, and without cattle or horses the family station wasn't worth a zack. Teague wasn't sure how or why the land was in dispute after all these years, only that the fight never seemed to end. His grandfather had fought the Frasers, as had his father, and now, his older brother, Callum.

But all that would have to be forgotten now that he was venturing into enemy territory. He had come to help an animal in distress. And if old man Fraser refused his help, well, he'd give it anyway.

As Teague navigated the rough road, his thoughts spun back nearly ten years, to the last time he'd visited Wallaroo. He felt a stab of regret at the memory, a vivid image of Hayley Fraser burned into his brain.

It had been the most difficult day of his life. He'd been heading off into a brand-new world—university in Perth, hundreds of miles from the girl he loved. She'd promised to join him the moment she turned eighteen. They'd both get part-time jobs and they'd attend school together. He hadn't known that it was the last time he'd ever see her.

For weeks afterward, his letters had gone unanswered. Every time he rang her, he ended up in an argument with her grandfather, who refused to call her to the phone. And when he finally returned during his term break, Hayley was gone.

Even now, his memories of her always spun back to the girl she'd been at seventeen and not the woman she'd become. That woman on the telly wasn't really Hayley, at least not the Hayley he knew.

The runaway teenager with the honey-blond hair and the pale blue eyes had ended up in Sydney. According to the press, she'd been "discovered" working at a

T-shirt shop near Bondi Beach. A month later, she'd debuted as a scheming teenage vixen on one of Australia's newest nighttime soap operas. And seven years later, she was the star of one of the most popular programs on Aussie television.

He'd thought about calling her plenty of times when he'd visited Sydney. He'd been curious, wondering if there would be any attraction left between them. Probably not, considering she'd dated some of Australia's most famous bachelors—two or three footballers, a pro tennis player, a couple of rock stars and more actors than he cared to count. No, she probably hadn't thought of Teague in years.

As he approached the homestead, Teague was stunned at the condition of the house. Harry Fraser used to take great pride in the station, but it was clear that his attitude had changed. Teague watched as a stooped figure rose from a chair on the ramshackle porch, dressed in a stained work shirt and dirty jeans. The old man's thick white hair stood on end. Teague's breath caught as he noticed the rifle in Harry's hand.

"Shit," he muttered, pulling the Range Rover to a stop. Drawing a deep breath, he opened the window. His reflexes were good and the SUV was fast, but Harry Fraser had been a crack shot in his day. "Put the gun down, Mr. Fraser."

Harry squinted. "Who is that? State your name or get off my property."

"I'm the vet you sent for," Teague said, slowly realizing that Harry couldn't make him out. His eyesight was clearly failing and they hadn't spoken in so many years there was no way Harry would recognize his voice. "Doc Daley sent me. He's in the middle of a surgery and couldn't get away. I'm…new."

Harry lowered the rifle, then shuffled back to his chair. "She's in the stable," he said, pointing feebly in the direction of one of the crumbling sheds. "It's colic. There isn't much to do, I reckon." He waved the gun at him. "I'm not payin' you if the horse dies. Got that?"

They'd discuss the fee later, after Harry had been disarmed and Teague had a chance to examine the patient. He steered the Range Rover toward the smallest of the old sheds, remembering that it used to serve as the stables on Wallaroo. Besides that old shack on the border between Wallaroo and Kerry Creek, the stables had been one of their favorite meeting places, a spot where he and Hayley had spent many clandestine hours exploring the wonders of each other's bodies.

Teague pulled the truck to a stop at the wide shed door, then grabbed his bag and hopped out. The shed was in worse condition than the house. "Hullo!" he shouted, wondering if there were any station hands about.

To his surprise, a female voice replied. "Back here. Last stall."

He strode through the empty stable, each stall filled with moldering straw. A rat scurried in front of him and he stopped and watched as it wriggled through a hole in the wall. While the rodent startled him, it was nothing compared to the shock he felt when he stepped inside the stall.

Hayley Fraser knelt beside a horse lying on a fresh bed of straw. She was dressed in a flannel shirt and jeans, the toes of her boots peaking out beneath the ragged hems of her pant legs. They stared at each other for a long time, neither one of them able to speak. It wasn't supposed to be like this, Teague thought, his mind racing. He'd always imagined they'd meet on a busy street or in a restaurant.

Suddenly, as if a switch had been flipped, she blinked and pointed to the horse. "It's Molly," she said, her voice wavering. "I'm pretty sure she has colic. I don't know what else to do. I can't get her up."

Teague stepped past Hayley and bent down next to the animal. The mare was covered with sweat and her nostrils were flared. He stepped aside as the horse rolled, a sign that Hayley's diagnosis was probably right. Teague stood and reached into the feed bin, grabbing a handful of grain and sniffing it. "Moldy," he said, turning to Hayley.

"I got here last night," she explained, peering into the grain bin. "When I came in this morning she was like this."

"She might have an impaction. How long has she been down?"

"I don't know," Hayley said. "I found her like this at ten this morning."

Teague drew a deep breath. Colic in horses was tricky to treat. It could either be cured in a matter of hours or it could kill the horse. "We need to get her up. I'll give her some pain medication, then we'll dose her with mineral oil and see if that helps."

"What if it doesn't?" Hayley asked. "What about surgery?"

Teague shook his head. "I can't do surgery here. And the nearest equine surgical facility is at the university in Brisbane."

"I don't care what it costs," she said, a desperate edge to her voice. "I don't care if I need to charter a jet to fly her there. I'll do whatever it takes."

He chuckled softly at the notion of putting the horse on a jet. "We'll cross that fence when we come to it," Teague murmured. "Help me get her up."

It took them a full ten minutes of tugging and prodding and slapping and shouting before Molly struggled to her feet, her eyes wild and her flanks trembling. The moment she got up, she made another move to go down and Teague shouted to distract her, slapping her on the chest and pushing her out of the stall.

He handed the lead to Hayley. "Keep her walking, don't let her go down again. I've got to fetch some supplies."

Teague ran toward the stable door, then glanced over his shoulder to see Hayley struggling with the mare. Thank God they had this to focus on, he mused. It was difficult enough seeing her again without demanding answers to his questions and explanations for her behavior.

He opened up the tailgate on the Range Rover and searched through the plastic bins until he found a bag of IV fluid, which he shoved in his jacket pocket. He took a vial of Banamine from the case of medication. Then he grabbed the rest of the supplies he needed—a hypodermic, IV tubing, a nasogastric tube and a jug of mineral oil—and put everything into a wooden crate.

When he got back to the stable, he saw Hayley kneeling on the dirty concrete floor with Molly lying beside her.

She looked up, tears streaming down her cheeks. "I couldn't stop her. She just went down."

Teague set the crate on a nearby bale of straw, then gently helped Hayley to her feet. In all the years he'd known her, he'd never seen Hayley cry. Not a single tear, not even when she'd fallen from her horse or scraped her knee. He'd never thought much about it until now, but it must have taken a great deal of strength to control her emotions for so long.

"Don't worry," he said, giving her hands a reassuring squeeze. "We'll get her up."

Then he brushed the pale hair from her eyes, his thumbs damp from her tears. It had been so long since he'd touched her, so many years since he'd looked into those eyes. But it seemed like only yesterday. All the old feelings were bubbling up inside him. His instinct to protect her had kicked in the moment he looked into her eyes and he found himself more worried about Hayley than the horse.

Teague didn't bother to think about the consequences before kissing her. It was the right thing to do, a way to soothe her fears and stop her tears. He bent closer and touched his lips to hers, gently exploring with his tongue until she opened beneath the assault.

Cupping her face in his hands, he molded her mouth to his, stunned by the flood of desire racing through him. They were teenagers again, the two of them caught up in a heady mix of hormones they couldn't control and emotions they didn't understand.

He drew back and smiled. "Better?" Hayley nodded mutely and Teague looked down at the horse. "Then let's get to work."

It was as if the kiss had focused their thoughts and strengthened their bond. Though he wanted to kiss her again, he had professional duties to dispatch first. And saving Molly was more important than indulging in desire. They managed to get the horse on her feet again and pushed her up against a wall to keep her still as Teague inserted the IV catheter into her neck. Drawing out a measure of the painkiller, he injected it into the IV bag.

"There. She should start feeling a little better. Once she does, we'll dose her with mineral oil. If it's an impaction, that should help."

They walked back and forth, the length of the stable, both of them holding on to Molly's halter. At each turn, he took the time to glance over at her, letting his gaze linger.

Without all the slinky clothes and the fancy makeup and hair, she didn't look anything like a television star. She looked exactly like the fresh-faced girl he used to kiss and touch, the first girl he'd ever had sex with and the last girl he'd ever loved. Teague clenched his free hand into a fist, fighting the urge to pull her into his arms and kiss her again.

"So you got home yesterday," he said.

Hayley nodded, continuing to stare straight ahead. He could read the wariness in her expression. If she was feeling half of what he was, then her heart was probably pounding and her mind spinning with the aftereffects of the kiss they'd shared.

"I've seen you on telly. You've become quite a good actress." This brought a smile, a step in the right direction, Teague thought. "I heard you won some award?"

"A Logie award. And I didn't win. I've been nominated three times. Haven't won yet."

"That's good, though, right? Nominated is good. Better than not being nominated."

"It's a soap opera," she said. "It's not like I'm doing Shakespeare with the Royal Queensland."

"But you could, if you wanted to, right?"

Hayley shook her head. "No, I don't have any formal training. They hired me on *Castle Cove* because I looked like the part. Not because I could act."

He wanted to ask why she had decided to run away from home. And why she hadn't come to him as they'd always planned. Teague drew a deep breath, then stopped. Molly had settled down, her respiration now almost normal. "See, she's feeling better," he said, smoothing his palm over the horse's muzzle. "That's the thing with colic. One minute the horse is close to death and the next she's on the mend. Have you ever twitched a horse?"

Hayley shook her head. "I don't want you to do that. It will hurt her."

"It looks painful, but it isn't if it's done properly. It's going to release endorphins and it will relax Molly so she won't fight the tube."

"All right," she said, nodding. "I trust you."

Three simple words. *I trust you*. But they meant the

world to him. After all that had happened between them, and all that hadn't, maybe things weren't so bad after all.

As they tended to Molly, they barely spoke, Teague calmly giving her instructions when needed. Hayley murmured softly to keep her calm, smoothing her hand along Molly's neck. Once the mineral oil was pumped into the horse's stomach, Teague removed the tube and the twitch and they began to walk her again.

"She is feeling better," Hayley said. "I can see it already." She looked over at him. "Thank you."

Teague saw the tears swimming in her eyes again and he fought the urge to gather her into his arms and hold her. The mere thought of touching her was enough to send a flood of heat pulsing through his veins.

He'd kiss Hayley again, only this time it wouldn't be to soothe her fears, but to make her remember how good it had been between them. And how good it could be again.

HAYLEY STARED OUT at the setting sun, her back resting against the side of the stable. A bale of straw served as a low bench. Teague sat beside her with his long legs crossed in front of him and his stockman's hat pulled low to protect his eyes from the glare.

They'd spent the last hour walking Molly around the stable yard, and to Hayley's great relief, the mare seemed to be recovering quite well. Hayley wanted to throw herself into Teague's arms and kiss him silly with gratitude. But she knew doing that would only unleash feelings that had been buried for a very long time—feelings that could sweep them both into dangerous waters.

She'd already turned into an emotional wreck over Molly. Since she'd returned to Wallaroo, she'd rediscovered her emotional side. It had disappeared after her parents died, when she'd stubbornly refused to surrender to sorrow or pain. But in these familiar surroundings, her past had slowly come back and she'd found herself grieving, for her parents' deaths, for her difficult adolescence and for her fractured relationship with Harry.

There was no telling what might happen if she and Teague revisited their past. With so many unresolved feelings, so many mistakes she'd made, she'd likely cry for days.

Now, it seemed so clear, his leaving. He'd been going off to university, starting his life away from home. But at the time she'd seen it as a betrayal, a desertion. Though she'd known he'd be back, Hayley's insecurities had overwhelmed her without Teague to help hold them in check.

From the moment she'd met Teague, she'd found a home, a family and someone she could trust. She'd come to depend on him. He had been the only person who loved her, the only person who cared that she existed and suddenly he was gone. She'd been angry. And though she'd tried to tell herself she'd be all right on her own, she'd been terrified.

So she'd run, away from the place that held so many memories, away from the boy who might not want to return.

She snuck a glance at him. He'd grown into a handsome man. Working in television, she'd met a lot of good-looking blokes, but none of them possessed Teague's raw masculinity. Teague Quinn was a flesh-and-blood man, seemingly unaware of the powerful effect he had on women.

"She looks almost frisky," Teague commented, nodding toward the horse.

"I don't know how I'll ever be able to thank you," Hayley said.

"Don't worry. I'm glad I could help. I know how much Molly means to you. I remember the day you got her."

"My sixteenth birthday," Hayley said. "My grandfather was never one for birthday celebrations. He'd shove money into my hand and tell me not to spend it on silly things. And then, he gave me Molly and I thought everything had changed."

"You rode her over to Kerry Creek to show me. You looked so happy, I thought you'd burst. You immediately challenged me to a race."

"Which I won, as I remember."

"Which I let you win, since it was your birthday. You were such a wild child. Looking back, I wonder how you managed to survive to adulthood. Remember when you were determined to jump the gate near the shack? You were sure Molly could do it. You even bet me my new saddle against your Christmas money."

"That wasn't my finest hour," Hayley admitted, wincing.

"She stopped dead and threw you right over the gate. It took a full minute for the dust to clear from your fall. And what about that time you decided to try bull riding?"

"Another embarrassing failure," she said with a giggle. "But at least I tried. You didn't."

"You were crazy. But I thought you were the most exciting girl I'd ever seen. You were absolutely fearless." He paused, then reached out and touched her face. "What's going on here, Hayley?"

She turned away, staring out at the horizon. "What do you... I don't know what you mean." Was he talking about the kiss? About the attraction that they still obviously felt for each other?

"Look at this place. It's a bloody mess. He's feeding your horse moldy grain. And she doesn't look like she's been exercised or groomed in weeks. Your grandfather used to take such pride in the place."

"I—I didn't know it was getting this bad," she said, grateful that she wouldn't have to analyze the kiss. "I haven't been home for three years. I thought Benny McKenzie was taking care of everything. I was sending money and they were cashing the checks. But then, I spoke to Daisy Willey last week and she told me Benny's mother had taken sick and Benny had left to tend to her. He's been gone a month. But this couldn't have all happened in a month."

"What about the other stockmen?"

"There are no others. My grandfather ran them all off. He thought they were lazy and not worth their pay. And when there was no one left to care for the stock, he sold it. Molly is the last animal on Wallaroo, besides the rabbits and kangaroos and dingoes." She forced a smile. "I'm going to try to convince him to sell the station. Or maybe lease out the land. His health is bad, he's still smoking and he hasn't been to a doctor since I came to live on the station thirteen years ago."

"You're not going to get him off this station," Teague said.

"I have to try," she said, her voice tinged with resignation. "And if I succeed, I want you to take Molly and find her a good home."

Teague nodded. "But until then, I'll bring some decent feed from Kerry Creek when I stop by tomorrow to check on her."

"You're coming back?" Hayley asked, unable to ignore the rush of excitement that made her heart flutter. She'd see him again. And maybe this time, she wouldn't be weeping uncontrollably.

"Follow-up visit," he said. "It's part of the service."

Joy welled up inside her and Hayley couldn't help but smile. Her arrival on Wallaroo had brought nothing but sorrow. And though she knew it would be best to get her grandfather off the station, she'd thought that selling the land would cut her last connection with the boy she'd once loved.

Now that connection was alive again. He was here with her, touching her and kissing her and making her feel as though they might be able to turn back the clock. "Thank you," she said again.

"You need to exercise her," Teague suggested. "Easy at first. A nice gentle walk. You could always ride out to the shack. That's not too far."

Surprised by the suggestion, Hayley couldn't help but wonder if it was an invitation. The shack had been their secret meeting place when they were teenagers. The place where they'd discovered the pleasures of sex.

"Maybe I'll do that."

"I mean, I don't know how long you're planning to stay, but—"

"I don't know, either," Hayley said. "My plans are… flexible. A week or two, at least."

This seemed to make him happy. He looked at his watch. "I really should go. Don't feed her tonight. Just water. I'll see you tomorrow."

She quickly stood up, wanting him to stay but unable to give him a good reason. "Tomorrow," she repeated. Hayley glanced down, wincing inwardly. There were so many things she needed to say, but now didn't seem like the right time. She looked up to find him staring at her. And then, acting purely on impulse, she pushed up onto her toes and kissed his cheek.

She slowly retreated, embarrassed that she'd shown him a hint of the emotions roiling inside her. But then, an instant later, Teague crushed her to his chest, his mouth coming down on hers in a desperate kiss.

In a heartbeat, her body came alive, her pulse quickening and her senses awash with desire. He was so familiar, and yet this was much more powerful than she'd remembered. Her knees wobbled but he was there to hold her.

They stumbled until she was pressed against the rough siding of the stable. His hands drifted lower, cupping her backside and pulling her hips against his. Hayley felt herself losing touch with reality. How many times had she dreamed of this moment? Over the years, she'd wondered what it might be like if they saw each other again. And now, the time had come and she wanted to remember every single second, every wild sensation.

Hayley clutched his shirt, fighting the urge to tear at the buttons. She wanted nothing more than to shed her clothes and allow him to have his way with her. She knew, just by the effects of his kiss, what he could do to her. It had been so long since she'd felt such unbridled passion. Was Teague the man she'd been waiting for all this time?

His palm slid beneath her shirt and up to her bare breast and she arched closer. Cupping her warm flesh, Teague ran his thumb over her nipple until it grew hard. God, it felt so good to have his hands on her body again. All the years between them seemed to drop away and the world was right again.

Hayley worked at the buttons of his shirt and when she pressed her hand against his chest, she could feel his heart pounding in a furious rhythm. "Make love to me," she pleaded.

Her plea seemed to take him by surprise and he stepped back and stared down into her eyes, as if searching for proof that she'd spoken at all. She saw confusion mixed with his desire. Had she made a mistake? Had she moved too fast?

"Hayley! Where are you, girl?"

The sound of her grandfather's voice shocked her

into reality. She quickly straightened her clothes and brushed her hair from her eyes. "Here," she called.

Teague reached for the buttons of his shirt as she turned to wait for her grandfather in the doorway of the stable. "We're watching Molly," she said with a bright smile. "She's better. See?"

He stepped out into the late-afternoon sun, shading his eyes as he searched the paddock. His eyesight had been failing for years, yet he refused to get glasses. Sometimes his stubbornness was downright silly, she mused. At this moment, though, it was convenient. "Where's that damn vet?"

"I'm here, sir."

Hayley steeled herself for what she knew would be a litany of harsh words between them. A Quinn setting foot on Wallaroo was unthinkable. "Grandfather, I don't think—"

"What's your name, boy?" he demanded.

Teague glanced at Hayley, sending her a questioning look and she frowned. Hayley quickly cleared her throat, stunned that her grandfather hadn't recognized Teague. "His name is Tom," she said. "Tom Barrett."

It was the name of one of the characters on *Castle Cove,* but her grandfather had never seen the program so there wasn't much chance of him recognizing the name.

"Dr. Tom Barrett," Teague said, holding out his hand.

"How much is this going to cost me, Dr. Tom Barrett?" her grandfather asked impatiently, ignoring Teague's hand.

"Don't worry, Harry," Hayley replied. "I'll pay for it. Molly is my horse. My responsibility."

"Suit yourself," the old man muttered. He squinted into the sun, then said something under his breath before turning and walking into the barn. Hayley released a tightly held breath. "He didn't recognize you."

"No," Teague said. "Good thing, since he was waiting on the porch with a rifle when I arrived."

She laughed softly, then shook her head. "I knew his eyesight was bad, but not that bad. For a second there, I thought I'd have to break up a fistfight."

"I think I could have taken him," Teague said. He slipped his arm around her waist, pulling her close. "Meet me tonight," he said. "I'll wait for you at the shack."

"I'm not sure I remember how to get there."

"There'll be a moon." He pointed toward the east paddock. "I'll meet you right there at the far gate. Just like we used to. Nine o'clock. We'll ride over together. Molly needs the exercise."

Never mind what Molly needed, she thought to herself. Hayley needed the touch of Teague's hands and the taste of his mouth, the feel of his body against hers. "What if I can't get away?"

"It's all right," he said. "I've been waiting for almost ten years. Another night isn't going to make much difference." With that, he kissed her again, only this time he lingered over her mouth, softly tempting her with his tongue.

A sigh slipped from her lips and Hayley lost herself in the sweet seduction. Every instinct she had cried out to surrender to him, to be completely and utterly uninhibited with her feelings. "Tonight," Hayley said.

He stole one last kiss, then walked backward into the stable, a wide grin on his face. "I sure am glad to see you again, Hayley Fraser."

At that moment, he looked like the boy she'd loved all those years ago. "Stop smiling at me," she shouted, a familiar demand from their younger years.

"Why shouldn't I smile? I like what I see." He picked up his bag and the crate of supplies and continued his halfhearted retreat.

She rubbed her upper arms, her gaze still fixed on his. When he finally disappeared through the door on the opposite end of the stable, Hayley sighed softly. She'd never expected to feel this way again, like a lovesick teenager existing only for the moments she spent with him.

She knew exactly what would happen between them that night and she had no qualms about giving herself to Teague. Of all the men she'd dated, he was the only one she'd ever really loved. And though time and distance had come between them, they were together now. And she was going to take advantage of every moment they had.

2

"WHAT DO YOU WANT to drink?"

Teague glanced up from the plate that Mary had placed in front of him. "Whatever you've got," he replied distractedly. "Beer is good."

She opened the refrigerator and pulled out a bottle, then twisted off the cap with the corner of her apron. Mary had been keeping house at the station for years, hired a few short weeks after Teague's mother had decided that station life was not for her.

He took a long drink of the cold beer, then picked up his fork and dug in to the meal. Dinnertime at the station was determined by the sun. When it set, everyone ate. But Teague had missed the usual stampede of hungry jackaroos tonight. The return trip from Wallaroo had taken longer than he'd planned after he stopped to fix a broken gate.

"Where is everyone?" he asked.

Mary shrugged. "Brody took some dinner out to Payton earlier. And Callum and Gemma disappeared after they helped me with the dishes. They said they were going for a walk." She sat down at the end of the table and picked up her magazine.

"Well?" Teague said. "Aren't you going to offer your opinion? I've met them both and they seem perfectly lovely."

She peered over the top of her magazine. "They add a bit of excitement to life on the station, I'll give them that. At least for Brody and Cal."

Teague chuckled. "Women will do that."

Women could do a lot of things to an unsuspecting man. Since he'd left Hayley at Wallaroo, his thoughts had been focused intently on what had happened between them. He'd replayed all the very best moments in his head, over and over again. The instant that he'd first touched her. The kiss they'd shared. And then the headlong leap into intimacy. His fingers twitched as he thought about the firm warmth of her breast in his palm. "There's nothing wrong with a little excitement every now and then, is there?"

"What about you?" Mary asked, slowly lowering the magazine. "Have you had any excitement in your life lately?"

Teague glanced up. "Excitement?" He chuckled softly. "Are you asking me if I've cleared the cobwebs in the recent past?" Though Mary had served as a mother figure to the three Quinn brothers, she was a bit of a stickybeak, insisting that she know all the relevant facts regarding their personal lives. "Not lately, but I'll let you know if my fortunes change."

She sighed. "I want to see you boys happy and settled."

"Why?" he teased. "So you can get off this godforsaken station and have a life of your own?" Teague watched her smile fade slightly. Mary had always been such a fixture in their lives that they'd hardly considered she might want something beyond her job at the station.

He took another bite of his beef and potatoes, then grabbed a slice of bread and sopped up some of the gravy. "You know, I think it's about time you had a little holiday. I'm going to talk to Callum about it. You could take a week or two and go visit your sister. Or go on a cruise. You could even rent a bungalow on the ocean. Get away from this lot of larrikins."

She shook her head. "There are too many things to be done on the station this time of year. Besides, we have guests. There's not a chance I'd leave those ladies to your care. Now, eat your dinner before it gets cold. My program is on in a few minutes." She stood up and wiped her hands on her apron, then slipped it over her head and hung it across the back of her chair. "Are you going to watch *Castle Cove* with me tonight?"

Teague shook his head. "No, I thought I'd take a ride. There's a full moon and I need to work off some excess energy." He pushed away from the table, then wiped his mouth on his serviette and tossed it beside his plate.

"You barely ate any of your dinner," Mary commented.

"I'm not hungry. Save it for me. I'll eat later." He pulled his saddlebags from the chair next to him, then crossed to the refrigerator. He'd already put the necessities—matches, bottled water, condoms—in the bags. He added a bottle of wine from the fridge and then tossed in a corkscrew from the drawer next to the sink.

He and Hayley had never shared a drink before, but they were old enough now. Maybe she liked wine.

Mary arched an eyebrow. "Do you plan on doing some entertaining tonight?"

"No."

She studied him for a time, then shook her head. "I heard Hayley's back on Wallaroo. But then, I expect you know that already, don't you?"

Teague shrugged, avoiding her glance. "I do. But how did you know?"

"I talked to Daisy Willey today. She called from the library to tell me my books had come in and she mentioned she'd heard Hayley was on her way home. Daisy's cousin, Benny McKenzie, helps take care of the place for old man Fraser, and Benny had to leave to see to his sick mum. So Daisy told Hayley she might want to check up on her grandfather while Benny is gone. Hayley makes a regular donation to the book fund at the library, so she and Daisy keep in touch."

"News travels fast," Teague said.

"Take care," she warned. "You know how your brothers feel about the Frasers. And with the lawsuit heating up again, you don't want to be stuck in the middle. Why Harry Fraser is starting this all over, I don't know."

Teague suspected he knew. If Harry planned to sell Wallaroo, it would be much more valuable with that land attached. "Hayley doesn't have anything to do with that mess," he said. "The land dispute is between Callum and Harry. Besides, I'm a big boy. I know what I'm doing."

"Like that time you did a backflip off the top rail of the stable fence and broke your wrist? As I remember, that was on a dare from Hayley Fraser."

"I'm older now." *But not much wiser,* Teague thought as he slung his saddlebags over his shoulder. He strode to the door and pushed it open, then stepped onto the porch.

He jogged down the steps and headed toward the stables. It was still early and the moon hadn't come up, but he could find his way to the shack blindfolded. When he stepped inside the stable, he flipped on the overhead lights. A noise caught his attention and he squinted to see Callum and Gemma untangling themselves from an embrace.

Gemma tugged at the gaping front of her shirt and Callum pushed her behind him to allow her some privacy. "What are you doing out here?" Callum asked.

"I'm going for a ride." Teague pulled his saddle and blanket from the rack and hauled it toward the paddock door. "Hey there, Gemma."

"Hello, Teague." She peeked around Callum's shoulder and waved. "Nice night for a ride."

He heard Callum mutter something beneath his breath and when he looked back, he saw his brother and Gemma making a quick exit from the stables.

Since the genealogist from Dublin had arrived, Callum had been besotted. Every free moment he could find away from running the station, he spent staring at Gemma. And Brody had brought home a girl of his own, Payton Harwell, a pretty American he'd met in a jail cell in Bilbarra.

Teague threw his saddle over the top of the gate, then whistled for his horse. A few seconds later, Tapper came trotting over, a sturdy chestnut gelding he'd been riding since he'd returned to the station a year ago. He held the horse's bridle as he led it through the gate and into the stable.

It only took a few minutes to saddle his horse and when he was finished, he strapped his bedroll on the back of his saddle, then slipped his saddlebags beneath the bedroll. Every month that he'd been home on Kerry Creek, he'd taken a ride out to the shack. Occasionally, he'd spend the night, sleeping in the same bed where they'd first made love, remembering their sexual curiosity and experimentation.

At least he and Hayley still had a place where they wouldn't be disturbed, a place that would conjure all the best memories. He pulled his horse around and gave it a gentle kick. It had been a long time since he'd felt this optimistic about a woman. And maybe it was silly to think they could return to the way things had been all those years ago. But he hoped they could start over.

As he rode into the darkness, Teague couldn't help but wonder what the night might bring. Would they discuss their past or would they simply live for the moment and be satisfied with that?

HAYLEY STOOD beside Molly, slowly stroking the horse's neck. She'd been waiting in the dark for ten minutes. And for every second of sheer, unadulterated excitement she felt, there was another of paralyzing doubt. Stay, go, wait, escape. She wanted to see Teague again, yet every shred of common sense told her she was setting herself up for heartbreak.

He'd called her fearless. But deep down, Hayley knew that wasn't true. Her childhood bravado had been a way to hide her fears, to divert attention from everything that terrified her. Though she still felt the urge to challenge him, to dare him to prove his devotion to her, she knew better than to risk bodily injury to get his attention, the way she had as a teenager. The only part of her body in peril this time around was her heart.

Over the years, the crazy memories had faded and she'd been left with just Teague, sweet and protective, loyal to a fault. She'd tried to convince herself that they had shared nothing more than a teenage infatuation. They'd discovered sex together and, naturally, there had been a bond between them. But they would have gone their separate ways sooner or later.

Teague had been there to help her through the difficult times. She'd been so confused and angry when she'd arrived on Wallaroo. Her life had been nothing but chaos since the death of her parents, most of the upheaval caused by her rebellious behavior.

Harry had been her only living relative, since her mother was orphaned at a young age, as well. But Harry had refused to take her, and she'd ended up in a series of foster homes. All of them had been fine places, but she'd wanted to be with her grandfather. She'd been constructing a perfect life for the two of them in her mind and was determined to make it happen.

But when he'd finally given in and allowed her to stay at Wallaroo, Harry had wanted nothing to do with her. He was cold and dismissive, barely able to carry on a conversation with her. It had been Teague who had given her a reason to go on with her life, a reason to accept her circumstances and make a place for herself on her grandfather's station—and in Teague's heart.

That's why his desertion had hurt so badly. For months before he'd left for university, she'd tried to tell herself their feelings were strong enough to survive their time apart. And then, after only a few weeks, he'd forgotten her. No letters, no calls. Every letter she'd written had gone unanswered.

Isolated as she was on Wallaroo, she'd assumed the worst of Teague. In the years that had passed after she'd left the station, she'd often wondered what had really happened. Maybe now she would find out the truth.

Hayley had wanted to go to him back then, to demand answers. She'd packed her meager belongings, said goodbye to Molly and hitchhiked as far as Sydney before she ran out of money. After a month there, she'd decided she didn't need anyone to depend upon—or love. She could fend for herself. And in the end, that's where she'd stayed, starting a new life, a life that didn't include anyone who could possibly hurt her.

The sound of an approaching horse caught her attention and she stepped out from behind Molly and peered into the darkness. She held her breath as he came closer, wondering how long it would be before he kissed her again.

Teague maneuvered his horse up next to her, then held out his hand. It had been forever since they'd ridden together. It had been this way when they'd spent nights at the shack. They'd ride out on the same horse, Hayley's body nestled against his so they could talk and touch on the ride home. A few hours before sunrise, Teague would return her to the gate.

He wove Molly's reins through the leather strap on his bedroll, then settled Hayley in front of him. Wrapping his arm around her waist, he gave his horse a gentle kick and they started off at a slow walk.

For a long time, they didn't speak. Hayley felt her heart slamming in her chest and she found it difficult to breathe with Teague so close. She focused her attention on the spot where his arm rested against her belly, shifting back and forth and creating a delicious friction as the horse swayed.

Even after all the time that had passed, this felt safe and comfortable and right. Hayley sighed softly and leaned against him. He nuzzled her neck and she tipped her head to the side to allow him more freedom. His mouth found a bare spot of skin.

Arching against him, Hayley wrapped her arm around his neck, drawing him closer. She was almost afraid to speak for fear she might break the spell that had fallen over her. There was no need to revisit past mistakes and dredge up old resentments. They were here, together, and that was enough.

Teague pressed his palm to her stomach, his fingers splaying across the soft fabric of her T-shirt. But as they continued their silent ride, he slipped his hand beneath her shirt to caress her breast. Hayley inwardly cursed her decision to put on her sexiest underwear. She wanted to feel the warm imprint of his hand on her flesh like she had that afternoon.

The night was chilly and the moon shone golden as it rose over the outback. She had lived so long in Sydney she'd forgotten how desolate it was on Wallaroo—and how incredibly beautiful.

By the time they reached the shack, the silence between them had become part of their growing desire. She didn't need to speak. There'd be time for words later. Teague slid off the horse, then held out his hands for her. Grasping her waist, he held tight as she dropped to the ground. Her breath caught in her throat as he looked down into her eyes. She couldn't read his expression in the dark, but the moonlight outlined his mouth and she fixed her gaze on it, waiting for him to make the first move.

He drew a slow breath, then reached down and ran his fingers through her hair. His lips met hers in a kiss so soft and sweet that it caused a lump in her throat. He took his time, drawing his tongue along the crease of her mouth, teasing until she allowed him to taste more deeply.

Her body pulsed with desire, a current racing through her bloodstream. She shuddered, anticipation nearly overwhelming her.

"Cold?"

Hayley shook her head.

"Scared?"

"Never," she replied, her voice breathless. It was true. She had nothing to fear from Teague. Whatever happened between them, she could handle it.

He took her hand and tucked it inside his jacket, pressing her palm to his chest. "Nervous," he whispered, a smile curling the corners of his mouth.

"It's been a while," she admitted. "For you, too?"

He nodded. Teague took his horse's reins in his other hand and led Hayley toward the shack. He untied Molly's reins and secured both horses to the hitching rail before grabbing his saddlebags. Then he took her hand and they walked up the steps. Hayley paused on the porch. If this shack looked anything like Wallaroo did, she wasn't sure she wanted to go inside.

"It's all right," he said, opening the door.

Hayley waited as he lit an oil lamp. A wavering light filled the shack and she walked inside. Nothing had changed. It was exactly as it had been ten years before. She'd expected cobwebs and dust, but the interior was surprisingly tidy.

"I come out here every now and then and do a bit of housekeeping," Teague said. He set his saddlebags on the small table in the center of the room. "I guess maybe I was hoping I'd find you here one day." He pulled her into his arms. "And here you are."

Teague pushed the door and it swung shut. He slowly drew her jacket down over her arms then tossed it aside. He shrugged out of his own jacket, letting it drop to the rough plank floor behind him.

When he paused, Hayley reached out and began to

unbutton his shirt. She wouldn't be satisfied until they both were naked and lying next to each other in the narrow bed against the wall. As soon as he saw what she wanted, Teague grabbed the hem of his shirt and yanked it over his head.

Hayley's breath froze as she looked at his body in the soft light from the oil lamp. This was no boy. He was Teague, but a different Teague—tall, broad shouldered and finely muscled. Where he'd once had a dusting of hair on his chest, there was now a soft trail from his collarbone to the waistband of his jeans.

Her hand trembled as she smoothed her fingers over his torso. He reached for her T-shirt and pulled it over her head. His gaze immediately dropped to her breasts and he smiled, running his finger beneath the lacy edge of her bra. "Pretty," he said. "I now have hair on my chest and you have expensive underwear."

"I guess we really have grown up," Hayley teased.

Slowly, they continued to undress each other, tossing aside items of clothing one by one. When he was left in his boxers and she in her panties and bra, they stopped. Years ago, she'd always been a bit apprehensive about getting completely naked. It was the only thing that made her feel vulnerable.

But Hayley wasn't a girl anymore. And she wanted to show Teague she was ready to make love to him as a woman, completely free and uninhibited. She reached back and unhooked her bra, then let it slide down her arms. Catching her thumbs in the lacy waistband of her panties, she pulled them down over her hips. Then, without hesitating, she reached over and skimmed his boxers down, his erection springing upright as the waist-band passed over his groin.

Hayley straightened and let her eyes drift over his body, taking in all the details. Teague had been a lanky young man, but now he was a fully formed male, with a body that would make any woman weak in the knees.

"God, you are beautiful," he murmured, reaching out to run his hand over her shoulder. "But then, you always were."

"We've both changed," she said.

"One thing hasn't changed," Teague countered. "I still want you as much as I did the first time we made love."

"And I want you," she said.

Teague pulled her against him, soft flesh meeting hard muscle. He was so much taller now, and stronger, and she was surprised by how fiercely he took control. But this was still Teague, still sweet and gentle as he laid her on the bed, then stretched out beside her.

How many times had she fantasized about this? And it had always been the same, the two of them, here in this place, lying naked in each other's arms. Now that her fantasy had come true, she didn't want it to end. Was it possible for the scene to play out again and again, not in her head, but in a brand-new reality?

THE SENSATION OF Hayley's skin meeting his set Teague's desire ablaze. Though he'd often thought back to their times together, he hadn't remembered feeling this incredible. Her skin was silk, her scent like an exotic aphrodisiac. And her body was made to be slowly explored.

Making love with her now would be different from when they were teenagers. They'd both had other partners, and experience was always the best teacher. He stretched out above her, bracing his weight on his hands as he kissed her. But he was like a man parched with thirst. There had been no other women for him, not like Hayley. Desire had been fleeting, something easily satisfied by a one-night stand. But this was much more. As their mouths met again and again, teasing, tasting, he challenged her to surrender.

Her hands smoothed over his face, and every time he drew back, her eyes met his. There was no doubt about what she wanted. Desire suffused her expression, from her damp mouth to her half-closed eyes.

Teague slowly moved his hips and the friction of his cock against her belly sent currents of pleasure shooting through his body. He was hard and ready and longing for the moment when he'd bury himself inside her. But there was no telling how he might react. It felt like the first time, as if every sensation were multiplied a thousand times over. And if he responded as he had that night so long ago, it would be over before it really began.

Her hands drifted down his chest, then grasped his hips, pulling him into each stroke. She moved beneath him, twisting and arching, deliberately taunting him with what she offered. He wanted to take it, right then and there. But Teague fought the impulse and slowly slid down over her body.

The bed was narrow, not made for full-scale seduction. In the end, he knelt beside it, his lips trailing kisses from her belly to her thighs. Everything about her was perfect. This was his Hayley, the girl who had owned his heart for all those years. And yet, she was something more now. She was a woman who had the capacity to break that heart all over again.

Teague didn't care. He didn't care if she disappeared from his life tomorrow. Tonight was all he needed. It was a perfect ending, a way to close the book on all the questions. He would be satisfied and he'd sure as hell make certain she was, too.

Hayley's fingers tangled in his hair as he continued to explore her body with his lips and his tongue. He waited, wanting her to guide him. And when she did, when she drew him to the spot between her legs, Teague didn't hesitate.

He knew exactly how to make a woman writhe with pleasure, how to bring her close to release and then draw her away from the edge. She moaned and whimpered as he took her there, controlling her pleasure with each flick of his tongue.

But Hayley was impatient with the teasing, and every time he slowed his pace, she tightened her grip on his hair. The pain only added to his need to possess her. Teague brought her close one more time, then slid up along her body.

He was breathless now, his need driving him to seek her warmth. She reached down between them to stroke his cock and Teague held his breath, determined to maintain control. He knew he'd have to retrieve a condom, but her touch felt so good that he didn't want her to stop.

She rolled on top of him, her fingers still firmly wrapped around his shaft, then straddled his thighs. Teague watched her as she bent over and placed a kiss on his belly. As she moved up his chest, his fingers tangled in her hair and he relaxed, grateful for the respite.

Yet Hayley wasn't about to stop. She was damp from his tongue and when she shifted above him, he found himself suddenly buried inside her. A tiny gasp slipped from her lips and Teague clutched at her hips, determined to stop her.

He should have known better. When Hayley wanted something, anything, there was nothing that could stand in her way, safety be damned. And it was obvious what she wanted. "Should we stop?" he whispered. "I brought condoms."

"It's all right," she said. "I'm on the pill. And you're the only person I've ever had unprotected sex with."

He smiled. "So are you. We're safe, then."

She didn't answer. Instead, she began to move above him. Hayley braced her hands on his chest, her hair tumbling around her face as she focused on her need. Her eyes were closed and a tiny smile curled the corners of her mouth. Teague watched her, taking in the sheer beauty of her face and body. It was as if she'd been made purely for his eyes. Everything about her was perfect.

Hayley slowed her rhythm, then rose on her knees, until the connection between them was nearly broken.

Then she opened her eyes and moaned as she slowly, exquisitely impaled herself once again. The sensation was more than he could handle and Teague felt himself nearing the edge.

She bent down and kissed him as she repeated the motion. He tried to stop her, holding tight to her hips, but she brushed his hands away, grabbing his wrists and pinning them above his head.

It was no use, Teague mused. She was in control and he had no choice but to enjoy it completely. Her breasts brushed against his chest and he found himself lost in the feeling. He refused to close his eyes, to shut himself off from her beauty.

As Hayley began to increase her rhythm, he knew she was close. He knew her body, her reactions, probably better than she knew herself. He'd taught her how to surrender, how to let go of her inhibitions and fears and experience her first orgasm. The signs were still there—her brow knitted and her bottom lip caught between her teeth.

Teague concentrated on her face, allowing himself to move as she did, closer and closer to the edge. He wanted to share in her release and when the first spasm hit her, he was ready.

She came down on him hard, arching her back as the shudders rocked her body and crying out in pleasure. It came just as quickly to Teague and he grasped her hips as he exploded inside her. He tried to maintain a grip on reality, but the sensation was too overwhelming.

He'd made love to a lot of women since Hayley, but

there was something about being with her that seemed
to go beyond mere physical gratification. When he was
inside her, he felt a connection deeper than shared pleasure and mutual passion. It was like a silent promise
between them, that this intensity, this release, bound
them together forever.

It had been nearly ten years since they'd made love,
with almost as many lovers in between, but here with
her again, time seemed to drop away. He pulled her
down beside him and ran his fingers through her hair.
Hayley kissed him, still breathless, her face flushed and
her lips pliant.

"I guess it's true what they say," she whispered. "It's
just like riding a bike. You never forget how to do it."

3

HAYLEY SNUGGLED into the warmth, floating between sleep and consciousness. She opened her eyes, waiting for her vision to clear before completely comprehending where she was.

It all returned to her in a rush, his body, his touch, the feel of Teague moving inside her. And then the overwhelming pleasure of her release. She had wondered what it might be like between them, now that they were both more experienced. But she'd never anticipated the earth-shattering encounter that they'd shared tonight.

How had she ever believed it would just be sex between them? She'd known her desire for Teague was undeniable, something so powerful it had to be satisfied. But she'd been so sure that, once sated, she'd be able to walk away. After all, they no longer loved each other. And without an emotional attachment, sex should be sex and nothing more. That's how she'd approached all the men in her life since Teague—they were useful for physical gratification, but she wasn't interested in emotional attachments.

Yet now that she was here, all she wanted to do was

stay safe in Teague's arms and in his bed. Hayley drew a shaky breath. This was not the smart choice, she reminded herself. It had taken her years to forget him, or at least put him out of her day-to-day thoughts. And now she'd be forced to fight that battle all over again.

It would be so easy to depend upon Teague, to believe that he'd always be there for her. But they lived completely separate lives now, with miles between them, both physically and emotionally. And the only person she could truly depend upon was herself.

Hayley pushed up on her elbow and stared down into his face in the dim light from the lantern. If she concentrated hard enough, she could push aside her memories of the boy she'd loved and see the man capable of breaking her heart. She was stronger now, independent and in charge of her own life. She had a career and plenty of money to assure her security. Everyone told her she had a future in films. There would be no time for a man in her life.

But all the money and fame in the world could never feel like this, Hayley thought—the pure exhilaration and freedom of being herself, the Hayley she'd been before her role on *Castle Cove* had made her a celebrity. She picked up the edge of the blanket and, holding her breath, slipped out of bed.

The early-morning air was chilly against her naked skin as she tiptoed around the shack retrieving her clothes. The sun was already brightening the eastern horizon and if she wasn't back at the house by the time her grandfather got up, he'd come looking for her.

Hayley dressed quietly, watching Teague as she pulled on her clothes and stepped into her boots. She fought the urge to wake him and kiss him goodbye before she left. But she wasn't sure what to say to him. Perhaps it was better to let this settle in before trying to explain it all.

Shrugging into her jacket, she turned for the door. Molly was tied to the rail next to Teague's horse. She unwrapped the reins, then swung up into the saddle, gently wheeling Molly around and pointing her toward Wallaroo.

Hayley drew a deep breath. Though she enjoyed living in Sydney, there were times when she missed the solitude of the outback. The air smelled sweeter and the sun shone brighter on Wallaroo. Though she'd run away from this place, she still considered the station home.

Hayley glanced over her shoulder, taking one last look at the shack, then prodded Molly into a slow gallop. The horse's step was quick and energetic and Hayley was amazed at how Molly's circumstances had changed from the day before. Once again, Teague had been there to save her from certain disaster, to set things right and to make her happy.

Hayley laughed softly. She'd dreaded her visit to Wallaroo. Since she'd first left, she'd only been back twice. But this trip was different. The last two times she'd returned, she had still been so confused and conflicted. This time, she was ready to accept her life as it was. She tipped her face up and whooped as loud as she could, startling Molly.

Teague had promised to return to the station to check

up on Molly and to bring over some fresh feed. She'd see him again in a few hours and maybe they'd make plans to spend the night at the shack again. "I can handle this," she assured herself.

She could, if she managed to maintain a bit of perspective. She wasn't in love with Teague anymore. They were old friends. Lovers who'd rediscovered each other. There would be no strings, no serious attachments. And when it was time to go their separate ways, they would part without anger or hurt feelings. They weren't teenagers. They were rational, sensible adults.

When she reached the stable, Hayley slid out of the saddle and held the reins, leading Molly inside. To her surprise, her grandfather was waiting, sitting on a bale of hay, smoking a cigarette.

"Where were you?" he demanded.

"I took Molly out for some exercise," Hayley said. "You shouldn't smoke in here, Harry."

How easy it was for her to lie to her grandfather. And to divert his attention by changing the subject. She'd done it throughout her teenage years. But now it bothered her. There was no reason to lie anymore. It was her right to spend the night with a man if she wanted, even if that man was Teague Quinn.

"I can smoke any damn place I want to," he said. "Answer my question."

"I couldn't sleep. I've been worried about Molly all night. I came out here to check on her and I thought I'd take her out for some exercise."

He squinted at her, his expression suspicious. "If

you want breakfast, you're going to have to make it," he muttered.

"I'll be in as soon as I get Molly settled. And you don't have to worry about taking care of her. I'll do that from now on."

"I would think so," he said, pushing up to his feet. "She's your damn horse." He walked off toward the far end of the stable with a stoop-shouldered gait.

"Harry, wait a second. I want to talk to you."

"We can talk at breakfast," he called, continuing his retreat.

"No!" Hayley shouted.

Her grandfather froze in his tracks and slowly turned to face her. She prepared herself for his anger, something that she'd become accustomed to in the past. But she wasn't afraid anymore. This man held no power over her. After all this time, she'd resigned herself to the fact that he'd never love her. So what did she have to lose?

"We need to talk," she said in a measured tone as she straightened her spine. "I've noticed your vision isn't what it used to be. I think it's time you go to the eye doctor and get a prescription for glasses. We're not going to argue about this. There's an optometrist that comes out to Bilbarra once a month. I'm going to take you to see him on Thursday."

"There's nothing wrong with my eyes."

"You've been feeding Molly moldy hay. If you couldn't smell it, you should have been able to see it. The station looks bloody awful, the house is a wreck, the yard is all overgrown and you don't see it. I know you wouldn't want Wallaroo to look like this, Harry. But you can't fix what you can't see."

He scowled. "You don't know what you're talking about, girl."

"I have eyes and, unlike you, I *can* see. So, go into the house and get yourself cleaned up and shaved and I'll make breakfast. From now on, I want you to take more care with your appearance. If I have to look at you over the breakfast table then you're at least going to make an effort to look decent. After breakfast, we're going to talk about getting this station back to rights."

Harry thought about her suggestion for a good ten seconds, then, to Hayley's surprise, gave her a curt nod. He turned and shuffled out of the stable, muttering to himself. Hayley smiled. Things had certainly changed. And maybe it wasn't such a long shot trying to convince her grandfather to move off the station. Her powers of persuasion had obviously improved over time.

"The first battle won. Now for the war," she said. She had to be in Sydney by the end of the month, when she'd film her character's return from a short stay in a mental institution, so she didn't have much time. As long as the station wasn't making money, Harry would continue to fall further and further into debt. No doubt her contributions were covering most of his expenses, but she had no idea how he was paying the taxes—if he was paying the taxes.

Though Wallaroo was a small station, just half the size of Kerry Creek, it was worth millions. At least four million, perhaps more. But Harry couldn't spend a dime of it unless he sold the station. He might be able to lease the grazing land, but he'd still be all alone on Wallaroo, without anyone to watch over him. By selling, he'd have enough money to buy a mansion in Sydney and live out the rest of his life in comfort.

And if he lived close by, she could keep on eye on him, make sure he was taking care of himself. After all, for better or for worse, Harry was the only family she had left.

As she tended to Molly, Hayley's mind wandered to thoughts of the man who'd shared her bed the previous night. There had been a time when she'd considered Teague family. When she'd first met him, he'd been like a brother. And then he'd become her best friend. But gradually, her feelings had changed, shifting from affection to sexual attraction.

Hayley smiled, remembering the confusion those emotions had caused. She could recall the exact moment Teague had gone from best mate to object of lust. She'd been fourteen, Teague fifteen, and it had been only days after his mother had left the station with Brody in tow.

She'd found Teague at the rock and he hadn't seemed to be happy to see her. He'd haltingly explained what had happened and Hayley had been surprised to see tears swimming in his eyes. For the first time since her parents had died, she felt the urge to reach out and touch another human being. She'd put her arm around his shoulders to comfort him and then wrapped him in her embrace.

They'd sat that way for a long time and then, when he'd finally gathered the courage to look at her, she'd done something incredibly stupid—or so it had seemed at the time. She leaned forward and kissed him, square on the lips. In the moments after the kiss, her mind had raced for some way to excuse her behavior. But she hadn't needed one. Teague had stared at her as if she'd suddenly sprouted horns and a tail. His face had gone beet red before he'd scrambled off the rock, jumped on his horse and ridden as fast as he could away from her.

Hayley's lips twitched into a smile at the memory. It was at that moment she'd realized her power over him. How something as simple as a touch or a kiss could render a boy speechless. That night, as she'd lain in bed, Hayley had replayed the day's events in her mind. But she'd come away with only one certainty—things had changed between her and Teague Quinn.

From then on, every time she saw Teague, she experienced a physical reaction. Her heart skipped or her stomach fluttered or her cheeks got all warm. That first kiss had led to many more and, eventually, to a slow experimentation in adolescent desire. The relationship had become their little secret, a secret that, if revealed, could bring an end to their time together.

All those silly feelings had come rushing back the moment she'd seen Teague standing outside Molly's stall. But Hayley wouldn't let herself be swept away by emotions this time. Losing her heart to Teague again was not an option. Sexual attraction did not have to include emotional attachment. She'd managed to prove that with the men who'd recently populated her social life. And she'd prove it with Teague.

Hayley took the porch steps two at a time, then

turned and surveyed the yard of Wallaroo station. She had plenty of work to keep her occupied for the next few weeks and plenty to keep her mind off the man who had made her ache with desire the night before. And when she found denial too difficult to bear, they'd meet at the cabin again for another night of unbridled lust.

She smiled as she pulled the screen door open, a delicious shiver racing through her. How long would it be before she saw him again? And what would happen when she did? The answers to those questions were far too intriguing to consider. For now, she'd focus on breakfast.

"WHERE ARE YOU GOING with that feed? And my ute?"

Teague heaved the bale of hay into the tray of Callum's pickup, then slammed the tailgate shut. "I don't have enough room in the back of my Range Rover. And I'll only be gone a few hours."

"What the hell is going on with you?" Callum asked. "I catch you sneaking in this morning before sunrise and—"

"I wasn't sneaking," Teague said.

"And now you're loading feed into my ute. You could at least tell me where it's going."

"To someone who needs it," Teague muttered. "Charity begins at home." He reached into his back pocket and pulled out his wallet. "All right, how much do I owe you? I'll pay for the bloody feed. I've got three bales of hay, a bag of oats and a bag of the premix."

"You don't have to pay me," Callum said, pushing the

money aside. "Hell, take what you need. I don't care where it's going."

"Thanks, brother," Teague said, patting Callum on the shoulder. "If Doc Daley calls, tell him to ring my satellite phone."

Callum shook his head as Teague hopped into the pickup. If his older brother suspected anything, he wasn't saying, Teague mused. Maybe he didn't really want to know. Callum had inherited their father's distaste for the Frasers and was even crankier now that Hayley's grandfather was making another play for the disputed land.

Of all the Quinns, Teague probably knew Harry Fraser the best, and the old man didn't like to lose, not his money, not his reputation and not his land. Oddly, he didn't seem to care a whole lot about his granddaughter.

Teague turned the ute onto the long, rutted road that led from Kerry Creek to Wallaroo. Though he and Hayley were only a half hour apart over land by horseback, it took a full ten minutes longer than that by road.

As he drove, he picked through his brother's selection of music. Callum had always been a country-music kind of guy, preferring Keith Urban and Alan Jackson. Brody went for hard rock, anything loud and obnoxious. Teague's taste in music leaned toward alternative, little-known bands and singers with interesting lyrics. He managed to find a Springsteen CD in the mix and decided it was the best he'd do. He popped it into the player then sang softly along with the tune.

Just yesterday, he'd taken the same route, his thoughts

filled with memories of Hayley and the time they'd spent together as kids. But now, those thoughts were a pale prelude to what had actually happened between them last night.

He still couldn't believe she was here, within his reach and eager for his touch. She was different, yet she was the same girl he'd fallen in love with all those years ago. The same pale blue eyes, the same honey-colored hair, the same lush mouth and tempting smile.

They hadn't spent much time talking, but there would be time enough for answering all his questions. As he drove, Teague thought about the circumstances that had torn them apart. For months afterward, he'd tried to figure out what he'd done wrong, why it had ended as it had.

But after beating himself up for mistakes he wasn't sure he'd made, Teague realized there had been other forces at work. Maybe her grandfather had driven them apart. Or maybe she'd decided that she didn't love him anymore. Whatever the reason was, he needed to know the real story and Hayley was the only one with the answers.

By the time he reached Wallaroo, Teague had made a mental list of all his questions. He was prepared to take the blame for whatever he'd done wrong and hope that she'd forgive him. As he drove up to the house, he caught sight of her standing on the porch, her hair blowing in the breeze.

The ute skidded to a stop and Teague jumped out, his eyes on Hayley. She hadn't changed in the few hours since he'd seen her last. If anything, she looked more beautiful. Suddenly, all his questions were replaced with an overwhelming need to kiss her. "Hi." The word slipped from his lips like a sigh.

"Hello," she said, a smile playing at her mouth.

Teague took a deep breath and found his voice. "I brought some fresh feed. And I phoned in an order to the feed store in Bilbarra, but they said they wouldn't be able to deliver until later this week. I'll bring more over if you run out."

They stood at a distance, staring at each other, as if afraid to approach. Teague knew that the moment he got within arm's length he'd want to pull her into a long, deep kiss. He glanced around. "Where's Harry?"

"He's inside. I've got him tidying up the house. He's not happy about it, but at least he's not sulking around."

"I'm going to go check on Molly," Teague said, pointing toward the stables. "Do you want to—"

"I'll come with." Hayley bounded down the steps.

He helped her into the ute, then jogged around to the driver's side. As he backed the truck away from the house, Teague glanced over at her, his gaze fixed on her mouth. Kissing her again had become an obsession, something that he couldn't get beyond.

As soon as the truck was far enough from the house, he slammed on the brakes and turned to her. Reaching out, Teague tangled his fingers in the hair at her nape and pulled her toward him. "I missed you," he murmured before bringing his mouth down on hers.

A tiny moan slipped from her lips as he deepened the kiss, his tongue teasing hers. Though the sensation of kissing her was familiar, the passion they'd shared as teenagers was only a fraction of what he felt now. He knew what he could do to her body and what she could do to his.

There was nothing standing in their way now, no silly insecurities or fears of pregnancy. He looked down into her eyes, a frown wrinkling his brow as he thought back to that time. They'd taken a lot of chances when they were younger. Chances that could have changed the courses of both their lives.

"What?" she asked, staring up at him.

Teague shook his head. "Nothing."

She drew a deep breath and forced a smile. "We should check on Molly."

Teague nodded. If they went much further, he'd have to make love to her in the front seat of the ute. Though it might be fun, they certainly could afford to find a more comfortable spot. "How is she doing?" he asked, throwing the pickup into gear and steering toward the stable.

"Good, I think. We had a nice ride back this morning. She doesn't seem to be suffering from any aftereffects of the colic."

"With proper feed, she'll be fine," he said. "And I brought some supplements you can add to her food."

"Thank you. You're a good vet. I knew you would be."

"You always had a lot of faith in me," Teague said, pausing as he stopped the ute at the wide stable doors. "Why didn't you wait?" The question came out before he could stop it. He was afraid to look at her, afraid he'd see anger in her expression.

"I had to get home before Harry woke up," she explained. "And you were sleeping, so—"

"I'm not talking about this morning," Teague said, keeping his eyes fixed straight ahead.

"I—I don't know what you—"

"You know exactly what I mean." He turned to face her, stretching his arm across the back of the seat. "I expected you to be here when I came home. And you were gone. You didn't even bother to let me know where you were."

Hayley stared down at her lap, twisting her fingers together. "I was supposed to wait, I know. And I tried. I was so angry when you left."

"I thought you wanted me to go. You said—"

"What was I supposed to say? I was confused. I thought I could survive alone but as soon as you left, I was…lost. I felt like part of me had been cut away. Once you were gone, there was nothing left for me at Wallaroo, nobody who cared whether I stayed or left."

"But we'd talked about it over and over. I wasn't going to be gone forever. And once you turned eighteen, you could leave on your own and come to Perth."

"My parents were supposed to come home, too, and they never did. I guess I was sure once you left, you'd find someone else, someone smarter, someone prettier. And I didn't want to wait around for that to happen."

"But we made plans, Hayley."

"I know. But the longer you were away, the angrier I got. I wasn't exactly thinking straight. I was confused and scared and a little self-destructive. It's taken three years of therapy to deal with all my rubbish and, believe me, it goes real deep."

"I tried to phone, but Harry wouldn't let me speak to you. And I wrote. Almost every day."

"Harry never told me you'd called, and I never got your letters," she said, frustration filling her voice.

"Would that have made a difference?"

"I don't know. I was in love with you and you left me behind and that's really all I could think about. It was like my parents all over again." She sighed softly. "We can't fix the past, Teague. There's no use talking about it now."

Hayley opened her door and hopped out of the truck. He followed her to where she stood at the tailgate. She picked up a bag of feed and carried it into the stable, and Teague hauled a bale of hay in, as well. An uneasy silence grew between them as he watched her feed Molly.

He sat down on the hay bale, bracing his elbows on his knees, refusing to let the subject die. "Tell me what happened. I mean, I've read the stories in the magazines, about how you were discovered. But tell me."

She stood next to Molly, smoothing her hand along the horse's neck as if it brought her comfort. "I got to Bilbarra hidden in the back of a feed truck. And from there I hitched to Brisbane and then to Sydney. I didn't have any money, so I did odd jobs where I could, mostly washing dishes at restaurants along the way. And then, when I got to Sydney, I found a job at a T-shirt shop on the beach. I lived on the streets and in the parks, in the bus station and the train station. And then one day, this guy walked into the shop and next thing I knew, I was standing in front of a camera, reading lines from a script."

"I came home for semester break and I rode out to

the shack and waited for you. Three days I hung out there. I didn't eat, I didn't sleep. And then Callum told me he'd heard you left Wallaroo two months before. I was…I was scared. Scared I'd never see you again."

"But here I am," she said, glancing over at him.

"That's not what I meant," Teague snapped. She seemed to be so unaffected by what had happened. Surely she must have felt something. She'd walked away from a relationship that had meant the world to him. It wasn't just a teenage crush. He'd loved her. He'd planned his whole life around her. Irritated, Teague stood and strode to the truck, then grabbed another bale of hay.

When he returned to the stall, she was vigorously grooming Molly, wielding the currycomb with careful efficiency. She was angry, too. He knew the signs—the stony silence, the refusal to meet his gaze, the haughty expression.

"I think I have a right to be angry," Teague said.

"I don't know what you want to me to say. I was a kid. I was seventeen. I didn't understand what I was feeling."

"And now?"

Hayley turned to face him, her arms crossed beneath her breasts. "We're both older and wiser. And just because we slept together last night doesn't mean— It doesn't mean anything."

Teague crossed the distance between them. He slipped his hands around her waist and spun her around, pinning her against Molly. His eyes searched her face, then focused on her lips. "I know you, Hayley. Don't forget that. You can't hide from me."

He leaned forward, his mouth hovering over hers, her breath mingling with his. He wanted to kiss her. But he thought better of it. Instead, he let go of her and stepped back. If she was so determined to push him away, then he'd be happy to oblige. "I have to go. I've got calls this afternoon."

"Thanks for the feed," she said.

"No worries."

Teague returned to the ute and dumped the last bale of hay in front of the stable door, then got inside and started the engine. He glanced in the rearview mirror to see Hayley watching him, her chin tilted up in a defensive manner so familiar to him.

She was like one of his wounded birds, so fragile, yet so frantic to escape. He'd been too stupid and naive to see the true depth of her pain when they were younger. But now, he could read it on her face, in the grim set of her mouth and the indecision in her eyes. She was terrified and he knew exactly what was frightening her.

It scared the hell out of him, too—the possibility that what they'd shared all those years ago was real. That the connection between them was still there, as strong as ever. And that she was the only woman he could ever love.

He had his answers now. And yet, Teague found himself plagued with a whole new list of questions.

HAYLEY STARED at the ceiling above her bed, watching a fly crawl across the painted surface. She picked up the script she'd been reading and attempted to finish the page she'd started an hour ago.

The house was silent. Her grandfather usually went to bed immediately after watching the evening news, still keeping stockman's hours even though Wallaroo no longer kept stock. Once the sun went down, there really wasn't much to do…except…

Tossing the script aside, Hayley sat up and brushed her hair out of her eyes. She walked to the bedroom window and looked out into the darkness. It was past ten and the moon hung low in the night sky, softly illuminating the landscape.

Though she and Teague hadn't planned to meet that night, Hayley knew he'd be there waiting. She'd spent the evening devising a litany of excuses not to go to him. Reasons why giving in to her desire was dangerous. But as the night wore on, the reasons became less and less important.

Turning from the window, Hayley retrieved her jeans from a nearby chair. She tugged them on, then stepped into her boots. Her jacket hung on a hook behind the bedroom door. She shrugged into it, buttoning it over her naked breasts, then tiptoed into the hallway.

The stairs squeaked as she made her way down to the kitchen. She slipped out the back door, then ran across the yard toward the stable. Molly's stall was near the door and there was just enough light to see the bridle hanging from the hook on the wall. Hayley grabbed it, went inside and slipped it over the horse's head. But as she reached for the buckle, she felt an arm snake around her waist and lift her off her feet.

She screamed and a hand came down over her mouth.

A moment later, she was outside the stall, twisting against the grasp that held her tight. His grip loosened and she spun around, ready to defend herself. But when his mouth came down on hers, the instinct to fight dissolved, leaving her heart slamming in her chest and her breath coming in shallow gasps.

He didn't say a word and every time she tried to speak, he covered her mouth in another demanding kiss. His palms smoothed over her body, finding bare skin beneath her jacket. Teague turned her around, tucking her against him as kissed her neck.

His touch seemed to be everywhere at once, teasing each nipple to a peak, sliding over her belly, then dipping beneath the waistband of her jeans. He wasn't in any hurry to undress her and in truth, Hayley found the seduction incredibly erotic.

His fingers fumbled with the button at her waist and when it was undone, Teague lowered the zipper. He found the damp spot between her legs and slipped his finger between the soft folds of her sex.

Hayley's breath caught in her throat as desire snaked through her body. Slowly, he caressed her, drawing her closer to the edge while he moved her backside against his hard shaft. They were like teenagers again, too impatient to undress, too desperate to bring each other to release. It was safe, but it was still seduction.

His breath was hot on her neck and she shifted against him, the contact causing a moan to slip from his throat. Hayley wanted to stop, to strip off all their clothes and begin again. But this headlong rush toward completion was impossible to resist.

Her knees grew weak as she lost herself in the pleasure he was providing. Rational thought was replaced by single-minded focus. A burst of sensation spread through her body and then she was there, quivering, waiting, then tumbling over the edge, the spasms too delicious to deny.

She arched back, and his lips found hers, possessing her mouth in the same way he'd taken her body. The orgasm seemed to last forever and Teague wasn't satisfied until she was completely spent and limp in his embrace.

When she could stand on her own again, she turned to face him, ready to return the pleasure that he'd given her. He was still hard, his erection pressing against the faded denim of his jeans. She ran her hand along the length of him and he sucked in a sharp breath.

There were so many ways she could please him, but in the end, she brought him to completion with her fingertips, teasing him, edging him closer and closer, until he came in her hand.

Teague chuckled softly as she continued to stroke him. "The things you do to me," he murmured, nuzzling her neck.

"How long have you been waiting for me?"

"Not long." He brushed her hair away from her temples. "I went out to the shack first and got tired of waiting there. So, I decided to come here and kidnap you out of your bed."

"That would have been exciting," she said. "Although, you may have ended up on the business end of Harry's rifle again."

"It would have been worth it." He looked into her eyes, his features barely visible in the moonlight. "I'm sorry about this afternoon. I shouldn't have gotten angry."

"And I shouldn't have been so irrational. Sometimes, I get a little scared."

"Hayley, you never have to be frightened of me. I would never hurt you."

"You already did," she said. "Once."

"But not deliberately. I was a teenager. I didn't know how you felt. Hell, I couldn't even figure out how I felt. But I think I understand now and I'm sorry I hurt you."

Hayley pushed up on her toes and kissed him softly. "I'm not sure I understand," she said. "But I know we need to be careful. It would be so easy to depend on you again, to feel safe. But I have a life in Sydney and maybe a life in Los Angeles. It wouldn't be a good idea to get all wrapped up in each other."

"Los Angeles?"

Hayley nodded. "My contract with *Castle Cove* is up in September. My agent thinks I could have a career in films, maybe even in Hollywood. He says Australian actresses are hot now. I'm supposed to go there and meet with some casting directors before the end of the month. And he's trying to set up some auditions, as well."

"Los Angeles," Teague repeated. "That's a long way to go for a job. Especially when you have one right here in Australia."

"And the work is good here, don't get me wrong. But if I got a movie, a good movie, then things would change. I'd make more money. My future would be more secure. I wouldn't have to worry. And maybe people would start to see me as a serious actress."

"Is that what you want?"

"I guess. I'm not really qualified to do much else. I didn't go to university. I don't have any other talents or skills. Acting is what I do."

Teague forced a smile. "Then I hope everything works out for you. I mean it, Hayley. I want you to be happy."

"This doesn't mean we can't see each other," she said, reaching up to rest her palm on his cheek. "I just think we should try not to…"

"Fall in love?"

She giggled. Teague didn't mince words. "Yes. Fall in love. I think we should avoid any infatuations. We have to be practical. You have your life and I have mine, and when I leave in a few weeks, everything will return to the way it was."

"But until then, we'll be friends. Friends who might happen to have sex occasionally?"

"Friends with benefits," she said. "I think that's the proper term."

"Ah. So this is a familiar concept to you?"

Hayley shook her head. In truth, she didn't have many friends and certainly no male friends. And the lovers that she'd had were temporary diversions at best. "I've heard it works."

"I'm willing to give it a try."

She held out her hand. "Come with me. I'm sleepy and I want you in my bed."

"Don't you think that's a little risky? With your grandfather in the house?"

"You've slept in my bed before, don't you remember? Two or three times as I recall. The first time was on a dare. You crawled up on the porch roof, then shinnied over to my bedroom window. I'll need to sneak you out before the sun comes up, but we should be safe if you don't act like a yobbo once your clothes come off."

"I can be very quiet," Teague said. "But we're too old to be doing this, Hayley. I don't want to have to watch what I say in bed or sneak out before the sun comes up. If we want to sleep with each other, then we shouldn't need permission."

"We can go back to the shack, then," she suggested.

"That's not exactly five-star accommodations, either," he said. "Hell, I have a plane. We can go anywhere we want."

"No, we can't," she said.

"Why not?"

"Because people recognize me everywhere. Anyone who has a telly knows who I am. My personal life is all over the tabloids. And yours will be, too, if you're seen with me."

"So what do we do?" Teague asked.

"We take what we can get. We ride out to the shack and spend the night together. And in the morning, we go our separate ways."

"Then let's go," he said. "We'll ride out there right now. I want you in my bed tonight."

She wanted to test her resolve, to prove that she could resist if she had to. But in the end, Hayley saddled Molly and they rode out into the moonlight. There'd come a time when she would have to refuse. It wouldn't be tonight. Tonight, she'd give him what he wanted—her body. But she'd take care to keep her heart safe.

4

"DAVEY SAID the colt in the next stall has been sold. He's beautiful."

Teague watched as Payton Harwell tended to his horse, cleaning the gelding's hooves with a pick. Since Payton had arrived on the station a few days before with Teague's younger brother, Brody, the stable had undergone a makeover. The tack room was tidy, the stalls clean, the feed arranged in stacks against the wall. Though Callum hadn't been enthusiastic about hiring the American, Teague could vouch that she knew her way around horses.

She moved with an easy efficiency, feeding and grooming and mucking out the stalls, all in a very orderly fashion. She wasn't afraid to work hard and seemed to enjoy what she was doing, curious about the breeding operation that he oversaw.

"He's going to be trained as a show horse," Teague said. "Some of our horses are used for polocrosse. And some for campdrafting."

At any other point in time, he might have been attracted to Payton. She was smart and beautiful and she seemed to be very well educated. The kind of woman he ought to want. But there was only one woman who captured his imagination these days.

Funny how a few days with Hayley could change his outlook so completely. He found himself anticipating the end of the day, searching for an excuse to see Hayley again. He'd spent the morning and early afternoon making calls, but he didn't intend to spend the evening alone.

Payton set the horse's hoof onto the concrete floor and straightened, brushing her dark hair out of her eyes. "What's that?"

"Besides Aussie rules football, polocrosse and camp-drafting are the only native Aussie sports. Polocrosse is a mix of polo and lacrosse and netball. And I reckon campdrafting is kind of like your rodeo riding. The horse and rider cut a calf from the herd, then they have to maneuver it around a series of posts."

"I'd like to see that," she said.

"I'll take you sometime," Teague promised. "There's a campdrafting event in Muttaburra in August if you're still around."

"I'd like to try it."

"Then I'll teach you."

"Teach her what?"

Teague turned to find Brody standing at his side. Though his brother was smiling, Teague sensed an undercurrent of aggravation. Brody was sweet on the new arrival and wasn't doing much to hide his feelings. "Hey, little brother. Where have you been?"

"I went out with Davey to fix the windmill in the high pasture," Brody replied.

"Good to see you putting in an honest day's work," Teague teased, clapping his brother on the shoulder. He smiled at Payton, then tipped his hat. "I've got a call. I'll see you later, Payton. Maybe you can give me a hand tomorrow morning. I've got vaccinations to do on the yearlings."

"Sure," Payton replied. "I'd be happy to help."

He nodded again. "I think I'll like having you here," he said. Teague turned to Brody. "Have you had all your shots?"

Brody's jaw grew tense and Teague decided to make his exit before his little brother decided to reply with an elbow to the nose. Brody had spent five years playing Aussie rules football on a pro team. Aussie rules was a mix of rugby, soccer and professionally sanctioned assault. There was no question who the toughest of the three Quinn brothers was.

"Don't mind Teague," Brody called as Teague strolled out of the stables. "He has a bad habit of yabbering to anyone who'll listen."

Teague pulled off his gloves and shoved them into his jacket pocket, heading toward the house. He had the evening to himself, with only one call on his agenda, a stop at Wallaroo to see Hayley.

Mary was preparing supper in the kitchen when he walked inside. He tossed his hat on the table and washed his hands in the sink.

"Where have you been?" she asked. "Or maybe I needn't bother asking."

Teague put his finger to his lips. "Let's make this our

secret, eh, Mary? I don't need to listen to any whinging from my brothers about my choice of companions."

"I don't think they're in a place to be complaining," Mary said. "They're a bit preoccupied with their own romances."

"I'm heading out," Teague said. "I'm taking my satellite phone, so if Doc Daley calls, tell him to ring me at that number. And I don't plan to be home for a while."

"You haven't slept in your own bed for the past two nights," she said.

Teague grinned. "Yeah. Well, I'm saving you the trouble of making my bed. You should be happy."

Mary shook her head and laughed. "You take care," she said. "I remember what happened the last time that girl broke your heart. You were impossible to live with."

"No one is going to break anyone's heart," Teague reassured her. He pulled open the refrigerator and searched through the contents. "I thought there was another bottle of wine in here."

"Brody took it last night," she said. "Wine consumption has gone up on the station since the ladies arrived." She opened the cabinet above the sink and pulled out a bottle. "Red. It should be served at room temperature."

Teague leaned over and kissed her cheek. "You're a sweetheart, Miss Mary." He strode out of the kitchen onto the back porch, then crossed the yard to his Range Rover. Callum approached from the opposite direction, wiping his hands on a rag as he walked. Teague slipped the wine into his jacket pocket, pushing the neck of the bottle up his sleeve.

"You leaving?" Callum asked.

"Yeah, I've got to drive into Bilbarra to pick up some medicine from Doc Daley."

Callum frowned. "Why don't you take the plane. You should be able to make it home before dark."

Teague shrugged. "I don't mind the drive. I thought I might spend the night. Do a bit of socializing. Since you and Brody have corralled the only two decent-looking women in this part of Queensland, I'm going to have to look elsewhere."

Callum stared at him for a long moment. "You are so full of shit," he muttered. "Who do you think you're fooling? I know Hayley Fraser is on Wallaroo and I suspect you've been seeing her."

"And what if I am?" Teague asked.

Callum shook his head. "Did you ever think that maybe Harry Fraser is using his granddaughter against us?"

Teague laughed. "I think you've got a few kangaroos loose in the top paddock there, Cal. The land is ours. He'll lose, whether I'm seeing Hayley or not. Unless you think he has a valid claim to the land."

"Doesn't matter what I think," Cal said. "Harry's the one raising a stink. He's gone completely round the bend thinking he'll win. This is costing money to defend ourselves once again. I'm ready to sue him right back for the fortune I've spent on solicitors."

Callum had no idea how close he was to the truth

about Harry. He *had* gone a bit berko. And maybe the lawsuit was part of that. "If you must know, Hayley is trying to convince Harry to sell the station."

Callum gasped. "What?"

"He's out there all by himself. He's got no stock, the place is falling down around him and he's probably spending his last cent trying to get that land back. I don't know what good the land will do him, unless he thinks it will raise his asking price for the station."

Callum frowned, shaking his head. "If you really think Harry will sell Wallaroo, you're the crazy one. The only way Fraser is leaving that station is in a casket."

"Hey, I'm just telling you what I know," Teague said as he pulled open the door on the Range Rover. "Hayley is not involved with what her grandfather is doing. She doesn't give a stuff about that land."

As Teague drove the road to Wallaroo, he thought about Cal's attitude toward Harry Fraser. Callum was a reasonable bloke and he always made decisions after careful thought. But his dislike for Hayley's grandfather seemed completely irrational. Yes, the land was valuable. But if the situation were reversed and Callum thought he'd been cheated out of the land, he would do everything he could to get it back.

What difference did it make? Teague mused. He and Hayley were friends. What Callum and Brody thought about their relationship was irrelevant. And if they became more than friends, then he'd have to deal with that when the time came.

When he got to the house on Wallaroo, he found

Harry sitting on the porch, his feet resting on the railing, his hands folded over his stomach. He sat up straight as Teague leaned out of the window of the Range Rover. "Hello, Mr. Fraser."

"She's in the stables. If you're here to collect on your bill, she's going to pay it. It's her horse."

"No worries," Teague said. "I'm sure she's good for it."

"If you're not back for money, what are you doing here?"

"Just another follow-up call," Teague said.

"Get on with it, then," he said, calling an end to their conversation.

By the time Teague reached the stables, Hayley was headed toward the house. He pulled up beside her and reached out, smoothing his hand along her bare arm. "Get in," he said.

"Where are we going?"

"Out," Teague replied.

"There is no out in the outback. We're already out."

"Well, I have a destination in mind. We'll have a little wine, maybe a bite to eat. After that, maybe we'll see a show." He reached over and opened the passenger-side door. "Come on. We're going to be late."

She gave him a dubious look, but hurried around the SUV and jumped inside. Instead of driving toward the road, Teague drove through the yard and past the stables. The Range Rover bumped along toward the sunset, dust billowing behind them. Teague had seen the landing strip from the air the last time he'd passed over Wallaroo and he wanted to see it up close. When he reached the long, flat stretch, he turned the SUV around, its tailgate facing west.

"What are we doing out here?" Hayley asked.

"The best show in all of Queensland," Teague said as he helped her out. He pointed to the brilliant pinks and purples on the horizon. "We're just in time." Teague opened the tailgate of the Range Rover, then lifted Hayley up to sit on it. Then he retrieved the bottle of wine from behind the driver's seat. "And I brought refreshments."

Hayley smiled. "Is this a date? Are you trying to impress me?"

"Is it working?" Teague asked.

"Yes."

"Then this is a date," he said. He took a corkscrew out of his pocket and opened the wine. "I didn't bring glasses. We'll have to drink out of the bottle."

"It's so much more sophisticated that way," Hayley teased. "That's the way they do it at all the best restaurants in Sydney." She crossed her legs in front of her. "You know, this is our first date. In all the time we knew each other as kids, we never went on a real date. No school dances, no parties. I wish we would have had something like that to remember."

"We'll have this," Teague said.

"Maybe we shouldn't." Hayley sent him a sideways glance. "Maybe we're getting ahead of ourselves. We're so anxious to rekindle a teenage romance that we aren't thinking about the effect it will have on our lives."

"Are you saying you don't want to be with me?" Teague asked.

"No. I'm saying, when this is over, I might not be able to cope with losing you again. I feel happy when I'm with you, Teague. The world seems right."

"You'll always have me," he said. "You don't have to worry over that."

She took a sip of wine, then smiled ruefully. "We'll be eighty years old and I'll show up on your doorstep wondering if our 'friends with benefits' deal is still good."

"And I'll invite you in for a cup of tea and a Vegemite sandwich and we'll watch a nice game show on the telly." He bumped her shoulder with his. "And you'll be wearing some of those sexy stockings that end at the knees and comfortable shoes and a nice hairnet and I won't be able to keep my hands to myself."

"Now you're making me really depressed," she said.

Teague took the wine and set it down beside her. Then he leaned forward and dropped a kiss on her damp lips. "I can make you feel better," he offered. "It's the perfect remedy. Have you ever had sex on the roof of a Range Rover at sunset?"

"I can't say that I have," Hayley answered.

Teague reached into the rear of the SUV and pulled out a blanket, then tossed it over his head. He stood up on the tailgate and pulled her up to her feet. Spanning her waist with his hands, Teague lifted her up to sit on the roof, then handed her the bottle of wine.

"I knew there was a reason I didn't get the optional roof rack," he said as he crawled up beside her. "Sweetheart, you are never going to forget our first date."

A MANTLE OF STARS filled the inky sky. Away from the lights of the city, Hayley was amazed at the sight, like a million diamonds scattered above her. Only in the outback, she mused. Snuggling against Teague, she sought the warmth of his body to ward off the chill of the night air. They lay facing each other, the blanket wrapped around them both, their noses touching.

"This was the nicest first date I've ever been on," she teased, her lips brushing against his as she spoke.

"I know what a woman likes," he said. "I'm pretty smooth that way. Wine directly out of the bottle, a beautiful sunset and really incredible sex on the roof of my car."

"So, how many other women have you had since me?"

"I don't remember," he said.

Hayley drew back. "You're lying."

"I'm saying that none of them were memorable. You were the one who stuck in my mind. I think I can recall every single time we made love." His hand ran up along her hip, then down again. "Would you like me to recall them all for you?"

Hayley shivered, nuzzling against his neck. "I guess it's true what they say. You never really forget your first love."

"Very true," he agreed.

"We should probably go. Harry is going to wonder where I am."

"It's not that late. We can stay a bit longer." He kissed her again, this time lingering over her lips. "I want to say something to you and I want you to listen carefully."

"What is it?" Hayley asked, wondering at his serious tone.

"I plan to spend as much time as possible with you, Hayley. I don't know how long you'll be here, but I'm determined to make every minute count. So when we're together, there'll be no talk of getting home or worrying about Harry or maybe we shouldn't be doing this or that. If you're not prepared to spend every free minute with me, you need to tell me now."

"You have to work," she said.

"I do. But I figure you can come along. That's why I wanted to check out the landing strip. I'll buzz the house and you can meet me out here and off we'll go. What are you doing tomorrow? I have to fly into Bilbarra to cover a couple surgeries for Doc Daley. After we're done we can fly to Brisbane for lunch."

"I have to take Harry into Bilbarra. The eye doctor stops there tomorrow and he has an appointment to get his vision checked. We're leaving first thing in the morning. Two hours in the car on the way to Bilbarra and two hours back. I'm not sure how that's going to go."

"Why don't you let me fly you both. It's about a half hour by air. Once I'm finished at the surgery, we'll have lunch."

"Harry would never get on a plane," she said. "I'm going to have the devil of a time getting him in my car. He's very suspicious of everything I suggest to him. He'll probably think I'm planning to dump him off at some retirement home."

"He must leave the station occasionally. Doesn't he?"

"From what I can tell, not recently. He'd been living off tinned food for a month before I arrived. This station was his whole life. It's kind of sad to see what's happened to it. Makes the feud seem a bit silly, doesn't it?"

"Why is he bringing this up again? He's lost the last two times in court. And the time before that, he only won because he found some old document that the judge thought was real."

"I don't know," Hayley replied. "He has no money to pay for this lawsuit. He's not using the land he has. He's so fixated on winning." She drew a deep breath. "Couldn't you let him win?"

Teague frowned. "You mean turn over the land to Harry? Cal would never go for that."

She nodded. "Why not? I'm beginning to think the feud is the only thing keeping my grandfather on this land. He simply refuses to leave until he wins."

"He's not going to win this time," Teague said.

"What if I bought the land from Cal? How much would your brother want for it?"

"He won't sell," Teague said. "Why do you care? Harry never did anything for you except drive you away from the only home you had left. You don't owe him anything, Hayley."

"You don't understand," she countered.

"Explain," he said. "Make me understand."

Teague waited, watching as she tried to put her thoughts in order. "You're right, I don't owe Harry anything. But he's the only family I have. And I can't continue to push him away. There's going to come a day when he isn't around anymore and I don't want to have any regrets about what I did or didn't do."

Teague caught her hand and drew it to his lips. "You can't make him love you. Even if you handed him that land on a silver platter, it wouldn't change who he is."

"I know." She drew a ragged breath. "He seems so old. And sad. And when he's gone, I won't have anyone left."

"You'll have me," he said in a fierce tone. "How many times do I have to say that for you to believe it?"

"Kiss me again," she said. "Then maybe I'll believe it."

Teague cupped her face in his hands and kissed her softly. Tears pushed at the corners of her eyes and she fought against them. She never cried. She hadn't cried since her parents' funeral. And now, twice in one week. Teague was the dearest friend she'd ever had, the only person in the world she could trust. Yet, she couldn't allow herself to surrender to those feelings.

He pulled away and Hayley swallowed the lump in her throat. Before he had the chance to see her tears, she rolled over on top of him, pushing the blankets aside. Goose bumps prickled her skin as the chilly night air stole the warmth from her body. She ran her fingers down his chest from his collarbone to his belly.

The cold magnified every sensation, the simplest touch warming her blood and making her heart race. Teague smoothed his thumb over her nipple and Hayley sighed softly, bracing her hands on his chest.

She moved above him, teasing at him until he began to grow hard with desire. And when he was ready, Hayley shifted and he was suddenly inside her. She moaned as he thrust deep, his hands clutching her hips.

She could lose herself in this passion. When he was

inside her, all her doubts and insecurities vanished. The connection became strong and the trust unshakable. But they couldn't spend the rest of their lives making love. They both had to live in the outside world, where other forces would pull them apart.

If only she knew what to do, how to commit to a man. Without an example to follow, without loving parents to watch, she'd been left to find guidance from romantic movies. But that wasn't real life.

Her parents had loved each other, against all odds. They'd met and fallen in love in the course of a day, then married young, just a year after her father had left Wallaroo. They'd started with nothing and built a life together. But how did it happen? She'd been too young to see the truth in their relationship. To her, they'd seemed perfect. Yet they must have had their problems just like any other couple.

Had it begun like this? Hayley wondered. With desire and passion and need? Or was there some other secret to making love last a lifetime? She looked down at Teague, his face cast in silver light from the moon, then bent closer and kissed him.

He twisted his fingers through her hair, holding her close, whispering his need against her mouth. Then he reached between them and touched her. She drew in a quick breath, then moaned, an unspoken plea for him to continue.

Hayley gave herself over to him, light-headed with desire and unable to think rationally. It felt so good to let go, to know that he would be there to catch her when she fell. She could allow herself to be vulnerable without the usual fears.

The seduction was slow and deliberate, a gentle climb toward release. And when it finally came, she and Teague found it together, their bodies joined in perfect pleasure. Hayley didn't know much about love, but she knew what they shared sexually was as good as it got.

He pulled her into his embrace again, tucking her against his warm body and wrapping the blanket around them. "We can't go on like this," he murmured.

"We can't?"

"I don't want to leave you. I want you with me."

"That's not very practical," she said.

"I'll find a way to make it happen. Twenty-four hours together with no one to get between us. Two days would be even better."

"I'm cold," Hayley said, anxious to change the subject.

"I think I'm going to have to find our clothes." Teague wrapped her up in the blanket, then slid off the top of the Range Rover.

She sat up and watched him, appreciating his body naked in the moonlight. He gathered his clothes first, pulling his shirt over his head before he tugged on his jeans. Then he searched for his boots and socks. When he was finished dressing, he returned with her clothes.

"So, tomorrow you have to take Harry into Bilbarra. I'll drive you. I'll be here at seven sharp. You can take care of your business in town while I stop at the surgery. We'll drive home in the afternoon and then spend the night at the shack."

"I don't think this is a good idea. A Quinn and a Fraser in the car together for four hours."

"Dr. Tom Barrett will be taking you to Bilbarra. Your grandfather loves me. I'm the one who saved your horse, remember? And I gave you a discount on the bill."

"You didn't charge me anything," Hayley said as Teague pulled her T-shirt down over her head.

He helped her find the sleeves, then gave her a quick kiss. "I prefer to get compensated in other ways."

"Where are my panties?" she asked, searching through the pile of clothes.

"I think a dingo ran off with them."

"This is awful. I lose my panties on our first date."

"I can hardly wait for the second date." Teague winked at her.

"Don't be so certain. Harry will be coming along tomorrow."

"Maybe I can find *him* a date," Teague joked.

TEAGUE FIXED HIS GAZE on the road in front of him. He fought the temptation to glance at the clock on the dashboard. No matter how much he wanted this day to be over, counting down the minutes wouldn't make it go any faster.

"Have you seen the horses they breed?" Harry asked. "Scrawny creatures. A wonder they manage to sell even one. But then, the Quinns have always been cheats—every last one of them."

Teague gritted his teeth. His jaw was beginning to ache with the effort to remain silent. He'd listened to

Harry blathering all the way to Bilbarra. The old man seemed determined to offload every imagined insult and slight that the Quinn family had ever perpetrated against him. Teague was beginning to wonder if Harry knew who he really was and was provoking him deliberately. Likening Teague and his brothers to con men was over the top.

Hayley sent him an apologetic smile. "How are your new glasses working, Harry?"

"I don't need glasses."

"Put them on. You won't get used to them if you don't wear them."

"They make me look like a fool," he muttered.

"They make you look very clever," Hayley countered.

"What would you know, girl?"

"Don't speak to her like that," Teague said, staring at Harry in the rearview mirror. "She doesn't deserve that."

"What do you know about what she deserves?" Harry snapped.

With a low curse, Teague slammed on the brakes. The Range Rover skidded to a stop and Teague twisted around to face Harry. But Hayley put her hand over his. "Nature break!" she said, sending him a warning look.

She jumped out of the SUV and ran around to Teague's door. "Come on," she said, yanking the door open and grabbing his hand. "I want you to watch for snakes."

They walked into the brush, Hayley clutching his hand and tugging him along behind her. "What are you doing?"

"What am I doing? What is *he* doing?"

"He's being Harry. That's the way he is."

"He's rude. And he treats you like crap. I'm not going to listen to him speak to you like that. I won't have it, Hayley."

"It's just the way he is," she said. "It doesn't bother me. I've learned to tune it out."

"Well, you shouldn't have to." He braced his hands on his hips and shook his head. "You're not staying on Wallaroo any longer. You're coming to Kerry Creek with me."

"What?"

"I won't allow you to be subjected to his tantrums. And you wonder why you're carrying around so much baggage? Well, there's one big windbag you can get rid of right now."

"He's family," she said. "You don't have any idea what it's like to have no one. You have two parents and two brothers. I have him. And yes, he can be a pain in the arse at times, but he's still my grandfather."

"He's also the guy you ran away from ten years ago. And the guy who refused to take you in right after your parents died."

"Well, I've had time to realize my mistakes," she said. "And now, I'm waiting for him to realize his."

"Why is it so important? He'll never be what you want, Hayley."

"I'm not going to argue about this," she said, turning to walk away from him. "Not here."

Teague followed her, grabbing her arm and spinning her around to face him. "We're not getting in that car until you agree to come to Kerry Creek and stay with me."

"Then we're going to be out here all day and night, because I'm not going to Kerry Creek. Do you think I'll be any more welcome under your brother's roof than I am under my own?"

"You won't even give *us* a chance, will you?"

"What is that supposed to mean? What do *we* have to do with me coming to Kerry Creek?"

"No matter what I do, you're never going to need me. You're too scared to need anyone, Hayley. That's why you ran all those years ago. And that's why you're still running right now."

"Don't try to analyze me. You're no good at it."

"I know you better than anyone in this world."

"You used to know me," she said. Hayley turned and walked toward the road. She got inside the Range Rover and slammed the door behind her.

Teague cursed, then kicked the dusty ground in front of him. Hayley was the most beautiful woman in the world, but there were times when he wondered what the hell he was doing with her. She stubbornly refused to acknowledge she might deserve a bit of happiness in her life. The closer he tried to get, the more she pushed him away.

Last night, under the stars, he'd felt as if they'd finally gotten past her insecurities. But then, hours later, she'd found a way to sabotage what they'd shared. They were running around in circles and he was getting dizzy.

Teague walked back to the SUV and got inside. He threw the car into gear and pulled out onto the road. The problem was he and Hayley would never get things right between them if there was always someone standing in the way. His brother, her grandfather and Hayley herself.

He glanced over at her and found her staring out the passenger-side window. Maybe trying to reestablish a relationship with Hayley wasn't worth the trouble, Teague mused. They'd be going their separate ways in a few weeks. The more time they spent together, the more they seemed to be at odds with each other.

The rest of the ride passed in silence. When Harry made a move to speak again, Hayley quickly shut him down. To Teague's surprise, the old man followed her order, slumping in the rear seat with his arms crossed over his chest. He'd seen that posture from Hayley too many times. Maybe they were closer than he'd thought.

When they reached Wallaroo, Teague pulled up in front of the house. Harry shoved his new glasses onto his nose and peered out the window. "Jaysus," he muttered. "That house needs to be painted." He got out of the SUV and walked up to the porch, examining the peeling paint, then disappeared around the corner of the house.

"Come home with me," Teague said.

"I can't. Thanks for the ride. I know he can be a horror sometimes. But I can handle him now. He doesn't bother me."

"You deserve better."

She forced a smile, then nodded silently. A moment later, Hayley jumped out of the truck and closed the door. She gave him a little wave, before turning and running into the house.

As the Range Rover bumped down the road, Teague tried to put the day in perspective. Life couldn't always be perfect. They weren't kids anymore and there would be differences between them. But he knew more now than he had ten years ago. It wasn't easy to fall in love or to stay in love. Sometimes the differences between two people were too large to overcome.

There was an upside to staying away from Hayley. He wouldn't have to think about her 24/7. He could get his work done without having to hurry home so he might spend the night with her. And he and Callum would be on better terms.

So that was it. He'd given seeing Hayley a go and it hadn't worked. "Nothing ventured, nothing gained," he muttered to himself. Would she be that easy to give up? Though it would be a challenge to stay away from her, he was determined to try. He had calls to make tomorrow and the next day, he'd promised to fly Gemma and Payton to Brisbane so they could do some shopping.

He wouldn't have time to even think about Hayley until Sunday. By then, maybe he'd be ready to forget her and go on as if nothing had happened between them. "Right," he said, knowing that was all but impossible. His attempts to stop thinking about Hayley would only lead to more thoughts about her.

All the way home to Kerry Creek, Teague tried to figure out a way around the walls Hayley had constructed. If anyone could breach them, he could. But as he was furiously taking them apart, brick by brick, she was frantically building them thicker on the other side.

It was her move, Teague decided. He would wait for her to come to him. She couldn't run away if he refused to chase her.

When Teague got to the station, he didn't bother stopping at the house. Instead, he drove directly to the landing strip. He had a few hours left until sunset. If he stayed on the station, he'd only be tempted to ride out to the shack. He'd have to put some space between himself and Hayley.

He'd fly back to Bilbarra. Once the sun went down, he couldn't land on the station. He'd be stuck where he was. He'd spend the evening getting pissed at the Spotted Dog, sleep it off on Doc Daley's office sofa and then make his calls tomorrow.

It was a decent scheme, with no room to make a fool of himself. And that's all he really wanted from here on out—to keep from playing the fool.

5

HAYLEY WOVE MOLLY's reins through her gloved fingers, then turned the horse away from the stables. With a gentle kick, she urged her into a slow gallop. The early-morning air was chilly, the breeze whipping at her hair. But a ride was exactly what she needed.

She'd spent the last two nights wide-awake, fighting the temptation to ride out to the shack and see if Teague was waiting for her. Her therapist would probably say she was reverting to the self-destructive patterns of her childhood, making a bad decision simply to punish herself. But Hayley knew it was something more than that.

Was she trying to test him? To see how deep his affection ran? Or was she trying to drive him away before he had a chance to leave on his own?

Her stomach fluttered as she thought about what she'd say if he was waiting for her. She managed to stay away from the shack partly because of the fear that he might not be there. If he wasn't there then he didn't care and it was all over. She'd half expected him to stop by the station with the excuse of checking up on Molly, even though the horse had recovered completely. And he hadn't come. In two days, no word from the only person in the world who claimed to care for her.

She urged Molly to gallop faster and faster. Hayley's legs ached and her breath came in shallow gasps, but she didn't want to stop. As she came over a small rise, she saw the shack in the distance. Two horses were tethered out front.

Drawing a deep breath, she headed toward the shack. Had he been there all night waiting? When she reached the porch, Hayley slid out of the saddle and dropped softly to the ground. She walked up the steps, then rested her hand on the doorknob. As she opened it, the hinges creaked. "Teague?"

Hayley froze as she saw the two naked bodies intertwined on the small bed. She felt her world shift, the ground moving under her feet. Teague had brought another woman to their special place. How could he have done this? Was he trying to punish her?

With a soft sob, Hayley turned and ran down the steps. She heard a voice call out behind her, but her heart was beating so hard and fast that it obliterated every sound around her.

She fumbled to put her foot in the stirrup, frantic to escape before he discovered her here. She swung her leg up and over the saddle, then reached for the reins.

"Wait!"

Hayley glanced up, tears swimming in her eyes. Slowly, she realized the man who stood on the porch wasn't Teague at all. Though the family resemblance was obvious, she found herself looking at a man who could only be Teague's younger brother, Brody. She'd only seen him once, when he was much younger, but she knew it was him.

"What are you doing here?" she demanded, her voice shaky and her hands trembling.

"We needed a place to sleep," Brody explained. "This was close by. Was Teague supposed to meet you here?"

"No," she snapped, keeping a tenuous hold on her emotions. "Why would you think that?"

He shrugged, then shoved his hands in his jeans pockets. "It was almost as if you were expecting him," Brody said, his eyebrow arched.

Hayley swallowed hard and tried to steady her voice. "I saw the Kerry Creek horses and I thought it might be him. But I was mistaken. Sorry. I didn't mean to wake you."

"Should I tell Teague you were looking for him?" Brody asked.

"Why?" Hayley shook her head, unwilling to reveal her true feelings to Teague's brother. "No. You don't need to tell him anything."

A moment later, a woman joined Brody on the porch, her eyes sleepy and her long mahogany hair loose around her shoulders. He turned to her and smiled, slipping his arm around her shoulders. "Morning," she said, nodding to Hayley.

"Payton, this is Hayley Fraser," Brody said. "Her family owns this place. Hayley, Payton Harwell."

Payton smiled warmly. "Thank you for letting us

stay here. I got lost last night and wasn't really prepared to sleep outside."

Hayley nodded, still suspicious of Brody's friendly attitude. She knew what Teague's brothers thought of her, what his whole family thought. She was trouble, a girl who didn't deserve a brilliant boy like Teague. His parents had tried to put an end to their friendship early on and when Teague had been forbidden to see her, they'd simply snuck around, taking whatever time they could find together.

"I—I have to go," Hayley said. "Stay as long as you like. I won't say anything to my grandfather."

Hayley couldn't contain her humiliation as she rode back to the house. Once again, tears flooded her eyes and she brushed them away with her fingers. What was wrong with her? She'd never been this emotional before. This was what romance did to her—it caused her heartache and pain.

But mixed with the humiliation was a large dose of frustration. She'd been the one to mess everything up. Teague had done nothing but offer her his friendship and affection and she'd thrown it in his face. He was right. She didn't owe anything to Harry. If it came down to a choice between Teague and her grandfather, she should have chosen Teague.

Harry may be family, but Teague was something more. Teague was a true friend. Hayley sighed. No, he was more than a friend. A lover. "A lover that I don't love." She groaned. A soul mate? Was that it? The notion seemed so sentimental, but it came the closest to describing how she felt.

There was no one in the world she trusted more. Considering she usually trusted no one but herself, that was saying a lot. And there wasn't one other man with whom she'd rather spend an evening. He knew what she was thinking before she said it, as if he could see right into her mind. And Hayley was certain that no matter how much time had passed, she could depend on him if she needed help.

As she approached the stable, Hayley noticed Teague's truck parked nearby. Her heart leaped and she kicked Molly into a quicker pace. When she got inside the stable, she saw him sitting on a bale of straw at the far end. He glanced up at the sound of Molly's hooves on the concrete and then got to his feet.

Hayley jumped to the ground and took a step toward him. For a long moment, they stared at each other, and then a tiny sob racked her body and Hayley ran toward him. Teague gathered her in his arms, lifting her off her feet as he kissed her.

"I'm sorry. I'm sorry," he whispered between kisses.

"No, I'm sorry," Hayley said. "I was such a bitch to you. And you didn't deserve that."

"I need to be more patient," he said, setting her on the ground. He held her face in his hands and kissed her again. "I've been miserable these last few days. All I could think about was you. I was in Brisbane yesterday and I was walking through David Jones and everything I saw reminded me of you. I wanted you there with me."

"You went shopping to get your mind off me?"

Hayley asked. "Don't men usually go to a pub and get themselves drunk?"

"I did that on Thursday night. Saturday I took Gemma and Payton shopping in Brisbane."

"I met Payton," she said softly. "I rode out to the shack this morning and she was there with Brody."

"So that's where they ended up," Teague said with a soft chuckle. "I guess that's not our private place anymore."

"She seemed nice," Hayley said. "Very pretty."

"I've never known Brody to be this far gone for a girl before and he's had lots of girls. And Cal, he's got a sweetheart, too. Though I'm not sure he knows what the hell to do with her. Her name is Gemma and she's a genealogist from Ireland. Things have changed at Kerry Creek in the past week."

"Is that why you asked me to come and live with you? So you'd have someone there, too?"

"No. And I shouldn't have asked. I know how you feel, and Cal and Brody haven't ever done anything to get to know you better. But that's going to change."

"How? Are you going to beat them up if they say anything nasty about me?"

"Yes," Teague said, nodding his head. "I will thoroughly thrash them to defend your honor. But before I do, I'm going to give them a chance to get to know you. I want you to come to Kerry Creek tomorrow. We're having a little celebration for the queen's birthday, a barbecue. And I'm inviting you to be my guest."

"I don't know, Teague. If I come, Callum and Brody will be upset and I'll ruin everyone's good time."

"But if you don't come, you'll ruin my good time," he said. Teague slowly rubbed her arms, searching her gaze until she couldn't help but smile at him. "It will be fun. We're going to have games and a campdrafting competition. It will give you a chance to show off your skills on a horse. And you can see Payton and meet Gemma and talk about…girl stuff."

In truth, Hayley would have been happy to avoid Callum and Brody for as long as she could. But Brody had been rather nice to her at the shack. Maybe their feelings had softened a bit now that they were older. "All right. I'll come, but if your brothers don't want me there, then I'm going home."

"I'll pick you up at—"

"No, I'll ride over," Hayley said. "In case I decide to leave early."

"You won't want to leave." He kissed her again. "I promise. You'll have a good time. Now, I have the day off. What are we going to do with ourselves?"

"We could go riding," Hayley said.

"We could fly to Brisbane to see a movie," Teague suggested.

"We could drive to Bilbarra and have lunch at Shelly's."

Teague bent close, his forehead pressed to hers. "Or we could ride out to the shack, kick Brody and Payton out and spend the rest of the day in bed."

"I vote for the shack," she said.

"Me, too."

He walked over to Molly, who had been munching on some loose hay in her stall, and led her to the door.

He swung up into the saddle, then shifted to make room for Hayley. He held out his hand and pulled her up to sit in front of him, then clucked his tongue.

Hayley settled against him, holding tight to the arm he'd wrapped around her waist. Everything was all right now. She hadn't made a mess of things. Teague still cared and she had another chance to show him how much he meant to her.

"I'LL GIVE YOU THIS," Brody said. "She's not hard to look at. I've watched her program a few times with Mary. They make her look like a real tart on the telly. She looks much better in person."

"They say the camera adds ten pounds," Callum said soberly.

"Who says that?" Teague asked, laughing at his brother's comment.

Callum shrugged. "I don't know. They. People who know that kind of shit. I'm not saying she's fat, because she isn't. And I think she's pretty enough, but Gemma is much prettier."

"Payton has them both beat. Dark-haired girls are always more attractive," Brody said. He nodded in the girls' direction. "What do you suppose they're talking about?"

The three women were standing along the far fence, their arms braced on the top railing as they chatted. The conversation must be going well, Teague mused, because Hayley was smiling.

Callum folded his hands over his saddle horn. "I

don't know. Maybe recipes. That's probably it. They're exchanging recipes."

This time both Brody and Teague laughed. "You don't know anything about women, Cal," Brody said. "They're probably talking about shoes or clothes."

"Or they could be talking about us," Teague offered. "The same way we're talking about them."

"What? Like they're discussing how pretty we are?" Brody asked. "There's not much to discuss. I'm a better-looking bloke than the two of you. End of story."

"Brody has always been the pretty one in the family," Callum said. "We've always thought of him as our little sister, haven't we, Teague?"

"And since you're the one with all the experience around women, little sis, you go over there and find out what they're talking about," Teague suggested.

"I'd guess they're probably talking about what a pair of dills you two are," Brody muttered as he rode away.

"You're not upset that I brought her here, are you?" Teague asked.

"No," Callum said. "My fight is with Harry Fraser, not his granddaughter. Besides, you could always marry her and then Wallaroo would be yours someday."

"What the devil are you talking about?"

Callum gave him a dubious look. "Don't tell me you haven't thought about it. She'll inherit. Harry doesn't have any other heirs. Though Wallaroo is smaller than Kerry Creek, it has some prime grazing land. And it would be the perfect place to raise horses. You've always wanted to do that. Isn't that why you went to vet school?"

"I told you, Hayley isn't interested in the station. She's going to try to convince Harry to sell it."

"You should talk her out of that," he said. "That land is worth a whole lot more than what anyone will pay for it now, especially since it borders Kerry Creek."

"You could always buy it," Teague said.

"Yeah. If three or four million dollars falls out of the sky tomorrow, I could. But I'm not holding my breath on that one."

They watched as the ladies climbed over the fence and walked across the yard toward them. Brody had talked them into taking part in the campdrafting competition. They'd compete as pairs against each other.

Though Callum was the best at driving cattle, it was obvious Gemma wasn't comfortable around horses. Payton, however, was an experienced horsewoman, but she'd never attempted campdrafting, so Brody's chances were about the same as Callum's—fifty-fifty. But Teague knew Hayley would throw herself headlong into any competition, especially if it involved riding.

"Two on a horse," Brody explained. "The girls steer, the guys work the stirrups. This should be fun."

Teague reached down and grabbed Hayley's arm, then swung her up in front of him. "We've got this won," he whispered in her ear.

"I don't know," Hayley said. "I think Payton might be a decent rider."

"And you could probably beat half the stockmen," he said. "With your hands tied behind your back."

"Oh, adding a little bondage to the competition might be fun," Hayley teased.

"Be careful," he warned, holding her close. "I won't be able to concentrate on winning."

Callum decided to go first and called out to Davey to release a calf from the pen. Payton and Brody watched from the other side of the fence, Brody's arms wrapped around Payton's waist and his chin resting on her shoulder.

Gemma screamed as she tried to maneuver Callum's horse. When Callum tried to grab the reins, the stockmen began to jeer at him for cheating. He finally told Gemma to drop the reins and he steered his horse using only his knees and feet.

Though the effort wasn't Callum's best, he did manage to get the calf through the obstacle course and back into the pen in under five minutes. Gemma looked as if she could hardly wait to get off the horse.

"Hey!" Brody called from the fence. "We're going to grab some more coldies. Who wants one?"

Both Hayley and Teague raised their hands, as did half the stockmen. Brody took Payton's hand and pulled her along toward the house.

"I sure hope you boys aren't too thirsty," Callum shouted. "They may be a while."

Teague gave Tapper a gentle kick and Hayley maneuvered the horse over to the gate. "Ready?" Teague asked.

"I'm ready."

Teague shouted to Davey and a moment later, the gate swung open and a calf ran out. Teague jabbed his heels into Tapper's sides and Hayley pulled the horse to the right, cutting off the calf's escape.

Over the next ninety seconds, they worked as a perfect team, anticipating each other's movements without speaking. Hayley was firm but aggressive with the reins, and Teague couldn't help but admire her determination. When they returned the calf to the pen and Davey slammed the gate shut, the stockmen erupted in wild cheers.

Teague glanced over at Callum to find his brother looking at the two of them in disbelief. "What?" Teague said. "You didn't think we could do it?"

"You beat Skip's time and he's the best on Kerry Creek," Callum said. "Ninety seconds."

"No," Teague replied, shaking his head. "You must have the time wrong. Skip Thompson's the best stockman we have. No one can beat him." He reached around Hayley and took the reins, then trotted Tapper over to the gate.

"It was only ninety seconds," Hayley said beneath her breath. "I think we won."

"I know. But we can't humiliate the boys. Skip will get the prize and everyone will be happy."

"What about my prize?" she said, turning around and sending him a sexy pout.

"I'll think of something I can do to make it up to you."

"You could rub my backside," Hayley suggested. "I've been spending too much time riding and I'm a bit sore."

When they reached the stable, Teague helped Hayley off his horse, then removed Tapper's saddle. He led him into the stable yard, then carried the saddle to the tack room. When he emerged, Hayley was waiting for him, a devilish smile on her pretty face.

"I'm not going to rub your bum," he said.

"Please," Hayley teased. She turned away from him, then looked over her shoulder, pursing her lips in another pretty pout.

Hayley was growing less wary of him, he mused. Allowing herself to tease and act playful. Maybe they were making progress. Teague was still unsure, but as long as their relationship kept changing for the better, he wasn't going to complain. "What if someone walks in?" he asked.

She pulled him into an empty stall. Then, taking his wrists, she placed both of his palms on her backside. Wriggling, she pressed up against him, her arms draped around his neck. "You do it so well when I'm naked. What's a little denim between friends?"

"Friends with benefits," he reminded her. "You really are determined to make me squirm, aren't you? Is this payback for my dragging you here in the first place?"

"No. Actually, I'm having a lovely time. Gemma and Payton are very nice and your brothers have been quite cordial."

"I told you you'd have fun."

"I'd have more fun if you rubbed my bum."

With a low growl, Teague grabbed her legs and picked her up, wrapping her thighs around his waist. Hayley yelped with surprise, then laughed as he stumbled. Pressing her against the wooden wall, Teague kissed her, his hands smoothing over the sweet curves of her backside.

"Oh, yes," Hayley moaned, her voice deep and dramatic. "Oh, that feels so good."

"I thought you were a good actress," Teague teased.

She pushed her hands against his shoulders and looked at him, a shocked expression on her pretty features. "And I thought you were a good lover."

"I am," Teague said.

"Prove it."

It was like one of those challenges she used to issue when they were kids—I can ride faster than you can, I can jump higher than you can, I can hold my breath longer than you can. He'd never refused one of her challenges in the past and he wasn't about to now.

"Here?"

"Are you afraid? Oh, don't be such a big girl's blouse."

"And you're going to get a reputation as the town bike if you don't watch out." He chuckled as he set her back on her feet. "I'm not going to start something here that might be interrupted, especially by one of my brothers."

"Then you'll have to work quickly," she said, reaching down and unbuttoning his jeans. "Ingenious design, these chaps. Good for riding and better for sex."

He moaned softly as she began to tease him erect. Strange how the prospect of getting caught made the desire even more intense. It was silly, this desperate need to hide their sexual relationship. Their romance was in the open now and there didn't seem to be any objections from the Quinn side of the equation. And sex was all part of that.

Still, Teague wasn't anxious for his brothers to know how obsessed he was with Hayley Fraser. She'd become the single point around which his universe revolved. And he was beginning to believe that he wouldn't want to live his life any other way.

"So what are you looking for in the way of a massage?" Teague whispered, his lips trailing along the curve of her neck.

She drew in a slow breath, then tipped her head to the side, inviting him to move lower. "I'll leave that up to you."

Over the next minute, they tore at each other's clothes, pulling aside just enough to allow the basics of sex. And when he slipped inside her, Teague was already on the edge. This was all he needed in life. That thought whirled round and round in his head as her warmth enveloped him.

And when he finally lost control and buried himself one last time, he made a silent promise. He would do whatever it took to make her happy, whatever it took to keep her with him. She was his—she always had been, from the moment they'd met out on the big rock until forever.

HAYLEY HEARD THE PLANE before she saw it. Shading her eyes from the sun, she stared up into the sky and caught sight of it coming in from the west. He flew low over the house and she ran out into the yard and waved. Teague wiggled the wings in response.

With a laugh, she hurried to her car and hopped inside, then made a wide turn toward the old airstrip. It had been a week since the queen's birthday celebration and she and Teague had seen each other only a few times. His work had called him off the station several times on overnight visits, and when he returned, he was off again within the next few hours. On top of that, he'd had to make a quick flight with Payton and Brody to Brisbane when they'd decided to visit Fremantle for a few days.

Though Hayley knew this was what a real relationship between them would be like, she'd found herself feeling more lonely than she'd ever imagined she could. No matter how hard she tried to convince herself they were involved in a purely physical relationship, it was becoming more delusion now than determination.

She and Teague weren't just sexual partners. They'd rediscovered their friendship and rekindled an affection that had never really disappeared. And though it might have been easy to say they were falling in love again, Hayley wasn't ready to take that step—not yet. Perhaps if they could meet the challenge of spending so much time apart, she might consider love.

The odds had been against them when they were kids and now that they were adults, not much had changed. She had her career in Sydney and the possibility of much more. And he had his new practice in Bilbarra. Perhaps if Teague had been free to practice in Sydney, it might work between them.

But he'd made a commitment to buy Doc Daley's practice. It was his chance to run his own business. And it could take years to establish himself in Sydney, especially as an equine vet. He'd probably be forced to join an existing practice and work for someone else. This had been his dream, to live in Queensland, to expand the horse-breeding operation on Kerry Creek.

He was standing beside the plane when she arrived at the airstrip, his arm braced on one of the wing struts. Hayley hopped out of the car and walked up to him. "Are you trying to impress me?" she asked in a teasing voice.

"Come on," he said. "Let's go."

"Where are we going?"

"We're getting away. You and me, alone, for a few days. I've made all the regular visits on my schedule and now I've got some time."

"I can't just leave," she said. "I don't have anything packed and I—"

"You won't need anything," Teague said.

"But—"

"But what? Where's your sense of adventure, Hayley Fraser? As I recall, you called me a big girl's blouse just last week. You used to do anything on a dare. I dare you to get in this plane."

"I can't leave without telling Harry I'm going to be gone. He'll notice I'm not there to make him supper."

"All right. Go," Teague said. "I'll give you fifteen minutes. If you're not back, I'm going to leave without you. I'll have to find another girl who's more adventurous."

Hayley frowned. Then she stepped up to him, threw her arms around his neck and kissed him. The kiss was long and deep and meant to show him that leaving her behind would be a big mistake. When she finally drew away, she looked up into his eyes to see desire burning there.

"Yeah, I thought so. You're not going to leave," she assured him. "And there are no other girls more adventurous than I am."

A smile curled the corners of his mouth and he sighed. "No. But I still want you to hurry."

"Are you going to tell me where we're going?"

He grinned and shook his head. "Do you have something against surprises?"

Hayley usually preferred to be in control, but she knew Teague would never plan a surprise she wouldn't like. "I'll be right back."

By the time Hayley returned to the house, Harry was already pacing a path along the length of the porch. When he saw the car, he stopped and stormed into the yard. "Where did you go?" he demanded as she jumped out of the car. "Was that a plane I heard?"

"Yes. I'm going to be leaving for a few days. I have…business. It's important, so they sent a plane." It was an outright lie, but Hayley didn't want to take the time to make up a more plausible excuse. She paused. Maybe she ought to tell Harry the truth. There was no use hiding it anymore. "That's not right," she said, facing him. "Teague Quinn has invited me on a holiday and I'm going. I don't care if you don't like it. I'm an adult and I make my own decisions."

Harry cursed and wagged his finger. "I'll not have you taking up with that Quinn boy again!" he shouted.

"I can do what I want, Harry. There'll be no letters for you to intercept and no phone calls for you to ignore. I've cooked and cleaned for you for the past two weeks and I deserve a bit of a break. I'll be home… when I get home."

She moved to the door, ready to return to her room and pack a few belongings. But then, Hayley realized she'd only have to put up with Harry's badgering the whole time. Teague said she wouldn't need anything, so she would trust him on that, as well.

"Goodbye, Harry." Hayley jogged down the steps and got into her car. She saw Harry in the rearview mirror, glaring at her from his spot on the porch. She'd never really stood up to him when it came to Teague and now that she had, Hayley realized Harry wasn't nearly as powerful as she'd thought he was. What was the worst he could do, kick her out of the house? She had a place of her own in Sydney. And a place with Teague, if she needed it.

Harry would have the next few days to cool off before she had to face him again. But there was no longer a reason for her to be ashamed of seeing Teague. He made her happy and she hadn't felt truly happy since the last time they'd been together. Nearly ten years of searching for the one thing she needed, and she found it in the place where it had all begun.

When she drove up to the plane, Teague was waiting. He helped her inside, showing her how to strap in, then circled around and climbed into the pilot's seat. A few seconds later, the engine roared to life.

"When did you learn how to fly?" she shouted.

"Four years ago," he said. "Figured I'd need a plane if I was going to be an outback vet. I bought it last year.

Lived like a pauper when I was working in Brisbane, saving everything I made. This baby comes in handy."

Hayley had never been in a small plane before. She drew a deep breath as they headed down the bumpy runway, the plane gathering speed. She was afraid it might fall apart with all the bouncing and bumping, but then they lifted off and the ride was suddenly smooth.

Teague reached over and captured her hand, then brought it to his lips to kiss it. She felt a familiar thrill, the same feeling she'd had when they were kids and they'd found an adventure to experience together. There was a certain satisfaction in sharing something new with Teague. As if it was something no one could ever take from them.

"Will you tell me where we're going now?"

He shook his head. "Look in the bags behind your seat."

She twisted around and found two huge shopping bags from David Jones, a department-store chain. "What's this?"

"I picked up a few things while I was shopping with the girls."

"How long have you been planning this?"

He shrugged. "Awhile. Well, ever since we spent that first night in the shack. I wasn't sure I'd be able to get away, but Doc Daley told me I could take a few days if I cleared my schedule."

She pulled out a tiny pink-flowered bikini and held it up. "We're going to the beach?"

"Yes." He nodded.

She found a matching sarong and a pretty pair of sandals in the same bag. In the other bag, she found two sundresses along with a pale yellow cotton cardie. In a smaller bag, a selection of underwear, bras and panties in pastel colors. "You bought these yourself?"

He nodded again. "I think they'll fit. I had to guess on the sizes." He glanced over at her. "I don't think you'll need more than that."

"I suspect I'll be spending a fair number of hours without any clothes at all."

"Yes," he agreed with a boyish grin. "I didn't pack much, either."

As they flew northeast, Teague pointed out all the major landmarks. They flew over Carnarvon National Park and then over the Blackdown Tablelands before turning directly north. Soon, the coast was visible, the turquoise-blue water shimmering in the afternoon sun. Hayley sat back in her seat, watching the landscape float by below them. When they got over the water, Teague brought the plane lower and pointed out the window at a pod of whales breaking the smooth surface. They circled once so she could get a better look, then he navigated north again.

"It's so beautiful," she said. "I love the ocean."

"I know." He turned and smiled at her. "You told me the day we met. You stood on the top of the rock and tried to see the ocean. And when you couldn't, I was afraid you might cry."

"You remember that?"

"I remember everything about that day," he said.

Islands dotted the coastline and Teague headed farther east until they could see waves breaking over the Great Barrier Reef. She'd never really appreciated the true beauty of her homeland, but here, with Teague, everything looked different somehow. The coast was greener, the sky bluer, the water sparkling with the light of a million diamonds.

How was it possible that life seemed so much more exciting when he was near? He was just a man, nothing more. Yet, when she was with him, she felt…complete. As if all the pieces that had been missing over the years had found their place again in her heart.

Her body buzzed with a strange anticipation. While they were on Wallaroo and Kerry Creek, it was simple to think of their time together in finite terms. But now that they were in the real world, the possibilities seemed endless. Could they continue after they both returned to their regular lives? Would there be shared holidays and weekends away? The more she thought about how it might work, the more Hayley realized that it could work.

Lots of people carried on long-distance relationships. And she and Teague had spent nearly ten years apart, yet it hadn't changed anything between them, except the intensity of their feelings for each other. What was a week or a month compared to ten years?

"Which beach are we going to?" she asked.

"Why don't you let me surprise you," he insisted. "I know it's not in your nature, but give it a try, just this once."

"I have to warn you again that wherever we go,

people will recognize me. They'll either ask for my autograph or tell me what a horrible person I am. They sometimes get me mixed up with my character."

"You *are* a very bad girl on the program. How many marriages have you destroyed?"

"Three, I think," Hayley said ruefully. "And two engagements. I seem to like sex far too much for my own good."

"How does that work?" Teague asked. "When you have to do those scenes?"

"Sometimes it's uncomfortable. Especially when you don't know the other person very well. But it's part of the job." She paused. "And sometimes, it creates a false sense of intimacy."

"And how did the men in your life handle you doing love scenes with other guys?"

"You mean my boyfriends?"

Teague nodded. "I know you've had boyfriends. I've read all the magazines. Whenever there was a story about you and some fella, I'd have to read it. You've had some very famous boyfriends."

"I suppose they didn't care. They never really knew me, anyway. I never let them get close enough."

"I know what you mean," Teague said. "It's never felt right with other women."

"So you were abstinent for ten years," she joked.

"No. And I don't expect you were, either. But I never found anyone that felt as…right as you did. As right as you *do*. With me."

"What are we going to do about that?" she asked.

"I don't know. I'm still figuring it out."

A long silence grew between them as Hayley considered what he'd told her. Everything he'd said had been the truth and she'd felt it as strongly as he had. They belonged together. But admitting that fact made everything so much more complicated.

She could figure it all out later, she decided. For the next few days, she was going to enjoy her time with Teague and not worry about the future.

6

TEAGUE SAT on the edge of the bed and stared out the open doors onto the bungalow's wide veranda. Hayley stood facing the ocean, her body outlined by the setting sun. The breeze caught a strand of her hair and he watched as she distractedly tucked it behind her ear.

She was the most beautiful thing he'd ever seen. And it was obvious to him that he couldn't consider a life without her. How was that possible? Had they really fallen in love as teenagers? Was this merely a continuation of those feelings? If he couldn't figure that out here, alone with her, then maybe he'd never know for sure.

They'd landed at the only commercial airport in the Whitsundays, on Hamilton Island, and then had hopped onto a helicopter for the ten-minute flight to the resort. Teague had heard of the resort when he was living in Brisbane and when he'd called to make a reservation, he'd been assured that it was very private. There were only sixteen bungalows, set near the water's edge, the lush rain forest spreading out behind them. This being the off-season, he and Hayley were the only guests midweek.

The bungalows were furnished in plantation style with high ceilings and polished wood floors. A fan whirred above his head, the sound mixing with the rush of waves on the shore. If they were going to fall in love all over again, this would be the place to do it, Teague mused. They had three days and nights together to figure out their relationship.

She turned to face him, her expression soft and her smile satisfied. "It's beautiful," Hayley said as she walked toward him.

"The helicopter pilot told me we're the only guests right now. We have the whole island to ourselves. Besides the staff, the wallabies, the goannas and—"

She put her finger to his lips, then sat down on his lap. "No people to bother me with autographs," she said.

"Nope."

"A real bed with a down comforter," she said, leaning back to smooth her hand over the bed linens.

Teague nodded.

"You know how to spoil a girl, don't you."

"I do my best," he said.

She gave his chest a gentle shove and they tumbled onto the bed together. "Now that we're here, what are we going to do with ourselves?"

"I have some ideas," Teague teased. "But they all involve taking off your clothes."

Hayley scrambled to her feet and, without hesitation, pulled the cotton dress up and over her head. Then she kicked off her shoes and jumped onto the bed. "Now what?"

"Use your imagination," Teague said.

She stretched out at his side, then ran her hand from his chest to his groin. She rubbed the front of his khakis, waiting for the customary reaction to her touch. As he grew hard, she smiled. "You're far too easy," she said.

Teague caught her wrists and rolled her beneath him, pinning her hands above her head. "What about you? It doesn't take much to make you all warm and wet."

"I can last longer than you can," she said.

Another challenge. Funny how he enjoyed these challenges so much more than the silly challenges of their younger years. He loosened his grip on her wrists and slowly slid down along her body, his lips pressing against her silken skin. He stopped long enough to dispense with her bra, then let his mouth linger over each tempting breast.

Hayley arched beneath him as he brought each nipple to a stiff peak, then blew on it softly. Teague's fingers twisted in the waistband of her panties as he pulled them over her hips and thighs. When she was finally naked, he lay beside her and gently caressed the damp spot between her legs.

Her eyes were closed and her lips slightly parted. When he looked at her, every detail of her face suddenly became important to him. Her bow-shaped upper lip, the long lashes that fluttered against her cheeks, the tiny mole on her chin. He'd known them all by heart so many years ago, but now he didn't want to forget.

Teague bent over and kissed her gently as he slipped

his finger inside her. Hayley's breath caught in her throat and she moaned. He knew she was close, but he wanted to prolong her pleasure. They had a comfortable bed and a long night ahead of them. There was no need to rush.

But Hayley wasn't ready to surrender. She gently pushed his hand away, then rolled over and straddled his body. Her hair fell in waves around her face and she smiled down at him as she tugged at his T-shirt.

Carefully, she undressed him, Teague touching her at every turn, his hands searching out the sweet curves of her body. He'd been so long without a woman before Hayley had come into his life again. And now that he'd grown used to having her near, Teague wondered if he'd ever be able to do without. There was something so comforting in knowing that, for at least this moment in time, she belonged entirely to him.

Her lips were warm against his bare skin. A shiver skittered over him as she teased his nipple. Then, her lips drifted lower until her hair tickled his belly. He knew her game but he also knew how close he was to losing control. Teague groaned as her mouth brushed along the length of his shaft.

There were certain aspects of passion that they hadn't enjoyed as teenagers and this had been one of them. But it was obvious that new skills had been acquired in ten years. Her mouth closed around him and Teague felt a current race through his body, making him flinch in response.

He slid his fingers through her hair, holding her back when he felt too close, then loosening his grip when he wanted more. Teague lost himself in the wild sensations her mouth and hands were bringing him.

"All right," he groaned. "You win."

"Not yet," Hayley said. "Not until you give up." She went to work and Teague knew she wouldn't be satisfied until he was. Did he want to surrender? Or would he rather find his release inside her?

In the end, Teague didn't have a choice. The feel of her tongue on his cock was more than he could handle. He held his breath and felt his body grow tense with anticipation. And then, a spasm shook his core. His fingers tangled in her hair, gently pulling her away as the warmth of his orgasm pooled on his belly.

When it was finally over and his body had relaxed, Teague opened his eyes to find her looking up at him, her chin resting on his chest. "I win," she said, a satisfied smile on her face.

"No. I'm pretty sure I won that round." He reached down and drew her up alongside him, tucking her into the curve of his arm. "If this is any indication of the rest of our holiday, I think I'm going to need a holiday from our holiday."

"I like this," she said, staring up at the ceiling. "It feels so grown-up."

"We are grown-up," Teague said.

"Sometimes I don't feel like an adult. I keep waiting for my life to start, as if there's supposed to be a big sign that tells me when I need to begin paying attention. Your Life Starts Now," she said, emphasizing each word with her hands.

"Your life has started."

"But it doesn't seem like it's mine," Hayley said. "It feels like it belongs to someone else."

"What did you think it was supposed to be?"

She considered his question for a long moment. "I thought that you and I would live on a station and we'd raise horses and spend all day riding them. And at night, we'd live in a little shack, like the one on Wallaroo. And we'd sleep in the same bed and wake up together every morning. And that would be our life."

"It sounds pretty nice to me," Teague said.

"Not very practical, though. Where would we have found the money to buy a station and horses? How would we have supported ourselves? It was a silly dream."

Not so silly, Teague thought to himself. He'd had the same dream himself when he was younger. Only, he'd have a job as a vet to help support them both. They'd work the station together and breed the best horses in all of Australia.

But as he looked at Hayley now, he wondered whether she'd be happy with station life. He'd seen what it had done to his own mother, driving her away after eighteen years of marriage. And raising a family in the outback wasn't a piece of cake, either.

Hayley had a glamorous life in Sydney, enough money to live quite comfortably. She was a celebrity, people recognized her. That wasn't the kind of life someone walked away from.

But he could walk away and join her. His deal with Doc Daley wasn't finalized yet. Though they'd reached a verbal agreement, they were due to sign the papers at the end of the month. If he backed out, there would certainly be other vets who'd jump at the chance to take over the practice. Teague could return to clinic work, like he'd done after he graduated from vet school. City life hadn't been that bad. He could get used to caring for dogs and cats again and forget about horses.

Teague closed his eyes. He'd promised himself that he wouldn't think about the future while they were at the resort. There was time enough for that later.

"There's a very large shower in the bathroom. I think we should try it out," he said.

"We've never had a shower together," she said. "Or a bath."

"Well, if you don't count the time you snuck over to the pond on Kerry Creek and talked me into skinny-dipping."

A smile spread slowly across her pretty face. "I remember that."

"Yes. You spent half the night laughing at the effect the cold water had on my bits and pieces. I was humiliated."

"Yes, but you forget that a few days later, we found something much more interesting to do with your bits and pieces." She dropped a kiss on his lips. "We had sex for the first time."

"That's right," he said. "And look where we are now. Still naked, still having sex. And you're still issuing challenges."

"We have come a long way," Hayley said. She rolled off the bed and held out her hand. "Shower. I think it's time we ticked that off the list. I'll wager you dinner that I can wash your back better than you can wash mine."

Teague followed her into the bathroom, his gaze fixed on the sweet curve of her backside. If this was the way their holiday was starting, three days and nights would never be enough.

HAYLEY SAT on the wooden lounge chair, her feet tucked under her. The sun was beginning to brighten the morning sky. The mist rising from the dense rain forest on the island would soon burn off, leaving them with another beautiful day.

She'd learned to love mornings on the island. Right before the sun came up, birds would awaken and begin chattering in the trees that surrounded their bungalow. Teague slept so deeply he never noticed. But for Hayley, they were like an alarm clock, reminding her that she had another whole day to spend with Teague.

They'd walk on the beach or take a trek on the paths through the forest. They'd sip fresh juice for breakfast and enjoy a gourmet meal for dinner.

Sadly, this was their last day on the island. At noon, they'd take the helicopter back to Hamilton Island and then Teague's plane home to Wallaroo. She didn't want their holiday to end. It had all been too perfect.

Was she wrong to believe that real life would never match the fantasy of their time on the island? It was easy to fall in love in this place. They had no responsibilities, no worries, no careers tugging them in different directions.

Was their relationship strong enough to survive time

and distance apart? If they didn't make any promises to each other, there wouldn't be any failures or regrets. Why couldn't she accept this for what it was—temporary?

If she knew what was good for her, she'd return to Sydney before she lost her heart completely. She had scripts to memorize and she hadn't been to the gym in ages. Plus, she'd promised her agent she'd make the trip to L.A. before she was due back on the set.

She pushed to her feet and walked inside the room, the dew from the veranda creating tracks across the wooden floor. Slipping out of the expensive robe that the resort provided, she crawled beneath the down comforter.

Teague was warm, his naked body stretched out beneath the cotton sheets. This was the third morning she'd awoken beside him without having to think about the repercussions of spending the night together. This was how it should be.

Hayley slid her arm around his waist and pressed her body against his, throwing her leg over his thigh. He stirred and then slowly opened his eyes, turning his sleepy gaze on her.

"Your feet are freezing," he complained.

"I was sitting out on the veranda. Listening to the birds."

"What time is it?"

"Early, she said. "The sun is just coming up."

"I like waking up with you," Teague said, drawing her closer.

"How would it have been," Hayley asked, "if I had come to Perth to be with you?"

Teague frowned. "What brought this on?"

"I'm curious. How would it have worked?"

He drew a deep breath then raked his hand through his tousled hair. "Well. We would have had to find a place to live. I don't think they would have allowed you to stay in my room at Murdoch. We would have found a flat in the city, something we could afford. I worked while I was in school, so we would have had some money, although my parents might have cut me off if they'd known we were together. You would have had to find a job. I'm not sure we could have both afforded to go to school, but I could have—"

Hayley reached up and pressed her finger to his lips, stopping his words. "Do you realize how complicated it would have been? Teague, it would never have worked. As much as we dreamed it could."

"You don't know that," he said.

"I found a job when I first got to Sydney and I could barely afford to eat, never mind rent a place to live. We were so young and so stupid. We thought love would solve all our problems. Love doesn't pay the bills. It was best that things turned out the way they did, don't you think?"

"We spent ten years apart," Teague reminded her.

"But we both made something of ourselves in that time. We're happy with our lives, aren't we?" she asked.

"Are you? You don't seem anxious to get back to yours."

"Don't try to analyze me," she warned. "Best leave that to professionals."

He sighed softly. "I wish I could find a bandage to

fix all the bad things that happened to you in your life, Hayley. I wish there was medicine or some kind of cure for all the pain that you've had to endure."

"I know I'm pretty much a wreck," she said with a weak smile. "It's a wonder you can tolerate me. But don't stop trying."

"You're not a wreck. You're a little banged up. A few dents here and there, but nothing that will stop me from wanting you."

"So do you think you can fix me, Dr. Feelgood?"

"I'm Dr. Feelamazinglygood." He pulled his hand out from under the comforter. "These fingers are magic. They can cure anything that ails you."

"What about what ails you?" Hayley slipped her hand beneath the comforter and smoothed it along his belly until she found his shaft, which was already growing hard with desire. "I think you have a problem. Something very strange is happening here. There's an unusual swelling. Oh dear, I've never seen anything like it."

"Very strange," he said, kissing her softly.

Hayley giggled, then felt a warm blush creep up her cheeks. "I remember the first time I touched you down there. I had absolutely no idea. I mean, I'd seen horses and cattle, but I never imagined that boys would function the same way."

"Are you saying I resemble a stallion? Or a bull?"

"Oh, definitely a stallion," she said. "Long legs, a nice mane, beautiful eyes."

"So, you want to go for a ride or what?"

Hayley gasped at his request, then gave him a playful slap. "You're terrible. All you think about is sex."

"No, all I think about is sex with you. There's a big difference."

"You don't ever think about other women?"

"Not since you came back into my life. You're it. All my fantasies, you're right there. Dressed in sexy lingerie, doing all kinds of nasty things to me, whispering in my ear, telling me how much you want me."

"We need to take another holiday together," she said. "This has been perfect."

"It would be this way all the time if we lived together," he said.

Hayley shook her head. "You'd toss me out in less than a week. I'd make a horrible roommate." She knew what he was offering, but if she made a joke of it, she wouldn't have to answer him.

She sighed inwardly. She'd like nothing more than to accept. It would be wonderful to share a place and to share their lives. But marriage was difficult enough, even without long periods apart. If she was going to commit to Teague, then she'd have to be prepared to give up her life in Sydney and start a new life with him.

"You haven't been a bad roommate these last few days. I wish we could stay longer," he said.

"Me, too. I'm not looking forward to my homecoming at Wallaroo. In fact, I've been thinking maybe you ought to fly me straight to Sydney."

"You want to go home to Sydney?" he asked, a trace of hurt in his voice.

"No. It's just that…I told Harry about us. Right before I left. That I was going away with you. I'm not sure if he's going to want me staying with him anymore."

"Why did you do that?"

"I was tired of pretending. It was silly. And you and I have nothing to do with the fight between him and Callum. So what difference does it make?"

"He won't see it that way," Teague said.

Hayley shrugged. "I expect all my things will be tossed in a big pile in the yard. Or maybe he'll have burned them. When he's given enough time, he can work up a pretty bad temper."

"The longer that feud goes on, the more ridiculous it seems."

"It's a matter of honor," Hayley said.

"What are you talking about?"

She pressed her face into his naked chest. "That's what Harry says. It's a matter of honor. Promises were made and promises were broken."

"What promises?"

"You don't know?"

"No. I assumed it was some mistake made on the deed years ago."

"According to Harry, his father traded a mail-order bride for that piece of land. Your great-grandmother fell in love with your great-grandfather and didn't want to marry my great-grandfather. So they made a trade. Only, your great-grandfather kept the land and the girl."

"Why did I never know that story?"

"Probably because it proves that Harry is right about

the land. It belongs to Wallaroo. Unfortunately, the paperwork was never filed. It was a gentleman's agreement, which doesn't count for much these days." She glanced over at him. "So, I guess that if it weren't for my great-grandfather and that little piece of land, you and your brothers wouldn't exist."

Teague frowned. "I'm not sure I believe anything Harry says. He'd do anything to have his way."

"It is a good story, though. Especially if it proves to be true."

"Maybe I should trade Harry the land for you," Teague teased, nuzzling her neck. "That would end the feud and we'd both get what we wanted."

"What about what I want?" Hayley said. "Doesn't that count?"

Teague pulled back, his gaze searching her face. "What do you want, Hayley?"

It was a simple question and Hayley ought to give him an answer. She could tell he was getting weary of always asking where he stood. And truly, if she knew, she'd give him an answer. But fabulous sex and long, romantic meals with Teague had only made her more confused. It wasn't just about a relationship now, it was about a lifetime together.

"Breakfast might be nice," she said.

"Don't do that," Teague warned. "Don't brush me off like that. Whenever I talk about the future, you seem to find a way to make a joke out of it. We've spent three incredible days together, just the two of us and no one else. Has that made any difference?"

She tried to twist out of his arms, but Teague wouldn't let her go. "Hayley, I'm falling in love with you all over again. But you've got to let me know if I'm making a fool of myself. Or if there's a chance for us."

"Don't do this," she said. "I can't— I don't know how—"

"What?"

"I can't go through that all again. Watching you walk out of my life. I can't do it."

"But you won't have to. That's the point. If we decide to be together, then that's it. Neither one of us will be walking out."

"I will be. All the time. My work doesn't exactly allow me to stay in one place for very long. Not if I want to be successful."

"Is acting what you want to do for the rest of your life?"

"I'm not sure. But my career is the only thing in this world that truly belongs to me. I made it happen. And I don't think I can give that up."

He exhaled slowly and drew her closer. "All right. At least I know where we stand on that. And I'm all right with a long-distance thing. You'll come home when you can. We can make it work, Hayley."

"Are you going to come to Sydney? Are you going to follow me around the world when I have work outside Australia? Would you give up everything to be with me?"

"I'm not sure I'd have to give up everything," Teague said. "We don't need to be together every minute of every day in order to be happy."

Hayley felt tears of frustration pushing at the corners

of her eyes. "Oh, brilliant," she muttered. "Now I'm crying again. I seem to do that a lot lately."

Teague ran his hands through her hair, then dropped a soft kiss on her lips. "Don't cry. There's no need for tears."

"I just…can't."

"I know," he murmured, pressing a kiss to her temple and then another to each of her eyelids. "I know."

Hayley drew in a ragged breath, then let the tears come. She had fought so long against her emotions. But now that they'd finally broken free, she realized how much good came of crying. It felt as if all the pain was draining out in her tears.

Teague held her close as she wept. After a time, she wasn't sure why she was still crying. Was it for her parents? For the perfect childhood she'd never had? For the love and loyalty that Teague was so determined to give her?

It didn't matter. All that mattered was that she was finally capable of crying. And whether Teague understood her tears or not, the ability to let loose her emotions meant more to their future than anything she might say.

"I CAN'T BELIEVE we have to leave in a few hours," Hayley said. She glanced up at Teague and then reached across the breakfast table to take his hand. "This was the best holiday I've ever had. Thank you."

"Next time it will be your turn to plan," he said. "I'll provide the plane."

"All right," Hayley agreed. "It's a date. No matter what happens, we'll have another holiday together."

"And then another and another," Teague said. "We

could survive on a string of holidays." He paused. "I would be satisfied with that if that's what you're offering."

Teague felt like a fool willing to settle for scraps when he might have the entire meal. But if it was what Hayley wanted, he didn't have much choice.

She nodded. "We'll choose a date and I'll make the plans. And this time, it will be my treat."

"Christmas," he said. "I'd like to spend Christmas with you."

"Christmas it is."

They finished their breakfast in silence. Teague was happy they'd managed to agree on future plans at last. But it hadn't escaped him that the plans didn't address the things standing between them and a real relationship.

In a few weeks, he would sign the papers that would give him ownership of Doc Daley's practice. When he'd first returned to Kerry Creek, Teague had been certain that taking over an established practice would be the perfect opportunity. Doc Daley had been ready to retire, and Teague figured he could make enough to buy Doc out in five years. He already had the plane, so he could handle much more business than Doc had ever managed, which would increase his income substantially. His future had looked brilliant.

But now Teague had to wonder if tying himself down in Queensland was really the answer. He could establish a practice on the outskirts of any large city—Brisbane, Sydney, Melbourne. Or he could work for another vet and not worry about keeping a business afloat.

Funny how he'd spent the last ten years of his life

happily cruising along, never worrying about his future. It was easy when he was on his own, with no responsibilities for another person. But he'd begun to see how complicated things could become once he'd decided on a life with Hayley.

Hell, there was no point thinking about it now. He had a few weeks. Things might be completely different between them by then. They'd just planned a holiday together. Who knew what could be waiting around the next corner?

"Mr. Quinn?"

Teague looked up at the waiter. "We're fine. The breakfast was great." He glanced over at Hayley. "Would you like more juice?"

She shook her head. "No. Thank you."

"Mr. Quinn, there's a phone call for you in the office. It's a Dr. Daley. He says it's urgent."

Teague frowned. He'd nearly forgotten they'd been without phones for the past three days. Messages were delivered in person. No telephones, no television, nothing to distract from the solitude.

He pushed away from the table. "This will only take a minute," he said to Hayley. "He's probably wondering if I can make a call on my way home to the station."

He followed the waiter to the small office where the manager was waiting with the phone. "Thanks," Teague said. "Doc?"

"Sorry to interrupt your holiday, Teague."

"No worries. Is something wrong?"

"I got a call from Cal early this morning. He's been

looking for you and thought I might know where you were."

He'd told his brother that he'd be gone until Friday afternoon. He hadn't given him all the details, but had assumed he wouldn't be bothered with station business. "I'll call him. I'm sorry that he—"

"No, he wanted me to pass along a message. This is for Hayley Fraser. She is with you, isn't she?"

"Yes," Teague said.

"Hayley's grandfather took a bad fall. He rode over to Kerry Creek and wanted to stir things up with Cal. He fell getting off his horse and broke his hip. He's in the hospital in Brisbane. Things aren't looking too good. He's refusing care and insisting that they let him go home. They want Hayley there as soon as possible to try to talk some sense into him."

"Which hospital?" Teague asked.

"St. Andrew's."

"Call Cal and tell him we'll get there as soon as we can."

"Take a few more days to be with your girl," Doc said. "I can handle things here."

"Thanks," Teague said. He returned the cordless phone to the manager. "Can we get an earlier flight to Hamilton? We've got a bit of an emergency."

"I'll call the pilot right now," the manager said. "Why don't you get packed and I'll send someone to let you know when the helicopter will arrive."

Teague hurried back to the dining room. This was going to be difficult. Hayley had finally asserted herself with her grandfather and now she'd get drawn in again by guilt. Teague wasn't sure how she'd react to the news.

She saw his expression before he had a chance to sit down. "What's wrong?"

He took a deep breath. "It's your grandfather. He must have rode Molly over to Kerry Creek. He was looking to mix it up with Cal, probably over the land dispute. He somehow fell off Molly and broke his hip."

Hayley gasped. "Oh, no. That's serious, isn't it?"

Teague nodded. "They've taken him to the hospital in Brisbane. But he's refusing treatment. They want you to come and convince him."

"He has a broken hip. He can't walk with a broken hip. What does he expect to do?"

"I don't know, Hayley. But we need to go there. The resort manager is calling for the helicopter. We can fly directly to Brisbane from Hamilton. We'll be there in a few hours."

"Could he die from a broken hip?" Hayley asked.

"No," Teague said. It was the truth. But Teague knew the complications that came with an injury like that. For a man Harry's age there was pneumonia and blood clots to consider. And if he refused treatment, he'd be stuck in a wheelchair for the rest of his life, probably living in a great deal of pain.

Teague stood and held out his hand and Hayley laced her fingers through his. "Everything will be all right," he said.

Hayley nodded, her face pale and her eyes wide. He walked to the room with her, then packed for both of them while Hayley stood on the veranda, looking out at the ocean. Without her grandfather on Wallaroo, there was little to keep her in Queensland.

Teague said a silent prayer that the old man would see reason and accept treatment for his injury. Maybe, with rehab, he could live on his own. But it was unlikely he'd be fit to run Wallaroo again. Chances were far better that Hayley would have to find him a place where she could watch over him.

A soft knock sounded at the door and Teague pulled it open. The resort manager stood there, a solemn expression on his face. "The helicopter will be here in ten minutes. Would you like me to take your bags?"

Teague nodded, then stepped aside to let him pass. The manager gathered up their meager belongings. "I'm sorry your holiday had to end so abruptly," he said.

"I am, too," Teague said. "But it's been wonderful. Truly, the best holiday I've ever had."

"We hope you'll come again soon."

Teague closed the door behind the manager and walked across the room to the veranda door. "Ten minutes," he said.

Hayley turned around. Her face was wet with tears. In three long strides, he crossed the veranda and gathered her into his arms. "Don't worry," he whispered. "Everything will be fine."

"Promise?"

"I promise. Harry is being stubborn. It always takes him a while before he gives in."

"He's not going to want to see me. He thinks I deserted him. For you."

"Well, now you're coming back. And if he doesn't forgive you, well…I'll have to set him straight."

Teague gave her a fierce hug, picking her up off her feet and shaking her. A tiny giggle slipped from her lips and he kissed the top of her head. "Come on. Let's go."

As they walked to the helicopter pad, Hayley held tight to his arm. This wasn't the way he wanted their holiday to end, but he couldn't help but wonder if it might finally breach the last wall between them. Hayley needed him right now, needed his strength and his counsel. He'd help her through this hard time and perhaps they'd come out better for it on the other side.

7

TEAGUE GLANCED UP from the newspaper he was reading as Hayley approached. She'd left him in the hospital waiting room nearly an hour ago. With a soft sigh, she sat down beside him, glad for a break from the endless conversations with doctors and nurses.

They'd arrived at the hospital and she'd gone directly into a meeting with Harry's doctors. Teague had asked if she wanted him there for support, but Hayley had prepared herself to deal with the crisis on her own during the flight to Brisbane.

In truth, Hayley knew Teague had his own opinions about her grandfather, none of them very good. He thought Harry was a cranky old bastard who seemed to take delight in making Hayley miserable. Teague would always stand up for her first, especially against Harry. And now was the time to avoid conflict at all costs.

"He's refusing an IV," Hayley finally said. "And he won't even consider surgery."

Teague took her hand. "He'll change his mind once he gets tired of lying in that bed."

She tried to control the tremble in her voice, but then

realized it didn't matter. She was talking to Teague. He could handle her emotions. He'd seen plenty of them over the past few weeks. "But if he doesn't get enough fluids, then they can't do surgery. And if he doesn't have surgery, he won't walk again. I don't know what to do. He won't listen to me."

"Would you like me to talk to him?"

"No! He'd probably break the other hip trying to chase you out of the room. They're bringing in a counselor to talk to him later today. They asked that I get some of his things from home. They think if he has some reminders of his life at Wallaroo, he'll be more apt to want to get well so he can return home." She turned to him. "I don't want to leave. I—I made a list and I was hoping you could go to Wallaroo and pick up a few things." She handed him the piece of paper.

"I'll do that," Teague said, taking the list from her. "But first, why don't we get you settled in a hotel, somewhere close by."

Hayley shook her head. "No, I'm going to stay here. They have a small room for family members. There's a bed if I need to sleep. I think I should try to talk to Harry again later tonight after the counselor leaves."

"Why is he doing this?"

"He told the doctor that he's finished living. He's done. If he can't ride a horse without falling off, then he's pretty useless on a cattle station."

"He's feeling sorry for himself."

"Well, he has good reason. Wallaroo isn't what it used to be. I think all of the troubles at the station might come from this anger of his. He's mad at his body, that it doesn't work the way it should, that he can't spend twelve hours in the saddle, seven days a week. He's seventy-five years old. What does he expect?"

"I suppose I can sympathize. I know I'd be pissed off with the world if I were stuck in that hospital bed. He's always been so independent and now he needs help. Harry Fraser has never needed another human being in his life."

Hayley leaned over and rested her head on Teague's shoulder. "I often wonder whether he would have been different had my grandmother lived. I never knew her, but he has a picture of her next to his bed."

"How did your grandmother die?"

"Complications after childbirth," Hayley replied. "Three days after my father was born. She gave birth on Wallaroo and I guess everything was fine until a couple days later. She got sick and by the time they got her to the hospital, it was too late." Hayley paused. "I can see why Harry hates hospitals. Can you blame him?"

"How come you never told me that story?"

"I didn't know it until just a few years ago. I asked Daisy Willey and she told me." She sighed. "Maybe Harry would have had a happy life and they'd have moved off the station in their retirement and lived in a cottage on the ocean. Or maybe they would have gone to the city, like your parents did."

She glanced at the clock on the wall. It was already three in the afternoon. Teague needed to leave for the airport soon or he'd be spending the night. "You should go. You're not going to make it to Kerry Creek before sunset if you don't leave now."

"I'm going to stay. I'll fly to Wallaroo tomorrow morning. We'll get some dinner and I'll get a room. That way, you could rest for a while before coming back here."

"No, you should go," Hayley insisted. "You've been away from work for three days. And you'll be back tomorrow with Harry's things, remember?"

Though it was generous of Teague to offer to stay, Hayley felt it was her duty to deal with Harry. He was her family, her responsibility. Besides, it felt good to do something. She'd been all but useless to Harry for most of her life. Now she could help him get through this, help him get well.

Teague pulled her hand up to his lips and kissed her fingertips. "Walk me down to the door?"

"I should—"

"Harry isn't going anywhere. He'll be fine." Teague stood, then drew Hayley up beside him. They headed toward the lift and once inside, Teague gathered her into his arms and kissed her softly. She held on as tightly as she could, hoping to draw some strength from him.

He always knew exactly the thing to make her feel better, to lift her spirits. She closed her eyes as he gently smoothed his hand over her hair, her face nuzzled into his chest. A memory of her childhood flickered in her mind. Her mother had often done that when Hayley had awoken from a bad dream, soothing her fears until she'd fallen back asleep.

But this wasn't a bad dream. It was bad reality. She

had no one to blame but herself for this disaster. She'd been the one to take off with Teague, leaving her grandfather to fend for himself. If she'd been watching over him at Wallaroo, he would never have gotten on a horse and ridden to Kerry Creek.

Hayley couldn't believe they'd run out of time. She wanted some of those years back, years that she could have used to get to know her grandfather better. She barely remembered her parents, had never known her grandmother and she couldn't face losing the last member of her family. Without Harry, she'd be utterly alone in the world.

The doors opened and they stepped out into the lobby of the hospital. She sat down while Teague walked to the reception desk to call a taxi.

If Harry agreed to the surgery, she was willing to deal with all the consequences. There would be a long rehabilitation, but the promise of going home might tempt him to work harder. And he would go back to Wallaroo, to live out his days on the station he loved.

Harry wouldn't sell. He had never looked at his land as a financial asset. It was part of his family heritage, something that didn't have a monetary value. In truth, the station was part of who she was, too. Whether she wanted to admit it or not, the land she'd played on as an adolescent was more a parent to her than Harry had been.

He'd always lived his life by his own rules and he had a right to make his own choices. Hayley closed her eyes. Maybe she ought to respect Harry's wishes now and let him do as he wanted—no IV, no surgery. Who was she to stop him? If he wanted this to be the end, then maybe it should be, on his own terms.

But she didn't want to lose him—not yet. Hayley had always held out hope that she'd find a way to make him love her. When she'd run away, she'd wanted him to come looking for her, praying he'd show that he really did care. But Harry had never once tried to find her. And when Teague had tried, Harry had stood in his way.

Grandparents were supposed to love their grandchildren. Yet she'd managed to get the world's worst set of grandparents. Three were long gone, her mother's parents unknown to her and her grandmother just a photo beside Harry's bed. And then Harry, who'd never come close to the kindly, indulgent old folks she'd seen on the telly.

"Hayley?"

Startled out of her thoughts, she turned to find Teague standing in front of her. "Yes?"

"The taxi's outside," he said. "I have to go."

She quickly rose, then pushed up onto her toes and kissed his cheek. "Thank you," she said. "For bringing me here. And for the holiday. With the rush to leave the resort, I never told you how much fun I had."

He grinned. "We're going to do it again. Remember? You're making the plans."

"And thank you for going to get Harry's things from Wallaroo. I feel like you give so much to me and—"

"Don't," he warned. "Don't even say it. If I didn't want to be here, I wouldn't be here. It's as simple as that."

"You're a good friend, Teague," she said. "My only

true friend." She suddenly wanted to drag him off to a dark corner and lose herself in a frantic seduction, anything to take her mind off her troubles. But the distraction wouldn't last. Harry would still be lying in a hospital bed once they were through.

They walked outside and stopped next to the waiting cab. "I've been thinking," Hayley said. "I wonder if Harry is the way he is because he's been alone for so long. Because he lost the one person he loved in the whole world."

"I think Harry was born mean."

"But what would you do if you lost the person you loved?" Hayley asked. "I mean, not if she went away. But if she suddenly died? Wouldn't you turn bitter like Harry did?"

He considered her question for a long time, lazily playing with her fingers as he did. "I can't believe I'm going to say this, but, yeah, maybe I would. I guess it does explain his behavior a little better. He had his reasons."

"He did," Hayley agreed.

Teague reached for the door of the taxi. "I'll see you tomorrow morning," he said. "Ring my satellite phone if you need anything. In fact, call me later and let me know how things are going."

"I will."

Teague pulled her toward him, his mouth coming down on hers in a deep and stirring kiss. Hayley felt her legs go weak and she clutched at his shirt to maintain her balance. When he finally drew back, she remained limp in his arms, her eyes closed. Just hours ago, she would have tumbled him into their comfortable bed at the resort. Now, he was leaving.

When she looked up, he smiled softly at her. "Love you," he murmured.

"I love you," she replied, the words coming without a trace of hesitation.

With that, he let go of her, the impact of his revelation slowly sinking in and stealing her breath away. He jumped into the taxi and then gave her a wave as it drove off.

Hayley fought the urge to run after him, to demand an explanation. What did he mean? How could he say such a thing and then leave? He loved her like a best friend loves a best friend, right? And what about her? What did she mean?

She sat down on a nearby bench, numbly staring down the driveway, a frown wrinkling her brow. Maybe he'd said it to make her feel better, to boost her spirits. Hayley swallowed hard. Or—or maybe Teague really loved her.

A shiver raced through her body and she rubbed her arms to smooth away the goose bumps. *Love*. Such a simple word, a word they'd used so many times as teenagers. But back then, they hadn't known what it meant, how deep the feelings could run, how strong the bond could be. Did they know now? Or was it still only a word with vague emotions behind it?

"Are you all right, miss?"

She looked up to see an orderly standing beside the bench, a wheelchair in front of him.

"Yes. I'm fine. Just getting a little air." Hayley drew in a deep breath, then let it go. From the moment she'd first seen Teague again in the stables at Wallaroo, she'd felt as though she were clinging to the neck of a runaway horse. She wanted to jump off, to take some time and reestablish her bearings, to clear her head and think. But if she got off, could she climb back on or would the ride suddenly be over?

She pushed to her feet, the weight of emotional exhaustion making it hard to move. Perhaps the hospital had a nice quiet psychiatric ward where she could spend the next few days sorting through her feelings.

"I'VE NEVER ASKED YOU for anything, but I need this."

"No," Callum said, shaking his head. He shoved away from his desk and began to pace the width of the room. "I can't believe you'd even ask."

Teague schooled his temper, knowing only a calm discussion would get him what he wanted. Callum could be so stubborn at times, but he was also a reasonable man. And though Teague was asking an awful lot, he hoped his brother would relent. "I'll give you whatever you want for it. You know I'm good for it. I have the practice. I'll pay you back with interest."

"That's Quinn land," Callum said.

"Harry Fraser would dispute that."

"Now you're taking Harry's side?" Callum cursed beneath his breath. "I should have known this would happen."

"She doesn't have anything to do with this," Teague said. "It's me. I'm making this request."

The door to the office swung open and Gemma

stepped inside before she noticed the two of them. "I'm sorry," she said, turning to leave.

Callum's expression softened. "No, come on in. We're done here."

Teague stood and walked to the door. "We're not done here. Could you excuse us?"

Gemma glanced at them both, then nodded and quickly made her retreat. Callum made a move for the door, but Teague blocked his way. "We're going to finish this," Teague said.

"We are finished."

"You forget that all three of us have a share in this station. You may have a larger share because you run it. But I've been providing free vet service for over a year now and that's worth something."

Callum sat down at his desk and pulled out his check register. "How much do I owe you?"

"I don't want to be paid. I want you to sell me the land at a fair price."

"I'm not selling that land," Callum insisted.

"If you don't agree, then I'm going to have to call Brody and we'll bring it to a vote. If he votes with me, then you lose."

Since his father had moved off the station and turned the operation over to Callum, he'd given his sons an equal vote in any major decisions that had to be made regarding their birthright. Though Brody might side with Callum, the threat of bringing any subject to a vote underscored the serious nature of Teague's request.

"If there was one thing you could do to make Gemma's life happier, you'd do it, right?"

"Yes," Callum said.

"And I'd do the same for Hayley. That's why I need to give her grandfather that land. I wouldn't ask if it wasn't really important. You'll need to trust me on this, Cal. It will all work out in the end."

Callum gave Teague a shrewd look. "You're not a stupid bloke. But I honestly think you're being suckered into this."

"You know when it comes to the land, we each own a third. That piece doesn't even come close to a third. I'll take it and you can have the rest of my share."

"You're mad. You're willing to give up everything for a few hundred acres and a water bore?"

"I am," Teague replied.

Callum shook his head. "No. I'm not going to let you do that." He slowly closed the check register. "I'll sell you the land. But for the next five years, anything comes to a vote, you vote with me."

Teague smiled. "Thank you. This will all turn out in the end. I promise."

"I'm going to hold you to that promise," Callum warned. "Now, get the hell out of my office. And tell Gemma she can come in."

Teague had one more request and knew it wouldn't go over very well. "If it's possible, I'd like the agreement today. Before I head to Brisbane."

"Today? Why today?"

"Because I need it today." He glanced at his watch.

"In the next hour or two would be good." Teague walked to the door, then turned and sent Callum a grateful smile. "Thanks, Cal. I owe you. Free vet services for the next fifty years."

"That would about cover it," Callum said. "As long as you throw in ownership of the plane, too."

Teague left the office and climbed the stairs to his bedroom. He'd have to pack for at least a week if he expected to run his part of the practice out of Brisbane and spend his nights with Hayley. Though he'd use extra fuel flying back and forth, he could extend his workday by at least three or four hours by landing in Brisbane at the end of the day, taking advantage of the illuminated runways there.

He wasn't the kind of guy who folded when times got tough. And he knew how fragile Hayley could be when she felt as if she'd been deserted. The deal he'd made to give Harry the land would make her smile. And it might change Harry's mind about checking out early. Teague gathered some clean clothes from the pile Mary had put on the end of his bed and tossed them into a duffel bag.

He'd gotten up at sunrise and driven over to Wallaroo. He'd felt a bit strange going through Harry's belongings, but he'd found everything on Hayley's list—a flannel robe, a battered stockman's hat, a framed photo of Harry with Wallaroo's prize bull and a key chain with a lucky rabbit's foot.

He'd thought about taking the photo of Hayley's grandmother, then realized why Hayley hadn't put it on the list. Maybe Harry was ready to be with her again and the photo would only remind him of that. Teague couldn't imagine how any of the other things would be important to Harry, but then, he didn't know Hayley's grandfather.

He'd also ventured into Hayley's room and packed some of her clothes into one of her designer bags. Teague had actually enjoyed picking through *her* things, remembering when she'd worn each item of clothing, inhaling the scent of her perfume and her shampoo, flipping through some of the scripts she'd brought along.

He hadn't spoken to Hayley last night and was left to assume she was all right. Sleep had been impossible, his thoughts rewinding to their time at the resort. It seemed as if their holiday was weeks ago, even though they'd just left the island the day before.

A knock sounded on his door and he turned to find Gemma standing in the hallway. "Hi," she said. "I heard about Hayley's grandfather." She held up a paper bag. "Mary and I baked some biscuits. Shortbread. I know she probably won't have time to eat, so… It's not much, I know."

Teague crossed the room and took the bag. "Thanks. I'm sure she'll appreciate it."

"Tell her I hope everything turns out well. And if she needs anything, she should call."

"I will."

"My grandfather passed on last year. I used to spend summers with him. He was such a kind man, always looking out for me. I was devastated. I cried for days."

"Hayley and her grandfather aren't really close," Teague said.

"But I thought she grew up on the station."

"She did. But—"

"No need to explain," Gemma said, holding up her hand. "And tell her I hope we have a chance to see each other again before I go home."

"You're going home?" Teague asked.

"I'm almost done with my work. I'm needed in Dublin."

"You wouldn't have to leave," Teague said. "I know Cal enjoys having you here. And you haven't learned to ride yet."

Gemma giggled. "I've tried. But I'm fairly certain that, even if I stayed for a year, I'd never be much good at it."

"A year? That would be about enough time," he said. Teague studied her for a long moment, wondering how much he ought to say, then realized that Callum could probably use as much help as he could get. "My brother has spent his whole life working this station. There's no one who works harder than he does to make sure this place turns a profit. He's not the most romantic guy in the world, or the smoothest, but he has a lot of good qualities."

"You don't have to—"

"I do, because I know Cal never would. He's a pretty humble guy. But he's steady and loyal and—" Teague chuckled. "And I'm making him sound like the family dog."

"I understand what you're saying. And I do appreciate all his fine qualities. It's just that…well, it would be a huge thing for me to leave my life in Ireland behind. And there's no question that I'd have to do that if we were to be together." She paused. "And he hasn't asked me to stay."

Teague nodded. He wasn't going to try to sell Gemma on life at the station. It wasn't easy and she and Cal would have to love each other deeply in order to make it work. His mother hadn't been able to take it, Hayley had left and even Brody and Payton had escaped to the city.

"Well, I'll leave you to your packing," Gemma said. "Enjoy the biscuits."

Teague nodded. How odd was it that all three of the Quinn brothers now had women in their lives? And that all three of them risked losing those women. Payton and Gemma were foreigners and would probably be returning home soon. And Hayley? He figured he still had a shot with her.

They, at least, lived on the same continent.

TEAGUE SAT ACROSS the table from Hayley, watching as she picked at the pasta salad he'd brought her for dinner. Shadows smudged the skin below her eyes, betraying her lack of sleep the previous night.

"You're not staying at the hospital tonight," Teague said. "I've got a room. After you're finished eating, I'm taking you with me and you're going to get some rest."

Hayley nodded and sighed. "All right." She glanced around the hospital cafeteria. "Do you think anyone would be bothered if I crawled over the table and curled up in your lap?"

Teague grinned. "That lady behind the cash register looks strong enough to toss us both out."

"I want to kiss you for an hour or two," she said, stifling a yawn. "And then I want to pull the covers over my head and sleep for a year."

"How is Harry?"

She shrugged. "Still stubborn. But I think the things you brought him made an impact. He was wearing his hat when I left his room. And I heard him joking with one of the nurses and Harry never jokes. I think they're flirting with him. The counselor was in again today and has made some progress. If Harry agrees, they'll do his surgery tomorrow morning."

"I have something else for you," Teague said. "Actually, for Harry. But you can give it to him." He reached into his jacket pocket and withdrew an envelope, holding it out to her.

"What is it?"

"An agreement to deed the land over to me. And another to transfer it from me to Harry. It's his."

Hayley gasped, her eyes suddenly wide. "You did this for Harry?"

"I did it for you," Teague said. "And Harry. Maybe it will help."

"Oh, it will," she said, excitement filling her voice. "The court fight was weighing on his mind and this makes it all so simple. Thank you." Hayley glanced down at her uneaten dinner and pushed it aside. "I want to go tell him. Now."

"Let's go," Teague said.

They rode the lift up to Harry's floor, but before they got to the room, Hayley took Teague's hand and pulled him into through a doorway in the middle of the hall. Three cots lined the walls of the darkened room. This was obviously where Hayley had slept the night before.

She pressed him back against the closed door, his body blocking the window and their only source of light. Then she wrapped her arms around his neck and kissed him, deeply and desperately. Her need to touch him seemed frantic and she pulled at the buttons of his shirt until she'd undone them all.

He tipped his head back as she smoothed her hands over his chest. Her touch set his body on fire, every nerve tingling with anticipation. His cock grew hard almost immediately.

Hayley nuzzled his chest. "I missed you," she murmured.

Teague chuckled as she trailed kisses along his collarbone. "It's been less than twenty-four hours."

"It seemed like days," she said. "Weeks."

"Maybe because we'd spent the previous three days in bed."

"We weren't in bed the whole time. We did walk on the beach and eat."

"But it was pretty much a sexfest."

She looked up at him, grinning. "I like that. A sexfest. I think we should have another one of those."

"I know exactly where to find one. My hotel room. Fifteen minutes."

She quickly buttoned his shirt. "Let me go give Harry

the news and then we can leave." She reached down and ran her fingers along the front of his jeans. "You can stay here if you'd like. Until you…calm down. I'll only be a few minutes." She pulled the envelope out of her pocket. "Harry is going to be so surprised."

Hayley slipped out of the room and Teague sat down on the edge of the cot. He drew a deep breath, trying to douse the fire that raged inside him. Would his desire for her ever fade? Perhaps a long-distance relationship would be the perfect thing for them. All that time apart for their need to increase and then coming together again for an explosion of lust.

Yet, there was something to be said for the everyday events, the tiny things in life they could share if they lived together. He could touch her and kiss her whenever he chose. He could read her moods and soothe her worries. They could build a real life, together, maybe have a family.

Teague wanted to believe it would happen that way. Maybe not tomorrow or even next year, but someday he and Hayley would be together for good. He pushed to his feet and opened the door, stepping out into the brightly lit hallway.

He stood outside Harry's room, trying to hear the conversation inside. There was no shouting, which was a positive sign. Maybe this scheme of his would work.

A few minutes later, Hayley emerged, a smile on her face. Teague breathed a silent sigh of relief. She was happy. That was all he cared about.

"How did it go?"

"Good," she said. "We had a really nice talk." Hayley shook her head in disbelief. "He said he wanted me to be happy. And he said he'd go ahead with the surgery." She reached up and pressed her palm to Teague's chest, right over his heart, her eyes fixed on the spot. They stood that way for a long time, silent, the heat of her fingers warming his blood. "And he'd like to see you."

"Me?"

She nodded then glanced up at him. "Try to be nice."

Teague gave her hand a squeeze, then reached for the door. He wasn't quite sure what to expect. Was Harry going to throw the agreement back in his face? Or was he going to accept the land graciously?

The room was dimly lit, the blinds on the window turned down. Teague was shocked by Harry's appearance. He was immobilized by traction, ropes and slings and pulleys keeping his right leg at an angle. The man had always seemed so powerful. But he looked so small in the big bed, his skin pale, his beard grizzled.

"Hello, Mr. Fraser."

"Quinn," he said. He pointed to the chair beside the bed, but Teague shook his head. "I'm good."

"Hayley showed me this." He waved the paper. "Is it real?"

Teague nodded. "Yeah. My brother gave me the land and I'm giving it to you."

"Does your brother know about this?"

"Yes. As soon as you're out of here, we'll get all the papers signed and make it official. But it's yours."

"Why are you doing this?"

"For Hayley."

"You expect me to turn her over to you because you gave me the land?"

Teague laughed. "Jaysus, Harry, she's not a horse. You can't trade her like a piece of property. I did this because I thought it might keep your arse alive. That's what Hayley wants and I want what she wants."

Harry scowled. "Are you in love with her?"

"Yes," Teague said. "I have been since I was a kid."

"So, I guess you figure once I leave this world, she'll get everything and you'll waltz right in and share in the wealth?"

Teague cursed beneath his breath. "Go to hell, Harry. I don't give a shit about Wallaroo. But after all you've put Hayley through, the mess you made of her childhood, I think she deserves the place after you depart this life. Although, I don't expect you'll be dying anytime soon since it's your goal to make her as miserable as possible."

"I don't want that," Harry said. He went silent for a long time, turning his head away from Teague to look out the window. "I know I didn't do well by her. But I didn't know how to take care of her any more than I knew how to care for my own son."

"It's not that hard to love her," Teague said. "I fell in love with her the very first time I saw her."

"I guess it's my fault, then. I never knew what to say to her. Hell, I drove her father off Wallaroo and I figured she wouldn't have any interest in sticking around, either. She proved my point when she ran away."

"I don't know why, but she does care about you."

Harry shifted, wincing as he tried to sit up a little straighter. "They have me so shot full of pain medicine, I'm not sure what I'm saying, but I'm going to say it anyway. If I don't make it through the surgery, I want you to watch over her. I may have had my troubles with your father and your brother, but you seem like a decent sort, Quinn. And Hayley likes you."

"I think she does," Teague said. "But you are going to make it through this operation. And then you'll go somewhere where they'll get you walking again. And then you'll go home to Wallaroo. And I'm going to see that you're a lot nicer to Hayley from now on."

"You seem pretty damn sure of yourself," Harry said.

"I am. And if you don't try to make that happen, then you and I are going to have a problem."

"Good enough," he said. "Then I guess we have an understanding?"

"We do," Teague said.

"Now get the hell out of my room and let me sleep," Harry ordered.

Teague turned and walked to the door, smiling to himself as he stepped into the hallway. Hayley was waiting for him outside the door. He wrapped his arm around her shoulders and walked with her toward the lift. "It went well. We had a nice talk. Now let's get out of here."

They found Teague's rental in the car park. Teague pulled the door open for Hayley, then circled around to the driver's side. The hotel was less than a mile away, but Hayley wasn't in the mood to wait. She ran her hand along his thigh as he turned onto the street, then slid it in between his legs.

He grabbed her wrist to stop her from going farther, but she just smiled and ignored him. By the time they reached the hotel, he was completely aroused, his erection straining at the fabric of his jeans.

When they pulled in to the hotel car park, Teague retrieved his jacket from the rear seat and held it over his groin as he and Hayley strolled into the lobby. He glanced over to see a satisfied grin on her face. "Thank you," Teague said. "I always appreciate walking around like this. It makes me look like a pervert."

They rode the lift in silence. When he opened the room door and stepped aside, Hayley trailed her fingers across the front of his jeans as she walked past him.

The moment the door closed, she began undressing him. He reached for her shirt, but she brushed his hands away. Teague decided to let her have her way with him, curious how far she would go to pleasure him.

By the time she had him stripped naked, he really didn't care what she did. The feel of her fingers wrapped around his shaft was enough to bring him to the edge. But Hayley had other plans. She kissed a trail from his mouth to his chest and then lower.

He felt oddly vulnerable. She was still dressed and he was naked. But the moment her mouth closed over him, he realized that this situation was fantasy material. She was in control, seducing him, and he could simply relax and enjoy the ride.

It hadn't taken Hayley long to learn what he liked,

exactly what stoked his desire. They'd had plenty of practice during their holiday. Teague drew in a deep breath and held it, her tongue sending him closer to release. But she read the signs and slowed her pace, smoothing her hands over his belly as she pulled back.

He was so hard, he wasn't sure he could be any more aroused. But then, Hayley stood. Her gaze fixed on his, she slowly stripped out of her clothes, as if performing for him. The striptease was even more intriguing than physical contact.

He reached for her, but she evaded his grasp. And when she was completely undressed, she didn't return to touching him. Instead, she ran her hands over her own body. Teague groaned, aching to touch her but still caught up in the game she was playing. But when she slipped her fingers between her legs, he growled softly and grasped her waist with his hands.

Picking her up off her feet, Teague wrapped her legs around him, holding tight to her hips. Her lips found his and she twisted her fingers through his hair as she kissed him. Slowly, Teague entered her, a surge of desire washing over him. And when he was buried deep, Hayley sighed softly, a satisfied smile curling her lips. "Oh, don't move. That feels so good," she said breathlessly.

"I have to move," he said.

"No, you don't."

"Let me move," he said.

She shifted above him and he gasped. Maybe he didn't need to move. But the pleasure was too strong to deny. Teague held her tight as he slowly withdrew, then drove forward again. She whispered his name, her lips soft against his ear.

This was all he needed, Teague thought. The only thing in his life he couldn't do without. Her body was the perfect match for his, her heart and her soul the prize he wanted to possess. And though he hoped to spend a lifetime with her, Teague knew he'd be happy with one more day and the night that followed.

8

THE SKY WAS GRAY and overcast as the plane flew low over the outback landscape. Hayley had thought about canceling the trip, leaving it for a sunnier day, but then decided that the weather matched her mood. It had been nearly a week since she'd last smiled, the evening after Harry's surgery, when she'd sat by her grandfather's bed and told him that she loved him.

Hayley looked down at the urn on her lap, running her hands over the cool ceramic surface. The numbness had begun to wear off and reality had set in. Harry was gone.

He'd written detailed plans before going into surgery, scribbling everything he wanted her to know on a small scrap of paper. She'd found it a day later, after the hospital had returned his belongings. No funeral, no mourning, scatter his ashes over Wallaroo.

His death had been unexpected. He'd survived the surgery and had been making plans to enter a rehabilitation center. She'd said good-night to him that evening, happy that things had gone so well, and the next morning, when she'd arrived at the hospital, the staff had told her Harry had passed away during the night.

It had been a quiet death, in his sleep, and though the doctors wanted to give her all the details and the cause, Hayley really didn't want to listen. She knew why Harry had died. He'd done as she had asked, and then chosen his own time, on his own terms. In the end, Hayley was grateful that he never had to know a long, debilitating illness.

She had wanted to grieve for him, but she knew Harry wouldn't approve. There had been tears, but after the tears had come comfort in knowing that Harry's spirit would always live on at Wallaroo, in the beautiful sunsets and wide, sweeping vistas, in the shimmer of light off the slow-moving creeks and in the soft breeze that brought the rain.

"This looks like a nice spot," Teague said. "With the creek and that outcropping right there. It's very peaceful."

"It is," Hayley said. "What should I do?"

"Open the window and take the top off once you're holding the urn outside. Then tip it toward the tail of the plane."

Hayley slid the window open. "Goodbye, Harry." She followed Teague's instructions and watched as the cloud of ashes flew past the plane and drifted down to the ground. It was difficult to believe Harry wouldn't be there when they got to the house, sitting on the porch, watching over his property. She'd never have to cook him supper or pick up after him again. She'd never have to listen to him complain.

Hayley had been so young when her parents had died that she barely remembered feeling anything then. One day, they were there and the next day they weren't. The minister had told her to be brave. The people at the funeral home had patted her on the head and whispered behind her back. And though she felt the loss, she hadn't been old enough to understand the true impact it would have on her life.

"He was all I had left," Hayley said.

"You have me." Teague reached for her hand and gave it a squeeze. "Cal asked if I'd bring you over for dinner tonight. Gemma is going to be leaving soon and she wanted to say goodbye."

Hayley smiled weakly. "I can't. I'd really rather go home. I've got a lot to do."

"Nothing that can't wait," he said.

"I have to make some decisions. I have to get back to Sydney. I'm supposed to fly to Los Angeles next week. And I'm due at the studio right after that to finish taping *Castle Cove*."

"So you're going to leave?"

"I don't have much choice," Hayley said.

"The station is yours now. You've watched Harry run it. You could do the same. You could raise horses, give the Quinns some competition. And you've got free vet services. There are plenty of station owners who'd kill for that."

"I can't live out here alone," she said.

"You wouldn't be alone," Teague replied. "I'd be here. I could move my things over and come and go from Wallaroo."

Hayley felt her cheeks warm. Was this a marriage

proposal or a business proposal? "And what would we be?"

"Whatever you wanted us to be," he said. "Friends? Lovers? Partners? Roommates?"

She turned away, her pulse racing at the thought of accepting his offer. She could have Teague with her for as long as she wanted. Or as long as he wanted, whichever came first. Though the thought of losing him terrified her, it wasn't half as bad as the thought of never having him in the first place.

"I know what you're thinking," Teague said. "Where's the parachute? I gotta get out of this plane."

Hayley couldn't help but laugh. "You planned this so I couldn't escape?"

"It looks that way. You don't have to give me an answer now, Hayley. But at least consider the option."

"Good. Because I don't have an answer now," she replied.

"But you'll think about it?"

Hayley nodded. It was the least she could do. Besides, it was a plan worth examining. She could imagine a life on Wallaroo with Teague. It would be simple, but satisfying. She could also picture her life in Sydney, her career, making movies and traveling the world.

If she decided not to stay, the sale of the station would provide her with the kind of lifelong security she'd always wanted. She could take the time to choose good projects, to build a film career slowly and carefully. And she'd never have to depend on another person for her day-to-day existence.

But Teague wouldn't understand that reason, her need to be able to survive without help from anyone. He seemed happy to have her dependent on him, to provide for her and make sure her life was easy.

They landed on the airstrip on Wallaroo, then rode to the house in Hayley's car. They bumped along the rough dirt track, Teague bracing his hand on the dash. "If you're going to live on Wallaroo, you're going to need a better way to get around. The suspension on this thing will last about a week."

"Right," she said softly. As she focused on the road ahead, she thought about the other changes she'd have to make. She'd have to sell her place in Sydney, give up acting and walk away from the life she'd built for herself. To live in the middle of nowhere.

But here, on the station, she would have love. And no matter how she turned it over in her head, there was no possible way she could have both.

When they reached the house, Hayley stopped the car and got out. But she couldn't bring herself to go inside. She'd spent the past week wandering around the station, cleaning the stables and the yard, taking long rides in the outback with Molly, sitting on the porch and memorizing her lines for the next three episodes of *Castle Cove*. She'd avoided the house as much as possible, knowing she'd have to face sorting through Harry's things.

Teague had been occupied with work and had only spent a few nights with her, sleeping by her side while she passed the night wide-awake and restless, her mind a jumble of disparate thoughts.

"I can't," she said, staring at the house. "I can't go inside. Not now. It's too sad."

He pulled her along, holding tight to her hand. "We don't have to go inside," he said. "Let's ride out to the shack. We haven't been there for a while. It'll be fun."

Hayley nodded and they walked toward the stables. She sat on a bale of straw as Teague saddled Molly. When he was finished, he gave her a knee up and then settled himself behind her. He gave Molly a gentle kick and they started out into the gray daylight.

"When I go home to Sydney, I want you to take Molly to Kerry Creek. Find someone to ride her every day."

"I can do that," Teague said.

She sank against him and closed her eyes. Exhaustion seemed to descend on her all at once, the gentle gait of the horse lulling her toward sleep. Everything seemed so right when Teague was with her. He was strong when she couldn't be and he made her laugh when she felt gloomy. He talked to her when she needed an opinion and listened when she didn't.

From the moment she'd seen him standing outside Molly's stall, Hayley had known what she was risking. And now, she was left to deal with the consequences of falling in love with Teague all over again. Only this time, she'd be the one to walk away and leave him behind.

Somehow, that didn't make her decision easier. It made the prospect of leaving almost impossible to bear.

"I'M NOT QUITE SURE why I'm here," Teague said, looking around the interior of the solicitor's office. Both he and Hayley had been summoned to Brisbane for the reading of Harry's will. Teague had assumed that it had to do with the land he'd given Harry.

The solicitor cleared his throat as he rearranged the stacks of files on his desk. "Since both you and Miss Fraser are mentioned in the will, it's customary."

Teague frowned. "I'm in the will? How can that be?"

"Harry made some last-minute changes. He called me over to the hospital the morning of his surgery so he could sign the new addendum."

"Let me guess. He left me the Quinn land that I gave to him."

"No," the solicitor said. "He left you half of Wallaroo."

Both Teague and Hayley gasped at the same time, then looked at each other. "Say that again," Teague murmured.

"You two are to share ownership in the station. Fifty-fifty. Harry decided if his granddaughter did not want to keep the station, then it should go to the Quinns. You are both required to live on the station for at least six months out of the year or you will forfeit your right to ownership. After ten years, if you both agree to sell, then you will split the profits from the sale fifty-fifty. If there is no agreement to sell, then this arrangement remains in force."

"But I can't live on the station," Hayley said. "I have a career in Sydney."

"Then I'm afraid the station will go to the Quinns, as long as Mr. Quinn is following the residency clause. Are you willing to live on Wallaroo?"

"Yes," Teague said.

"Of course he is," Hayley said. "It's perfect. The Quinns have always wanted Wallaroo. And now they have it." She turned to Teague. "What kind of deal did you make with him? Did you talk him into this?"

"No!" Teague said. "I'm as surprised as you are."

"You're sure you didn't figure out some way to force the issue, to make me stay on Wallaroo? Because this seems awfully suspicious to me."

"Well, it seems downright crazy to me. Harry asked me to take care of you, but I never thought—"

"And what did you say?" she demanded. "Did you tell him you would?"

"Of course."

"See. That's what it was. He assumed you'd marry me and we'd live happily ever after on Wallaroo."

"Well, it's not such a bad idea," Teague said. "Didn't you say you'd always dreamed we'd have a station together, with horses?"

"I was a kid," Hayley said. "And it was just a stupid dream. I have a life of my own now. I don't need you making decisions for me."

"Would you two like a moment alone?" the solicitor asked.

"No!" Hayley said.

"Yes," Teague answered.

The solicitor got up and Hayley shook her head. "Why do you listen to him and not to me?"

When the solicitor shut the office door behind him, Hayley turned to Teague. "You can't force me to live on Wallaroo."

"I'm not forcing you to do anything, Hayley. This was Harry's deal, not mine. But I can understand his thinking. Wallaroo has been in your family for years. He didn't want to see it sold. And you shouldn't, either. It's part of your heritage."

"I make my own decisions about my life. Not you, not Harry, me."

"So you don't want to be with me?"

"Not because of some scheme you and Harry cooked up," she said.

"I see." Teague shrugged. Hell, there were times when Hayley's ability to reason flew right out the window. Instead of thinking things through, she reacted. They could make this arrangement work. Teague could run the station and she could come and go as she pleased. He wouldn't hold her to the residency clause— at least not down to the letter.

But if he did decide to enforce the rules, he'd have her for six months out of the year. If he couldn't convince her they belonged together given that amount of time, then maybe they didn't belong together at all.

"If you don't like the terms, then don't follow them."

"I'd lose my share of Wallaroo," she said.

"You hate Wallaroo."

"I don't hate it. I just never appreciated it until I came back this last time."

"What do you want me to do?"

"Give me your half," she demanded. "That's the only fair thing to do."

"No," Teague said. "You aren't prepared to run it

alone. And it's the perfect place to raise horses. What land we don't use for that, we can lease to Callum for cattle."

"You have it all planned out, don't you? This plays right into your hand. Why don't we both agree to break the rules and sell it. You can come to Sydney with me and start a practice there." She raised her brow. "How about that scheme? Now you have to turn *your* life upside down for me."

"Would that make you happy?" Teague asked. "Would that mean we could spend the rest of our lives together?" He waited for her answer, knowing it wouldn't come. The question actually seemed to make her even angrier.

Had he really expected the fairy tale to last forever? Everything had been going so well for them, beyond Harry's passing. Hayley had been quiet and thoughtful, though a bit confused. But here was the Hayley he'd always known. Scrappy and opinionated, a girl who didn't let anyone push her around. Until she was backed into a corner. Then she clawed like a tiger to escape.

"I'm going to fight this in the courts," Hayley said, snatching up her bag and getting to her feet.

"Great!" Teague replied. "Now that one feud is finally over, we'll start another one."

"Tell your solicitor that he will be hearing from mine," she said as she strode to the door.

"How are you going to get home?" he shouted. "It's a long walk."

Hayley slowly turned. "I am perfectly capable of getting to Wallaroo on my own. I see you share Harry's rather low opinion of my intelligence. You two should have made friends long ago. You're so much alike."

She yanked on the door. At first, it didn't open, and when it did, it hit her on the head. Teague winced, jumping to his feet to help her. But Hayley warned him off, waving her finger at him.

Teague sat down in the chair, cursing softly as she slammed the door behind her. A few moments later, the solicitor returned, a file folder clutched in his hands. "I suspected she might be upset," he murmured as he took his place behind his desk. "These last-minute changes are always a problem. But the doctors assured me that Harry was of sound mind and all the necessary signatures were made. If there is a lawsuit, I'd be happy to testify."

"I don't think that will be necessary," Teague said. He stood and held out his hand. "Thank you. I'll be in touch."

Teague half expected Hayley to be waiting in the reception area, but when he got there, she was gone. Her behavior wasn't surprising. He'd been expecting it for some time. It was Hayley's way of coping when she felt herself growing too close to someone, depending too much on another human being.

She'd done it when they were teenagers, refusing to speak to him for days after some silly fight. He'd always figured that must be the way all girls behaved. But now he saw it for what it was—a defense mechanism. It probably would have come earlier had her grandfather's death not delayed her.

It was the "love you" he'd mumbled to her outside the hospital that probably set it off. Too much, too soon.

It'd seemed like the proper thing to say, considering the situation. He'd wanted to reassure her, not box her into a corner. But his declaration and then the will were enough to convince her that he expected to be a part of her future—and she had no say in the matter.

"What the hell were you thinking, Harry?" Teague muttered as he walked to the car park. Though he suspected Harry had noble motives for changing his will, it only proved that he'd never really known his granddaughter. If he had, he'd have realized she'd see the move as another attempt to control her life.

Harry had suspected Hayley wouldn't want to run the station, so he'd given half of it to a Quinn. He'd thought Hayley might sell the station, so he'd made it impossible for her to do so without a Quinn's permission. If Hayley did want to run the station, then she would have help…from a Quinn.

Harry's attempt to keep the two of them together, in at least a legal and working arrangement, may have driven them apart emotionally. But Hayley would have to see the sense in it. She had a career away from the outback. And Teague was in the perfect position to make something out of Wallaroo. If he succeeded, she would profit from it, too.

Teague walked up the stairs to the second level of the car park and searched the rows of cars for his rental. He spotted it parked at the far end, right where he'd left it. As he approached he noticed Hayley leaning against the passenger-side door, her arms crossed over her chest, an annoyed expression suffusing her pretty face.

Teague ignored her, unlocked the driver's side and got in. Two could play this game. If she wanted a ride home, she'd have to ask. He wasn't going to offer.

God, she could be so exasperating. There were times when he almost believed they'd be better off giving up on their romance and beginning a chaste friendship. She wouldn't be half so skittish and any disagreements between them could be worked out in a rational fashion.

"Are you going to get in or will I have to drive over you?"

She turned and pulled on the door handle, but the passenger side was still locked. Hayley sent him a withering glare and he pushed the button to unlock it. She got inside, looking straight ahead and refusing to speak.

"You're really beautiful when you act childish," he said.

"You don't think I have a right to be angry?"

"No. Because you've assumed things that aren't true. I didn't ask Harry to do this. I was as surprised as you were. And I understand why you're angry, but don't take it out on me."

"Why not? I'm sure you think this is a perfect solution. With the station between us, you'll have exactly what you want."

"And what is that?"

"Me," she snapped.

Teague shoved the key in the ignition and started the car. "And what's so bloody wrong with me wanting you? I happen to like spending time with you. I think you're the most beautiful woman in the entire world.

And I think we'd make a good team. We could make a success of Wallaroo, turn it into something really grand. But you've got your knickers in a twist because of the way it happened."

"I can't be tied to that station."

"It's not only the station. It's everything. You're like a mare that can't be broken." As soon as the words were out of his mouth, he realized his mistake.

"Oh, that's lovely," she retorted. "As if I should want to be tamed, so I can live with a bit in my mouth and haul your arse around all day long."

"All right, maybe that wasn't the best comparison. But there are some benefits to settling down and making a commitment."

"I don't want to talk about this right now," she said. "I would rather we pass the ride to the airport in complete silence. Can you manage that?"

He felt her pulling away and there was nothing he could do to stop it. She'd been under so much stress, the weight of Harry's injury and death bending her to the breaking point. But now, with the will, she'd cracked. The wall was back up and they'd returned to where they began.

Maybe Hayley wasn't capable of a long-term relationship. He'd always wanted to believe she was perfect, but the more time he spent with her, the more he understood the ghosts that haunted her. No matter how hard he pushed, she simply pushed back.

It would be up to her to decide if they had a future. And nothing he could say or do would change that. He just hoped he wouldn't have to spend the rest of his life waiting for her to realize she loved him…and wondering what might have been if she had.

"HAYLEY!"

Teague's voice echoed through the empty house. Hayley folded the T-shirt and tucked it into her bag. Then she bent down and picked up the sandals Teague had bought her and placed them in the plastic bag with her other shoes.

"Hayley!"

She found the letter she'd written to him and tucked it into the back pocket of her jeans. His footsteps sounded on the stairs as she closed the zipper on the tote and set it beside the bed. Then she sat down and folded her hands in her lap, knowing that the next few minutes might be more difficult than she'd ever imagined.

"Hayley?" He stepped inside her bedroom. "Didn't you hear me calling?" His gaze dropped to the bag at her feet. "What's going on?"

"I have to go," she said.

"You don't have to be back in Sydney until next week."

"My agent got me an audition for a television series. They want me in Los Angeles right away. I have to go now."

He frowned, shaking his head. "A television series? In Los Angeles?"

She nodded.

"But you're not going to do it, right? You have a job like that right here in Australia."

"This would be different. This would be a lot more money."

"Hayley, you own half this station. You don't have to worry about money anymore."

"But I can't sell my half unless you agree to sell yours. So I really don't have anything except a lot of land and no money."

"If you need help, you know I'll be there to help you. Do you need money?"

"See, there's the problem." She stood up and returned to her packing, grabbing her tote and stuffing a pair of jeans inside. "Any actress would kill for an opportunity like this."

In truth, she still hadn't decided whether it was a good idea. She was *supposed* to want a better career. Her agent had said so and she usually listened to her agent. This might open the door to American movies or at least a big role in an Australian movie.

But since she'd returned to Wallaroo after the reading of the will, she hadn't thought much about her acting career. There had been long stretches of time when it hadn't even entered her mind. If acting was her passion, wasn't she supposed be obsessed with it?

Instead, she'd spent her time wandering around the house, making a mental list of the changes that needed to be made, imagining life at Wallaroo with Teague. With so much time alone, she'd found herself fantasizing an entire existence—and she'd liked what she'd seen in her head.

"I need to find out what it's all about before I get too excited," Hayley said in an indifferent tone.

"You were going to leave without saying goodbye?"

"I wrote you a letter." She risked a glance up at him. "I want you to make sure you look after Molly. And if you need any money, call me. We should share the expenses of fixing this place up. If you don't want to do that, then just keep a tally. If we ever sell the place, you can take it out of my share."

Teague cursed softly. "You're not coming back."

"That's not true. I have to come back. I'm under contract with *Castle Cove* through September."

"I meant to Wallaroo. You're not coming back here."

"I'll visit when I can." She sat down on the edge of the bed. "When are you moving in?"

"I brought some of my stuff over today. Callum is coming later to pick me up and then I'll fly the plane over here. I can't very well get this place in shape if I don't live here."

"No. There is a lot to do."

"I figure we ought to upgrade the homestead a bit while we're looking for stock. I spoke to Cal and he's interested in leasing some of the grazing land for Kerry Creek cattle. So we should have some money to invest."

He made it sound as if she was going to be part of it all. Was that wishful thinking or did he believe he could change her mind about leaving? "That's brilliant," she muttered. "You have it all figured out."

"Not all," he said. "There are still a few pieces missing, but I'm working on those."

"I don't know when I'll be able to come to Wallaroo

again," she said. "Our production schedule is always really busy. Maybe sometime in September."

"No worries. You'll be surprised when you come the next time. I'll have this place in top shape."

Hayley drew a deep breath and flopped back on the bed, staring up at the ceiling. What did he want from her? Was she supposed to feel guilty for leaving all the work to him while she ran off and became a movie star?

Teague lay down beside her, turning to face her. He reached out and toyed with a lock of her hair. "We can make this work," he said.

"Can we?"

"Only if you want to, Hayley. Do you? If you don't, then you should get up and leave right now. Because I'm not sure I'm going to be able to say goodbye without making myself look like a damn drongo."

Hayley rolled onto her side. "Kiss me," she said, saying a silent prayer that one kiss would make everything clear in her head.

"Why? Do you expect that to change anything? I could tear all your clothes off and make love to you and you'd still leave. You decided to leave the day you got here and nothing that's happened since has made a bit of difference, has it?"

"That's not true. You don't have to be cruel."

"I'm being honest," Teague said. "We've always been honest with each other, haven't we?"

Hayley heard the anger in his voice, the bitter edge that sent daggers through her soul. Teague understood her too well. He knew exactly what was running through her mind right now, the desperate need to run away and the overwhelming temptation to stay.

He rolled over and threw his arm over his eyes. "Get the hell out of here, Hayley. You don't belong here. You never have. The same way I don't belong anywhere *but* here."

"I'm—"

"Don't. I don't need any explanations. Just go."

Hayley sat up. Bracing her hand beside his body, she leaned over and brushed a kiss across his lips. "Goodbye, Teague." When he didn't reply, she slowly stood and picked up her bags. He was still lying on the bed, his arm over his face, when she turned to take one last look.

As she walked down the stairs, she slowed her pace, waiting for him to come after her, to drag her back to the bedroom and make love to her for the rest of the afternoon. By the time she reached her car, Hayley realized he wasn't going to come. He was going to let her walk away.

Drawing a ragged breath, she tossed her bags in the rear seat and got behind the wheel. She glanced up at her bedroom window, where the breeze ruffled the plain cotton curtains. He wasn't there watching.

Hayley reached for the car door, then let her hand drop. She shoved her keys into her pocket, turned and walked toward the stable.

Molly was in her stall, munching on fresh hay. She watched Hayley with huge dark eyes, blinking as Hayley smoothed her hand over the mare's nose. "You be a good girl," she said. "Teague will take care of you now. He'll make sure you have plenty to eat and get exercise. He's good with horses and you'll like him."

Hayley's eyes swam with tears. How was it she could walk away from Teague, yet the thought of leaving Molly made her cry? She kissed Molly's muzzle, then turned and ran out of the stable.

As she approached the house, she saw Teague standing on the porch, his arm braced against one of the posts, his expression unreadable. Hayley stood next to the car, watching him. Their eyes locked for a long moment. Then she smiled and gave him a small wave.

He didn't respond. Gathering her resolve, she got into the car and started the engine, then slowly drove out of the yard. She couldn't bring herself to look in the rearview mirror. No, from now on, she couldn't focus on the past. She had to look forward. Without regrets and without doubts.

This was her life and she'd make her own decisions. And whether they were right or wrong, she was willing to live with the consequences.

9

HAYLEY HAD NEVER SEEN anything like it. Miles and miles of traffic stretched out in front of the taxi, the landscape of cars wavering in the heat from the freeway pavement. Though traffic could be slow in Sydney, the government had quickly moved to fix the problem. Here in Los Angeles, people seemed to accept it as part of the lifestyle.

The airport had been worse than the freeway. Her flight had been delayed twice. She'd been scheduled to arrive twelve hours before her audition, giving her time to settle into a hotel and get some rest. Instead, she'd arrived with just two hours to spare and had to go from the airport to the studio directly.

"How long will it take to get there?" she asked the cabdriver.

He shrugged. "Maybe hour, two, could be," he replied in a heavy accent. She glanced at his name card. Vladimir Petrosky. She'd heard that all the cabdrivers and waiters and store clerks in L.A. were aspiring actors. If that was true, she'd probably have plenty of competition.

"You call," he said. "Tell them you be late."

"I don't have a phone," Hayley replied.

He passed a mobile through the window between them. "Use mine," he said. "No problem."

Hayley pulled out the copy of her itinerary and searched for the number of the studio. When she found it, she punched the digits into the phone. A receptionist answered and put her through to the assistant producer's assistant. Who put her through to the assistant producer. Who politely informed her that the producer had another appointment in an hour and if she didn't make it, they would have to reschedule for next week.

"I'll be there," she said. Hayley handed the phone to the driver. "Is there another way? Perhaps we could get off this highway and find another route?"

"Other could be bad," Vladimir said. "You have audition, yes?"

"Yes?"

He twisted around in his seat and looked at her. "You give me producer's name and phone number, I get you there on time."

Wasn't this extortion? Not a very serious case, but an actor had to do what an actor had to do. "All right," she said. "But I'm going to write it down and leave it here on the seat. If anyone asks, you don't mention my name. Deal?"

"I not know your name," Vladimir said.

"Good, that works out well for the both of us."

True to Vladimir's word, he managed to get her to the studio in under a half hour, taking the first exit off the freeway and then winding through busy city streets.

She paid him with the cash her agent had given her, then hurried through the doors of a plain two-story building on the studio lot, dragging her bags along with her.

The receptionist pointed to a long sofa and Hayley sat down. The office was decorated with photos from the programs they produced. Like her show in Australia, this was an hour-long weekly drama. Set in an American hospital, the show had launched movie careers for three of its lead actors, so a place in the cast was considered a stepping stone to bigger things.

Bigger things, she mused. Was that really what she wanted? Her mind flashed back to the room she'd shared with Teague on the island, to the perfect solitude of their waterfront bungalow. All that seemed like a dream to her now, stuck in the middle of this noisy city with a haze of smog all around it.

She closed her eyes and pictured Teague in bed, his naked limbs twisted in the sheets, his hair rumpled. That's what she wanted. Teague, naked and aroused, his lips on hers, his hands exploring her body, making her ache with desire. She wanted to go to bed at night knowing he'd be there in the morning. She wanted to talk to him about little things she'd discovered in the course of her day. And she wanted to be assured that he would always love her, no matter what.

But wasn't that exactly what she'd walked away from? Hadn't he offered that life to her? Why was it so easy to see, now that she was miles and miles away from him? Hayley pressed her palm to her chest, trying to ease the emptiness that had settled in her heart. Though she'd tried her best to convince herself otherwise, something had changed inside her.

The thought of loving him and then losing him no longer frightened her. Anything truly important always came with risks. Her real fear was that she'd go her entire life and never find another human being who would understand her the way Teague did. Had she deliberately ignored her true feelings simply because they'd begun when she was a child?

It was so easy to consider their connection a teenage infatuation, something never meant to survive to adulthood. But it had survived. And they did still love each other. And she'd been a… "Fool," Hayley whispered.

She glanced up to see the receptionist watching her with an odd expression. "Is everything all right?"

"No," Hayley said with a groan.

"Are you going to be ill?"

Hayley shook her head. "I don't think so." She stood up. "I have to leave. Can you call me a taxi?"

"But, Miss Fraser, Mr. Wells hasn't seen you yet."

"I know. But I don't want to be seen. Tell him I'm grateful for the opportunity, but I'm not interested in doing American television. I don't want to live in America. It's too far away."

"Are you sure?"

Hayley smiled. "I am. I've never been more sure of anything in my life. Isn't that crazy? I walk away from him a few days ago and now all I can think of is getting home to be with him."

The receptionist smiled. "Oh, I understand. Love?"

"Yes!" Hayley cried. "I think it might be. And I don't want to be living here while he's there. I'm not even sure I want to be in Sydney. I mean, that's at least fifteen hours by car. Although he has a plane, so he could probably come for visits. But I don't like the idea of not seeing him every day. I think if you're in love, you should be together. Don't you?"

"Yes?"

"Exactly," Hayley said. "I need to get to the airport right away. How long will it take for a taxi?"

"I'll call right now," she offered. "It will only be a few minutes."

"That would be brilliant," Hayley replied, picking up her bags. "I think it would be best if I waited outside."

She didn't want to have to make her excuses to Mr. Wells. After all, what would she say? I'm sorry, I can't audition today because I just realized I'm still in love with my childhood sweetheart. "I'm such an idiot!" Hayley cried as she shoved open the main door and stumbled out.

She stood beneath a wide awning for five minutes before she saw a taxi approach. The car stopped in front of her and she got inside, only to find Vladimir behind the wheel. He got out and tossed her bags in the boot. "It went well? You smiling."

"No," she said as she crawled inside. "It didn't go at all. But that's all right. I've got something really good waiting for me at home."

Vladimir got behind the wheel. "Where can I take you?"

"To the airport," she said.

"Quick trip," Vladimir said. He started the meter and Hayley sat back and sighed softly. Her agent was going to be furious, but she didn't care. He'd get over it. As for her acting career in Australia, she still had obligations, but once she'd fulfilled her contract, she was free to take projects she found interesting and exciting, and not just projects that would pay the bills.

Teague had been right. She owned half the station and though it wasn't money in the bank, it was financial security. She'd always have a place to live, work that she found satisfying and the chance for a comfortable future. That was all she'd ever wanted from her acting career.

What would it feel like to leave celebrity behind? She'd never really enjoyed the notoriety that her career had brought and it wasn't something she'd miss. And perhaps, someday, someone would ask what had happened to that girl who used to play the vixen on *Castle Cove*.

They'd find her living on Wallaroo with her childhood sweetheart, raising horses—and maybe a few children, as well. Although Hayley wasn't sure about the children. How could she be a good parent when she'd never had a good example to follow? But, though she barely remembered her own parents, she did remember being loved. There had been smiles and hugs and giggles.

She let her thoughts drift, images flowing through her head, all of them comforting, happy, the pieces of her life she wanted to remember. There was no reason to always expect the worst, to be waiting for some disaster to befall her. Teague had tried to tell her that, but she hadn't listened.

The next thing Hayley knew the driver was calling out to her. She opened her eyes and realized that she'd fallen asleep. Rubbing her face, she sat up and looked around. They were at the airport again, in the same spot from which Vladimir had picked her up. "Qantas?" he asked.

"Yes," she said. She fumbled with her wallet, then withdrew the rest of the American money she'd brought along. "Here, keep the change."

He frowned. "But this is too much."

"Don't worry. I don't need it. I'm going home. And I'm not going to be leaving again anytime soon."

"IT'S GOOD GRAZING LAND," Callum said, staring out across the landscape toward the horizon. "If we have more land, we can increase the size of the mob. How many hectares do you want to lease?"

"As much as you want. I plan to start small," he said. "Maybe twenty-five mares. Good stock. We won't need a lot of grazing land. I'm hoping you'll sell me five or six Kerry Creek mares."

"I don't know if I should be helping you. You're going to be competing with us."

Teague drew a deep breath, ready to lay out his plan. "You never wanted the horse-breeding operation in the first place. I'm the one who talked you into it. Why don't you let me move the whole thing over here. You'll get your pick of stock ponies at a good price and you can concentrate on cattle."

Callum thought about the offer for a moment. "He won't go for that," Brody said, his hands folded over his saddle horn, his hat pulled low over his eyes. "Cal would never pay for anything that he could get for free."

"There's where you're wrong, little brother." Callum turned to Teague. "All right. It's a deal. I'll trade you the Kerry Creek horses for lease rights on Wallaroo grazing land."

Teague glanced over at Brody. "What's wrong with Cal?"

"Lovesick," Brody said. "Right now he'd say yes to just about anything. Gemma has turned him into a shadow of his former self."

"Not only me," Cal countered. "Look at poor Teague. We're both alone again. You're the only lucky guy in this bunch. How does that figure?" He paused. "And what the hell are you doing here with us when you have Payton waiting back at the homestead?"

"She has a serious case of jet lag. I think she's going to be sleeping for the next week," Brody said.

The three brothers turned and silently surveyed the land in front of them. Teague found it odd that three women had swept into their lives in a single week, turning their lives upside down before sweeping back out. What were the chances of that happening to one of the Quinn brothers, much less all three? Well, at least Brody's girl had come back.

"Yep, we're a pretty pathetic pair," Teague said, patting Callum on the shoulder. "Do you think it's something in the genes?"

"Must be," Brody muttered. "I have plenty in my jeans to satisfy a woman."

"Genes," Teague said. "G-E-N-E-S. You know, DNA? Not your trousers, you big boof."

"Right," Brody said. "Leave it to you to get all scientific on us, Dr. Einstein."

"So, Casanova, what do you propose we do about this mess?" Teague asked.

Brody shrugged. "Why do you think you should do anything? Gemma and Hayley went home. Obviously they weren't interested in living out here in the middle of nowhere. Do you blame them? Our own mother couldn't handle it. Why would they even try?"

"It's not that bad," Callum said, leaning forward in his saddle to look at Brody. "Payton likes it here."

"She does," Brody agreed. "With Teague over at Wallaroo all the time, you're going to need some help running the place. We thought we'd stick around and give you a hand."

"But you're going to take the tryout, right?" Cal's expression turned serious. "You can't give up that chance."

Brody nodded. "Once the knee is stronger."

"Hell, if I could pick this station up and move it to Ireland, I'd do it straightaway," Callum said. "Without a second thought." He turned to Teague. "And you. Why should you even be worried? Hayley has a job in Sydney. At least for a few more months. If that's not enough time to convince her to move in with you, then you're not as smooth as I thought you were."

Callum was right. At least he and Brody had more

options. Cal was pretty much stuck. He'd never walk away from the station. He'd dreamed about running Kerry Creek since he was a kid. But then, he'd never been in love before.

"Maybe you ought to try and convince Gemma to come back," Teague said. "Go to Ireland. Explain to her how you feel and ask her to come home with you."

Callum shook his head. "She wouldn't want to live here."

"Why not? If she loves you, she probably won't care where you live. And Brody and I can watch over the station while you're gone."

"No, I'm fine."

"What did she say when you asked her to stay?" Brody inquired.

Callum frowned. "I didn't ask. She had to go home. She didn't have a choice. Besides, I didn't want to deal with the rejection."

"Jaysus, Cal," Brody and Teague said in unison.

"You don't get anything unless you ask." Teague chuckled. "This is the problem. You've been trapped on this station for so long, you've never learned to deal with women. You are completely clueless."

"If you know all the right moves, then why are you alone?" Cal countered.

"Point taken," Teague muttered.

"I have an idea," Callum said. He pushed his hat down on his head. "Follow me." With a raucous whoop, Callum kicked his horse, and the gelding took off at a gallop. Teague and Brody looked at each other, then did the same, following after him in a cloud of dust and pounding hooves.

Teague assumed they were going to Kerry Creek for a few coldies and some brotherly commiserating. But instead, Callum veered north. As they came over a low rise, he saw the big rock and instantly knew what his brother had planned.

Brody looked over at him and laughed, then urged his horse ahead, overtaking Callum to reach the rock first. He threw himself out of the saddle and scrambled to the top, waiting as Teague and Callum approached.

Brody gave them both a hand up and when they were all standing on top of the rock, he nodded. "Doesn't seem as big as it used to, does it?"

Teague couldn't believe it, either. The rock had once seemed like a mountain, but now he could understand how it might have been rolled here from another spot. "So what do we do? I'm not sure I remember."

"We have to say it out loud," Callum replied. "One wish. The thing you want most in the world."

"How do we know it will work?" Teague asked.

"It worked for me. Remember? I wished I could be a pro footballer. And it happened."

"And I wished I could run a station like Kerry Creek," Callum said. "And I'm running Kerry Creek. I remember what you wished for. You wanted a plane."

"Or a helicopter," Brody said. "I guess you got your wish, too."

"So what makes you think it will work again?" Teague asked.

"We won't know unless we try." Callum drew a deep breath. "I wish Gemma would come back to Kerry Creek for good."

"I wish Hayley would realize I'm the only guy she will ever love."

"I wish Payton would say yes when I ask her to marry me," Brody said.

Teague and Callum looked over at him in astonishment and Brody grinned. "You don't get anything in life unless you ask."

"Well, I guess that's it," Callum said in his usual down-to-business manner. "We'll see if it works. Are you riding back to Kerry Creek with us?"

"I've got work to do on Wallaroo," he said. "But I'll come by tomorrow to talk about our deal."

They jumped off the rock and remounted their horses. Then Brody and Callum headed toward Kerry Creek and Teague toward Wallaroo. The ride to the homestead was filled with thoughts of Hayley. She'd left for L.A. four days ago and he hadn't heard from her since. He'd tracked down her phone number and tried calling, but had gotten her voice mail and hung up.

He thought if she answered, he would know what to say. Something would come to him. But he couldn't leave a message. So he called occasionally, hoping that she'd answer. And when she did, he'd be able to put into words how he felt about her.

But didn't she already know how he felt? Hadn't he made it clear? Or, like Cal, had he forgotten to ask her to stay? He rewound every one of their conversations. No, he'd asked, over and over. And she'd refused.

"Guess I'll have to find a better way to convince her," he murmured.

When he reached the stable, he groomed and fed Tapper then sent him out into the yard with Molly and two other horses he'd brought over from Kerry Creek. As he got the operation running, he'd bring over more and more stock until all the breeding mares were stabled at Wallaroo.

There were still repairs to make on the paddock fences and supplies to buy. Between working on the house and the stables, he spent his time making calls, flying out of Wallaroo and returning each evening before sunset. The airstrip on Wallaroo was much closer to the house than the one on Kerry Creek had been, and he'd considered running electricity out for some crude landing lights. Then he wouldn't have to worry about the length of his workday.

But that was a project for a later date. There were too many things to be done. He strode to the house, slowing his pace when he reached the porch. He'd managed to paint the facade a bright white and the trim a deep green. When he'd chosen the colors, he'd thought about what Hayley might have picked and wished she'd been there with him. But without her input, he'd depended on an old color photo of the place.

It looked good. In fact, he couldn't remember ever seeing the house looking quite that nice. He planned to get flowers and bushes for around the porch in spring. And he'd put a porch swing up and buy some comfortable chairs so they could—

"They," he repeated out loud. He was still thinking in terms of "they." He and Hayley, together on Wallaroo. It was always good to be optimistic, but when did optimism turn into delusion? "Give her three months," Teague said. "No, six." After that, he'd be forced to come to terms with the possibility that she wouldn't come back.

He pulled open the front door and walked inside. The interior smelled like fresh paint. He'd finished the front parlor and rearranged the furniture, bringing over his favorite chair from his room at Kerry Creek.

He walked across the parlor to the small desk that Harry had used to keep the accounts for the station. He'd been meaning to go though the papers and see if there was anything he should keep.

Grabbing a chair, he sat down and started with the top drawer. He pulled it out, then dumped it at his feet. A packet of letters caught his attention and he picked them up and examined the envelope on the top.

His breath caught as he recognized his name and his old address at Murdoch University, all written in Hayley's careless scrawl. He slipped the string off the packet and flipped through each envelope. There were letters to him and from him, all of them unopened.

Teague rose and walked out the front door to the porch. He sat down on the step and opened a letter in his handwriting.

As he read the text, memories flooded his mind, memories of a nervous teenager, alone in a strange city, wishing he was home with the girl he loved. Teague chuckled at the clumsy declarations of love, the silly questions, the assurances that they'd be together again soon.

Harry had obviously intercepted his letters, probably meeting the mail plane himself each week. And he'd obviously searched through the outgoing mail for Hayley's letters, as well. Teague had never imagined her grandfather might interfere with the mail. Would things have been different if the letters had been delivered? There was no way of knowing.

He opened a letter from Hayley, written on stationery he'd given her right before he left, stationery decorated with an ink drawing of a horse. It was nearly the same as his letter, declarations of affection and news of her days on Wallaroo.

He stared out across the yard. It was a bit ironic. Now he was the one left waiting and wondering when he'd see her again, hoping for any type of communication. "Come home, Hayley," he said softly. "Come home soon."

HAYLEY'S EYES drifted closed. She shook herself awake and squinted at the deserted road in front of her. She'd landed in Sydney about fifteen hours earlier. She'd lost an entire day on the trip back, but she'd managed to sleep most of the way home. After landing, she'd packed the car and headed north on the Pacific Highway.

A breakfast stop outside of Brisbane provided the opportunity for a short nap before heading west toward

Bilbarra and Wallaroo. The drive had been pleasant when she'd made it a month ago. She'd taken her time, traveling over two days, rather than driving straight through.

But she was anxious to get home, to see Teague again and to try to repair the damage she'd done by leaving. They hadn't spoken for a week and Hayley hadn't bothered to call and warn him of her arrival. She didn't want to explain her actions. She just wanted to walk up to him, throw herself into his arms and kiss him until she was certain he understood how she felt.

She felt like a fool for leaving him in the first place. Teague had put up with a lot of foolish behavior from her, but she hoped he would forgive this one last mistake. She wasn't about to walk away again, at least not until they'd come to an understanding.

They needed to discuss whether they would live together at Wallaroo as friends, as lovers or as two people who were planning to spend the rest of their lives together. Hayley preferred the latter, but she was willing to settle for the other two choices.

As she passed the road to Kerry Creek, she slowed her car, wondering if she ought to stop there first. Over the past week, she'd wondered if Teague had changed his mind about living on Wallaroo. The house was a wreck and it would be a lonely place to live compared to the hustle and bustle of his family's station.

If he wasn't at Wallaroo, she'd take the time to clean up, maybe catch a few hours of sleep and then drive over to see him later in the day. She glanced in the rearview mirror then groaned at the sight she saw.

Dark shadows smudged the skin beneath her eyes and her hair was a mess of tangles. The makeup she'd worn for her audition was long since gone. She hoped he'd be so happy to have her home he wouldn't notice the details of her appearance.

As she drove down the road to Wallaroo, her energy began to surge and she felt a jolt of adrenaline kick in. She was about to change the course of her life for the second time. Only this time, she was steering directly toward what she'd left behind.

She stopped the car at the end of the long driveway into Wallaroo, then got out and retrieved her bag from the rear seat. She tugged off her T-shirt and jeans and slipped on a soft cotton dress. Then she found her brush and tamed her unruly hair, tying it back with a scarf.

When she bent down to look at her reflection in the side mirror, she thought about lipstick and a bit of mascara, but then decided against it. Teague had always preferred her without makeup. She didn't want to look like Hayley, the television star. She wanted to look like Hayley, the girl he'd fallen in love with years before.

Gathering her resolve, she hopped back into the car and started off down the driveway. As she got closer to the house, she noticed something odd. It seemed to gleam in the morning sun. It was only when she entered the yard that Hayley realized the house had been painted.

A tiny gasp slipped from her lips. The two-story clapboard structure looked so shiny and new she barely recognized it. Teague had painted the trim around the windows and the porch floor a deep green. And she noticed a row of new green shutters drying in the sun.

She stopped the car and slowly got out, taking in the other changes that had been made in the course of a week. The yard was clean and raked, the various bits of junk that had collected over the years hauled away. Teague had dug up the ground along the front side of the porch as if to make a garden. And the weather vane that had once perched on the roof at a precarious angle was now fixed and functional.

The front door was open and she peered through the screen, wondering if Teague was inside. She hesitantly opened the screen door, calling out his name, but the house was silent. Hayley looked around in astonishment. He'd worked miracles on the interior, as well. The walls had been painted and the woodwork had been oiled. The plank floors now gleamed with a fresh coat of wax and all the furniture had been rearranged.

It was Wallaroo as it had been, back in its early days, when everything was bright and new, back in the days when her grandmother had been alive and this had been a real home. She walked into the parlor and sat down in a soft leather chair, a chair she recognized from Teague's bedroom at Kerry Creek.

Hayley noticed a pile of mail on the table nearby and reached for it. A tiny sigh slipped from her lips as she realized what she was holding. Her letters to Teague! They were all here, all neatly addressed with the stamps unmarked. She pulled one out of the envelope and read it, each word ringing in her mind as if it had been yesterday.

"I found them in Harry's desk drawer."

She glanced up to see Teague watching her from behind the screen door. He was dressed in work clothes, his stockman's hat pulled low over his eyes. She couldn't read his expression and didn't know if he was pleased or displeased that she'd returned.

Hayley slowly stood and dropped the letters onto the chair. "Hi," she said.

"Hi, yourself," he replied.

"I'm back." She swallowed hard. It wasn't sparkling conversation, but it was the best she could manage between her pounding heart and her dizzy head.

"I can see that."

"I thought I should come home."

"To check up on me?"

She frowned. "No. I mean, yes. To see you. I wanted to see you."

"Why are you here, Hayley?"

She sighed impatiently. "Can we at least be standing in the same room when we have this conversation?"

"What conversation is that?"

"The one where I tell you that I was stupid to leave and that I'm in love with you and I hope you're in love with me." The words came out in a rush and after she said them all, she felt a warm blush creep up her cheeks. So what if it hadn't been scriptworthy romantic dialogue. This wasn't a scene from a television program, this was real life. And real life wasn't perfect.

"Say that again," he murmured.

"No," she said. "Not until you come inside."

He reached for the door, then thought better of it. "I'm going to stay out here."

"Why?"

"Because if I come inside, I'm going to have to kiss you. And once I start, I'm not sure I'm going to be able to stop."

"That sounds nice," Hayley said, smiling at him. "Please come inside." She walked to the door and pushed open the screen door. "Come on." She stepped aside to let him pass. But as he did, his arm slipped around her waist and he pulled her against him.

In a heartbeat, his mouth came down on hers in a deep and soul-searching kiss. He left no doubt about his feelings. In a single instant, Hayley knew he was glad she'd returned. She ran her hands over his shoulders and arms, enjoying the feel of his body. She hadn't realized how much she'd missed touching him.

Teague scooped her up in his arms and walked into the parlor. She grabbed his hat and tossed it aside, taking in the details of his handsome face as they continued kissing. He sat down in the leather chair, settling her on his lap, molding her mouth to his until she felt as if she might pass out.

Hayley smiled as she teased him with tiny kisses, first on his mouth, then his jaw and finally on his neck. "So you're happy to have me home."

"That depends on how long you're planning to stay."

"I was thinking maybe the rest of my life." She looked up at him.

He drew back, then held her face between his hands. "What does that mean?"

"Exactly what I said. This is my home now. I'm going to come and go from Wallaroo. I'll have to return to Sydney to finish up my contract on *Castle Cove*. Then I'll sell my place and move everything up here."

A grin broke over his face. "You're going to live here with me," he said, as if to reassure himself that he'd heard her right.

"Yes. It's my house, too."

"What about your career?"

"Well, if something interesting comes along, then we'll discuss it. We may need money for buying stock. Or for fixing up the station. I'm not going to make any plans right now, except to spend the next week with you. Then I have to go back."

"We have a week? What will we do with ourselves?" He cupped her breast.

"You'll have to work and I'm sure I'll find something to do around here." She chuckled.

"About that. Work, I mean. I spoke with Doc Daley and we've made a few changes in our plans. I'm not going to take over his practice, at least not all of it. I'm going to do the equine cases only, so I can spend more time on the station. And he's going to find someone else to take over the rest of the work. I figured, if we wanted to make a go of Wallaroo, I needed to be here as much as possible."

"So, I guess it's all settled then. You and I are business partners."

"And friends," he said.

"Lovers, too," Hayley added.

"Roommates."

She smiled. "Soul mates."

"And the rest will come," he assured her. He ran his fingers through her hair and pulled her into another kiss, lingering over her mouth. "I love you, Hayley. I always have and I always will."

"And I love you, Teague."

He smoothed his fingers through her hair. "You must be very tired from your trip. I can tell you'd like to lie down."

"Oh, you can tell?" she teased. "I think you want to get me into the bedroom."

"Actually, I want to show you the bed." He stood and pulled her along to the upstairs, past the door to Harry's old room, past the door to her room, to the largest of the bedrooms. Harry had used it for storage, like an attic, filling it full of old furniture and things he couldn't bear to throw away. She'd always suspected it was the room he'd shared with her grandmother. The beautiful bedroom set was too fancy for a single man to use.

But Teague had cleaned the room out. The old bed was there, but dressed with brand-new linens. He tossed her onto it, then flopped down beside her. "Do you like it?"

"Yes." She turned and ran her hands over the down

comforter. It was exactly like the— "These are the bed linens from the resort."

"I liked them so much that I bought some. They sell the bed linens and the soap and the shampoo right from the hotel. I bought the sheets and the down comforter. Oh, and the down pillows. And I got one of those nice showerheads, too."

Hayley rolled over and threw her arms out. "It's perfect. I could spend all day in this bed."

"Is that a request or a demand? Because I'd be quite happy to keep you in this bed all day."

She rolled over and wrapped her arms around his neck, remembering that first day at the big rock. He'd saved her life that day. Without Teague, Hayley probably wouldn't have survived her teenage years. But he'd made every day an adventure, every moment something wonderful to be shared.

"Promise me you'll love me forever," she said.

"I will love you forever and beyond," Teague said, his declaration simple and direct and honest.

"My life starts today," Hayley said. "No more fears, no more running away. And if I ever get a little crazy again, I want you to drag me back into this bedroom and prove to me why we belong together."

"Can I do that now?" Teague asked.

Hayley laughed, then kissed his mouth. "Yes," she said. "And don't stop doing it until I tell you."

As Teague began to seduce her, Hayley closed her eyes and gave herself over to the man she loved. How something so complicated had suddenly turned so simple, she would never understand. It was like a switch had been thrown and a light turned on, illuminating all the things she knew deep in her heart yet had never acknowledged.

She was exactly where she belonged now—in Teague's arms. And after so many years of searching, she was finally home.

* * * * *

There's only one single Quinn brother left.
Callum's head over heels for Gemma, but what will he
do when he learns she has a secret that could change
his life forever? Find out in the final
QUINNS DOWN UNDER *book,*
available in May 2010 from Mills & Boon® Blaze®.

ONE GOOD MAN

BY

ALISON KENT

Alison Kent is the author of several steamy books for Blaze®, as well as a handful of fun and sassy stories for other imprints. She is also the author of *The Complete Idiot's Guide to Writing Erotic Romance*. Alison lives in a Houston, Texas, suburb, with her own romance hero.

To HK, WD, k2, JM and SF, who made me laugh at least once every day while writing this. And to Walt, who makes me laugh every day whether I'm writing or not. You, dear, are the best of all good men.

1

GRUDGINGLY ACCEPTING her repetitive routine as a sure sign of impending spinsterhood, Jamie Danby still began every day the same way—with a two-mile run, a shower and clothes change, then a large cup of coffee, a banana-bran muffin and the front page of the *Reeves County News*.

The paper and the breakfast she picked up each morning on her way to work. When weather permitted, she walked.

It was only six blocks from her two-bedroom cottage to the Cantu Corner Store—Dolores Cantu baked the muffins herself and saved the plumpest of the batch for Jamie—and only another ten to Weldon Pediatrics, the small West Texas practice where Jamie had worked as office manager for six years.

Because she walked, she usually finished her coffee before she arrived. Her mother knew this, being as familiar with Jamie's daily routine as with her own.

On those days, Dr. Kate, as she was fondly referred to by the county's residents, would bring Jamie a refill, picking it up with her own breakfast—an egg, potato, cheese and chorizo burrito, loaded and folded by

Dolores's husband, Juan—before making the drive five miles north to the Danby Veterinary Clinic.

This morning, Jamie was still outside the pediatrics office, a boxy building of brown siding with rock beds of succulents hugging the front, fitting her key into the door, when her mother's black Suburban pulled into the lot that would soon be teeming with bilingual mothers and children.

Jamie turned briefly, squinting against the sun as she watched Kate swing the SUV in a semicircle, the big vehicle's tires grinding on the gravel and creating a cloud of dust thick enough to gag a horse. Jamie's mother had always been more focused on her destination than the journey of getting there, and it showed in the way she drove.

Once the clinic's door was unlocked, Jamie dropped her keys into the bulky hobo bag hanging from her shoulder, and walked to where her mother waited. She took the coffee Kate handed her, removed the top from her empty cup, and settled the new one into the old.

After a quick sip, she smiled and said, "Where would I be without you to look after me?"

The corner of Kate's mouth, her lips smooth and free of added color, quirked to one side. "Married with children?"

It was an ongoing joke between overprotective mother and a daughter who had been through hell and only by a miracle survived. Though could Jamie really call it surviving?

Ten years later she was still in hiding, existing not as

her own woman, but as a creation of the horrific crime she'd witnessed when she'd been just nineteen years old.

Not having kids or a husband was, in her case, for the best. Should her memories of what she'd seen return, she didn't know if she'd be fit to live with, or if the remembered trauma would send her over the edge.

No, the future Jamie saw for herself was one spent alone. And, really—she was okay with it. Independence. Doing her own thing. A woman, an island unto herself. Seriously. How bad could spinsterhood be?

Another sip, and she thought back to what her mother had said. "I'm too spoiled for marriage and children. I like getting my own way all the time."

Kate shook her head, and reached for her own coffee where it steamed from the holder built into the Suburban's center console. "I'll cop to being a hovering nuisance, but the spoiling is your own doing. I was always too busy working and worrying to waste time seeing to your every whim."

Jamie nearly choked, but managed to swallow and come up laughing. "Are you kidding me? Where do you think I learned the art? You were the best teacher a girl could have." She raised her cardboard cup as proof. "You still are."

"Humph." Kate shook her head, fought a smile with a frown. "It would only be spoiling if I were stopping at the Cantus' just for you. But since I'm stopping for my own breakfast, it's not."

"You keep telling yourself that," Jamie said, lifting a hand to wave at Roni and Honoria, two of her coworkers who carpooled to Weldon from Alpine, and had just arrived in Honoria's sedan. "And I'll keep enjoying being single and an only child."

Kate arched a brow, studying her daughter's face as if the right angle might show her something new. "Sounds to me like you learned more from me than spoiling. You learned the art of self-deception as well."

Jamie tilted her cup against her mother's in a toast. They were two of a kind, gracefully accepting what life had served them. And though both would rather things had turned out differently, neither would give up the bond they now shared to make it so. "You have a busy day ahead of you?"

Kate nodded, pushing up the brim of the Danby Veterinary ball cap that covered the short wedge of her silvered brown hair. "The Barneses are bringing in their litter of shepherd pups. Two spays and six neuters."

"Which means you'd better get going."

"Which means I'd better get going. Besides—" Kate angled her chin in the direction of the clinic "—it looks like your staff has something on their mind."

Jamie followed the direction of her mother's gaze. Just inside the plate-glass entrance, Roni and Honoria stood facing each other, gesturing dramatically in Jamie's direction. She couldn't imagine what had them so animated this early. The day's first patient had yet to arrive.

She backed away from her mother's Suburban and hefted her bag more securely over her shoulder. "I'd better see what's going on. And you've got a dozen testicles calling your name. Thanks for the refill."

As her mother pulled out of the parking lot, leaving with a full-arm wave, Jamie headed for the front door.

She opened it to the sound of scurrying feet squeaking on the tiled floor as Honoria disappeared down the hallway toward the examination rooms.

Roni had obviously been in a similar hurry to take her seat at the front desk. Her headset was on crooked, and as Jamie came closer, she saw an insurance file open in front of the other woman. A tall blonde Laurel to Honoria's short dark Hardy, Roni stared at her computer monitor, doing her comical best to pretend she was hard at work.

Jamie blew the other woman's cover by reaching across the reception counter and turning the file right side up. "Might as well spill it now before the two of you explode. With Dr. Griñon here only half a day, I won't have time to clean up the mess if you do."

"Why are his half days the busiest of the week? And why don't we get to leave at noon, too?" Roni asked, forcing a light laugh as she situated the folder to her liking. She refused to meet Jamie's gaze. "I swear, Wednesdays should be relaxing, but they can really suck."

They could, but Jamie knew when Roni was grabbing for a distraction. The spots of color high on her cheeks told the tale. "You're changing the subject."

"Am I?" The color brightened. "I thought I was commenting on what you just said. You know, making conversation?"

"I'm not going away, so you might as well fess up." Jamie set her bag and her breakfast on the counter that rose in front of the desk, and her gaze on Roni, snapped open the single-section newspaper.

No sooner had she smoothed it out than Roni grabbed

it, hiding it beneath the desk in her lap, ignoring the "gimme" motion Jamie made with her hand. "Honoria said she wanted to talk to you first thing."

"What about?" And more importantly, how much of Jamie's paper was salvageable, and how much was smeared on Roni's pink scrub pants?

"I don't know, I mean, I don't remember." Flustered, Roni stood and leaned across the counter to call out, "Honoria! Jamie's here!"

As if Roni's partner in crime wasn't already aware. Jamie sighed. "This better not be some early surprise birthday-party thing…" Surely her mother would still be outside if it was, ready to come in and sing and blow noisemakers with the other two.

Roni met Jamie's gaze, frowning for a moment before her brown doe eyes went wide. "If there's a surprise party, I don't know anything about it, and this isn't it. Honoria! Get your butt out here now!"

Jamie sighed. Dear Roni, giving it away without admitting to a thing. Jamie's birthday wasn't for another two weeks, but she knew no one was going to let the momentous occasion of her turning thirty come and go quietly. That's how it was for old maids.

Honoria emerged from the file room, the morning's patient charts clutched to her ample chest. *Ample* was Jamie's word. Honoria considered herself short and dumpy and copy-paper plain—but then she'd never seen herself light up like the desert sky when her husband, Vicente, swept her away from the clinic for a private lunch.

Right now, the only thing bright about her were her eyes as her gaze bore into Roni's, broadcasting her disbelief that the blonde couldn't handle things on her own. Obviously, the two hadn't had time to get their story straight.

Whatever they were up to, it would have to wait. Jamie was hungry. "I'm going to the break room to eat my breakfast and read whatever part of the paper I can. Come get me when you've figured out how to tell me whatever it is you don't want me to know."

She lifted her bag by the shoulder strap, grabbed her coffee with the same hand, and reached with the other for the newspaper Roni still held captive.

Roni, having sat again, remained as silent and smiling as long-faced Laurel. Jamie turned to the Hardy of the duo. "I need my morning news. You know how I am without my morning news."

Honoria nodded, not a strand of her short wavy hair moving. Neither did her lips, not right away, and her eyes had gone flat. For the first time since walking into the comedy routine, Jamie was not amused. "What's going on, guys?"

"You don't want to see the newspaper today, *mija.*" Honoria pulled a copy of the latest *O Magazine* from her stack of files. She worshipped Oprah like she would a goddess. "Read Oprah instead. She has good, positive, cheery things to say."

Meaning whatever was in the *Reeves County News* was a bad, negative downer. Jamie thought quickly. Her mother was fine. She had yet to see Dr. Griñon today, but if something had happened to the clinic's pediatrician, Laurel and Hardy here wouldn't be hiding it. And they were both here, so there was nothing going on with their families.

Families. Jamie's father. He hadn't been a part of her life for ten years. Not since she'd been nineteen, attending Texas Tech University at Junction, living with her parents on their struggling ranch between Junction and Sonora, and working on Interstate 10 as a waitress at the Sonora Nites Diner. It had been his choice to walk out of her life, to leave her and her mother to deal with the things he hadn't been strong enough to handle. That didn't mean bad news wouldn't hurt.

"Is it my dad?" She knew it wasn't. Her mother would have told her had something happened to Steven Monroe. Which left only…that other thing.

Once more, Jamie set down her belongings and waited for the paper. This time, she wasn't taking no for an answer. Sharing a sad look with Honoria, Roni placed the folded and wrinkled sheets into Jamie's shaking hand.

There was only one thing that could have happened. Only one thing her friends would keep from her. Not because they didn't want her to know—she would find out eventually no matter what—but because of the wounds the news would reopen.

What her friends didn't understand was that the wounds had never really closed.

She crushed the paper, looked from Roni to Honoria, tears filling her eyes and blurring her vision, emotion lodged in her throat like a red rubber ball. "They found the last body, didn't they?"

Both pairs of brown eyes held distress and sympathy and fear. Jamie felt only one of the three. Her hands continued to tremble, her stomach twisted and gripped. Her friends nodded, first one, then the other, tears rolling down Honoria's cheeks as Roni choked back a sob.

Neither woman had known Jamie at the time of the murders—she and her mother had moved to Weldon not long after—and no one other than Jamie's parents and the authorities involved knew the details of that night.

Not even the families of the other victims—the victims who had died, and the one who had been dragged from the diner against his will. Jamie had been a victim, too, but that fact seemed lost on those left behind.

They'd demanded answers, had called her a liar, a coward, when the truth was she'd had no answers to give. She knew their lashing out was a coping mechanism; it gave them something to do when they felt so helpless. They wanted to know why she had been the one to live instead of their children, their siblings, their spouse. But most of all they wanted to know why she couldn't remember enough of that night to help authorities catch the person who'd destroyed so many lives.

She breathed deeply, tasted bile at the back of her throat and spread the newspaper open to the headline on the front page.

FIFTH VICTIM OF SONORA NITES DINER
MURDERS IDENTIFIED
Remains discovered in the Davis Mountains State Park this past March have, through dental records, been positively identified as belonging to Kass Duren, the hostage taken at gunpoint from the Sonora Nites Diner ten years ago following the

after-hours robbery and shooting spree that left all
but one employee dead.

Jamie had been that one employee. She stopped
reading and thought back, trying to remember what she'd
heard about the discovery of a body. Nothing came to
mind. Either she'd blocked it out, or she'd read nothing
about the find. The former seemed likely, but still…

Kass Duren. The cook. His wife's name was Helen.
He'd been what he'd called peasant stock. Sturdy and
solid. Descended from potato farmers from the old
country. Jamie, at nineteen, had never asked which one.

"I remember so little about it." Her voice came out
soft, words she heard in her mind more than with her
ears. "Colors, sounds. Flashes of light. It's all one big
mess. Like sharp bursts or abstract pieces." She closed
her eyes, felt the tingle of perspiration bite at her skin.
"They had to tell me that Kass had been taken away."

She looked back at her closest friends, the only two
people with whom she had trusted her story when she
could no longer hold it in, knowing they would never
betray her, or reveal the truth of her past. Both were silent,
pale. And when her cell phone played like a country-
western band in her bag, they both jumped along with her.
She dug it out, glancing at the number on the screen.

"I'm fine," she told her mother without waiting for
Kate to speak. "Go to work. There's nothing you can do
here."

"Jamie. I'm so sorry."

Jamie found herself shaking her head. "Don't be.
Kass's wife needs this closure. It's taken way too long."

"I know, sweetie, but there's going to be so much press, and so many reporters digging into that night. You've been safe here. Goddammit." There was a pause while Kate made a turn; Jamie heard the signal click on and off. "I should've moved you across the country, or at least across the state."

"We're in Texas, Mom. Half the state *is* almost half the country." Jamie forced a laugh, hoping it sounded better on the other end of the call because she was not buying the humor here.

"We need to talk about this. If your name shows up in the paper…"

Panicked, Jamie stopped listening. She hadn't read the whole article, and skimmed it quickly, finding no mention of who she was now, or who she'd been then. "It's not there. My name's not there."

"Not in this article, no, but what about the next, because you know this will renew interest in the case. They'll reopen the investigation. They'll figure out that Stephanie Monroe fell off the face of the earth and go looking. And someone with the right connections, or a big-enough gun, can find out that Dr. Kate Danby used to be Dr. Ruth Monroe."

Another pause and her mother was talking again. "I'm coming back. We need to talk to the authorities. And how the hell did the news make it into the paper without someone in law enforcement giving us a call?"

At the sound of the clinic door opening, Jamie turned, one arm hugged tightly around her middle that was roiling and surging in advance of the oncoming tidal wave she feared would sweep her away. "Oh my God."

"What is it? Jamie? What's happening?"

"They're calling now, Mom. In person," she added as the door swooshed closed, leaving Jamie face-to-face with the long arm of the law.

2

A SERGEANT with Company E in Midland, and assigned to the Unsolved Crimes Investigation Team, Texas Ranger Kellen Harding felt like a bull inside the china shop of Weldon Pediatrics—though the way the three women in front of him were staring, he might be well on his way to becoming a steer.

"I'll have to call you back, Mom," said the one Kell had already pegged as Jamie Danby, the one who had lived the first nineteen years of her life as Stephanie Monroe. The Hispanic woman was too short and, well, Hispanic. The blonde was the right height, and hair was easily colored, but she didn't have the same snap as the brunette—the brunette who was giving him a hell of an evil eye.

He stayed where he was, just inside the door, removed his white Stetson and sunglasses, and held her gaze. "Jamie Danby?"

Her face blanched, but color quickly returned to her cheekbones, and her mouth barely trembled when she asked, "And you are?"

"Ranger Sergeant Kellen Harding, ma'am, of Unsolved Crimes." He added the extra to break the ice that was taking too long to thaw. It was time he didn't want to waste, and she might not have.

"Can we help you with something, Sergeant Harding?" She faced him squarely, her chin up, her gaze direct. She didn't even bother looking around for a sick child. She knew he was here for her, and because of the recent break in the Sonora Nites Diner case.

He wondered if she was aware of the crumpled newspaper she held. He gave a nod toward it. "You've seen the story?"

"Of Kass being found?" she asked, her hand tightening around the strap of her bag, her knuckles turning white.

It was a rhetorical question, but it answered his, and he nodded again just the same. "Is there somewhere we can talk? Privately?"

"You can use the break room," the blonde hurried to offer, straightening the headset slipping down one side of her neck.

"Or there's a table and chairs on the back patio," the Hispanic woman added, a stack of folders in her arms. "It's a covered patio. With a ceiling fan."

Kell looked at Jamie. Jamie looked at Kell. It was her call, but he had a feeling no place on the clinic grounds would qualify as private. To tell the truth, he mused as the air-conditioning kicked on and the building's windows rattled, he had a feeling no place in Weldon would.

That was the thing about small towns. Folks liked to keep up with their neighbors' business, even when that business was none of their concern. Since authorities had never had a suspect to arrest and bring to trial for the murders, witness protection hadn't been an option for Stephanie Monroe. Her mother Ruth, now Kate Danby, had taken matters into her own hands, choosing to protect her daughter by changing their names and hiding in plain sight.

If anyone came after Jamie, the whole town would be waiting. Weldon's eleven hundred residents didn't need the details of her past spelled out before they'd come to her aid; she was one of their own and nothing else mattered—a fact Kell was sure Kate had counted on.

As plans went, it wasn't a bad one, but Kell liked his better. He was here to put an end to any and all threats this case still posed to her as the only witness to the Sonora Nites Diner murders. He just needed Jamie to hear him out, and then to go along with his proposal. Now that he saw her as more than a name in a file, he figured he was in for a fight. She might be rattled, but she was not down for the count.

Without looking toward them, Jamie spoke to the women standing behind her. "Can you two manage the patients and the doctor and the phones for a while?"

At her question, they both nodded, the blonde adding, "They invented voice mail for a reason, Jamie. We'll be fine. Go."

"And don't worry if you can't get back. It's a short appointment day anyway. We can handle the afternoon on our own." This from the darker woman.

Jamie took them at their word, folding the newspaper into her purse hanging from her shoulder, then reaching for her coffee and what Kell assumed was her breakfast in a brown paper bag.

He followed as she headed for the front door, catching it once she'd shoved at the glass, and returning his hat to his head, his sunglasses to his face, as he stepped onto the front walk behind her.

She held up one hand to shade her eyes, looking first at his four-wheel-drive SUV, then off down the block. "Can you leave your truck here? And take a walk?"

He could. "How far?"

"The Cantus have a covered deck with picnic tables at their market. Have you had breakfast? Juan makes awesome burritos."

Kell had poured himself a cup of coffee for the road when he'd left Midland before dawn, but that was it. "A burrito sounds great."

Jamie set off toward the sidewalk. Kell fell into step at her side. He was six foot one; he judged her to be about five foot eight and a whole lot of that height to be leg. She matched him step for step as they silently hit the end of one block and crossed the street to the next.

From behind the sunglasses he wore, he studied her. Her determination—she never faltered. Her focus—she trained it ahead, but that didn't keep her from paying attention to movement on all sides.

She was sharp, aware. She wasn't going to fall apart at the first sign of trouble. No, if Kell was going to have trouble with this case, it would no doubt have to do with the way she filled out the flower-pink bottoms of her scrubs.

He'd always been an ass man, and he'd never seen a tighter one than Jamie Danby's. Combine that with the rest of what she had going for her, and it was going to take a whole lot of discipline to keep his eye on the prize.

He pulled his lingering gaze away, catching the quirk of her mouth as they crossed one last intersection into the parking lot of the Cantu Corner Store. She didn't admit to knowing he'd had his eye on her backside, but then she didn't have to. That wicked half grin was her tell.

They stepped up onto the raised cedar deck; he let her take the lead and choose the table farthest from both the store and the street. She left her coffee and her bag behind and went inside. Again, that kind of town. One where she didn't have to worry about purse snatchers or identity theft.

Instead, she had to worry about a killer following the media coverage of his handiwork discovering who and where she was and hunting her down.

While Jamie heated what turned out to be a muffin in the small store's community microwave, Kell ordered two breakfast burritos and doctored a large coffee as they were being made. Once he and Jamie were back outside and settled at their table—and out of earshot of the curious onlookers inside the store—Jamie pounced.

"You're here because finding Kass's body reminded you that there's still a killer out there. Is that right?"

Kell stopped with his first burrito halfway to his mouth. "I've never forgotten there's a killer out there. Not once in ten years."

She met his gaze, hers not so much disbelieving as challenging. He knew it would take more than words to dispel her feelings that she'd been alone all this time, on her own, abandoned.

"You know I don't remember anything about the killer, so whatever you're hoping to find out, you can stop." She broke her muffin in half. Wisps of banana-scented steam rose, and she broke one of the halves again. "There's nothing there. My noggin broke. It didn't retain a thing about what he looked like, what he wore, nothing. You may have found Kass and solved the mystery of what happened to him, but the mystery of who's responsible remains." She paused, frowned, stared at the chunk of muffin she was ready to eat. "Unless that's why you're here. To tell me you have a suspect. To *warn* me you have a suspect, and that he knows where I am."

"No suspect," he said to set her at ease, biting off a quarter of his burrito while she calmed enough to eat the mangled muffin square. But she was wrong.

Just because she didn't remember anything about the killer didn't mean her noggin had broken, or that nothing was there. It *was* there. That much he knew, just as he knew it was hiding. He'd come here to get inside her head and coax it out.

She nodded thoughtfully as she ate, and he figured it was best to let her stew while he filled the hungry hole in his stomach. He was happy to answer any and all of her questions before getting to the reason he was here. But since he'd shown up unannounced, he didn't imagine she had many ready and waiting on the tip of her tongue.

She surprised him by having one, and with the way she took him in, her gaze causing the hair at his nape to stir. "Why did no one let us know about the identification before it hit the papers? Did you people lose the list of contact numbers you've had for us all these years?"

He'd only been assigned the case after the ID had been made and the files had been transferred from storage to the UCIT. The case was one he'd been aware of at the time of the killings, but he'd been in training academy then, and not yet a state trooper, much less the Ranger he was now.

Until the UCIT had been put in charge, he'd had no authority over how things were handled. He did now, and she was right. Jamie and her mother should have been informed.

He pulled his BlackBerry from its holster at his waist, punched up her contact information and showed her the screen. "I have all of your numbers. You're in the loop from here on. I promise."

He hadn't really answered her question, only guaranteed a similar lapse wouldn't happen on his watch. Whether or not that satisfied her, he couldn't say. She'd dropped her gaze and was back to picking at her muffin. It was hard not to watch her fingers at work, so precise, so nimble. So sure. "If you'd like to eat something besides crumbs, I'm happy to buy another round of burritos."

She shook her head, her eyes coming up, searching, soft, a little bit sad. "Go ahead if you want. I don't have much of an appetite."

He breathed deeply, hurting because she did. "Another coffee then?"

"No thanks." She pressed her fist to her sternum. "I think all that acid and caffeine was a mistake. It's going to take an Alka-Seltzer or Tums to get me through the rest of the morning."

Kell was pretty sure any stomach issues she was

having had less to do with what she'd put in it than with what she'd had to swallow when she'd seen the paper's front page. His showing up couldn't have made the news go down any easier. And what had he done since but make everything worse.

He got up from the table, and returned to the store to refill his own coffee and get Jamie a roll of antacids. Seeing a stack of *Reeves County News* copies in a rack next to the door helped him decide how to resume the conversation.

Once outside, he handed her the Tums and settled across the table from her again, folding his sunglasses into his shirt pocket before asking, "What's the first thing that went through your mind when you saw the headline?"

She peeled back the paper from the end of the roll. "There wasn't a first thing. It was more like a tumble of one thing on top of another."

Kell was good with going slowly, taking his time. "Such as?"

"That Roni's and Honoria's behavior made sense. They'd been going through all sorts of machinations to keep me from reading the news."

Roni would be the blonde, Honoria the Hispanic woman. Jamie had obviously shared some of her background with them. He made a mental note to add the info to his phone before prodding again. "What else?"

"That I needed to call my mother. That it wasn't going to be long before the media figured out Jamie Danby used to be Stephanie Monroe. This is the first movement the case has seen since it went cold, and investigative reporters these days are able to ferret out just about anything they want to know."

She shrugged, thumbed one of the tablets free and put it in her mouth, her fingers worrying the roll the only indication that her nerves weren't as calm as her voice. "My mother is the one who changed our identities. Once she realized we were on our own, she packed us up, sold the few head of livestock still on the ranch, filed for divorce, and we vanished. But her resources were way more limited than those available to whatever government agency handles witness protection. So I figure if reporters can find me after this break in the case, then the killer can, too.

"Except…" She paused, frowning as she gouged a thumbnail into the paper between the antacid tablets. "I've always assumed he knows. That he's left me alone because my amnesia means I'm not really a threat. That coming after me when it's clear he's gotten away with murder would be the stupidest move he could make."

The stupid ones didn't stand a chance. The smart ones, well, they could take longer to track down and bring to justice. But Kell *would* bring this one to justice. Jamie's family, Kass's family, the families of the other victims— they weren't the only ones who had suffered because of the killer who'd rampaged through the Sonora Nites Diner.

There was another man, the man who had taught Kell what it meant to be a Texas Ranger, who had lived and breathed the investigation, who had wept at every brick wall. As much as Kell was here for Jamie and Kate Danby, he was here for the man who had sworn to see this case through to the end, but who'd been hit and killed by a drunk driver while pulling over another on a long solemn stretch of Interstate 10.

This was Kell's job to finish now.

"On the other hand," she continued, popping a second antacid before closing the bits of paper around the roll's open end and tucking it into a pocket of her purse. "How smart could he possibly be to have left the diner that night without making sure there was no one still alive?"

Kell returned his cup of coffee to the table, holding it in place between both of his hands. "You're the one who outsmarted him by playing dead. You saved your own life, Jamie."

"Too bad I couldn't do the same for anyone else."

Her voice was flat, almost unfeeling. It didn't break with sadness over the loss of life, or sting with survivor's guilt. Though she'd walked out of that diner covered in blood, she spoke of the experience as would an outsider.

Locking away her emotions with her memories was a coping mechanism. Kell reached for the key. "What if you could do something now? For those who are left?"

Her eyes snapped, her breathing quickened. He'd hit the nerve he'd hoped for. "I told you. I told the cops and shrinks who questioned me then. I told the counselors I saw for months after. I can see splatters of color, and fractals of light and shadows as he moved through the diner. But I don't remember him. The last thing I see clearly is parking in the lot behind the diner before work. I barely remember opening the door and going inside."

She had gone inside. She had punched the time clock at 5:52 p.m.—eight minutes before her shift began. She had completed her six hours and—this was where Kell's imagination kicked in—had been joking around, maybe blowing off steam with her coworkers when the killer had slammed through the front door and opened fire.

Behind the register, Jamie—she'd been Stephanie then—had fallen to the floor. The killer had kicked her body out of the way to get to the cash register. Her ribs had been bruised so badly, the impression of his shoe's heel was visible in the blues and purples marring her skin.

She hadn't even moved when the killer had dragged away her boss. When the authorities arrived, she'd been lying exactly where she'd fallen, covered in her own blood and that of the others, her wounds fortunately no threat to her life.

What the crime scene photos and mock-up staging revealed, however, was that Jamie's position had her facing the front windows and the parking lot. If she'd opened her eyes even once, she might have seen… something. Car color, make or model. Numbers on the license plate. Killer's clothing, height or build. Age or ethnicity.

She might not have seen anything, but there was a very good chance that she had—and that she knew she had. Not consciously; the Jamie she was now wouldn't know anything about it. That's why Kell needed to ask Stephanie.

But he had to tread carefully to get from here to there. "I know you don't remember. Your mind is doing what it's supposed to do."

She gave a sharp snort. "It's supposed to fritz out? Really?"

"Not fritz out. Protect you. Amnesia is a coping mechanism." Just like her sarcasm.

"So it's all there. I'm just not thinking hard enough, or trying often enough to find it? Is that what you're saying? Because if you've come all this way for that—"

He cut her off before her accusations grew more strident, and got in the way of her listening to him. "That's not what I'm saying. Not at all. The memories are there, yes. But thinking hard or trying often is not how you'll find them."

She didn't believe him; he knew she was humoring him at best. "And I suppose you have the magic touch to make that happen?"

"Not me," he said softly, "but I know who might."

She waited, silent, expectant, as if bracing against him throwing a bucket of cold water in her face.

He got it over with as quickly as he could. "I'd like you to see a forensic hypnotist."

3

HE WOULD LIKE. *He* would like. Well, she didn't give a rat's ass what he would like. He wasn't the one whose head would explode if those memories ever came back.

"I'm sorry. I'm not sure what to call you. Sergeant? Ranger? Trooper?"

"Call me Kell," he said with too much twinkle in his green eyes for the subject at hand.

Murder needed to be looked at with serious intent. And if he was hoping to soften her up, to win her to his side with that sparkle, well, it was time he had his hopes dashed.

She started to do just that, but was stopped by the squeal of tires as her mother's Suburban took the turn into the Cantus' at a speed that would have scared a stunt driver straight. Jamie flinched, bracing for the SUV to ram the front of the store.

But the vehicle skidded to a stop, fishtailing to the left and throwing gravel, causing the Texas Ranger to surge to his feet with a deep "Holy hell."

"It's my mother," Jamie told him, enjoying the way his eyes went wide as much as she appreciated the width of his shoulders beneath his sharp white shirt. He was, in a word, hot. Disturbingly so. Big and intoxicating and lusty. Okay, more than a word, she thought, and cleared her throat. "I forgot to call her back."

Kate jumped out of the cab and came at them, waving her arms and yelling the very same thing. "You were supposed to call me back. Jamie. What's going on?"

On her feet now, too, Jamie made the introductions. "Mom, this is Sergeant Kell Harding with the Texas Rangers. Kell, my mother, Kate Danby. Dr. Kate."

Jamie's mother looked at the man in the Western-cut dress shirt, white hat, boots and jeans, then turned an inquiring gaze back on her daughter to wait for more than an exchange of names—a gaze filled with as many fears as questions.

Her own heart aching over the worry her mother had suffered all these years, Jamie took her hand and pulled Kate to sit on the bench beside her. "Kell came the moment he was given the case files. He came in person. He wanted to make sure we were okay. To answer our questions."

Jamie turned then to look at Kell. He again sat on the other side of the table, but rather than sit directly across from either her or her mother, he had positioned himself in between, giving them equal consideration. She liked that as much as she liked the creases fanning out from the corners of his eyes. They seasoned him with wisdom, not age, and spoke of experience Jamie knew was needed.

His attention on Kate, Kell inclined his head. "Your daughter's right, Dr. Danby. Any questions you have, ask—"

Kate cut him off. "You being given the files—does

that mean the case has finally been brought out of cold storage to thaw? That maybe we can put an end to this once and for all? Or are we going to have to spend the rest of our lives the way we've spent the last ten, fearful and looking over our shoulders, searching for whatever it is that's spooked us?"

Kell didn't look away. He pressed his lips together, and Jamie watched the muscles in his neck tighten as his jaw held taut. Around his coffee cup, his hands also tightened. She heard the plastic squeak. But he kept his frustration in check. And she knew it was frustration, not anger, not insult, and frustration with the case, not with her mother's accusation that he wasn't doing his job.

Finally, he found his words and spoke. "What Jamie didn't mention is that I work with the UCIT, the Unsolved Crimes Investigation Team. Cold cases are what I do, where I pour one-hundred percent of my energies. Right now, this case, Jamie's case, is my top priority."

"But only because of Kass Duren. Not because of Jamie," Kate said, and Jamie stiffened.

"Mom—"

"No, it's okay. She's right. Anytime there's activity on a case, it gets moved to the top of the list. That doesn't mean without movement it lies dormant. We're always looking for a break, a lead, new clues and witnesses."

"Looking?" Kate asked, her mouth grim and turned down, her Danby Veterinary Clinic ball cap pulled low. "Or waiting for them to fall into your lap? Because I don't see how you can give one hundred percent to any single case when you've got dozens of others still unsolved and demanding your time."

"He didn't say he gave one hundred percent to any single case. He said he prioritized." Jamie didn't know why she was defending the Texas Ranger.

She should be siding with her mother. They were the ones living this hell, the ones forgotten by law enforcement and left to their own devices, starting over, creating new identities, protecting themselves however they could because if they didn't, who would?

She decided it was because of Kell that her loyalties were wobbling. His sincerity. The pit-bull determination that had brought him all this way. He could've written a letter. He could've picked up the phone. He hadn't done either one. He'd driven the three hours between his office and hers.

Since the initial investigators had packed up and moved on, he was the first officer from any law enforcement agency to involve himself with Jamie and her mother directly. Now that she'd had a few minutes to cool down, she wanted to hear what he had to say.

If she'd learned anything over the last ten years it was to keep her eyes, mind and ears open. She told herself that she owed him that much. She told herself, too, that it wasn't because of his eyes. Or his shoulders. Or the size of his hands.

The fan whirring overhead stirred the hot dry air into a semblance of a breeze, pushing loose strands of her hair into her face. She plucked them away, ignored the heat stirring low in her belly and said, "Sergeant Harding— Kell—was about to explain forensic hypnosis to me."

Kate squeezed Jamie's wrist. "What?"

"I'm pretty sure he wants to jog my memory."

"The same memory you've told everyone repeatedly is blank? Does no one believe you?" Kate shifted on the bench, closer to Jamie and away from Kell. "Or since they're at a loss to solve this thing, are they now putting the onus on you?"

Kell had been sitting silent all this time, absorbing the exchange between mother and daughter as if searching for the best tack to take, or as if waiting his turn because, law enforcement or not, he knew he was the outsider.

But Kate's accusation obviously riled him. His pulse throbbed in his temples, and he had barely swallowed the rest of his coffee before he crushed the cup.

"The onus is on us, Dr. Danby. On me. Completely. Coming to Jamie is not a shifting of responsibility—"

Her skin pale, Kate pulled her hand from Jamie's and waved it to cut him off. "Then why are you talking to my daughter about hypnosis? Why—"

"Let him talk, Mom. Please." Jamie so understood what her mother was feeling.

It had been Kate's job to protect her daughter, to see Jamie from traumatized teen to a woman standing on her own, recovered, able to view the past from the distance she'd come in ten years. And she'd done it alone, while building a new life as a divorcée, coping with all of it at once because she'd had no choice. As much as Jamie did not want to return her to where this whole nightmare had started…

She tamped down the fear rising in a dark cloud around her and turned her attention on Kell. "Let him talk."

His gaze captured hers, held, a potent thank-you for not writing off his proposal before he'd had a chance to explain. A brief nod, then he looked at her mother, as if her permission was as important to him as was Jamie's.

She liked that. Found she was liking many things about him when the only thing that mattered was whether or not he would be the one to put an end to her hell.

Kate hadn't objected, so Kell cleared his throat. "Before you arrived, I was explaining to Jamie that the memories she thinks she's lost, well, she hasn't. Not really. Selective amnesia is a coping mechanism—"

"Selective amnesia? Are you saying she's forgotten on purpose?"

He shook his head. "Her subconscious won't let her remember. Her mind is protecting her from reliving the trauma of that night's events."

"And yet knowing that, you want to hypnotize her and have her suffer them again?" Kate shook her head vehemently. "No. No. It's not going to happen. Absolutely not."

"Mom—"

"Jamie, no." Kate's voice grew shrill. "I won't let you go through that again. You can't—"

It was time for Jamie to take charge. "I can, but I haven't said that I will. I want to know more before I agree to going back there."

Kell's expression changed, growing accommodating, respectful yet urgent, as if he was at her disposal for any little thing. "What do you want to know?"

Jamie wasn't even sure where to begin. "What makes you think this will work? This forensic hypnosis?"

"I'm not sure that it will," he told her, and she appreciated his honesty. "You may not recall anything we can use in our investigation. On the other hand, you might remember the very thing we need to track down this bastard and put him behind bars."

"Such as?" Jamie couldn't help but fear, what was for her, the unknown.

Her mother spoke before Kell could answer. "A license-plate number? Isn't that what that bus driver in California remembered under hypnosis?"

"You're talking about Chowchilla," Kell said, and nodded.

"What's Chowchilla?" Jamie asked.

"A town in California," Kell explained. "In 1976, three men kidnapped a busload of students and their driver, and held them hostage in a moving van buried in a quarry. A ransom note was found in the house of the quarry's owner. His son and two others were eventually charged."

Bury? A van? For a kidnapping? In the movies, sure, but for real? "You're kidding," she said, and when he shook his head, asked, "Were they rescued?"

"They were," Kell answered. "They dug themselves out, but by then, the kidnappers were long gone. The driver eventually underwent forensic hypnosis to see if he could remember anything helpful."

Bizarre. "And it worked?"

"He remembered enough of a license-plate number on one of the vehicles involved, that authorities were able to track the men down through the registration, I think it was. Hypnosis was also used in Ted Bundy's case. In the Boston Strangler's. In Sam Sheppard's. His was made into a movie. *The Fugitive.*" Kell's expression fell into a goofy smile. "With Harrison Ford."

Kate had been listening, and asked, "Are the memories refreshed during hypnosis even admissible in court?"

"Not everywhere, no. In Texas, they are, but we use them in conjunction with other investigative tools."

Meaning a conviction or acquittal wouldn't rest solely on what Jamie might manage to recall. "So if I remember seeing a license plate through the diner's window…"

"Then we'll track down what car those plates were on at the time and who it was registered to."

And to play devil's advocate. "Someone other than the owner could've been driving it."

Kell nodded. "Which is why we don't stop with the refreshed memory. We use it as we would any new lead. To help us find the irrefutable evidence that will put the perpetrator away."

He was making this sound simple, logical. Making it sound like the right thing. Making it sound as if she would be smart to let him do his job. "If I remembered something that helped, would I have to testify at a trial?"

"You might be asked to, yes."

"Would she *have* to?" Kate asked.

"Compelling her to do so wouldn't be my call." Kell turned his attention from her mother to Jamie. "Going into this you should think worst-case scenario to make sure all bases are covered."

Yeah. This was the part she'd been afraid of, what she'd been waiting to hear. She reached for the antacids, stared at the strips of torn wrapper and said, "Worst case being the killer comes after me before he goes to trial."

"That is my bailiwick. And that won't happen."

How could he know? How could he be sure? Things

could go so wrong… "And if I go insane reliving that night, does the court pay my asylum costs? Because as much as I want this bastard behind bars, I'm not sure I won't need bars of my own if those memories come back."

Kate slapped her hand against the table, and dust bloomed in tiny clouds. "Then you're not going to do it. I won't have you spending the rest of your life suffering."

If only it was that simple. Say no, and save herself the horrors those who had lost their loved ones would never put to rest. Or say yes, and hope that closing the case would allow her to do the same.

She looked up at Kell. "If I were to agree, who would do it? Hypnotize me?"

"The Department of Public Safety has officers licensed by the state and trained to use hypnosis in the investigation of crimes. Not a lot. Last I heard, out of sixty thousand officers, only three hundred were certified."

"Would I go to a police station somewhere?"

"You could, or the team would bring the equipment to you."

"Team?" Kate asked.

"The hypnotist, a technician to man the recording equipment and an officer to witness the questioning."

Jamie frowned. "An officer? Not you?"

"I'll be observing, yes, but not in the same room."

Her heart was racing. She didn't know why. She didn't know him well enough to want him there; wouldn't any officer do? "Why wouldn't you be in the same room?"

"I'm working the case—I'm invested in a way the officer witnessing wouldn't be. A neutral witness is best so there's no reaction to what you might reveal."

"And you might react."

He nodded, and she watched his pulse jump at his temple.

Her own jumped in response, then jumped again for reasons that had nothing to do with the case, and everything to do with the look in his eyes. "So it's videotaped, and I can do it anywhere I'm comfortable, and you'll be nearby even if you're not in the room."

"I'll be there, too," Kate said.

"You can observe," Kell was quick to say. "But no family members or anyone connected to the case can be in the room during the session. The rules are set up to make sure the memories recalled are clean, not influenced by observers or by suggestion, that sort of thing. Otherwise, anything recalled is considered tainted, and anything turned up during a follow-up investigation questionable."

"But as long as the rules aren't broken…" Was she that strong? That brave? Would she be able to live with the memories if they came flooding back? Would she be able to live with herself if she didn't give Kell's suggestion a try? She wanted so badly to help; she always had.

All these years, she'd felt so impotent, unable to remember details with enough significance to break the case. Because of her own frustration, it wasn't hard for her to understand that felt by the victims' families. Their accusations had stung, yes, but she'd never taken them to heart. And now she had a chance to give them the one thing they most needed.

How could she not at least try?

Kell had been holding her gaze all this time, and he

finally spoke. "As long as we follow the rules, this is our best shot to shut down this nightmare for good."

We. He'd said we.

Jamie knew her mother was as torn as she was, and that Kate's vote would most likely be no. She didn't want her daughter to have to suffer the horror the refreshed memories could bring. As a mother, that was her right. Kate didn't care that her baby was an adult.

But Jamie *was* an adult. She was the one who had to make this decision, weighing her mother's worries and Kell's assurances against her own counsel.

Really, though, there was only one course of action her conscience would allow her to take—and it would be as much for the other victims as for herself.

"I'll do it."

4

WHILE JAMIE AND HER mother talked privately in the air-conditioned cab of Kate's idling Suburban, Kell walked to the far end of the covered porch where the air stirred by the overhead fan had more room to move.

It was hot, but it was August, and it was Texas, the Chihuahuan Desert swath of West Texas to be precise.

He'd lived in Texas all his life. He'd grown up in Austin where his parents and younger brother still lived. His youngest brother had moved to Houston to work after graduation, exchanging the landlocked central Texas heat for the Gulf Coast humidity. Complaining about the state's weather was as much a part of being a Texan as waving the Lone Star flag.

But the heat sweating its way through Kell now was of a different sort. A heat wrapped up in pink scrub bottoms and long nimble fingers and an intelligence that wouldn't quit. Jamie Danby was an amazing woman, and his gut knotted up thinking of what she'd been through.

Even more gut-wrenching were the questions he kept asking himself. What if the hypnosis backfired and Jamie got burned? What if he got his man, brought him to justice, yet Jamie spent the rest of her life scarred worse than she was now?

He adjusted his sunglasses, staring at the haze fogging his view of the Davis Mountains dipping and rolling in the distance. He owned property on the other side of those hills, in the Guadalupe range, to be exact, a hefty number of acres that were home to coyotes and white-tailed deer and javelinas.

He had a cabin there, a simple log structure where he spent long weekends when he needed to escape the horrors he dredged up and the pain his dredging caused the victims of the original crimes. The sort of hell Jamie would be going through once her mind released its hold on her memories.

She was a cute one, Jamie Danby. Tall and willowy, the scrubs she wore hiding the curves she did have, except for her very fine ass. Her hair was long enough for her to pull up into a ponytail, and though he supposed she'd call it brown, it held a whole lot of dark red. The color probably accounted for the smattering of freckles on her nose and cheeks.

What he liked about her was a combination of things—all of them speaking to the depth of who she was. The way she considered Kate's feelings about the hypnosis; it couldn't be easy to peel back the protective layers her mother had wrapped her in, not knowing what waited on the outside of the cocoon. The way she had chosen to do what was right, though she'd had to fight herself to get there.

He had a feeling she was strong enough to get through whatever happened, but he would damn sure stick around to make sure that she did. That sort of follow-up might not be in his job-description manual, but Kell didn't need a book of rules and regs to tell him how to be human.

Neither did he need a shrink to tell him that his history with the officer who'd fought to keep the case from going cold made his involvement as much personal as professional. He was going to have to toe a fine line, and not cross over into the kind of emotional territory that led to costly mistakes. But that was between Kell and his conscience.

Behind him, one of the SUV's doors slammed closed. He didn't turn, but continued to stare at the rocky mountainside, the trees and scrub growing on the face, their roots finding and clinging to meager patches of soil that neither time nor Mother Nature had eroded away.

Soon enough he heard—and felt—footsteps on the deck as Jamie returned, heard the crunch of ground gravel and the squeal of burning rubber as Kate Danby left her daughter alone with him. Still, he didn't turn. He waited for Jamie to make the first move.

Her agreeing to the hypnosis was huge. He wasn't about to rush or press or insist they had no time to waste. Giving her the time she needed was the best way for Kell to accomplish his goal, and accomplishing his goal was paramount.

Her steps brought her closer. He sensed her at his side, her body heat, her tension, the sound of her sigh. When he caught her scent, his body tightened, and his conscience told him not to be a fool. "It's a rough one. I know."

He didn't, of course. At least not what she was going

through now. Or even what was to come. But he'd made his own share of tough calls, decisions he would rather have not come to. So in that regard…yeah. He knew.

"About that," she said, stepping on the tail end of his thoughts. "What *do* you know?"

He shifted enough that his elbow grazed hers. "What do you mean?"

She stayed there, brushing his shirtsleeve, and followed the direction of his gaze. "Some of the things you said. I get the feeling this case is more than just another left unsolved."

What had he said? What had he let slip? It had to have been something in his tone of voice. He knew he hadn't given anything away with words. She was his reason for being here, and he didn't want her to think otherwise should she discover his connection to the original officer on the case.

"Unsolved cases take a toll. Not that fresh ones don't. They do. I know that." He ran a hand over the back of his neck, wiping at both the stress and the sweat that it— more than the day's temperature—had caused. "But cold cases require the people involved, the victims, the bystanders, the witnesses…they all have to open closed doors, turn keys in locks they thought were keeping them safe."

He kept it at that. Hoped she'd leave it at that. She didn't need to know his professional interest came with a personal bent. The man who'd convinced Kell of his calling, the man who'd been a lifelong friend of his father, deserved better than to have this case go unsolved. But that was Kell's cross to bear. And it was his responsibility to make sure it didn't get in the way of his doing his job.

She didn't respond except to return to their table where she'd left her purse. Kell watched her sling the strap over her shoulder, her expression thoughtful, her eyes beneath frowning brows full of so many things she obviously wanted to know.

He walked toward her, detouring to the opposite side of the table from where she stood. It would be easier to talk to her from here. "Ask me."

Her gaze came up. Her chin, too. She tilted her head to one side, toyed with the end of her ponytail where it fell over her shoulder. He got a kick out of her scrubs top, with its teddy bears wearing firefighter gear, wielding hoses, mounted on ladder trucks.

Finally, she spoke. "I'm not sure you being so perceptive is a good thing or bad." She added a smile; shy, he thought. "I mean, it's good since you're an investigator…"

"But it's bad because it's your case I'm investigating? And I might pick up on things you prefer keeping close to the vest?"

She nodded, released her hold on her shoulder strap and lowered slowly to sit again on the picnic table's bench. "Something like that. Though Roni and Honoria know where I came from and what happened, my mother has made sure that I'm anything but an open book."

And here he was turning her pages. He sat, too.

"It's strange having so few friends to confide in. Living a solitary sort of life." She looked off into the distance, smiling, but for her own benefit, not his. "I was just thinking this morning that I'm a hop and a skip away from turning into a crazy cat lady. Or I would be if I had the cats."

"I hope you're not going to. Hop and skip in that direction." He wanted to give her a reason not to. A reason, instead, to reach for the full life she'd been denied. He couldn't imagine what things had been like for her, existing, not living, within a bubble he doubted was insulated against fear.

She looked back, and shook her head, laughing. "I've been tempted, but so far I've resisted the lure of feline ownership. And of covering a multitude of sins with lace doilies."

She had a sense of humor. Dry, self-deprecating. Even a little bit black. He liked that. Laughter cured a lot of ills. "If this works out, you might just be spared a future of cats, doilies and tea spiked with Jack."

This time when she laughed, it was at his expense completely. "Known a lot of crazy cat ladies, have you?"

She was going to get close. He knew that as surely as he knew he was going to let her. Let her, hell. The way she was hitting his buttons, he'd probably roll out the red carpet before they were done.

"I'm happy to say my experience has been limited to movies and TV."

"Then maybe I'll be your first."

Hoo-boy. The thought of her being his anything… He shook it off. All of it. The temptation, the attraction, the heat that had him wanting to do more than sweat.

He cleared his throat, pulled off his hat and set it on the table, brim up, crown down. "What I'm hoping is that you'll be my first forensic-hypnosis success."

There. He'd successfully switched them back on course. And just as successfully doused her good mood.

"You haven't done this before?" Her voice cracked at the end of her question.

"I'm not the hypnotist, remember? But, no. I've never had cause to use hypnosis on a cold case before."

She looked down, tugged her purse into her lap and held it close, toying with the rings that anchored both ends of the strap. "What if it doesn't work? If I don't remember anything that helps? Or anything at all?"

It was a very good possibility that would be the outcome. He knew that going in. She deserved to know it, too. But the way she'd withdrawn, pulled in on herself as if seeking shelter… She was asking for more than a simple answer.

He'd do his best to give her what would help. "As far as the case goes, I'll rework what's been worked before. New questions, a new investigator, it can make a difference in what memories are jarred. We've got the credit-card receipts from that night. We've got the same from the gas station next door. Those from the motels on either side, too. Someone who was there, working, gassing up, staying the night, stopping for a meal…I hit them again. My angle. My methods."

She was listening. She wasn't looking at him, but she was still, attentive. He took a deep breath and went on. "But as far as what will happen with you…"

Her head came up then, her chin trembling. Tears welled in her eyes and threatened to spill. She reached toward him with one hand, her fingers, her face imploring.

"If I can't remember anything that helps, it'll be hard, but I can live with it. What I can't live with is having to leave here. I'm making it. It's not the life I would have chosen, small town, small job, but I'm happy enough. If that little bit gets taken away…"

She closed her fingers, made a fist, held her lips pressed tight. "This is all I have, Kell. My life in Weldon. I'm safe here. I can't mess that up. I can't start over. There is no starting over."

He wasn't sure why she thought not remembering would mean starting over. What did she think would change? "If you don't remember, things will go on as they have been—"

"No. They won't." She pulled away, sat straighter, taller. She didn't need to dry her tears. They were already gone. "Going on as they have been would require that I not risk the sort of exposure my involvement in your investigation will bring."

"It won't be public—" he started to say, but she cut him off again.

"You can't keep my involvement from going public. You'll try. I know you'll try. But it'll leak out. Someone who knows about it will say something offhandedly, nothing they think twice about. But some listener will pick up on the news, and that spark will become a wildfire that's out of control before you have a chance to blink. You know how these things are, Kell. How they happen."

He did, but he wasn't sure what to say. She seemed certain that whatever the result of the hypnosis, things would change. And since there was no guarantee that her refreshed memories would bring an end to the manhunt—or even give him a place to start—he couldn't argue the validity of her concern.

All he could do was protect her to the best of his ability, and make sure she knew that he would be there anytime she needed him, for as long as she needed him, even after the case was closed.

He circled the table to sit beside her, their thighs close though he faced away from the store while Jamie faced forward. Rather than meet her gaze, he let his nearness assure her while he leaned his forearms on his knees and stared at what he could see of Weldon from here.

The town wasn't small enough that he could stand at the southern city-limits sign and see all the way to the north, but that was only because the main drag took a left and a right before splitting at a fork. One way led to Alpine, the other to Marfa, with not much of Weldon beyond.

Sonora, Texas, the place where Jamie, as Stephanie, had done her growing up was only about three times the size of Weldon, but it wasn't off the beaten path and tucked away in the craggy mountains as was her home for the last ten years.

He understood the lonesome appeal of the place; his cabin was similarly isolated. But he didn't know if he and solitude got along well enough to spend their lives together. He wondered how Jamie did it. He was just about to ask her, when she scooted away.

"I need to get back to work before Honoria and Roni send out a search party." She swung one leg then the other over the bench and stood.

Kell stood, too, hands at his hips. "Do you want me to make the arrangements?"

The look she gave him was full of so much sadness his gut started second-guessing his years of experience.

"How long will it take?" she asked, hitching her shoulder strap higher.

"To set things up? I can do it this afternoon."

"And how soon would it happen?"

"As soon as you want." He couldn't tell if she wanted to get it over with or put it off.

"Tomorrow? Is that too soon?"

Not if it was up to him. "Do you want me to have the team come here?"

"No," she hurried to say, shaking her head vehemently. "I don't want anyone here to know I'm doing this. Or for anything about that night to touch my life here. At least no more than it already has."

He gave a single nod, one of agreement but also of sympathy. Her part was to be brave. His part was to make her bravery easier. "I can set up the session at the Ranger station in Midland."

"That's fine."

He could tell she wanted to get away from this conversation. "I'll get a room for the night and make the arrangements, then give you a call this evening. We can drive up together tomorrow, and I'll bring you back when we're done."

Finally, a smile found its way to her face. "There's not much in the way of overnight accommodations in Weldon. You can try to get a room at the Cordoba Inn, though it's usually booked solid through Labor Day by summer vacationers, as is Indian Lodge. There's the hotel at the state park in Balmorhea, but same thing, especially with the spring-fed pool there, and it's about thirty-five miles away anyway. Of course, there's always my extra bedroom if nothing pans out."

He'd take it. "If I don't have to drive half the day looking for a room, I'll have more time to make sure we can do this tomorrow."

She considered him for a long moment, as if wondering for the same fiery reasons he was how truly wise her offer had been. But rather than take it back, she left it there, an opening, an offer, a heady invitation that ripened in the air simmering between them. "I can walk you over, or we can go back to the clinic for your SUV."

"Why don't we do that," he said, barely able to breathe. "I've got some files I'll need anyway, and my laptop and fax machine."

"Have electronics, will travel?"

"Not to worry," he told her, smiling. "I still carry a gun."

5

BY THE TIME JAMIE made it back to the office, the short clinic day was in full swing, and the hustle and bustle of colds and coughs and ear infections so crazy that she barely had time to think. Neither did she have time— nor opportunity—to tell the story of Kell's visit to Roni and Honoria.

She knew both of her coworkers were curious, but the women also respected Jamie's privacy; they let her know with smiles and quick hugs that anytime she might need them, and for whatever reason, they were there.

Once the noon hour arrived and the clinic's doors were locked for the day, leaving the women the rest of the afternoon free for phone calls and paperwork while Dr. Griñon drove to Alpine to golf, Jamie quickly explained that she'd be taking Thursday and Friday as personal days. Both women were more than willing to pick up the slack while she was gone.

She didn't spell out what it was she would be doing, only that she had to go to Midland to do it. Assuring them she was not in any trouble and there was nothing for either of them to worry about, Jamie worked quietly until five, going through the most pressing items on her desk before heading home.

Where Kell was waiting.

She had tried—and failed—to forget he was at her cottage, sitting at her kitchen table with his laptop, pacing the short hallway while making his calls, perched on the edge of the sofa watching cable news while adding details of their trip to his BlackBerry.

All of that was her imagination, of course, because she had no idea how he'd been spending his time. The only thing she knew for sure was that he'd be staying the night. Just the thought had her slowing her steps as she crossed Brick Avenue and continued her walk to Lamplighter Lane.

As Jamie Danby, she'd had very few men in her life. For a year she'd dated Stuart Pearson who managed the Village Greenhouse Co-op south of town. Stuart had been nice, a great guy, patient and kind, and because he'd been all of those things, Jamie hadn't thought it fair to load him down with her baggage. They'd parted amicably and remained friends; she took the fact that the breakup hadn't caused more than an uncomfortable twinge as a sign she'd done the right thing for both of them.

Things had been much different when she'd still been Stephanie Monroe. During those days, girlfriends, boyfriends and her social life had been her number-one priority. She'd never spent a Friday or Saturday night alone, and spent more weeknights partying than in study or sleep.

It was hard to believe she'd been that girl, to think back on the number of friends she'd had then when she had so few now. And as far as not having men in her life, or even one good man to make her forget those who'd come and gone, well, at least as Jamie she was safe.

Or she had been until Kell Harding had walked into the clinic. Now she didn't know what she was. There wasn't a doubt in her mind that he would do his best to make sure she came to no harm. The doubts crept in when she began to wonder if his best was good enough.

Would anyone's best be good enough? Or was her best bet for keeping danger at bay to continue as she had been, relying on herself and her mother and their combined instincts for survival?

It was the thought of Kate Danby that had Jamie's steps slowing. As much as she owed it to herself—and to the families of those who had died the night she had lived—to help close the Sonora Nites Diner murder case for good, she owed it to her mother most of all.

Kate had given up everything to keep Jamie safe, including the Sonora veterinary practice where she'd gone to work after graduating from Texas A&M, and where she'd eventually become a partner.

For ten years, Kate's life had been Jamie's life, and it was time Jamie released her mother from the obligation to protect her Kate had assumed. Of course, Kate had done so out of maternal love; Jamie got that. But now it was time for the mother to let the daughter give back.

That left only Kell. The part where he was going to work her case wasn't an issue; she was committed to following his lead, his suggestions, his orders. He was a professional, unsolved crimes his business.

No, she found herself dreading the next couple of days in his company because having accepted her fate as a singleton, it wasn't easy to come face-to-face with what she was missing in such a very big way. In such a fit and gorgeous and amazingly kind way.

When she turned the corner onto Lamplighter Lane and saw his big four-wheel-drive vehicle hulking in front of her cottage, she stopped walking and stood there, imagining for a moment what it would be like to come home to that sight every day. Come home to him every day.

Was it something she would ever grow used to? Or take for granted? Having a man like Kell Harding in her life? Being resigned to living alone, she couldn't imagine doing either one, but he wasn't in her life, not in that way, and her daydreaming wasn't productive. She shook it off, continuing down the sidewalk to her back door.

That was when the fantasy and the reality collided. She stopped on the top of the three concrete steps that led from her driveway into her kitchen; the screen door bounced against her rump because she had yet to move. The room smelled like heaven. She rarely cooked. She was one person, easily pleased with a sandwich, and she hated the heat of the stove. But the smell was only half the picture.

The real picture was Kell.

He'd taken over her kitchen. He was tall; his boots made him taller. She'd seen his jeans and white dress shirt before, but this was different. He was in her house, cooking, his long sleeves cuffed up his forearms. He had nice forearms, dusted with dark hair, muscled, a road map of veins in relief beneath his skin.

His hands were large, dwarfing the slotted spoon he held as he lifted home-cut fries from a skillet to drain. He salted them, peppered them, added garlic and what looked like paprika, but could just as easily have been cayenne.

He opened the oven door then, and slid two steaks beneath the broiler before pulling a big bowl of tossed salad from the fridge. That was when he turned, when he killed her with his smile, and with his eyes that twinkled like the stars over the mountains at night.

"Looks like I timed things pretty well."

He had. Perfectly. She came the rest of the way into the kitchen and shut the door on the heat of the day. The heat in the kitchen she could handle. As long as she kept it in the kitchen, and didn't start wondering if Kell was as clever in the bedroom. She was a spinster, remember? And he wasn't here to have sex.

Before she could do more than set her bag on the antique washbasin where she kept her keys and her cell charger, and where she dropped the day's mail, Kell had returned to her cupboards for salad bowls, dinner plates, and grabbed knives and forks from the right drawer without second-guessing.

Just as if he lived here. Just as if he'd been the one to decide where things would go.

She arched a brow, tried not to show all of the appreciation she was feeling. She couldn't let herself get comfortable having him here when it was only for one night. "I see you've made yourself at home."

"Only in the kitchen. I swear," he said, giving her a wink before turning back to the broiler and the steaks. "Well, I did use the facilities, but I washed my hands and aimed true."

Oh God. He was cute, and funny, made jokes at his

own expense, and confident enough to take over her kitchen without asking. She really needed to stop noticing, to remember he was a Ranger sergeant and here for only one thing. And that one thing wasn't dinner, nor was it her.

She headed for the fridge and the pitcher of tea there, was reaching for two plastic tumblers in the cupboard when she and Kell touched. He turned from the stove with the basket of home fries. She took a step in the same direction at the same time, and he reached to stop her from tripping over his feet.

It was nothing but his hand on her arm, his thumb brushing her breast accidentally, yet she felt the shock of electricity deep in her core, saw the same jolt spark in his eyes. She wanted to shake it off, to smile and put the tea on the table, to talk about the weather or the case. He still held her, however, his fingers flexing, as if he didn't know how to let her go, and when he finally did, she sensed regret.

"Sorry about that." He set the fries on the table, and made sure to step around her when he went back to turn the steaks. "I'm used to navigating a one-man kitchen."

She gathered herself close. "Hey, at least you're navigating. I don't do much more than make a beeline through the room to the door."

"You don't cook?" he asked, closing the broiler.

"How much of what we're about to eat, and thank you for that—" she stopped to add along with a nod "—did you have to go out and buy?"

He laughed. "All of it. Well, not the ketchup. Or the salad dressing."

"Exactly. You need condiments, I'm your girl. I can even build a mean sandwich," she hurried on, so the girl thing didn't hang in the air. "But I get my breakfast at Cantus', and usually skip lunch unless Roni or Honoria pack enough for two."

"Let me guess." He leaned a hand on the countertop, parking his other at his hip "They take turns, and it's been years since you've skipped lunch."

"I walk to work," she said before she realized he wasn't commenting on her weight. God, she was not cut out for this...this...banter. Or even small talk. Not with a man who shopped and cooked and set the table, and was going to fix her upside-down life. "I guess they think I don't pack anything so I won't have to carry it with me."

"And you let them think that." He took her in as if there was much about her to be learned in what she'd just said.

She was pretty sure there wasn't much to be learned about her at all, and so she shrugged and poured two tumblers of tea. "I don't want to hurt their feelings. And they both pack a mean lunch."

"Well, I hope my cooking measures up." Kell turned off the broiler to pull out the steaks.

"The way everything smells, that's not a worry." She sat in her regular chair as Kell forked a rib eye onto her plate.

He slid the second onto his own and sat across the table, dropping his napkin into his lap before picking up his fork and knife. "I figured with the lunch meat in the fridge, you weren't a vegan or anything."

Right. Because the lunch meat couldn't be for anyone else. She sighed—though his jumping to the right conclusion about her living alone shouldn't pinch like a nerve. Being unmarried didn't mean she was unmarriageable, but that was her projecting her own issues with being single at thirty, which was her problem, not his.

She loaded her plate down with fries. "One hundred percent carnivore, and this looks so good." She squirted a big pool of ketchup between the potatoes and the meat. "It's almost like you're fattening me up for the kill or something."

Kell remained silent, cutting into his steak and chewing a bite as he sliced off another, frowning all the while as if processing his thoughts as thoroughly as his food. Jamie ate two fries and watched him think, wondering if he would take this much time to respond if she had been anyone other than the sole survivor of a crime.

Finally, Kell laid his utensils along the edge of his plate and sat back, his gaze locking on Jamie's. "Is that how you really feel? That this is all about the hypnosis?"

It was safer to think that way, not to imagine he'd done it for other reasons. Of course, the simplest one was that he'd been hungry…

"That's why you're here, right? And it's not that the meal isn't appreciated." It was so appreciated, he couldn't even know. "I'm just saying, if not for the hypnosis, if you'd just come here to ask me questions to further the investigation, then no. I don't think I'd be sitting down to this feast."

He smiled then, the sort of smile that deepened the laugh lines around his eyes, that had dimples appearing beneath the day's growth of beard on his face. It was a sexy, scruffy look, not the look of a lawman working a case, but that of a man enjoying good food and the company he was keeping. It made Jamie's stomach do all sorts of things, none of them conducive to getting through this meal...or the night ahead.

"If I were here to ask you questions and was making use of your guest room?" He sat forward again, arching a wicked brow. "You can bet I'd be doing then what I'm doing now. For one thing, a man's gotta eat. For another, I'd never be able to face my mother again for fear she'd find out I hadn't properly thanked my hostess."

Mothers. A topic much safer than Jamie giving Kell a bed. "Sounds like your mother raised you right."

Nodding, Kell went back to eating, looking away from Jamie and down at his food. "Mother and father both. They raised three of us boys, and lived to tell the tale."

"Are you the oldest?" she asked, breathing better without his smile stirring her into knots.

"I am," he said, laughing before he asked. "Do I have big brother written all over me or something?"

Brotherly was not at all how she saw him, but she was pretty sure that wasn't what he meant. "You have 'in charge' written all over you. I can't imagine you being the little brother who got bossed around, or the middle child who acted out to find his place."

"Rather deep observations on siblings, coming from an only child."

"What can I say. I paid attention to how my friends fit in with their families while growing up," she said, before finally taking a bite of her mouth-melting steak and barely suppressing a groan.

"And that's why you're working in pediatrics?"

She shook her head. "I'm working in pediatrics because it was the only job I could find after we moved to Weldon."

"What was your major at Tech?"

"How did you know—" She stopped herself, feeling stupid. Of course he would know the details of her life. The case files probably held details not even her mother knew. "I hadn't decided. I was in their general business program, but only because I wasn't sure what I wanted to be when I grew up."

"And?" he prompted.

"Things took an unexpected turn before I ever got my act together," she reminded him, getting back to her food before she confessed things he wouldn't want to hear. He made her want to talk; she didn't know why. But she was pretty sure he wouldn't want to listen to her ramble on about lost dreams.

"What about now?" he asked. "From ten years away. If you could go back to school, what would you study?"

She'd thought many times what she'd give to go back to those days. Not once had she thought about her forgotten degree. "What would Jamie Danby study? Or what would Stephanie Monroe have ended up doing with her life?"

He paused with his fork halfway to his mouth. "Do you not think of yourself as Stephanie?"

"I don't really differentiate between—"

He stopped her from saying more with a knowing shake of his head. "You just did. When I asked about a field of study. You made the distinction between who you are now, and who you were then."

This was something she didn't think she could explain. She'd been Jamie for ten years, Stephanie for nineteen. Sometimes she felt more like one than the other. But always, always, she was both. "Are you the same person you were ten years ago?"

He chuckled. "I'm older, grayer, more stubborn, but mostly I'd have to say yes."

"You've always wanted to be in law enforcement?"

"Since the first time I wore a white hat and straddled a stick horse."

She laughed at that, quickly halted the sound because it rang so strange, then laughed again, unable to help it. She laughed with her mother, she laughed with Roni and Honoria, but this wasn't either of those giggles or girly titters.

This came from the center of her chest. It was deep and heartfelt, and brought on by the picture of Kell as a child riding a broomstick stuck into a stuffed plush head. It felt good. It felt honest.

And she realized that Kell was right. These were Stephanie moments, not Jamie moments. Jamie had been scared, and lonely, for so long. She missed Stephanie's laughter and heart. "I'm sorry. I'm really not laughing at you."

"I'd say that's exactly what you're doing. Or at least doing so at my two-year-old self dressed in nothing but hat, boots and a diaper."

She laughed harder this time, her chest aching, her eyes wet. She didn't know why she found the visual so funny. "Do you have a picture?"

"Even better. I have the video on a DVD. I'll show it to you tomorrow when we're in Midland."

A yanked rug or a thrown bucket of water couldn't have sobered her any faster than the mention of tomorrow's trip. She hadn't wanted to bring the hypnosis to Weldon. This was her home, her sanctuary. She had to keep as much of her past out of her present as she could.

The fact that she was going to have to go back there at all was unsettling, but at least she'd have this place, her place to come back to. Until she didn't anymore.

"Sure. That would be fun." She started to expand her less-than-enthusiastic response, to move on, but Kell reached across the table and took hold of the hand holding her fork.

She looked at his fingers where they spanned from her knuckles to her wrist, felt his thumb where it pressed into the heel of her palm. He was so big, so strong. He could overpower her if he wanted, but all he did was wait for her to meet his probing gaze.

So green, his eyes. Like spring in the mountains. Like leaves unfurling. Like life returning from winter's dead. She felt her throat closing around the words waiting there. This man. He scared her with the way he saw what she was thinking, with the way he made her remember what she'd lost of herself and wanted back.

"It's going to be okay, Jamie. You have every right in the world to dread the unknown, to be frightened of what's coming." He stroked his thumb along her skin as he spoke, tightening his grip on her hand that was shaking. "What you're doing takes enormous bravery."

She blew a sharp snort, pulled her hand free and stabbed her fork into three stacked fries. She couldn't deal with his kindness breaking her down. She needed her armor, Jamie's armor, and she set about pulling it tight. "What about me makes you think I'm brave?"

Kell shrugged, and got back to eating as if nothing had passed between them. "You get up and go to work every day. You do so while looking over your shoulder. And you've done it now for ten years. What about that wouldn't make me think you're brave?"

"The first few years…" She shook her head, toyed with her salad, scooting the multicolored lettuce shreds around on her plate. "I didn't get up every day. I didn't work or go to school. I didn't eat. I honestly don't know how I came out of that darkness with anything left of my mind."

Except she did know. Her mother—her voice, her hands, her heartbeat, her love—had been the only one able to penetrate the inky blackness that had swallowed Jamie whole, that had wrapped tentacles around her, into her, and pulled her away from the light.

"I'm sure Kate had a lot to do with that," Kell said, reaching for his iced tea and staring at Jamie while he drank.

God. Again, he was there with the right words. Kind and perceptive and stealing her breath every time their gazes collided. Jamie nodded. "She had everything to do with it. She's been my rock all these years."

As if entertaining fond thoughts, his expression grew tender. "From what I saw of her earlier, she reminds me a lot of my mother."

A topic of conversation that was safe. She breathed a sigh of relief. "Tell me about her."

Having cleaned all but a strip of gristle and a bite or

two of salad from his plate, Kell sat back. "My folks live in Austin. They retired early. My dad sold his dot-com start-up back when doing so still netted a mint. He golfs. My mom paints. It's a nice life."

"Very cool. Sounds like it would be, retiring when still young enough to enjoy it."

"What about your mother? Would she enjoy an early retirement? Or does she love being a vet too much to hang up her, uh, whatever a vet would hang up?"

Smiling, Jamie reached for Kell's plate, scraped his scraps into hers and carried both along with their flatware to the sink before she answered. "My mother will probably die surrounded by canine testicles and hair balls, a scalpel or laser in her hand."

Obviously fine with Jamie doing cleanup, Kell rocked his chair back on two legs. "Yeah, my mind's eye probably shouldn't go there on a full stomach."

"Sorry," she said with a laugh, bending down for the squeeze bottle of dish detergent beneath the sink. "I forget not everyone grew up talking surgery over dinner."

"Nope. The Hardings talked baseball, football, basketball, girls and food."

"And which sport was yours? Besides the girls?" she asked, turning in time to catch Kell's gaze on her ass. He looked up then, his eyes smoky hot, and she wondered how she was going to get through the night with him sleeping but one room away.

"Football. And baseball. Brennan played hoops and Terry came this close to winning the Heisman," he said, returning his chair to the floor and holding his palms an inch apart.

She loved watching the Olympics every two years, but that was her only interest in sports. "No thoughts of going pro? The lure of the white hat and stick horse too strong? Dazzling dozens of damsels in distress with your big shiny star worth running into the occasional basket case?"

Kell got to his feet, carried the ketchup and salad dressing from the table to the fridge, but he didn't speak until Jamie had filled the sink with soapy water and turned off the tap.

When she looked over her shoulder, she found herself backtracking over what she'd just said. She couldn't find anything wrong…but the flare of temper in Kell's eyes, and the pinch of displeasure around his mouth told a different story.

6

"WHY DO YOU DO THAT?"

"Do what?" Jamie asked, turning back to the sink, though Kell had seen a slip of guilty "ya got me" in her eyes.

She could run, but she couldn't hide—even in a sink of dirty dishes. "Make fun of yourself like that."

She shrugged, a tense roll of one shoulder beneath her teddy-bear scrubs. "I always make fun of myself. It's no big deal."

"Not taking yourself too seriously is one thing. I've seen you do that more than once today. I've seen you get emotional over the situation you're living in and make light of it." He waited a minute to see if she would respond. She did so by turning on the hot rinse water full blast. "But putting yourself down is not the same thing."

"Ten hours, and you know me so well."

He reached around her to shut off the gushing splash of water. He hadn't been ready for the silence, her stillness, her pain. The way she smelled like soap made of grapefruit and lemon zest. The sadness surrounding her.

He knew he should move, should give her space and time to work through what she was feeling, but he stayed close, noticing the fine hairs that curled into copper pennies at her nape. "I don't know you. But I know crime. I know people. I know…victims."

She bristled, tightened, lifted her chin to look out the window over the sink, but didn't look at him. He moved to her side, leaning an elbow on the countertop to get a look at her face. "I know you don't think of yourself that way, that you think of the people who died, of Kass Duren and Lacy Rogers and Julio Alvarez and Elena Santino as the victims. Of the Duren and Rogers and Alvarez and Santino families as the ones who suffered the most."

"They did suffer the most," she shouted, whipping her gaze toward him, her ponytail flying with the motion of her rage, her eyes angry, hurt.

He shook his head, softened. "They got the most sympathy. They were painted in the press as heartbroken. They lost loved ones. But your suffering has been just as great. You lost friends. You lost your innocence. You were accused of keeping things from the authorities. You had your life ripped away like a bandage off an open wound. I would say you've suffered just as much as anyone else."

She hung her head, leaned forward on hands that were buried to her wrists in sudsy water. "I should have died. I played dead. He thought I was, and left me there. I should have died."

Survivor's guilt. Common. Not unexpected. And such a burden for her to have carried for ten years. Kell hoped he wasn't about to make things worse. "I'll bet your mother's glad you didn't."

"She is," Jamie said, choking back a sob.

"I'll bet you're glad, too."

She nodded, squeezing her eyes shut as tears dripped to salt the dishwater and her skin.

"It's okay to be glad, Jamie." He straightened, took a step closer.

She shook her head, saying nothing. She didn't have to. He knew from interviewing victims as part of his work with the UCIT the things going through her mind. Knew, too, many who had given up.

"I'm sorry that I opened the old wounds. Hurting you wasn't my intent."

"I know that," she said, snuffling softly and hunching a shoulder to wipe her eyes and nose. "It's okay. I'll be fine."

He thought she would be, thought, too, that revisiting the past would enable her to get rid of it for good. That didn't mean it was going to be a painless process. But he wasn't going to push beyond what was needed. He wouldn't. That much he swore.

He hesitated, but in the end couldn't bear to see her crushed, so he wrapped an arm around her shoulders and pulled her into his chest. She didn't want to lean, shaking the soapy water from her hands and sniffing back tears. He handed her a dish towel and didn't let her go.

They stood like that for several moments, looking through the window and past her driveway to her neighbor's property beyond, Jamie finally relaxing, her breathing growing steady and deep. Kell remained where he was, letting her move away even though he could've stayed there a lot longer.

"Wow," she finally said, brushing back her hair with

one wrist and getting back to the dishes. "Sorry about the meltdown. You would think after all this time my armor would be completely without chinks."

It said a lot that it wasn't, and as he set about clearing the rest of the dishes and food from the stovetop and table, he had high hopes that her vulnerability would lead to success tomorrow—no matter how mercenary it sounded.

THE BED IN JAMIE'S GUEST room was a full and required Kell sleep with his head at the top left, his feet at the bottom right. He didn't sleep a lot, but he couldn't blame the size of the mattress. Not completely.

He'd been known to sleep in the driver's seat of his SUV, on the ground without a sleeping bag, in his chair at the office for a quick take five. Tonight, his inability to get to sleep and stay there was due in a large part to anxiety about tomorrow.

It was due even more to the woman asleep in the room next to his, and the things he was feeling about her, because of her, for her, even. Things that had nothing to do with her cold case, and yet had everything to do with who she was because of what had happened in the diner that night.

He'd studied the crime scene photos repeatedly, read through her statement so many times that, lying here now in his boxer briefs, covered to the waist by a sheet and cooled by the ceiling fan, the events of that night played in his mind as if he'd been there to see it unfold.

Jamie had been behind the counter running the day's register tapes, and counting and bagging the money in the till to drop in the bank's night deposit. The lights in the diner had still been burning, the neon sign above the front door spelling out Closed in a nostalgic red font.

Julio Alvarez and Elena Santino had been out front mopping the black-and-white-tiled floor and scrubbing down the white Formica tables and red Naughahyde booths.

Kass Duren and Lacy Rogers had been scouring the kitchen, storing food, gathering the trash to take to the Dumpster. The bags and cans, spattered with Kass's and Lacy's blood, had still been sitting by the back door when the authorities arrived.

Julio and Elena had crumpled one on top of each other, their blood pooling into a shared circle of death. Jamie had been spared from seeing her friends die, having dropped to the floor when the first shots were fired.

The bullet that had grazed her scalp and the one that had gouged her shoulder had bloodied her and the floor around her enough to fool the killer into thinking she was dead. But she hadn't been dead. She'd been quite alive, drifting in and out of consciousness, hearing the screams, the pleading, the voices choking in terror, drowning as her friends died.

His chest and throat tight, Kell tossed off the sheet and sat up, reaching for the jeans he'd left on the floor. He pulled them on, needing fresh air, water, a long walk with only coyotes and javelinas and the moon to watch. What he didn't need was to think about Jamie revisiting the scene he'd just imagined. And doing it because of him.

He headed for the kitchen, barefoot and shirtless, figuring he could grab a glass of water, take it outside, and pace her driveway for now. If that didn't help, well, a sleepless night wouldn't kill him. He had his laptop. He could go over his notes and files again and—

The kitchen should've been dark, but the back door stood wide open, allowing the light of the moon to spill through. His first thought was his gun, his second, Jamie. But a couple of silent steps into the room and he saw her sitting outside on the concrete stairs that rose to the back door, a bottle at her hip, a glass in her hand.

Uh-oh.

He made sure she heard his next steps. He even nudged a chair with his hip, scraping the legs on the floor and knocking it against the table. Jamie startled, but quickly settled, reaching for the bottle and hiding it between her feet. Tried to hide it, anyway.

Kell stood in the doorway behind her. "You planning to drink all of that yourself?"

"Grab a glass," she told him, scooting forward and leaning over enough for him to get through the screen door without pushing her off the top step.

He found a bottle of water and a glass that he filled with ice, and joined her. The night was warm, clear, the stars overhead like tiny twinkling Christmas-tree lights. It was a good night to get drunk. Tomorrow's agenda made it an even better one—except tomorrow's agenda required sobriety, ergo, the water and ice.

"Can't sleep?" A stupid question since here they both were, barefoot and half dressed, Jamie wearing a skinny-strapped tank top with pajama shorts that came nearly to her knees. He thought they were blue, but they might've been a soft green. He thought, too, that she wasn't wearing a bra.

She lifted her glass. "I will soon."

He reached for the liquor bottle between her feet, poured just enough into his glass to balance the ice then added water, offering her the same. She gave a nod, and he diluted her drink to match his, keeping his mouth shut. This wasn't the time to preach. Besides, he couldn't blame her for wanting to take the edge off.

"The nights are my favorite part of living in West Texas," she said after sipping her drink. "It's so quiet. And so clear. Have you seen the stars from the observatory?"

The McDonald Observatory, on top of Mount Locke and Mount Fowlkes, was about seventeen miles away, and provided astronomers some of the darkest night skies in the forty-eight contiguous states. "I have. Amazing the things the human eye can see with nothing in the way. Satellites, the Hubble, the International Space Station."

"And those are all man-made. Think how much farther away the constellations and even the Andromeda Galaxy are." She sipped again, swirling the liquid in her glass. "It sounds stupid, but even if things hadn't gone so wrong, I don't think I'd have ever moved away from this part of the country. I love the nights too much."

"Too bad the days are so miserable," he said, though really, living in Texas meant living with the heat, and he was Lone Star born and bred.

"You grew up here, right? You should be used to it."

He nodded, and swirled the ice in his glass. "I am, but weather always makes for easy conversation."

For a moment, she was silent, then she sighed with a deep resignation. "Easier than asking why I can't sleep?"

Or telling her what was keeping him awake. He nodded, sipped the Jim Beam and let it warm the parts of him left cold by the thoughts that had driven him from bed.

Jamie stretched out her legs, spread her toes, then bent to brush away something he couldn't see. "I don't lose a lot of sleep anymore over…everything. At first, I didn't think I'd ever sleep again. I had a prescription that helped. Or it did once my doctor upped the dosage a couple of times."

"Made for some fuzzy days I bet." He sat forward, his wrists on his knees, looking away from the smooth skin of her legs toward her detached garage and the moon shining in the windows there.

"Time was a big blur for months. I couldn't go back to school. I couldn't work. I did good to eat and bathe myself, though it took a while to care enough to do even that." She brought her glass to her mouth. "I honestly don't think I would've come out of it if my mother hadn't been with me."

She'd been so young, a kid, really. A very young woman at most. Either way, she'd been a girl who'd needed her mother, and had been lucky to have one so devoted. "She sounds pretty amazing."

"You have no idea." Jamie sat straighter, stretching her back, left then right, popping her spine before she leaned back against the frame of the screen door. "She did all of it herself, the taking-care-of-me stuff. Making sure I got through."

He'd known from her file that her father had split about that time, but didn't know the why. The way she said it… "Was it too much for your dad…what happened to you?"

"Something like that. I guess." She lifted her glass, and stared at the contents where the moonlight glinted off the amber liquid. "It's always been weird the way he bailed."

"How so?"

"He'd been a perfect dad my whole life, though somewhat taciturn, I guess. He helped with my science homework and showed me how to fix a flat on my bike. Oh, and how to run the lawn mower."

"The lawn mower?"

"I was the son he never had, taking care of a lot of things around the house while he and the seasonal workers handled the ranch chores."

Kell found himself chuckling. "Terry, my baby brother, got the same treatment. Except in reverse."

"How so?"

"My mother was determined one of her children would cook. Terry was the youngest, left behind when Brennan and I were in school, so he had a lot of one-on-one time with Mom." He stared down at the concrete step between his feet, his bare soles soaking up the stored heat from the day. "It seems to have stuck."

"He's a cook?"

"He owns a restaurant. A pub. In Houston. Not sure he still does much cooking, but he has. And he can."

"Runs in the family then."

"The steaks?" He shook his head. "That's bachelor food. Steaks, burgers, eggs. Nothing but the basics."

She was quiet for the next couple of minutes, not drinking, not moving, just sitting, letting the night wrap them in its cloak, letting the darkness keep them rooted, letting the heat of the drink lull them into a sense of easy comfort until the solitude finally loosened her tongue.

"Have you always been a bachelor?"

"I've never been married, if that's what you're asking."

"Why not?"

He guessed she was waiting for him to tell her he'd never found the right girl. Wasn't that usually the reason? And while it was true, it wasn't the whole story of why he was alone. "I haven't had the time to invest in a relationship. Not that sort of time."

"That sort of time? What do you mean, that sort of time?" She leaned across him to snag the bottle from where he'd set it on his side of the steps. Her unbound breasts, firm, full, brushed his knees. "You make it sound like a job, or a chore. Like work."

What he was working on right now was keeping his hands wrapped around his glass of throat-searing whiskey and melting ice. He wanted so badly to touch her. "You don't think relationships are work?"

"I wouldn't want to go into one thinking that, no." She sat forward again, gesturing with her glass. "I mean, I watched my mother work her ass off to salvage what she had with my father. She wheeled and dealed and begged, even agreed to let him do his man-alone-with-nature thing while she took care of me. He left anyway. Just loaded up his truck and his horse trailer and drove off into the sunset."

Hmm. Was she basing her feelings about relationships on one couple? Her parents? She had to know that marriages rarely survived something so horrific as what had happened to their child. Or…wait. Was Jamie blaming herself for her father's desertion?

Kell looked over at the strands of hair blowing into her face, catching on her lips and lashes. He reached for them, brushed them back over her shoulder, but then he let his hand linger there, let his fingers drift softly over the skin beneath her ear.

It was a big mistake, touching her, and even though he pulled away, he knew he'd done so too late. He'd crossed a line he shouldn't have, and even if he'd wanted to he could never go back. "If your father didn't work just as hard, then their marriage didn't stand a chance. There are two people in a relationship, and if only one is working, it's hard to imagine that it wouldn't fail."

Jamie sat shaking her head, before pushing to her feet and walking to the center of the driveway, as if she'd reached her limit on sitting still. She wobbled a bit, swayed a bit more, found her footing and stood in profile, her hair lifting on the warm night wind.

The moon bathed her; Kell could see the globes of her breasts, her nipples, the long line of her back to the gorgeous swell of her rump, the hint of her sex beneath the cotton of her pjs that was very very thin. Just like she wasn't wearing a bra, she wasn't wearing panties.

"The problem with my parents' relationship is that it grew to be about a third person, not just the two my father signed on for. The third, me," she said again, this time her voice cracking like glass, "was what ended up tearing them apart."

Kell didn't know the details, he had no right to assume or intrude. But Jamie's state of mind was a crucial component in what he was hoping would be tomorrow's success—though he knew what was going on here, tonight, between them had nothing to do with the case.

"It wasn't your fault, Jamie—"

"Of course it was," she shouted back, the sound like an explosive blast in the stillness.

If she'd had neighbors living close, he would've expected lights in windows to come on, curtains to sweep aside, concerned eyes to peer out and see if she needed help. But her closest neighbor on Lamplighter Lane was half a block away, and the house remained quiet and still.

Inside, Kell was anything but, his stomach and heart battling a surge of emotion, and he had to force his frustration into calm. "If your father left because of what happened to you, it was his problem, not yours. You were in the wrong place at the wrong time. That's all."

"A wrong place he didn't want me to be," she said, and finished off her drink, heaving her glass toward the garage, where it shattered, the slivers and shards scattering on the pavement.

Kell didn't move. He waited—though he would stop her if she even thought about cleaning up the glass. She was barefoot, a little bit drunk, and it was dark in the shadow of the garage.

She stayed where she was, however, dropping down and wrapping her arms around her knees, rocking back and forth, her back and shoulders arched like a turtle's protective shell.

So her father hadn't wanted her to work at the Sonora Nites Diner? Because of the late hours? Because of the easy access to the interstate? Because he'd wanted her to focus on her studies? Kell hadn't met her father, had only read about Steven Monroe's abandonment years after the fact. He had no way of knowing what the issue was between Jamie and her father.

He did know that it was time for sleep. For Jamie, and for him, too, so he capped the bottle, set his glass beside it next to the steps and went to bring her inside.

7

JAMIE KNEW BETTER than to drink. She had no tolerance for alcohol. She was an easy drunk, the cheapest of cheap.

And a barefoot Kell Harding, wearing nothing but his jeans, was going to make her cheaper and easier than she'd been in years. She could feel it in her blood, in her bones, a fire of lust and stupidity and Jim Beam.

She knew he was standing in front of her, but she kept her eyes closed. It had been hard enough not to touch him when he'd been sitting on the stoop beside her. She could smell him then, and now.

He'd showered before bed, and the heat of the night had carried the scent of his clean skin until she wanted to crawl beneath it, and wrap it around her like a cloak, and remember what it had been like to live without looking over her shoulder. She wanted that back, all of it.

"Let's go in. You need sleep. I need sleep. The glass will wait till morning."

Still hunkered down, she shook her head. "If I sleep, I'll dream, and it won't be one I can stomach alone. Not tonight. Not with…all of this happening. And with tomorrow." *Don't cry, don't cry, don't cry,* she told herself. *Please, please, don't cry.*

"I'll be in the next room. And I'll be with you tomorrow." He touched her hair then, brushed his knuckles against her temples. "I'm here now."

But he wasn't here in the way she needed him. He was here as a cop, a watchdog, here to keep her smart and sober and on time, though he was running late on the first two counts. She grabbed his wrist to stop him from moving his fingers along the shell of her ear, using her hold as leverage to gain her feet, rising along his body.

And then she couldn't help it. He was in front of her, looming, his chest big, bare and magnificent and calling her. She placed her hands there, the heels of her palms just beneath his pectoral muscles, her fingertips skating the edges of his nipples.

The wedge of hair in the center of his chest was soft, thinning as it descended his abdomen. She followed it with her thumbs, her eyes wet, her cheeks wet, her belly tight with wanting him, with wanting.

He stopped her when she reached his waistband. She felt him there, just beneath, swelling, full and firm, but he kept her from enclosing him in her hand, and held her arms at her sides. "Not a good idea."

His body said otherwise. "Are you sure? I'm getting some mixed signals here."

"I'm sure," he told her, his grip tightening when she tried to pull away and prove him wrong. "Another time, another place, maybe."

"You're saying no because of tomorrow?" Not because she was an old maid, damaged and broken and lost, with nothing to offer a man? Not because she was ugly and drunk and pathetic? Not because he didn't want her?

"I'm saying no because we both need sleep," he re-iterated, his voice rough, rougher than the hands holding her, than the concrete driveway she was standing on. "And because the reasons right now are all wrong."

What did that mean? That he could only tumble her into forgetfulness if it fit his white-hat sense of right and wrong? How fair was that, when she was the one who wanted no strings attached?

She pulled against his efforts to keep her at a distance, lifting her hands to his chest again, to his shoulders, lacing them around his neck.

She shimmied close, pressed her nipples to his chest and rubbed against the cotton of her camisole until sensation swept her to the edge of oblivion. "What do the reasons matter?"

He groaned. The rumble rose from a spot just beneath his ribs and made it all the way up his throat before stopping. His heart drummed, a thudding, primal, near-violent beat. "We can't. Not now. Not…like this. Here. It's late. You've been drinking."

Exactly. She could do anything she wanted to do. She had Jim Beam on her side. Eyes closed, she leaned her forehead against him and breathed.

His chest hair tickled her nose, her lips. She licked them, caught the edge of his nipple and licked that, too, smelling the alcohol in his pores, the heat of the night, something wholesome and sweet. All of it right, and hers.

"Jamie."

He ground out her name like a curse. Or a caress. She wasn't sure which one. She didn't care. She brought her mouth to the hollow of his throat, drank of his taste and his scent. He lowered his head, nuzzling his chin to her temple.

It was soft, but it was still need, and she turned into it, finding his mouth, biting until he parted his lips and bit back. Oh, he was going to be good, greedy and giving, hungry, hard.

She cupped his head, kneading the nape of his neck as she kissed him, her tongue on his, her chest against his, her sex aching where the ridge of his pressed, his hands on her ass lifting her like a puzzle to fit his pieces.

It was her whimper that ruined everything. He was hard everywhere, his fingers bold and questing, and it had been so very long since she'd wanted anyone to touch her as intimately as Kell was doing now. And so she whimpered, but just barely, with pleasure and need and an appreciation for the bad-boy way he kissed.

Kell's hands on her bottom stilled, then dropped her cheeks like two hot potatoes. He broke the kiss, found her wrists and broke her hold on his neck, cursing to himself as he took a step away. His face was in shadow, but his darkness was more than the lack of light.

He was angry. At her? At himself? And his whole body raged, stiff and tight and pulsing. "I said no, Jamie. Not here, not now, not without a better reason than dreading tomorrow."

If he didn't think dreading tomorrow was reason enough, then he was right that this wasn't the time or place. And he wasn't the man. Good thing Jim Beam wasn't so righteous.

"Good night then, Ranger Sergeant Kellen Harding," she said, walking away with a wobble, but without a single look back, and picking up the whiskey bottle before opening the screen door. "I'll do whatever it takes to deal with tomorrow. And I'll get help from whomever will give it."

No matter how very very much I want it to be you.

KELL HAD ARRANGED FOR Jamie's session with the forensic hypnotist to happen in Midland at eleven. The hypnosis was their sole purpose for making the trip; there was no excuse to put it off until later in the day.

The claustrophobic three-hour drive would've had her worrying herself into a state of exhaustion had she not been struggling to keep her stomach from upending all over the floor of Kell's SUV.

Spending the night with Jim Beam had not been particularly smart, but it had worked as a preemptive strike against freaking out; all she had on her mind this morning was not getting sick. Thankfully, Kell hadn't brought up her drinking, or anything about last night.

"I don't drink like that very often." She closed her eyes, opened them quickly when her nausea insisted on looking at something besides the blood-red interior of her eyelids.

"That's good to know." And that was all he said, his right hand on the steering wheel, his left elbow on the padding where the window met the door. His face was close shaved, his shirt starched and pressed. He wore his white hat and dark sunglasses. Jamie hadn't seen his eyes all day.

He hadn't had as much to drink last night as she had, so she didn't know if he was hiding bloodshot whites or dark purple half-moons beneath. Maybe he just didn't want her to know when he cut his gaze toward her, if he did, how often, how thoroughly he looked her over, what he was visually searching for. Maybe he just didn't want her to see his disillusionment.

"I mean, I'm not an alcoholic or anything. I drink sometimes, when I can't sleep." Or when I do sleep and the nightmare comes back.

"You don't have to justify anything to me, Jamie."

Right. He was going to turn her life upside down, but didn't want an explanation for her reaction to having that happen. Well, she didn't want him looking back and thinking her a slutty little lush.

"I'm not justifying anything, Kell. I'm explaining what went on last night, what you saw. That wasn't… me," she said, though the words rang false because the woman he'd seen was exactly who she was.

She put on a good front for her mother, her neighbors, her coworkers and friends, the world, but the real truth was too sad and broken to let anyone see. Anyone, apparently, but a man in a white hat with a gun.

He looked over at her, his jaw taut, his mouth grim. She couldn't see his eyes or his forehead, but could tell his face wasn't happy. She could tell, too, from his voice that was gritty and sharp. "Don't you think I get that? Yeah, we just met, but I know your case inside and out, and that includes the person you are."

She wanted to believe him, but it sounded a lot like he was making nice to get her to shut up about it. And, really, she wanted to shut herself up about it. She didn't know why it mattered so much that he think good things about her.

Except she did know. It mattered because of that kiss. Last night's blood-alcohol level hadn't kept her from remembering, reliving the feel of his mouth, his hands, his…everything dozens of times since rolling her protesting body out of bed this morning.

She wanted to kiss him again. She wanted to kiss him while sober. She wanted to kiss him in broad daylight or with the room's lights blazing. She wanted to kiss him and remember things the Jim Beam meant she'd forgotten.

None of that would happen, however, until he remembered something other than his disappointment in her. At least she assumed it was disappointment that had him keeping such a stiff distance between them.

"Did all that reading about me make you curious?"

"About?"

Oh, now he was being purposefully thick. "Anything in particular? What author I most like to read, or my favorite restaurant, or where I've traveled, or if I like to go fishing, or maybe know how to kiss?"

The corner of his mouth twitched. His hand on the steering wheel tightened, his knuckles like jagged peaks. "Who's your favorite author?"

Sigh. It was better than talking about the weather, or traveling in complete silence, though she'd much rather know what he thought about kissing her. "I'd have to say Tess Gerritsen. She writes a suspense series about a Boston police detective and medical examiner."

"Hmm."

"What does that mean, 'hmm'?"

He shrugged, continued to face straight ahead.

"I would've thought you'd prefer something less... gruesome."

Because of what she'd been through? "It's storytelling. It's entertainment. I'm not looking to forget what happened to me by escaping my reality. Or to work my way through it by projecting my experience onto a piece of fiction. It's just...reading."

"If you say so."

He didn't buy it, or else he was being contrary to keep her at bay. And that really didn't make any sense when everything else he'd done was about keeping her close...unless the kiss had made him change his mind.

"What's your favorite restaurant then?"

Fine. She'd play along, but only because she wanted to see if he'd make it through all five of her options, or if he'd stop when he reached the last one. "I'm not sure I have a favorite, but there's one in Junction called Isaack's where the cheeseburgers are the best I've ever had in my life."

He chuckled at that, a funny, rough sound, glancing in his side-view mirror before signaling and changing lanes. "How do you feel about fishing?"

Moving right along here...though he'd skipped asking about where she'd traveled. Was he in a hurry to talk about kissing her? Or just wanting to get it over with ASAP? "I've never been."

That earned her a glance, one she couldn't read because he was still hiding behind his dark glasses.

"I'm not sure I've ever met anyone who's never fished," he told her, then asked, "No opportunity, no interest, what?"

"Both, I guess. Though I've eaten my fair share of things that live in the sea. And lakes, streams, rivers, swamps."

"Swamps?"

"Crawfish. Frog legs. Alligator. You know. Swamp things."

Kell shook his head, giving a soft snort that she interpreted as disbelief. He didn't seem the type to be disgusted by things that weren't everyday food. "You've never been fishing, but you've eaten frog legs and alligator."

"I didn't have to catch them, just order them," she said, her headache easing along with some of the tension causing the drive to be so uncomfortably difficult. Funny how talking helped simplify things, when keeping them bottled up and hidden away made a more "out of sight, out of mind" sense.

And, no, she was not going to stop and apply that realization to the last ten years of her life. Or wonder why she'd talked more about what she'd seen and suffered to Kell Harding than she had to another soul in years. Crawfish and frog legs and alligator. That was the ticket, the always safe subject of food.

She leaned into the corner of the seat, shifting to see him better. "In case you didn't notice at dinner, I've got a big thing for food. I'll try anything, and I love almost everything. My mouth was definitely made for eating."

"That must be why you taste so good."

And just like that, there was the kiss.

8

THE KISS. They had to get it out of the way or today was going to be a bust, which was why Kell had put it out there. Thinking about Jamie's hypnosis to come had gotten lost in thinking about her mouth. But she was wrong.

Her mouth was not made for eating.

It was made for the way she'd used it last night, and he was surer than he was about never wanting to eat alligator, that she could use it for even more. Those things, all intimately imagined, were giving his body hell.

"I don't think I've ever had anyone tell me that I taste good," she finally replied, and as he glanced over, he saw her face color with the implications of what she'd just said. "Though I'm sure it had something to do with the JB."

Nice recovery, he thought, amused, though they both knew he hadn't been talking about the booze. "I swear, Jamie. If it had been any other time or place…"

He let the sentence trail, not sure why he was giving even more air to the subject instead of allowing it to breathe its last and drift off to die. Unless that wasn't what he wanted, to let it go, to forget.

"Yeah. You said that last night," she reminded him.

"I wasn't sure you heard me."

"I was drunk, but I was right there."

"I know." Where she'd been, the way she'd tasted, how she'd felt in his hands would stick with him a long, long time. "I just wanted to make sure we were clear."

"Oh," she said, then after a pause, went on to ask, "Why aren't you in a relationship? I mean, I'm assuming you're not…"

"I'm not, no, and I guess for the same reason I'm not married. My mother nags about grandchildren, but I'd rather not tackle parenthood on my own." His line of work had convinced him of that, as had his childhood. Sure, some single parents did a better job than two, but he wasn't cut out to try it.

Smiling, Jamie tucked her feet beneath her to sit cross-legged. "Your mother and my mother must be reading from the same script."

He wondered if what she'd been through had changed how she felt about starting a family. Maybe she'd never wanted one at all. Maybe she wanted one now more than ever. He didn't ask because he didn't want to stir things that had settled.

But then she went on. "The married-with-children thing is a long-running joke between me and my mother. She takes the blame for me being single."

Coming up on a slow-moving vehicle, Kell eased the SUV's cruise control to coast before changing lanes. It gave him time to let what Jamie had said sink in. "Why would she think it's her fault?"

"Because of her hovering."

Strange, he mused, passing the car on his right, the sun

that shone through the window glinting red through Jamie's hair. "She seemed concerned, protective even, but I didn't get a sense of her hovering. Or of you letting her."

Jamie laughed, a wonderful sound, fearless and full of life. "Trust me. There's no letting involved. She does it. I put up with it. And we love each other to death. End of story."

"Love makes all the difference," he heard himself saying before he thought better of going soft. "Between crowding and caring, I mean."

"It can still be crazy-making," she said, the smile on her face wry.

Kell understood. He had a few crazy-making memories of his own. "I lucked out being the oldest. My mom still had Terry and Brennan at home to fuss over. Then Brennan left for school and Terry got the full baby-of-the-family treatment."

Jamie chuckled. "And you weren't jealous at all."

"Jealous?" He shook his head. He didn't begrudge either of his brothers anything. "But I did miss the attention." And then he heard himself admitting, "I liked being spoiled. Still do."

Several seconds passed before Jamie responded, and Kell began to wonder what the hell he was doing. Getting the kiss out of the way had been one thing. Turning the conversation back to the personal was another, and not very smart.

He did not like the direction the attraction between them was driving him. He'd told her twice now another time, another place, and was thinking he should tattoo a reminder on the inside of his eyelids, a road sign telling him where not to go before he found himself unable to shift gears.

Finally, she moved, shifting in her seat, her voice low when she said, "The right woman will do that, you know. Spoil you."

It wouldn't do any good to pretend she was talking about someone's mother when she was talking about all the things he'd wanted from her last night, the things he'd denied himself, the things he could've had right there in her driveway.

He couldn't let himself think she was making him an offer, or read anything into the one she'd made him last night. She was a case he was working. That's all they had between them. "Yeah? The right woman and a Faustian bargain?"

She sat back with a huff. "No wonder you're still on your own."

He wanted to laugh, to tease her, to play until they reached their destination, but mostly he was desperate for a way out of this detour, so he grabbed the opening she'd given him instead. "I'm not so good at leaving my work at the office. I've never thought it would be fair to saddle someone with my life, what I have to deal with, what I see. I'm not always the best of company."

He knew she would understand his concern. Because of what she'd lived through, it had to be something she'd considered. He didn't for a minute believe she'd never been in a relationship, though he wouldn't be surprised if her lovers had been only casual.

Anything more would mean letting someone in, and neither one of them lived in a place that was very inviting. Jamie lived with the horror of her past, and would for the rest of her life; even if the killer was caught and put away, she'd carry with her what had happened.

And Kell… He carried his cases in his head; his subconscious was always stewing on the ones he'd backburnered while he feverishly stirred those that were hot, leaving very few of his brain cells for anything else.

Funny when he thought about it, but in a lot of ways, he and Jamie were two of a kind, their lives forever bound to the heinous offenses of others. It sucked in so many ways.

"So it's easier to be a martyr than to trust a woman to have what it takes to deal. Is that it?"

Biting down on a lot of words best left unsaid, Kell maneuvered toward the Midland exit. He knew he should've kept his mouth shut, because now he was going to have to go on the defensive, and that was not the mood he'd been working so hard to set. "It's not about being a martyr. Or about trusting or not."

"Then what's it about?" she demanded, because she obviously couldn't leave the subject alone.

He decided to turn it back on her, let her spin it from her own point of view. "Don't you find it hard to let men get close?"

She looked away from him and stared out her side window as they passed the Midland city-limits sign. And then she crossed one leg over the other and scooted closer to the door. Since she'd answered with her body, he didn't expect her to give him a verbal response.

"I let you get close. I would've let you get even closer if you hadn't put a stop to things."

He knew that. The reminder was not exactly welcome when he was trying to forget what he'd said no to. "I'm not talking about…sex."

"I know. You're talking about emotional intimacy. Caring and affection and eventually love. And, yes, I have found that hard. Mostly because I'm very careful when talking about my past." She paused, pushing the hair she'd left hanging loose away from her face. Color tinted her cheekbones, as if her admission didn't come easy. "It's been a deal breaker more than once. Men ask, I refuse to answer, they think I'm hiding something. They're right, but I'm not going to risk exposing myself just so some guy feels better about what he's getting into. A guy wants something long-term, he should be willing to accept my timetable for sharing what happened."

A knot of anger balled like a fist in Kell's stomach. He knew men like the ones she was describing, men who demanded everything go their way, men who made it hard for women to cut the rest of the male gender a break, a few of whom deserved to be strung up by what passed for their balls.

He started to tell her she deserved better, that the right man would be there for her past, present and future, but stopped. He didn't want the sentiment to come out sounding as patronizing as he feared it would. Besides, he felt strangely protective, possessive even, and didn't buy it when he told himself it was all about the case.

Before he could round up what he was feeling and force it into some kind of sense, Jamie took a deep breath and went on. "The thing is, making an intense connection with someone who knows those things about me, even one tangled up with a dark night, a bottle of JB and a killer kiss… Let's just say, it's not something I'm going to walk away from. And I'm sorry you felt you had to."

Kell was only human, and he couldn't take it anymore. He swerved the SUV into a parking lot, slammed on the brakes and shoved the transmission to park. His chest heaving, he stared straight ahead, his hands gripping the steering wheel so he didn't reach for her. "A little late to be spelling out the rules, don't you think?"

She gave a sarcastic grunt. "Better late than never. Besides, last night I was too self-involved to think you might need a playbook."

That didn't sit well. His blood began to boil. "I know all the plays, Jamie. I just don't like running them when I'm the only one with his head in the game."

Jamie was leaning toward him, a move that gave him a really good look down the front of her shirt. A gentleman would have looked away.

Kell was no gentleman. He unhooked her seat belt and pulled her to sprawl across his lap, reached for her breasts and brought his mouth down hard on hers. She pushed his hands away and unbuttoned her blouse. He felt her smile as his erection swelled to bump her thigh, and he wasn't sure which of them groaned the loudest.

The fire they'd set last night had burned. This fire exploded, an incendiary rush of heat and flame that sucked them both into its back draft. Jamie's mouth was hungry, her lips and teeth and tongue involved, her free hand warm against his cheek and holding him still.

This was wrong. So very wrong. But there was no way Kell was going to move when nothing in his life had felt this right. Jamie was a case, a victim of a crime, his job. He had no business wanting her at all, much less in ways that had him losing his mind. Yet he didn't care.

How could he when she fit him and wanted him and kept him from being able to draw enough breath? Men dreamed of this. Men paid for this. Hell, men killed for this. And here it was his, and all he'd done was broil her a steak and share her Jim Beam beneath the light of the moon.

Her breast in his palm was sweetly heavy, rounded like a peach, ripe and firm. He cupped and molded, leaving the fabric of her bra as a barrier teasing them both. She wiggled against him, pressed against him, nipped at his lower lip to tell him to move it out of the way. He kissed her harder instead, gripping tightly to the little bit of sanity he hadn't surrendered.

Her mouth. It was wet and warm, and she tasted like the coffee she'd sipped as they'd traveled, tasted, too, like a feverish panic and…fear. When he slowed the kiss, softening the pressure of his mouth, pulling back, she trembled and moved her hands to his shoulders to hold on.

"I'm not going anywhere, Jamie." He whispered the words against her cheek. "I'm right here. You're safe."

"Safe's not exactly what I'm feeling," she said, and tried to laugh, releasing her grip as if knowing he was close enough for now.

"If you're feeling what I'm feeling…" He watched as she buttoned her shirt, her skin flushed, her fingers fumbling, her expression as dazed and confused as he was feeling. They were headed down a dangerous road here, with neither one of them in a position to enjoy more than the physical trip…or were they?

Was that the danger he was sensing? An emotional connection neither one of them could have anticipated and braced for?

He gave her a hand as she returned to her seat and belted herself in. He then put the vehicle in gear and pulled out of the lot into traffic. He was so screwed. Sex between them was one thing. The complication of hearts and minds was another. The first he could deal with. The second…not now.

Maneuvering through the streets toward their destination, he did his best to put what had happened out of his mind. When he failed at that as miserably as he had at keeping his distance, he forced himself to visualize the crime scene photos from the murders at the Sonora Nites Diner.

It was what he should have been focusing on all along. His work. The job. Solving the case. Using Jamie to do it.

"Is that where we're going?" she asked, and Kell looked up in time to realize he was about to miss his turn.

He pulled into the parking lot and drove around to the rear of the building. They'd be using an office away from the high-traffic area of the station, one set up to look more like a cozy den with the high-tech recording equipment discreetly mounted on a bookshelf between leather-bound volumes, bronze sculptures and dishes of potpourri.

Glancing over at her as he shifted the SUV into park, he gentled his voice and asked, "Are you ready for this?"

"No." Her voice cold and flat, a mere whisper of

fear, she unbuckled her seat belt, climbed down from the vehicle and slammed the door. And there was nothing gentle in the way she did it at all.

9

THE ROOM REMINDED Jamie of a furniture-store showcase. That, or one of the many therapists' offices she'd seen from the inside over the years. From the framed cowboy art, to the saddle-tan leather overstuffed chairs, the den-size area would've made the perfect setting for a John Wayne western, an episode of *Bonanza,* a book written by Louis L'Amour.

She did her best to imagine that's where she was, in a ranch house on the plains, with cattle penned for branding, hands chewing chaws of tobacco, horses corralled and ready for a ride. The only thing that ruined the fantasy was the big picture window behind the half-drawn blinds. No one had told her it was one-way glass, but she knew it was. Knew, too, that Kell would be on the other side while she went back to a place she'd never expected to revisit.

In the deepest part of herself, she knew she was doing the right thing. Knowing so didn't make the process any easier, but interestingly, having Kell there did. Examining why he made all the difference would mean exposing thoughts that were no one's business, and since she was here to open a vein and bleed for the benefit of strangers, she just accepted his strength without question. She even smiled to herself while she did so, breathing deeply to settle her nerves, and sent him a silent thank-you she hoped his heart could hear.

"Miss Danby? Are you comfortable? There's a quilted lap throw folded on the lower shelf of the table there if you're cold."

"I'm fine, thank you," Jamie said to the female technician who would be observing the session and monitoring the recording equipment. From her seat in the recliner against the back wall, Jamie had a full view of Kell's window and the chair from which the male DPS officer would be conducting the session. A second officer would join them, strictly as an impartial observer.

With a nod, the tech moved to her position, a desk situated off to the side, and the two officers, a Sergeant Jay Ready and a Captain Norm Greenley, entered the room. Once introductions had been made, Ready moved to a chair in the corner, easing the door closed behind him, while Greenley, the hypnotist, signaled to the technician to begin the tapes. He gave Jamie a smile.

About sixty, he was dressed similarly to Kell, in boots and jeans and a western-cut dress shirt of starched khaki. His mustache was thick and as white as his hair, his face ruddy, his skin pocked, a testament to many years spent in the sun. He wore a simple wedding band on his left hand, a hefty gold University of Texas class ring on his right.

When he sat in the other recliner, Jamie found her fingers digging into the armrests of hers, her body stiff, her neck and jaw tight, her head beginning to ache.

Telling herself to relax didn't do a bit of good. Her heart was racing, her skin tingling, her stomach threatening to heave up her coffee-and-muffin breakfast.

Captain Greenley squared one leg over the other, folded back the cover of a legal portfolio and pulled a pen from his shirt pocket. He clicked the end and gave the time and date for the tape. "I'm Captain Norman Greenley with the Texas Department of Public Safety. I'm here in Midland, Texas, at the Texas Rangers Company E headquarters, along with media technician Megan Holly and Sergeant Jay Ready. The purpose of this recording is to document an investigative-hypnosis interview with Miss Jamie Danby of Weldon, Texas, also present. Ranger Sergeant Kellen Harding, of the UCIT, is observing from the adjoining room."

For the next thirty minutes, Captain Greenley engaged Jamie in what he explained was a prehypnosis interview. He stated for the record the few basic facts Kell had told him about the case, and established by questioning Jamie that the two of them had not met prior to today.

She listened intently as he advised her of his training and credentials, making sure she understood that he was certified and authorized to conduct the interview, and doing it all in a kindly, genial manner, his tone what she thought of as grandfatherly, his approach that of a natural storyteller, setting her at ease.

"Have you been hypnotized on any other occasion, Jamie?"

"No," she answered, shaking her head.

"Have you ever seen anyone be hypnotized?"

She laughed softly. "Only on TV and in movies."

Captain Greenley laughed, too. "Believe it or not, those demonstrations are actually responsible for the perceptions, and misconceptions, most people have of hypnosis."

Jamie assumed he was going to explain, but prompted him anyway with a curious "Such as?"

"While under hypnosis, you won't be asleep or unconscious. You won't divulge secrets, and you won't be compelled to tell the truth." He clicked his ballpoint again. "Hypnosis is not sodium pentothal."

"You mean it's not truth serum," Jamie said, pulling her legs comfortably into the seat of the big chair.

"Exactly. You won't get stuck in your hypnotized state, and unless you're already of a mind to do so, you can't be made to do anything foolish."

"Like flap my wings and cluck?"

Again, he nodded, smiling. "In a Vegas show, maybe, but not here."

"The real deal," she said, and wondered what Kell was thinking, if he was grinning in that way he had of making her insides quiver.

"Yes, it is," he said, clicked his pen one more time and jotted down a note. "You also need to know that you may remember additional information about the Sonora Nites Diner murders, but you may not. You will, however, remember everything about the session once I bring you out of hypnosis."

She nodded her understanding, relieved to know no one would think her a failure if her memory didn't return, not so relieved to know she'd remember everything after the fact. Over the years, she'd found solace in her amnesia. She'd hate to lose that tiny comfort even though she knew it was time.

"Now, Jamie. I want you to close your eyes, relax and picture your kitchen at home. Think about it for as long as you need to, then describe to me the visualization."

O…kay. "Well, looking into the kitchen from the living room, there's an exit to the right that leads into the hallway, and the refrigerator sits on the other side of that. There's a small strip of countertop, it's a light oak butcher block, between the fridge and the stove, then another larger section that runs into the corner. On the next wall is a window that looks out over the driveway. The sink and dishwasher are there, then the back door.

"The table butts up against the third wall. It can seat four people if pulled out, but I usually eat alone, so I don't bother." She stopped herself from mentioning that she'd eaten there last night with Kell. Even thinking about that right now was too much. "Against the last wall, the one with the door into the living room, is a desk with drawers and shelves. It's where I pay bills and keep cookbooks, stuff like that. The walls are a buttery yellow, the floor white tile, the cabinets the same light oak as the countertops." She opened her eyes, met Greenley's gaze and shrugged. "I guess that's it."

"Good. Very good." The captain nodded. "While you're under hypnosis and I ask you to describe a scene the way it looks in your mind's eye, that's what I want. A detailed visual account of what you see. Understand?"

"Yes. I understand," she said, exhaling deeply as he handed her a form to read through and sign, giving her voluntary consent to participate in the session for the sole purpose of aiding in the criminal investigation.

That done, Captain Greenley went over what she assumed was a standard cover-your-ass checklist, determining that she was not under the treatment of a psychologist or psychiatrist, suffering from any serious physical ailments, taking any stimulants or sedatives without her physician's consent, or subject to any phobias.

The last one made her laugh, but she answered no, and assured him when he reached the end of the questionnaire that she was not wearing contact lenses either. He finished making his notes, then considered her seriously, his brows lowered, and asked, "Do you know where you are right now?"

"Yes, I'm in the Texas Rangers station in Midland, Texas."

"Who asked you to come here today?"

"Ranger Sergeant Kellen Harding."

"What is your understanding of the purpose for coming here?"

"I'll be hypnotized to see if I can remember anything about the murders at the Sonora Nites Diner that will help Sergeant Harding in his investigation of the case."

Greenley's frown softened. "Before we get started, do you have any questions?"

"No, not really. You've been very thorough."

"Very good. Now, Jamie, using your own words, I want you to review for me what you do remember about that night and the events that occurred, in order, exactly as they happened."

"Where do you want me to start?" she asked,

shifting in her chair, fighting the return of the tension along her spine.

"Wherever you would like," he said, then sat back as if he'd paid for a show.

She told him the same story she'd told anyone who'd ever asked. The time she'd clocked in, how she'd waited tables and manned the register with Julio and Elena while Lacy worked in the kitchen with Kass. She'd told him about the last customer they'd never thought would finish his burger and leave, how he'd taken an hour to read the paper, how Julio and Elena had danced up and down the aisle with their mops and brooms after they'd locked the door behind him.

She told him about Kass hurrying all of them to finish because he wanted to get home to Helen. His wife had made his favorite black-forest cake, and he wanted to sit back with a glass of milk, a huge slice of the chocolate-and-cherry layers, and watch the Celtics NBA game on his VCR. He missed Boston a lot, Kass did.

She told Greenley about it being her turn to run the day's closeout tape on the register while balancing the till and preparing the nightly deposit of cash and checks. The credit-card slips went into a separate bag for Kass's bookkeeper, and Jamie had been sorting them, reaching for a paper clip, when the front door's glass had shattered from a spray of bullets and the killer had walked through.

She'd dropped to the floor, her forehead grazed and bleeding, her shoulder, too. The blood from her head wound had puddled around her profusely, and she'd taken short shallow breaths and held them as long as she could, her eyes closed the whole time. That was all she could remember, and she told Greenley that, too.

What she didn't tell him was how she'd felt then, the fear that had been like icy fingers crawling over her skin, the blood that had trickled into her mouth and tasted of death, fearing she would vomit and the killer would realize she was alive, hearing the screams of her friends, the choking, gurgling sounds Elena made as she died.

Those things she kept to herself because they were the hardest memories, the ones that sat like a crushing weight on her chest until she could no longer breathe and went numb. It was the numbness that she hated. She should suffer unbearably for those who had died; the fact that she couldn't caused an embarrassing guilt.

"Good. Very good," Greenley said again, his tone attentive, respectful, his pen silent as he took notes. He looked up then, and met her gaze, smiling as if they had all the time in the world, as if they were old friends catching up on things that had happened in their lives. He made it easy not to give in to her fears and panic.

"Now, Jamie, I want you to relax. Sit back, get comfortable and close your eyes. Good, just like that," he said when she leaned into the chair and let the cushions swallow her up, the feeling heavenly. "Let the tension drain from your limbs. Let your eyelids grow heavy. Breathe in slowly, exhale. That's it. Very good. Become aware of your arms. Allow them to relax. Your hands, too, and your fingers, one by one. That's right. You're doing just fine. In a moment, I'll ask you to count backward from ten. With each number, you'll become even more calm and relaxed until your mind feels like it's floating on a cotton-ball cloud."

That's exactly how Jamie felt, like she was on a cloud, the sky around her calm and blue. She heard her voice from a distance, counting, "Ten, nine, eight… seven…six…" Then she heard Captain Greenley again, telling her there was a television set in front of her, and it would play the movie of the Sonora Nites Diner murders while she told the story again, just like before, only this time she held a remote that could control the picture, speeding it up or slowing it down or pausing it when she needed a closer look.

She went through the same narrative as before, the captain asking her the occasional question about what she was seeing. She saw things she hadn't mentioned the first time, tiny little things she couldn't imagine were important, but were clear and easy to spot when the replay slowed.

And though she'd expected to feel the need to fast-forward through the worst of that night, the truth was she felt detached with Greenley's calm voice assuring her she was safe. Viewing the gory parts was no worse than watching an episode of *CSI*.

When the killer grew closer, however, her heart gave its first jolt, her breath catching in the constriction of her chest. Captain Greenley calmed her, encouraging her to breathe deeply and relax, to take her time describing the scene from her mind's eye.

Wearing blue jeans with ragged hems, the killer stood over her, smelling like diesel fuel and patchouli, and unzipped the deposit bag before banging the register. Coins rained down and pummeled her, the leather pouch landing in front of her face, the sharp corner of the till glancing off her elbow when he knocked it from the counter.

Cursing in Spanish, he kicked her to move her out of his way, and she saw the bloody heel print he left on the floor Elena had mopped and the Nike swoop on his untied black-and-red shoe. His next step, he slipped in a puddle of soapy mop water, reached out to catch himself on the edge of a table, and she saw the tattoo of a coiled rattler on the inside of his wrist.

Once he was out the door and she'd reached the end of the story, Greenley's questions stopped, and in a voice as soothing as ever, he said, "I'm going to bring you back to the present, Jamie, by counting to five. When I finish, you'll remember all of your refreshed memories, understand? Good. Now, one, two, three, four…five."

Jamie opened her eyes, and saw Captain Greenley's smiling mouth beneath the brush of his mustache. He studied her a moment—or maybe he was just giving her time to orient herself in the present—then asked, "How do you feel?"

"Fine," she said as she scooted to sit on the edge of her chair. "I never realized that I'd opened my eyes while I was on the floor. I thought I'd kept them closed until the police arrived and found us. I thought that's why I didn't remember anything but flashes of colors and sounds."

Greenley spent a few more minutes talking to her, then signed off officially for the tape. He got to his feet, and Jamie did the same.

The technician continued to concentrate on her monitor as Jamie turned to follow the captain, leaving the room where she'd spent the last hour and a half and walking into the one where Kell had been watching the hypnosis session—and was now waiting for her.

10

"I'M SORRY." Jamie knew she had nothing to be sorry for, no reason to apologize. She was just saying the words because she knew Kell was disappointed and she had nothing else to give him to take that away.

"Don't be. What you saw is what you saw," he said, clicking the key fob that unlocked his SUV, then walking to the passenger side and opening her door.

She put her hand on the frame, but turned to him instead of climbing into the seat. "But a tattoo? Who doesn't have a tattoo these days? Finding it, or the artist, will be the pro-verbial needle in a haystack. So much time has passed, not to mention he could very well have had the ink done in Mexico rather than Texas. And let's not even talk about the population of Hispanic males in the state."

Kell nodded toward her seat, most of his expression hidden in the shadow of his big white hat. "Get in."

She started to obey but stopped, put off by his bossy issuing of orders, even more put off by the fact that she was spinelessly following them. "Where are we going?"

He shook his head, looking off over hers into the distance. "I'm not sure. Back to Weldon, I guess. To take you home."

"Can we eat first?" She wasn't ready to go home, but more than that, she was starving. She'd been too nervous this morning to eat more than her usual muffin, but the bran and the banana were long gone. The coffee, too. "A late lunch or early dinner? Either one will do."

"Sure," he said, and when she still didn't move, wanting more of his attention than his vacant stare, he shook off his distracting thoughts and looked down. One brow went up wryly as he added, "But unless you're in the mood to walk, you'll have to get in."

If she'd known her way around, she might've done just that. Walked to the closest restaurant. Physical motion was the best way she knew to clear her mind and harness useless worry. But she was unfamiliar with Midland, so she gave Kell a small bow and climbed into her seat, wishing she hadn't forgotten her sunglasses. The late-summer sun was blinding as it reflected off the vehicle's bright white hood.

By the time Kell slid behind the wheel, she was belted in and thinking about food, having pushed aside thoughts of the hypnosis for now—or that was the case until she realized he'd made no move to start the engine.

Food slipped from her mind, and she frowned, asking, "Are you okay?"

He let out a sigh that was heavy, but she couldn't interpret what the weight of it meant. He could've been feeling almost anything, and holding it back.

But then he said, "Give me a second here," and she knew something somewhere was very very wrong.

"Is everything okay?"

He nodded, his hands on the wheel as he stared down,

his chest rising and falling as if he was struggling to breathe. As if he was fighting down words he wanted to say that she might not want to hear.

Was he angry? Disappointed? Frustrated that she'd recalled so little? Whatever it was, she was now officially worried. "Kell?"

His head came up. "I've read your case file dozens of times. I know from your statement everything that happened that night. But hearing your story in your own words…thinking about you going through that…" A shudder ran through him, seized him. "Jamie, what you just did…"

She waited a moment for him to go on before saying, "It was nothing, Kell. As in literally, nothing. Refreshing my memory didn't net you anything but a tattoo."

"I'm not talking about what you remembered." He turned to face her; his gaze caught hers, held, pulled. "I'm talking about how brave you were to do that. It looked effortless, but I know it wasn't. No way was that easy."

It had seemed easy enough at the time, which surprised her, but mostly she was glad it was over and done. She wasn't feeling haunted, or fearing that she might later suffer nightmares. The whole thing was more like a dream than a return to that horrible night. She started to tell him that.

And then she stopped. He hadn't yet put on his sunglasses, and he was studying her closely, his eyes heated, his lips parted, his jaw held taut against the tic of tension she saw there. Suddenly, all she could think about was what had happened two hours ago, when he'd pulled off the road and into the parking lot and she'd nearly stripped out of her clothes. She wanted to strip out of them now.

She forgot about being hungry, about the hypnosis, about everything except the feel of his mouth and his hands. His touch was a memory she knew she would never need help to recall, and her skin began to burn with wanting him.

Before she could think of all the reasons this was a bad idea, she asked, "Do you live far from here?"

His nostrils flared. He shook his head. Except to reach for the key and turn the ignition, it was his only response. He didn't shift into gear. It was as if he was waiting for permission, wanting to be sure they were on the same page, thinking, craving, the same thing.

Oh, but they were. They were. And she told him so, her heart lodged in her throat, as she softly asked, "Maybe we could go there instead?"

KELL WASN'T GOING TO be able to focus on anything else until he had her. Whether he'd be getting her out of his system by bedding her, or entrenching his desire for her inextricably, he didn't know.

He couldn't know without moving inside of her, without feeling her move beneath him.

She humbled him. He wanted to soak her up and show her more pleasure than she could bear. And it was taking too long to get home.

The drive from the ranger station to his house was one Kell made most every day. Only when away on assignment did he not cover this same stretch of road. Never before had the trip dragged so interminably.

Both the distance and the time were intensified by the impatience eating a hole in his gut. He could smell her, the soft scent of citrus he'd caught on her skin last night.

Was it only last night when she'd crawled all over him in her driveway? Was it only two hours since she'd unbuttoned her blouse in his lap?

He groaned audibly, and he felt her gaze when she looked over. He made the mistake of doing the same, and groaned again when he saw her teething her lower lip, her skin flushed, her eyes wide and dark, the pulse beating in the hollow of her throat synced with his.

He pulled to a stop at a traffic light, sat and stared straight ahead, his blood pressure rising, his body growing stiff. "I didn't plan for this to happen. This isn't something I do."

"What's not something you do? Sex?" she asked, the word sizzling on her tongue.

She'd said it. It was out there. Sex. There was no mistaking where this was going. "I don't…seduce women whose cases I'm working."

"I know," she told him. "That goes against your code. So I'm seducing you instead."

The light changed, and he floored the accelerator, burning rubber into the pavement behind him and feeling like a fool. He was too old to be this desperately horny, but all he could think about was getting his hands on Jamie's ass without her pajama bottoms in the way.

She didn't say anything for the remainder of the drive, but gripped the armrest on her door with one hand, curling the fingers of the other into the denim covering her thigh. He imagined her growing wet for him, and bit off a curse when he took the turn onto his street too fast.

He hit the remote on his visor that opened the garage door, and watched it go up as he pulled into his driveway. Once inside the garage, he shifted into park, shut off the engine and used the remote to send the door back down. And then all he could do was wait.

A curtain of darkness descended, enveloping them and heightening Kell's senses, yet he made no move to leave the SUV. His legs were shaking, his palms sweating, his heart aching, and he could hear Jamie shifting, breathing, kicking off her shoes, getting ready to ease this thing pulsing with a life of its own between them.

The air smelled of heated leather and perfumed skin and hunger, and he couldn't take it anymore. He reached for the telescoping lever and pushed the steering wheel into the dash, reached for the button that controlled his seat and moved it all the way back.

And then, finally—finally!—he turned in the near blackness and reached blindly for her.

She was waiting, and she fell into his arms, her mouth seeking his, her hands finding his shoulders, her fingers digging in and holding on as if she couldn't bear the thought of letting him go.

Her lips were soft, her tongue eager to please. She tasted like sweet desperation, like sex on fire. When he moved his hands from her biceps to the crease where her hips met her thighs, he found skin. Smooth skin. Bare skin. Warm and sleek and taut.

He groaned into her mouth. The sounds he'd heard as she'd scooted around were more than her getting rid of her shoes. But she had yet to get rid of her top, and he wanted her naked more than he wanted to breathe. He started on her buttons while she lifted her hips and straddled him.

He could smell her now. With her thighs parted, he could smell the damp musk of her sex, and he wasn't going to be able to wait, or take this slow, or give her time to catch up. As much as he wanted to seduce her, romance her, his body's demands were much more base.

He needed her now, and once he'd jerked open her blouse, he ordered her to "Raise up."

Their position was awkward, the conditions cramped, but Kell managed to lift his hips, push his pants to his knees, find his wallet and a condom. Once sheathed, he grasped Jamie by the ass and urged her into place, catching his breath when the head of his cock brushed her belly.

While she settled her knees on either side of his hips, he fumbled for the catch that released the seat and laid it flat. Jamie hovered above him, her hands gripping the padded leather on either side of his shoulders, her bent legs pressed tightly to his.

He reached between her thighs with one hand, slid his index finger through her wet folds, parting them, then pushed his middle finger inside her as far as he could. He added a second, and she gasped, then gripped him.

His cock throbbed. His blood heated. He struggled to breathe. His heart beat in a rhythm that further constricted a chest already tight with emotion. It was a rhythm brought on by this thing with Jamie. This thing that was more than sex. A more he didn't know what to do with yet. A more he wasn't sure his life was ready for.

His free arm across her back urged her down, and he found a nipple with his tongue and drew it into his mouth, rolling it and latching on. This he could do. This he knew how to enjoy, to savor, to give. He sucked on her, he fingered her. He smiled against her when she squirmed.

And when she begged, "Kell, please," he let her go, held her hips, and guided her body into place above his. She lowered herself slowly, found the head of his cock, opened for him and slid all the way down. Then she sat, stilled, did nothing but squeeze him with her muscles inside.

This time, he was the one to beg. "Jamie, don't."

She leaned over him, planting her elbows and forearms on the seat above his shoulders, her mouth hovering inches from his as she began to move. She lifted her hips until only the head of his cock was inside her. She lowered her sex until she'd swallowed the length of his shaft. She gyrated in a slow figure eight. She pumped up and down in piston-like strokes, fast, then slow, then slower. She made love to him as if she wanted to make sure he'd never forget.

As if that would ever happen. Kell swore he was going to die before he got a chance to come. He clenched the muscles of his legs, crunched his abs and grabbed Jamie where her ass met her thighs, pulling them open, thrusting up and burying himself all the way to his balls.

She kissed him then, covered his mouth with hers and sent her tongue seeking, her lips nibbling, her teeth nipping. She kissed him like kissing was the best part of sex, and he wasn't sure he could disagree. She let him into her mouth, giving him that pleasure as she gave him her body. He was ripe with waiting and ready to burst.

He pulled his mouth away, needing it to breathe, and drove himself into her again and again. She rested her forehead on his, breathing just as hard as he was, breathing his air, breathing him in and riding him, up and down, meeting his strokes.

And then she came, arching up and crying out as if the sudden rush of sensation caught her unawares, drowning her, sucking her into the same whirlwind that had tightened around him and squeezed.

That was it. He was done. One last thrust and he let everything go, feeling as if he were being turned inside out with each pulse of semen he shot. He grunted. It was the only sound he could make, the only sound that fit with the primal urge he had to own her.

She collapsed against him, her breasts flat on his chest, her face in the crook of his neck and shoulder. He wrapped her up in his arms and held her there, still connected, cocooned safely together in the darkness, thinking it might just be a very long time before either of them wanted to move.

11

BY THE TIME JAMIE finished pulling herself together in Kell's bathroom, he'd whipped up a huge lunch of bacon, lettuce, tomato, onion and cheese sandwiches, with tomato soup and Cheetos. Bachelor fare. Because he was a bachelor. A confirmed one at that.

She was surprised at his house, the very Martha Stewart decor. She wondered if his mother had decorated the place because she'd visited and found him living out of boxes or with dorm-room furniture or even with no furnishings at all.

Then she wondered how long he'd lived here, how many women he'd brought home to share his bed. She didn't know why she was wondering that; it was none of her business, and this strange sense of possessiveness stirring her made little sense. It wasn't as if they'd exchanged vows while in the garage.

The bathroom Kell had pointed her to when they'd finally made it inside had perfumed soaps and guest towels and nothing to indicate the shower had ever seen use. She'd thought at first he might join her. She had almost asked him to.

He'd hesitated in the doorway as if he wasn't ready

to walk away, or to let her out of his sight, or to lose her. His belt had been hanging loose, his crisp white shirt untucked, his expression as rumpled and used as the rest of him, uncertain, spent. But then he'd backed away, and told her he'd clean up in the master bath. Said for her to take her time, he'd have their very late lunch ready when she was.

And so she hadn't said anything, just nodded and closed the door, leaning against it and shutting her eyes, hoping to calm the rush of blood through her veins and catch her breath. She'd tied up her hair and stayed beneath the warm spray for twenty minutes. But her legs were still shaking when she followed the smell of the food to the kitchen and found him setting the table for two.

Soupspoons in hand, Kell looked up. He was freshly shaven, his skin glowing, his hair still damp and sticking up here and there. As usual, he had on jeans, but he was barefoot instead of in boots, and wearing a faded maroon Texas A&M T-shirt that showed off his shoulders and arms in ways his dress shirts never could.

He straightened and smiled, stopping what he was doing to stare at her as she stood in the doorway. The moment went on too long, the silence, the snap, crackle, pop of tension in the air, and he cleared his throat, saying, "I wasn't sure what you'd like. If you're not into bacon, I've got turkey. Or chicken noodle soup instead of the tomato."

"The tomato is fine. The bacon is fine. And I love Cheetos more than any other chip." She came farther into the room, pushed from behind by urgency, feeling the sizzle between them nipping at her skin. She wasn't sure if she should sit, or help, or get drinks…

"Do you want me to—"

"I'm sorry. I shouldn't have—"

"Don't be sorry. I was just as much—"

"Waiting was just too hard—"

"I know. It was. It still is. I want—"

"You want? What? Tell me—"

"To eat?" she ended with because otherwise they were going to linger here forever, wanting each other, and starve.

"Yeah," he said, dipping his head with a small laugh. "That's probably a good idea."

Jamie took a big breath, felt better when she blew it out and most of the stress she'd been holding in with it. She padded the rest of the way across the cool red brick tiles to the circular table and the chair Kell had pulled out for her.

He sat in the chair to her right. There was enough distance between them that neither their arms nor their thighs brushed, but she still felt the heat of his body, the pull of his nearness, the draw. It was hard not to remember the way he'd touched her, the way he'd filled her. He'd been so thick and full, and he'd reached so deep.

She tamped down a rising flood of desire and forced her trembling hand to still before picking up her spoon. She couldn't, however, stop herself from clenching the muscles of her sex. God, but she wanted him again. "This all smells so good. Thank you."

"It's soup and sandwiches. Took all of ten minutes to throw together," he said, but then when he noticed the arch of her brow, added, "You're welcome."

"That's better. It may be just soup and sandwiches, but you prepared it, and all I have to do is eat." She dipped up a spoonful of soup, blew softly across the surface, and before she ate, added, "And that makes me very happy."

"Good. I like making you happy," he came back with, and she thought she was going to choke.

She took a minute to clear her throat. "So far, you've done just about everything right. But then, in case you haven't noticed, I'm not hard to please."

This time he was the one who almost spit sandwich crumbs everywhere. He got up and grabbed two bottles of water from the fridge, handed her one and gulped down a big swallow of his before responding. "I guess there's something to be said for low maintenance."

"Exactly." She set down her spoon, popped back a Cheeto and chewed. "If I were high maintenance, I'd prefer a pomegranate cocktail to the Jim Beam, a salad of arugula and mixed greens to the Cheetos, and Egyptian cotton to GMC's leather beneath my knees."

He tensed, lifted his spoon and let it hover over his bowl. "I don't think you have to be high maintenance to prefer soft sheets to a truck seat."

He stopped, though she could tell he had more to say. She prompted him to go on. "But?"

He set down his spoon, rested his wrists on the table's edge, stared down at his food. "I'm just wondering if you being easy to please means you won't slap me silly when I tell you I really don't want to eat."

Oh. My. It was a struggle to find her voice, what with the way her heart was lodged in her throat. "Why don't you tell me and find out."

"I want to take you to bed." He looked up and met her gaze; his was hungry, unsatisfied and frighteningly dark. As if having her in the truck hadn't been enough of a taste of all the things he wanted to know and to feel, to learn of her. "Now."

She licked her lips, wanting the same thing, wondering if she'd be smart to resist, or if giving in would be enough to get him out of her system so she wouldn't miss him after he took her home and left her there.

Because that was her biggest fear, that when she looked back on today, it wouldn't be the hypnosis that scared her, but the thought of what she'd missed out on with Kell. She slid her palms down her thighs and told him without flinching, "I'd like it very much if you did."

He got to his feet, held out his hand. She laid her fingers on his palm, and he closed his over them, tugging until she, too, stood. Still, he didn't say anything. She watched the muscles in his throat work as he swallowed, watched the tic of his pulse in his temple as his blood surged. She wondered if he could see similar signs in her, signs of wanting and impatience and need. Tingles tightened the skin over her chest, like tiny electric charges shocking her.

Kell nudged away their chairs, and she thought briefly that they should cover the sandwiches so the bread wouldn't grow stale, the bacon cold, the vegetables warm. Thought, too, about returning the soup to the pan, the caps to the bottles of water. Then she thought about nothing more than following Kell to his bedroom.

The food could wait. The things she wanted from him had waited too long already. Whatever happened after today, she was through putting her life on hold, and if nothing else, she'd have him to thank for that.

His bedroom might have been decorated originally by the same person who had put Martha Stewart's touch on the rest of his place, but he'd put his own mark on the room since. It was lived in, a man's room, but not a pizza-box, beer-can, dirty-clothes pigsty. Just cluttered with his things.

Boots and athletic shoes and copies of *Time* and *Wired*. T-shirts were rolled, rather than folded, and piled on top of his chest of drawers as if he hadn't had time to put them away. Socks, too. Not matched or bunched into pairs, but dropped into a clothes basket with clean boxer shorts.

His furniture was the color of pecan, the pieces large, his curtains and duvet an abstract geometric pattern in shades of rawhide and rust. He had a bookshelf filled with paperbacks, jug lamps with wide-bottomed shades and a single framed print of a cattle drive she knew was a Frederic Remington.

There was no TV, and for some reason that surprised her. It occurred to her to ask if he read himself to sleep, but he stopped at the foot of the bed, and once there, turned to face her. "Look at me, Jamie."

She took a deep breath, eased it out and lifted her gaze. It was the hardest thing she'd ever done. Sex in the garage had been easy. The darkness had been the perfect shield, hiding her physical flaws, her huge case of nerves, masking all the things she knew his eyes would say if she could see them.

She couldn't escape any of that now, though the flaws

and the nerves were nothing when compared to the impact of standing so near, face-to-face, both of them barefoot, and remembering the feel of their joining, of being one. Of knowing a return to that pleasure was as close as his bed.

He brought his free hand to her cheek, stroked a thumb along the ridge of her cheekbone, tucked his fingertips behind her ear and made her shiver. Then he lifted the hand he was holding and pressed her palm to his chest.

"Feel that?"

His heart. It was wild, a flock of birds beating their wings on liftoff, horses' hooves pounding across the wide-open range. The wind, powering through tree boughs, whitecapping once-calm waves. She nodded, breathed, "Yes."

"It's been doing this since I walked into your office yesterday. I can't make it stop."

Smiling, she widened the spread of her fingers. His muscles beneath her hand were taut, firm, his flesh resilient. "I don't think you want it to stop. That would mean you were dead. And I would like you alive for a little while longer. Until I get my fill at least."

He slid his palm down the side of her neck to her shoulder. "Any idea how long that will take? Because I'll need to schedule recovery time. I have a feeling you're going to wear me out."

"You can tell that already?" She moved both of her hands over his rib cage and settled them at his waist, cocking her head to the side. "After only one time?"

He reached for the hem of his T-shirt, pulled the garment over his head and let it fall to the carpet. Then he waited until she was touching him again, her hands back at his waist, his skin burning, before he went on. "I knew what you'd be like before I had you. It's there in your eyes, in what you say, what you think and do. It was there last night in your driveway."

"I wanted you last night. It wasn't the JB. It wasn't the moon. It wasn't fear. It was me. I wanted you."

"I know," he told her, reaching for the buttons down the front of her blouse, pulling it off and dropping it. Then he reached for the buttons of her fly.

"But you put me off." She kicked out of her jeans.

He shook his head, then leaned close, soothing her with tiny kisses to her collarbone, his fingers molding her breasts. "We needed today out of the way. And barely managed that."

She shivered, her nipples tightening, the stirring in her belly now nothing but desire, anticipation, a readying of her sex. She knew how he fit, and she wanted him there, and found her hands cupping his erection where it strained.

"Not yet," he said, winding their legs like braided strands and backing her into the mattress. Her knees hit, and he lowered her, then left her, taking her panties with him and kneeling at her feet.

She closed her eyes, chilled by the ceiling fan circulating the air, but oh, the heat between her legs. Kell had spread her knees, exposing her sex, and was licking and kissing and biting his way the length of her inner thighs. His mouth was hot, his lips and tongue sure, his teeth sharp enough to sting. She loved it. She wanted more, and curled her fingers into the duvet to hold on.

A butterfly. Tickling, flitting, brushing air as it fluttered its wings. That's what Kell's mouth felt like when he reached her sex. He licked her, wet her, blew warm breath to bring her to life, and then he caught her clit with his lips and tugged.

She arched into him, her hips and pelvis coming up off the bed. Oh, he was good as he worked her with his mouth, slipping a finger inside of her to thrust. He knew what he was doing, and she was so close to the edge that she almost let go, but even more than coming again, she wanted to have him with her when she did.

Bringing her heels to her hips, she used her feet to push herself farther up the bed. She wanted him to cover her, she wanted to feel his heaviness, she wanted to have all of him naked, not just his mouth and his hands and his cock. And without her having to ask, he followed, standing first to shuck out of his boxers and jeans.

Their eyes met and held as he crawled over her on his hands and knees, resting his weight on his forearms above her shoulders, and lowering his chest, then his belly, then his hips to align with hers. Though she was half his weight, she welcomed the feel of his body pressing hers into the mattress, because for reasons she didn't want to stop and examine, he kept the outside world and its threats at bay.

The thought should have made her smile. It sobered her instead. And whatever change came over her expression as she realized the true danger she was facing, Kell saw it and stopped.

12

"THIS ISN'T WHAT you want?" Kell wasn't sure if he was making a statement or asking a question. He did know there was something wrong here. That wherever they'd been moments ago, the world had shifted and dumped them in a place where he'd yet to find his footing. He was hard, and wanting, and feeling rejected. This wasn't good.

"Oh, no," she said, holding on to his arms. "Don't think that. Please, this *is* what I want."

She was shaking her head where it rested on the bed between his arms, and he thought she was reassuring him that things were okay, but the sliver of what looked like uncertainty, maybe even regret, left him hanging.

He couldn't do this if she wasn't sure. "Jamie, what's wrong?"

She squeezed shut her eyes, and when she pulled in a breath, it caught as a sob she couldn't laugh away. "I'm sorry. This is so humiliating."

For her or for him? He rolled to the side, left one leg on top of hers to keep her beside him. He wasn't going to let her get away until he knew why she was falling apart.

And then it hit him, the things she'd been through today,

the things she'd relived and remembered. Her emotions had to be ragged, and all he could think of was rutting.

He was a toad. "Are you cold?"

She wiped her eyes. "I'm fine, really. I don't even know what happened. I was thinking about being in danger, and you making me feel safe."

Yeah. Not a good thing. "And that made you cry?"

She tried to laugh, managed what came out sounding like a hiccup, covered her mouth and turned her head, their gazes connecting. "If I tell you the truth will you promise not to run away scared?"

Why would he run away scared? "I promise not to run away, but I can't promise not to worry."

She stroked her thumb over his mouth, then rolled onto her side to face him. They were so close that her nipples brushed against his chest when either of them breathed.

"You don't need to worry about anything," she said. "I'm not going to fall apart on you, more than I already have, anyway. Or try to trap you into a relationship just because we've slept together."

Now he was simply confused. Was she crying because she wanted a relationship, or because she didn't? "You trying to trap me hasn't crossed my mind even once."

"Good, because that's not who I am." She wedged both of her arms between them, plucked at his chest hair with her fingers, twisted her mouth to one side as if trying on the fit of her next words. "It's just…"

That was all she got out before she started twisting again, plucking again, plucking harder. He grabbed her busy fingers, kissed their tips, then held them still instead of transferring them to the part of his body that, even softened, ached for her touch. "It's just what, Jamie? You feel this is a mistake?"

She frowned, and cuddled even closer to him, her lips grazing the skin just this side of his armpit. "Why would you think that?"

"I don't think that, but when a woman starts crying on me in bed…"

"I accepted a long time ago that I was going to live my life alone." She pushed out the words in a rush, as if it was the only way she could let them go. "I've tried on a few men, found them comfortable enough, but none of them were men I could see myself still wearing at the end of my life."

A strange dressing-room metaphor, but he got it. He'd decided to remain a bachelor for much the same reason. Dates offered him company and conversation, and occasionally the chance to share his release instead of flying solo in the shower at the end of the day. But sex wasn't a relationship. At least not the sex he'd had before.

And that was the problem here, wasn't it? What he and Jamie had going on was more than physical involvement. "So you don't want me to run away scared because I feel like I could turn into an old shoe. Is that it?"

She giggled as if picturing a funny image. But then she sighed, growing pensive again. "That's part of it, yes. But the other part is knowing that after this, we're going to get up and dress, and hopefully eat, and then you'll be taking me home. You might touch base every few months to keep me posted on the investigation, but that's it. I'm never going to get the chance to break you in. I feel like I finally found the buy of a lifetime, and the store closed its doors before I could get inside."

Because she'd seen the same potential between them that he had. Because she'd quit the idea of exploring it before starting the climb. He had, too. Neither of them wanted to risk screwing up their perfectly good lives. But both feared the real screwup would be in letting this go.

What to do? "You really know how to make a guy feel like a bargain. And how to stretch a metaphor."

"Hey, at least I didn't compare you to a piece of meat," she said, and winked, winding her legs in and out of his. "Thank you for not running away. For letting me spill all of that."

"Is that it, then?" he asked, though he knew "it" was a whole lot more complicated than getting things out in the open. They were still there to be dealt with. "You stopped me from finishing what I started because of your shopping woes?"

"I was overwhelmed." She draped one arm around his waist, slid her hand lower, spread her fingers over the cheek of his ass and nuzzled her nose to his throat. "Since living in Weldon, I haven't done much shopping. It can take a lot out of a girl."

She'd been living in Weldon ten years. A waste of so much time she could have been doing whatever twenty-somethings were doing then. But he couldn't think about that now, not when her fingers were walking into places he'd never before allowed anyone access. "I've got something to put in you, if you think it'll help."

"I think you're exactly what I need right now." That

was all she said as she urged his lower body closer with the press of her hand to his hip.

The thought of a future with many such days spent in bed beside her… As he rolled on top of her and lowered himself into her welcoming cradle, Kell forced the thought from his mind. They were here together now, and he didn't want their shared longing for anything else getting in the way of making this memory unforgettable.

Threading his fingers into her hair, he held her still for his kiss, blinding himself to all sensation but that of her mouth. His tongue found hers waiting, eager to please, found it bold. They pressed against each other, rocking, seeking, her lips tugging at his to keep him from moving away.

He moved anyway, kissed her jaw, her neck, from her shoulder to her collarbone to the hollow of her throat. To her breasts. She kneaded his biceps and kept him there, pulling him up her body when he tried to go down. He smiled against her skin, then returned to nuzzle his face to hers as he slid his sheathed cock inside her.

When he hit bottom, he stopped, feeling her tighten around him, feeling her shudder, still and release. She pulled her hips away, withdrawing to make him follow, pushing down into the mattress, and he did. He didn't want to lose the feel of being cloaked within her, of being lost inside her, of being one, and he surged deeper.

Jamie gasped, and he wanted to kick himself for not thinking of her comfort, focused only on the things he craved, but then she shifted, tilting her hips to accommodate him more fully.

And then she whispered hoarsely, "Give me more."

He laughed, growled, a deep gravelly noise that felt as rough in his chest as it sounded in the air. "How much of me do you want?"

"How much you got?" she came back with, digging her heels into his rump and holding him tightly in place.

It was no longer a question. In this woman, he had met his match. He crawled farther up her body. "How much do you think you can take?"

She arched her back, ground her clit against the base of his shaft, her hips rolling beneath him and drawing shuddering groans from them both. "I think we'd better just stick to the sex."

He laughed again, this time as a cover-up, because knowing it was too late for just sex, he was going to lie. "That I can do."

"Then do it," she told him.

With his forearms above her shoulders bearing the bulk of his weight, he began to stroke, his mind on what his body was doing, his thoughts centered on his cock, on her sex, his concentration on nothing but physical pleasure. Or so he told himself as he drove deeper, harder, pumping long and slow, a piston firing, sparking to life.

Her breathing told him how close she was, and he moved where she told him to with a nudge of her knee, a bump from her fist, a bucking up of her lower body into his. She made sounds, anxious sounds, moans of desperation, mindless huffs and grunts, squeaks of impatience as she reached for the end.

She found it, crying out as she came, her head and shoulders pushing into the bed, her chin lifting. He watched her face; tension drained in a rush, and the smile that followed sent him over the edge. His orgasm ripped through him, a blast of sensation that staggered him, pulsing waves that flattened him. Even his knees betrayed him. He collapsed like a rag doll, spilling himself in a flood.

Jamie held his weight, held him, soothing him with her hands that rubbed his back and shoulders, quieting him and bringing him back with her voice that whispered, "Shh," over and over again.

As if he had the energy to speak, the brain to search out coherent thought, the need to say anything besides words of emotion he knew were best left silenced. For now, anyway. Telling her what he was feeling while her body still claimed his was cliché. Sex talk. Heat of the moment. Endorphins tickling his tongue. Not truth.

He wasn't ready for the truth. The truth scared him. He'd known since childhood what he wanted to do with his life. He accepted that chasing bad guys brought him into harm's way more often than he liked.

He'd decided that was a risk he was willing to take, but not one he was sure was fair to ask a partner, a lover, a wife, to take on. He wasn't going to give up his calling, so he'd given up hoping to share his life.

He came with a lot of heavy baggage, though that wouldn't stop him from taking on the baggage of someone he loved. He'd just never thought he'd find someone in similar circumstances, a partner, a soul mate, someone who understood, who could take on all his baggage in return.

And so it scared him to think that he had. In Jamie.

13

WHEN JAMIE AND KELL finally left his house, the sun was long set, the street lamps shining down along with the light of the moon. Jamie wanted to stand in Kell's driveway and wrap herself up in him as she'd done only twenty-four hours ago in hers. Only twenty-four hours? Could it be?

And all that had happened in it. The way she'd climbed over him naked in his garage, in the dark, in the seat of his SUV. The way he'd fed her, cared for her, listened to her fears, and loved her as if...as if he meant it.

He didn't. He couldn't. She knew that. He was her Texas Ranger and she was his case. More fraternization than they'd already engaged in was asking for more trouble than they were already in. And she was pretty sure that they were in a lot. A very big lot.

With his SUV idling beside her, she stood watching his garage door slide closed, then climbed up in the passenger seat of the vehicle. He'd been sitting there waiting, the engine running. She'd had to talk herself into going home. Being here with Kell...she felt closer than she had in years to Stephanie Monroe.

And how weird was that? she mused, buckling her

shoulder strap into place. She'd made her life in Weldon, had felt safe in Weldon, knew the lay of the land there, the people in town.

Was that the problem? As much as she loved her home, was it more the place she'd run to escape her past? More a prison instead of a harbor? Being with Kell made her feel safe, secure, as if she belonged, instead of as if she'd had to forge a good fit. This was strange, wrong, so very—

"Shit!" Kell slammed on his brakes, adding, "Sorry, sorry," when she surged forward and choked on her shoulder strap. "I almost backed into that car. Across the street. I knew I'd cleared the mailbox, but...shit. Sorry. Guess the Feagans have guests."

He shifted from Reverse into Drive and they traveled toward the intersection. There they stopped, and Kell readied to turn. Jamie checked her side mirror, and saw the car's headlights come on before it pulled away from the curb.

Her nape tingled. "Would their guests be waiting for any reason for you to leave?"

"What?" Kell looked into his rearview and saw the car approach. "Hmm" was all he said as he made his turn, watching to see if the car followed. It didn't, heading in the opposite direction. Still, Jamie couldn't look away, staring until the car's taillights vanished.

So much for feeling safe. Suddenly, the reason for her being in Midland to begin with came rushing back, and she wished they were returning to Weldon in broad daylight, not in the dark of night that made her think too much about the memories refreshed during hypnosis.

Maybe if she talked it out? "Once you drop me off

and get back to work tomorrow, what's your first step? On the case? Assuming you don't have new evidence come in on another. Since I gave you nothing to work with on this one."

He reached across the console and took hold of her hand. "I'm not writing off this case just because the hypnosis didn't give us as much as I'd hoped."

"As much? It didn't give you anything." A tattoo. A Nike swoop. Orders issued in Spanish, a language she had a better grasp of now than she did then, but not enough of one to make sense of what the killer had said.

There were more Hispanic men in this part of Texas than there were Caucasian, and all she'd seen of the killer was his wrist, the ragged hem of his jeans and the shoes that had left bloody footprints on the diner's freshly mopped floor.

She closed her eyes, leaning her head back against the seat. "I wanted so badly to give you the answers you needed."

"Jamie, listen to me. What you gave the investigation was exactly what it needed. You gave it the details of what you saw. You can't be faulted for not seeing more than you did. God, woman." He squeezed her fingers. "The fact that you had enough in the way of wits to see that much is nothing short of amazing."

"You're just being nice." She wished she could believe him, but she felt like a failure. She'd failed Kell, herself, her friends who'd lost their lives that night.

"You're right. I am nice, but that's not what I'm doing."

"What are you doing?" Because, if he had a magic answer, she wanted to know.

"I'm telling you how I really feel. About the outcome of the hypnosis. About how you've handled living with this all these years. I don't think I've known another woman as brave as you are."

"Is that 'known' in the biblical sense?"

"No," he said, and laughed. "Though I'd include those in the total."

"What about your mother? She raised three boys." She paused, pictured Kell as the oldest of three adolescent males running through the Harding family home. It made her smile, and she bounced their joined hands on her thigh. "A woman would have to be brave to take on more than one like you."

"My mother is brave, but trust me when I say I gave her and my dad less hell than my brothers combined."

"What, were you the perfect son? Bossing your brothers around? Ruling the sibling roost with an iron fist?"

"Something like that," he said, pulling his hand from hers to turn the steering wheel. She tried not to feel bereft, but the contact made such a difference, so she reached across and laid her hand on his thigh.

Kell went on. "I was six when Brennan was born, and Terry came along the next year. The two of them being so close in age was like having twin heathens running wild. As they got older, they looked to me, rather than to our parents, for answers, like having been there already, I would know what they could get away with before someone with real authority put down a foot."

Cute. A mini Texas Ranger, ordering the younger two boys to stand at attention. She could imagine the respect and admiration shining in their eyes. "You were their role model."

"I guess so," he said, shrugging as he guided the SUV onto the highway that would take them back to Weldon.

The man was too modest, but then, she liked that about him, the way he saw no need for braggadocio, machismo. He was a man secure in who he was, the best sort. "What do you mean guess? A big brother who knew the lay of the land? Whose parents afforded him extra privileges and responsibility because he'd earned them?"

He chuckled. "Assuming a lot there, aren't you?"

She was, but she knew she was right. "Am I wrong? Were you not a younger version back then of who you are now?"

"Yeah, I had a thing about rights and wrongs. I stood up for more than one bullied kid in school. Also lost some friends because I wouldn't go along with their pranks. Papering houses was about as criminal as I ever got." He checked his mirrors, changed lanes, set the cruise control and got comfortable. "I wanted to play ball, have the respect of my coaches and team, and not have my college admission threatened by the stupid stuff teens do. Not sure if that made me a wet blanket or a Goody Two-shoes."

"I'd say it made you perfect for what you do." Surely he saw that. "There are lots of people who like to straddle the line between right and wrong, to see what they can get away with, or pull off as long as no one gets hurt."

"But that's the thing," he said, launching into something she could tell he felt passionately about. "Someone always gets hurt. Pranks, pyramid schemes, public intoxication, whatever. There's always a victim. Even if it's just the sanitation worker hosing away the drunk's vomit. Or the guy who has to clean the damp toilet paper out of his yard the next morning."

Huh. He'd kept that memory with him for a while. She shifted in her seat to better see him, the amber lights from the dash catching his jaw, his cheekbones. "You went back and helped, didn't you?"

"Went back?"

"And helped him with the toilet paper. You drove by on your way to school or football practice, saw the unholy mess, and your conscience made you stop."

He snorted. "Like I said. Goody-Two shoes."

"No, Kell Harding. You're a good man," she said, and meant it more than he could ever know.

He, of course, had to share the credit for his becoming the man he was. "I had a couple of role models of my own."

"Your father, and who else?" she asked, letting her eyes drift shut. She was beyond exhausted. The sex, the hypnosis, the identification of Kass's body, her cold case once again hot... It was amazing she hadn't fallen asleep while she and Kell ate their reheated food.

"Captain Warren Sheets," he told her. "My first supervisor as a Ranger, and a longtime friend of my father's. He convinced me to go into law enforcement just by being the man that he was. Respectful as well as respected. Upstanding and honest. A man you could count on."

Warren Sheets. It sounded so familiar. "I know that name. Why do I know that name?"

Kell paused, letting the question hang several seconds

before answering. "He was the original investigator on the Sonora Nites Diner case."

Jamie's eyes popped open. Her heart blipped, and she was suddenly wide, wide awake. "Oh my God. He was. But you didn't work it then, did you? I don't remember you being there at any of the interviews."

Kell shook his head. "Not officially, though I spent a lot of late hours with Warren combing through evidence."

"So when you said you were familiar with the case—"

"I wasn't kidding. Finding the killer has been a personal crusade, I guess you could say. Warren swore to see the man behind bars if it was the last thing he did. The crime scene…it really got to him. All the years I knew him, he never could let it go. The department might've called the case cold, but Warren—" Kell shook his head "—he never did. He died with this case still haunting him."

And Kell had sworn to finish his mentor's work, Jamie realized, realizing, too, that he had his own stake in this case, one driving him that had nothing to do with her. For the first time she wondered how this thing between them would impact him doing his job.

Would he make choices he might not have made otherwise? Would it be harder for him to put it away if it grew cold again? Would he suffer more guilt should he not be able to close it because of what they'd shared? Would she always wonder if this interlude had been, for Kell, a professional misstep?

God, her head hurt from thinking of all the ramifications of what they'd done. "You've taken up where he left off, then."

"I'm doing my job, Jamie," he reiterated. "If Kass Duren's body hadn't been found and identified, I'd be working on whatever case had the newest leads. It might've been this one, it might've been another."

It sounded good. She just had trouble buying it. He'd said Warren Sheets had influenced his life as greatly as his father. Finishing what the other man had started would be more than a job. It would be a calling. A vow.

"Why don't I believe that?" she asked softly.

He huffed once, twice, then cursed under his breath, the words self-directed, not meant for her. "Because somehow you've learned to read my mind? Or at least read me?"

"At the very least," she told him, because even *she* hadn't yet figured out the depth of their involvement.

"I used to be better at keeping my mouth shut."

"With women, or in general?" she heard herself asking.

He gave her another of his laughs that she loved hearing, then sighed. "Always back to the women with you, isn't it?"

She felt as if she had a vested interest in him now. And with the Weldon city limits looming, her time with him was too swiftly coming to an end. She wasn't ready to lose him.

She wasn't ready to let go. "You're staying over, aren't you? You're not driving back to Midland tonight?"

They hadn't talked about their parting, whether he'd drop her off at her front door, or tell her goodbye in the morning. They hadn't talked about keeping in touch, whether he'd check in with her on a regular basis, or if she should just wait for his updates as they came.

They hadn't talked about the end at all. Did that mean neither one of them wanted it to come?

Finally, Kell broke the silence that was eating her alive. "If you want me to stay, I'll stay."

Oh, she did, she did, but... She twisted her fingers together; she didn't want to reach for him too soon. "Only if that's what you want."

He leaned over, settled his hand at her nape, threaded his fingers into her hair and kneaded her there. Tingles of longing tightened her breasts. "I want it more than anything."

14

WHEN JAMIE HAD PURCHASED her cottage and moved out of the house she'd shared with her mother their first five years in Weldon, she'd also bought the four-poster bed she'd dreamed of since seeing it in a home-decor magazine as a teen.

It was a simple wrought-iron frame in matte black, the canopy draped with sheer white lace panels that made her think of harem curtains, umbrellas with privacy veils, tinted windows—all hinting at the secrets being kept behind.

Waking up along with the dawn and beside a sleeping Kell, Jamie realized her canopied bed now held secrets of its own—secrets she would keep close, share with no one, relishing them in private when life left her lonely.

Sure, she would fill her days with work, and have her mother, her friends and neighbors for company. And she would not feel sorry for herself, embracing instead every moment of joy that came her way, even creating them. But this time with Kell would never be far from her mind.

Their paths had crossed on this one particular road, but wishing for more would be folly. His knowing about her past didn't mean he wanted to live with it, to have to face down her ghosts when they drifted in, unannounced and unexpected, to haunt her.

Still, she'd be forever grateful for the way he'd helped her connect to lost pieces of Stephanie, for the way he'd helped her find the answers to the lingering questions about the night of the murders.

And he'd given her so much more…laughter and deep conversation, tenderness and fiery passion, honesty and hard truths. With every fiber of who she was, she knew she would never get the same from any other man.

She turned onto her side to watch him. He lay beside her on his back, the sheet she clutched beneath her chin draped across his torso, leaving his chest bare. One of his arms rested on top of the bedclothes between them. The other hand was spread low on his belly.

He wasn't a cuddler, she'd discovered, and that was okay. Just knowing he was there during the night had made her dreams serene, and every once in a while when she'd adjusted her position, she'd brushed up against him, her knee, her heel, her fingers when she'd stretched, and she'd roused enough to smile, somewhere between wakefulness and sleep.

Now that she was awake, she refused to allow herself to drift off again and miss any more of this time. She wanted to move closer to him, to enjoy his warmth, his weight sinking into the mattress, his bulk beside her lifting the sheet when she was so used to it lying flat around her.

She scooted toward him, quietly, an inch at a time, doing her best not to rock the frame or pull the covers. She watched his chest rise and fall, felt the heat of his body as she drew near, and then he moved the arm blocking her way, and mumbled, "I'm awake, you know."

"I know," she whispered back, though she hadn't been certain.

"Hard to sleep with you thinking so hard over there."

She laughed to herself, a soft sound that came out on her next breath. At least he couldn't hear *what* she was thinking. She didn't want to scare him away.

"It's okay," he mumbled. "I'm not going to shoo you off and roll over."

Or could he hear it all? His eyes were still closed, his lips barely parted. His cheeks were covered with a dark shadow of beard, and she liked this scruffy, disheveled Kell as much as the clean and pressed Texas Ranger version. "I didn't want to disturb you."

He peered at her through one slitted lid. "Too late. I'm disturbed."

A tingling set up in the pit of her belly. "Maybe I'll just stay where I am—"

"Don't even think about it," he said, and reached for her, tugging the sheet out of the way as she climbed on top and straddled him. "My disturbance needs attention."

So she'd noticed. "A trip to the facilities maybe?"

"I made one an hour ago," he grumbled. "This is all you."

Hmm. She hadn't even heard him get out of bed. "Feels to me like it's all you."

"Then you're obviously not doing enough feeling."

She was feeling with her inner thighs, with her belly. The head of his cock pushed there, hot, sticky with the moisture of his arousal. She knew this would be their last time, and she didn't want to rush through loving him.

The sheet was white and cool on her back, a contrast to the warmth and dark hair she encountered along her front as she moved down his body to take him into her mouth. He exhaled, a long slow potent groan that thrilled her, rumbling beneath her, a rocky surface, as it did.

He tasted like rich wine and salt and dark earthy musk, and she savored him, breathing him in, finding the seam that split the underside of his glans, her fingers ringing around him just beneath. She teased him with the tip of her tongue, curled it and cradled him.

He reached for her hair, tugged, biting off words that were gritty and raw, sex words, nasty words. She felt her sex swell and open, her juices ready to ease the way. She wanted him now and forever, filling her, beside her, with her.

Holding her mouth just so, she took him to the back of her throat, pressing her lips tight to his shaft as she pulled her way back to his cock's head. She stayed there, circling her cupped hand and her tongue over and around until she felt his balls tighten, his thighs and ass clench.

It would be so easy to give this to him, to let him finish, to come in her mouth, a pleasure they had shared last night, but she didn't. She let him go, crawling over his body, dragging her breasts, her belly, then her sex the length of his engorged cock.

"You're a cruel woman, Jamie Danby," he told her as she nuzzled his throat, his right armpit, his closest nipple that was as hard as hers. She flicked her tongue over it, massaged the muscle around it, the tips of her breasts skating through his chest hair as she moved from side to side. "Know I'll be getting back at you for this."

"I hope so," she said as she reached for a condom from those remaining on her nightstand. Throwing off the sheet, she sat on her knees and rolled the protective sheath to the base of his shaft. "If you don't, I'll have to hunt you down like a rabid dog."

He laughed, a guttural blast of sound, and grabbed both cheeks of her ass, urging her to take him, no, demanding that she did until she lowered her hips. Softly, she sat, impaled. Then she began to move, bracing her hands on his knees behind her, grinding, rotating, using her hips and her pelvis to dance, her clit sliding through the springy hair surrounding his thickness.

Sensation consumed her, sent her flying. Kell bucked his knees and she fell, planting her palms on either side of his pillowed head. He cupped her breasts, pushed them together, bit and kissed and licked his way from one peak to the other while she pumped up and down.

And then his eyes caught hers, held hers, refused to let her look away. All the things she saw… It was too much, the hope and the longing and the wishing and the want. How was she supposed to survive without him in her life? How was she supposed to pull out this memory years down the road and be happy when he wasn't with her?

Because she had no answer, she came, completely, giving herself up to the physical bliss of their joining. It was the most glorious pain, a beautiful ache.

She had him, but she didn't, and when he growled out, "Hands and knees," she gladly did his bidding, crawling off of him and onto the bed, punching a pillow beneath and anchoring her arms around it.

He knelt behind her, dug his fingers into her hips to position himself, then slid his palm over her sex, cupping her, slipping a thumb inside of her. His cock nudged his hand away, and he pushed into her slowly, releasing a groan that rattled her as his cock filled her up. He slid deeper, deeper, withdrew and returned, then reached around to toy with her clit, seeing to her pleasure while finding his own.

His strokes grew swifter, his breathing shallow; when he pulled his hand away to hold her hips, she replaced it with her own, working herself to completion as he came. He shuddered, stiffened, cursed coarsely and called her name. It made her cry, that sound, those words, though she buried her sobs in the pillow, hiding them.

Seconds later, the muscles of his thighs relaxed, and he moved away, easing himself from her body, then wrapping an arm around her waist and lowering them both to spoon.

They calmed together, no other words spoken, and then they showered, cleaning each other, Kell rinsing her, toweling her off, dressing while she dried her hair, fixing breakfast while she donned her weekend wardrobe of a tank top and shorts, and when time could no longer be forgotten, kissing her goodbye in her driveway.

It was a kiss full of tenderness, beauty, and she pressed her fingers to her lips to hold it there when he put his SUV into gear and backed into her street. He lingered, shaking his head as he settled his sunglasses in place. And when he finally pulled away, he burned strips of rubber into the pavement in front of her house.

A long black reminder of what she'd had and lost, one she'd see every day when she left for work and when she came home.

She returned to the cottage and spent the rest of the day—Saturday and Sunday, too—doing next to nothing but missing him. She didn't call her mother to tell her she was home. She did little more than move from the bed to the bathroom to the refrigerator, opening the door and staring inside.

When Monday morning arrived, she gathered her things, then exited through her half-acre backyard, opening the gate that led into Mr. Floyd's equally large yard behind and walking down Paul Revere Street instead of Lamplighter Lane.

Mr. Floyd wouldn't mind if she used his property as a shortcut in order to avoid the mark Kell had left in front of hers. It was either that, or never leave her cottage again.

As THEY'D PROMISED, Roni and Honoria had indeed taken care of things while Jamie'd been gone. That didn't mean she'd returned to find nothing to do. On the contrary. Her coworkers taking care of things simply meant they'd handled the daily chores that usually fell under her purview. It didn't mean they'd done her work, and she was glad.

Keeping busy meant she didn't have time to dwell on Kell's leaving her, or answer any questions Roni or Honoria had about what had happened while she was away. She didn't want to think about Midland. She didn't want to think about Kell or the hypnosis.

She didn't even want to think about what was going

on today—or had over the weekend—with the investigation into the Sonora Nites Diner murders. She wanted to think about the unpaid insurance claims and their deadlines staring her in the face. That was all.

She'd finally gone over everything about the trip and the hypnosis with her mother when Kate had stopped by the pediatrics clinic on her way to work. At least everything but the sex. Though Kell had called Jamie's mother while Captain Greenley had been conducting the exit interview following the session, Kate had wanted to hear the details firsthand.

As much as Jamie wanted to leave the last few days behind, she couldn't blame her mother for her curiosity or her concern. And though Jamie was certain her mother knew things with Kell had gone as they had, Kate didn't say a word. She just handed Jamie her coffee refill and told her they'd have dinner at Buck's Burger Barn tonight.

A burger sounded great, Jamie had to admit, heading to the lobby to cover the phones while Roni went on break. A burger wasn't a steak. A burger wasn't a bacon sandwich with Cheetos and tomato soup. A burger wouldn't make her think of Kell standing at her stove frying fresh-cut potatoes.

In fact, she was hungry enough that she didn't know how she was going to make it the two more hours until the clinic closed and she could get dinner, return to her sleepathon and start picking out names for her future cats. Gah, she had to stop. She was getting on her own nerves now.

When the front door opened, she welcomed the distraction from her depressing thoughts, smiling at the Hispanic man who approached. "May I help you?"

A shock of black hair falling over his forehead, he looked around, leaning his forearms on the reception counter, then finally gave Jamie his attention. "This office. It's the only kid doctor in Weldon? Me and my son, we just moved here."

Jamie nodded. "We are, yes. There's a general practitioner here as well, but you'll have to go to Alpine or Fort Stockton for another pediatrician. Were you wanting to make an appointment for your son?"

"School's coming up. He's going to need shots and things," he said, frowning, distracted, his dark eyes flitting but never to hers.

Jamie wondered if he was on drugs. "Sure. Do you have records from his last doctor? So we can see what he's had and what he needs?" she asked, opening the appointment-scheduling program and pulling the keyboard in front of her, prepared to input his information.

"His mother did all that. In Midland. I'll have to check."

"Did you want to go ahead and make the appointment? With school starting soon, we don't have a lot of openings in our schedule."

He shook his head, reached up to push back the fall of hair. "I'll just wait."

O…kay. She grabbed one of the clinic's cards and handed it across the counter. "Here's our number. Just give us a call when you're ready to come in."

He nodded, took it with a shaking hand, making Jamie think again of drugs. Or at least she thought of drugs until the cuff of his sleeve slipped up as he reached for the card and she saw his tattoo. The tattoo. The snake. Then she couldn't think of anything but not giving herself away.

For one short second, she considered asking for his name for their records, then thought better. She wouldn't do that with any other parent who wasn't ready to bring his child to see Dr. Griñon. This man might know that. This man might have been in here previously, before the hypnosis, and know that. And so she smiled and waited for him to go.

He studied the card, tapped it on the counter, then finally pushed away and headed for the door. Once he'd left the building, Jamie counted to thirty. She didn't want to jump up while he was right outside. She didn't want to start digging through the desk drawers for a letter opener or knife. She didn't want to pick up the phone and call for help until he couldn't walk back in and catch her.

Just as Jamie hit twenty-nine, Roni returned from her break. The other woman hadn't taken but one step into the lobby when Jamie whispered, "Lock the front door. Now. Turn the sign to Closed. And shut the blinds."

Roni frowned, but hurriedly did as she was told. Jamie picked up the phone, searching the desk for a weapon while she waited for Kell to pick up.

It took four rings before he did, and she could hear laughter in the background. His own voice sounded buoyant, upbeat. "Jamie?"

"He was here," she cried out with before he could say another word. "Here. In the office. I saw his tattoo."

"What? When? Maybe it was similar or—"

"Kell, it was it. The same one. I remember."

"Shit. Are you there alone?"

"No. Roni just locked the front door, and I'm holding a letter opener."

"Was he driving? Walking?" he asked, and Jamie could hear him shuffling his phone, slamming drawers.

She shoved out of Roni's chair and rushed to the door, flattening herself against the wall beside it to peer through the slats of the blinds. "There's a car pulling out of the lot. The glare's bad and the angle's wrong. I can't see if he's behind the wheel, but it's the only one."

"Can you get the tag numbers?"

Jamie gestured toward Roni who'd been standing and listening to her side of the conversation wide eyed. "Roni, help! Can you read the plates on that car?"

They talked over each other, Jamie seeing an eight where Roni saw a six, a three where she saw a five. It didn't matter. She rushed back to the desk, leaned across the counter, scrambled for a pen and wrote all of them down on her hand.

Then she read them to Kell. "I'm sorry. He was pulling away. That's the best we could do."

"You did good, sweetheart. We'll see what a mix and match turns up. Hang on a sec—" More shuffling sounds, cabinets banging, footsteps pounding, keys jangling, muffled voices in the background, until Kell came back. "You still there?"

"I'm here." She leaned her elbows on the counter, one hand holding the cordless phone, the other rubbing the bands of stress squeezing her forehead. She felt like a tomato ready to pop in a spray of red flesh and seeds.

"Okay. Troopers are on the way. No more than fifteen minutes. You stay in lockdown until they get there. Make sure all doors are secured. No one comes in or goes out."

She turned around, met the worried gazes of Roni and Honoria, who'd joined them, knew Mrs. Hernandez and her four-year-old-son would be right behind. "We've got patients here—"

"They can wait. No one, Jamie, you hear me? That door opens for no one unless they have a gun and a badge."

15

ON HIS RETURN TRIP to Weldon, Kell broke all land-speed records and abandoned every bit of common sense while behind the wheel. He'd been in his office at the ranger station when he took Jamie's call. His heart had yet to return to its normal rhythm. After the shock it had taken, he was surprised it was beating at all.

He'd kept her on the line until the first two troopers had arrived at Weldon Pediatrics. It had been a hell of an agonizing wait, working to keep his calm while insisting she do the same. A wait made worse by his being torn between doing the right thing as a ranger, and doing the right thing as a man whose woman's life was at risk.

He knew there was a DPS unit that regularly patrolled Texas 17 between Weldon and Balmorhea. Knew, too, they were his best hope for tracking down the suspect. If the Sonora Nites Diner killer was in the car Jamie had seen, he hadn't had time to get far.

It had been a gut-wrenching decision to make, but Kell had given those officers Jamie's description of the two-door sedan, the possible combinations of tag numbers, the location and look of the driver's tattoo. The unit that worked the stretch of highway between Weldon and Alpine was the one he'd sent to see to Jamie at work.

He'd been three hours out when she'd called. Three hours he'd cut to almost two by running with his grille lights flashing. He'd waited until hearing that the troopers were at the clinic before he'd let Jamie go and called Dr. Kate.

When he pulled up in front of Weldon Pediatrics, a sheen of sweat dampening his skin, his heart still pumping high-octane fuel, he found Jamie's mother waiting for him in her Suburban just like he'd asked. He pulled his SUV alongside hers and got out, staying her from doing the same with the wave of his hand.

She rolled down her window instead, and beneath the brim of the ball cap she'd pulled low to shield her eyes from the sun, her frown furrowed with fury. "What the hell is going on with my daughter?"

He'd told Jamie not to call her mother, or let the others in the office call family members or friends until the troopers assessed the situation. He wanted to avoid a flood of concerned loved ones descending and raising a battle cry.

This wasn't the scene of a crime. It was unlikely there was evidence to disturb outside; gravel dust didn't hold tire tracks. Fingerprints, shoe prints, strands of hair left inside were a different matter. But keeping a lid on things until he knew what they were facing would keep speculation from blowing like seeds on the wind.

"She's fine. Did you pack her things and enough food for a week?" Kell asked, thumbing his hat up his forehead. Whatever the investigation brought to light, he was not leaving Jamie here. And he was not bringing her back until the bastard was behind bars.

"I did, but I'm not handing them over until I get an answer," Kate said, her hand gripping the strap of the duffel bag in her passenger seat. Two boxes and an extra-large cooler took up most of the back. "When you called me from Midland? Right after the hypnosis session? You told me she didn't remember anything you could use."

Kell wanted to get to Jamie, but her mother deserved consideration. She was the one who'd brought Jamie safely this far. He propped a forearm on the roof of the Suburban, staring into the distance at the Davis Mountains rolling like waves in the haze.

"I told you she remembered the tattoo on the killer's wrist."

"Right. And?"

"And, she just saw it again."

"What? Where? Here?" Kate looked around frantically. "I want to see her. Now."

He held the door handle, preventing her from climbing down from her seat. "Wait. Hear me out. The man is gone. Jamie is fine. She and her coworkers are inside, and the troopers have secured the building. We can't let anyone else go in until we get the place dusted for prints, and see what other trace evidence he might've left behind."

Kate didn't like hearing what he had to say, but she didn't fight him for the door. "But you're bringing her out?"

He nodded. "And then I'm taking her someplace

safe. I know she'll argue, so having you on my side would go a long way to helping convince her."

With a huff, Kate sat back, crossed her arms over her leopard-print scrubs and glared. "I'm not so sure she'll be safe with you. He found her just days after you brought her home? Hardly a coincidence. I'd say your office needs to be checked for leaks. And I don't mean just some careless talk," she added, her tone brutally condemning. "What if someone there has known the killer's identity all these years? And not turned him in for that horrific crime? What kind of person could do something that unconscionable?"

Kell had imagined the same worst-case scenario seconds into Jamie's call, and had asked himself the same questions, though he was still weighing the possibilities. "He could've been here all this time, keeping an eye on her to see if her memory returned."

He could tell from the shake of her head that Kate wasn't buying it. "Or the story in the paper last week could have brought him here." Though this conversation was one he should be having with the authorities on the scene instead of with Kate, sounding it out with Jamie's mother couldn't hurt as a first step.

"Yeah, he could've come because of the article, to see if his face rang any bells," Kell said again. "But if he knew about the hypnosis… That was when Jamie remembered that he was Hispanic and tattooed. Either he knew that and wanted to see her reaction to his ink, or he didn't know, and was looking for any reaction, any refreshed memories at all."

"Six of one, half dozen of the other," Kate said with

a dismissive wave of her hand. "He came here to find out if she could ID him."

"And assuming she didn't give anything away—"

"I hope you're not basing your investigation on assumptions," she interrupted him to say. "We've assumed all this time she was safe here. We've assumed he had no plans to risk exposure by coming after her. I'm done with assumptions."

"No, ma'am. No assumptions. From here on, we work with solid evidence and facts."

"Sergeant Harding!"

Kell took a step in reverse and glanced over the hood of his SUV toward the officer flagging him down from outside the clinic's door. He waved that he was on his way, then told Jamie's mother, "I'll bring her out. Can you throw her pack and the supplies in the backseat with my things?"

Kate opened her door, turning on her seat to face him. "Only if you promise me you'll bring her home in one piece, and only when it's safe."

"Yes, ma'am. I promise." He slapped the hood of his vehicle then jogged toward the clinic. Enough of a crowd had gathered that two of the officers were positioning their cruisers to form a barricade.

He wanted to get Jamie out of here, but he first had to speak to the officers on scene and the civilians still inside. Doing so would go down a lot easier without any distractions—which meant sending her with a trooper to wait with Kate. He pulled Deputy Aronson aside and asked him to take care of that while Kell did what he needed to do.

Though it took an hour to finish his questioning, Kell learned nothing from Jamie's female coworkers, or from the doctor, or from the patients who'd been in the clinic when the man with the snake tattooed on his wrist had come in. Jamie had been the only one to see him.

Kell was interrupted twice during his interviews, hearing first from the troopers who'd gone after the car. No luck yet with them, or with the technician at the ranger station running the tag numbers on her end. Hitting dead end after dead end did not sit well with Kell.

This case had gone unsolved too long already. He'd be damned if he let this first solid lead they'd had in years go cold. Once he finished his initial investigation and made sure the officers knew he'd be in touch, he headed for his SUV, Jamie and Kate.

The two women were standing between the two vehicles, heads together, Kate's arm around her daughter's shoulders, Jamie holding on to her mother's free hand. Aviator sunglasses covering his eyes, Deputy Aronson stood next to the rear of Kell's SUV, arms crossed, stance wide, blocking the only entrance to the triangle of space where the Danby family stood.

That was what got to Kell. Jamie and Dr. Kate were the entire family, a fictional family created to save Jamie's life. They were two alone, depending solely on one another. Kell had his parents, his brothers, plus aunts and uncles and cousins he saw only a couple of times a year but knew he could tap in an emergency. He also had the Texas Department of Public Safety at his back, coworkers in numbers dwarfing what the Danby women had, and his carried weapons.

The injustice of their situation rankled. Seeing them as victims left him vexed. Yes, their circumstances were only unique to them; he'd dealt with dozens, hundreds of human casualties as he fought the war against crime, each with their own story, their own nightmares, but from those he'd kept his distance. Why he hadn't kept it this time...

Oh, hell. Who was he kidding? He knew exactly why he hadn't kept it this time. He'd walked through the front door of Weldon Pediatrics and seen that ponytail swinging, those big eyes dancing, those freckles spattering that nose, and that ass. She'd done him in, right then, right there; the teddy-bear scrubs hadn't helped.

And then he'd seen the fear, the devastating realization that her life was coming undone, that her carefully constructed wall of Jericho was tumbling down around her. He was a lawman, a savior, a rescuer. The fact that she was a damsel in distress in name only didn't keep him from wanting to be a full-fledged, bona fide white knight.

Once he'd released Deputy Aronson from guard duty, Kell approached the two women who, ready or not, were now going to have to say their goodbyes. As he passed, he glanced through his open driver's-side window into the SUV's backseat. Good. Jamie's pack was there with the cooler and boxes.

She looked up at his approach. Her face was pale, her eyes red-rimmed but dry. He needed to question her in detail, but they had a long drive waiting and plenty of time. For now, all he asked her was, "Ready?"

Her nod was brief. She knew nothing of where they were going. All he'd told her while they'd been on the phone was that he was coming to take her away.

"Give me a minute?" she asked.

"A minute," he said, concern a whetstone making his voice sharp, then walked around to the passenger door. He opened it. He waited. Through the window on the other side, he watched as she hugged Dr. Kate. As gripped as his gut was, he couldn't imagine what the Danby women were feeling, and when one minute became two, he still didn't move.

Minute three ticked around, and now his impatience caused him to clear his throat. Jamie stepped back, letting her mother's hand linger in her own until the distance grew and Kate's fingers slipped away. She climbed into her seat without saying a word to Kell.

He stayed where he was, waiting, and when she met his gaze, it was all he could do to nod toward her seat belt and tell her, "Buckle up."

The emotion in her face socked him in the solar plexus as hard as any hit he'd ever taken. Fists, football helmets, baseball bats. Brennan wailing on him after Kell had gone out with Lauren Randall, Brennan's crush. Terry wiping out his skateboard in front of Kell's and sending them both to the pavement where they'd broken bones. None of those incidents had left him feeling as hammered as the feelings Jamie couldn't hold back, a mixture of anger and fear and loathing.

He closed her door, made his way around to his and stopped to offer Kate his hand. She shook it, said nothing as she released it, just climbed behind the wheel of her Suburban and sprayed rooster tails of gravel as she drove away.

Kell remained silent as well, putting on his seat belt,

adjusting his visor, settling his hat so low that it bumped his sunglasses' frames. The sun would be hanging on the horizon a couple more hours, but the day was still bright, hot, dry. Outside, anyway. Inside the SUV, he swore he could safely store a side of beef.

He understood Jamie not being happy with the state of things. Working this case wasn't remotely how he'd hoped he'd be spending his time. They were both going to have to deal, and cross their fingers that they'd come out in one piece on the other side.

Once Weldon was behind them, he breathed deeply and nudged up the brim of his hat. "I know you told me everything on the phone, but I want you to tell me again."

"Why? Nothing's going to change," she said, her gaze fixed out her window, one hand gripping the edge of her seat, the other doing the same damage to her armrest. "I remember it all. I don't need to give you a mind's-eye narrative to have my memory refreshed."

Part of him wanted to growl. Another part wanted to laugh. He grabbed for middle ground. "I need the narrative. I know you told me everything, but I had a lot of things on my mind when you did. Mainly, securing your safety. I might've missed a detail that could've sparked a question with an answer that would help."

She seemed to give that consideration because she released her hold on the SUV's interior and sank into the seat. "It was a little bit after three. Roni goes on break then and I cover the front desk. I'd been on the phone with a sales rep wanting to schedule time with Dr. Griñon, and was late relieving her. Five or ten minutes."

Good. An established timeline.

"She headed to the break room—"

"Were there any patients in the lobby then?"

"No. The Irigoyen twins were due at three-thirty for their six-month checkup. Emilio Duran should've been there, but rescheduled his school sports physical." Jamie's voice softened. "Dr. Griñon has been his pediatrician since birth. I think the other guys on the team give him a hard time about a baby doctor clearing him for football."

Kell was intimately familiar with high-school locker-room razzing. "So you were there by yourself when this guy came in. And he didn't set off any bells? Fidgeting, looking around, avoiding eye contact? Asking questions but not really paying attention?"

"He looked around, yes, but as far as I knew, he'd never been in the clinic, so I didn't think anything of it. He was rather…twitchy, though. I wondered if he might be on drugs, yes. It wasn't the normal inquisitiveness of a father dealing with child custody for the first time, immunizations for school, stuff like that. It was more like…he didn't want to be there."

"Why did you think he was dealing with child custody?"

"When I asked if he had his son's medical records, he said his wife had taken care of all of that in Midland."

Midland. Kell wondered if the man had pulled that location out of thin air, or if he had a connection to the city Kell called home. The city where Company E was headquartered. And in light of his earlier conversation with Jamie's mother, the speculation about a leak in the department…

His gut souring as it churned, he checked his rearview and side mirrors before prodding Jamie for more. "Tell me about seeing the tattoo."

She took her time responding, staring out the window at the endless acres of yellowed grazing land, acres too dry to sustain more than the few head of cattle dotting them. "I saw it when I handed him a card with the clinic's phone number and office hours. He didn't want to make an appointment then, or have me open a file for his son. So I told him if he wanted to have him seen before school started, to call soon. Our schedule's always full this time of year. He was wearing long sleeves, and the cuff slid up when he took the card."

Long sleeves. In August. Laborers wore them, in the oil fields, on farms and ranches. Construction and road crews even. "Did he look like he'd been working? Or smell like it? Sweaty, dusty, anything?"

"Not that I noticed." She paused, added, "Oh, but his hair was clean. It kept falling over his forehead. Why do you ask?"

"The long sleeves. Whether he's our guy or not, he could be working in the area."

"An illegal?"

He grimaced, nodded. "Yeah, most likely. And if he smelled like plywood or diesel fuel or fertilizer or road tar, it would give us an idea of where he might be employed, who to question that might be able to identify him…"

"You don't think he was on his way to work, do you?"

"I doubt it," Kell said, shaking his head. "Were the cuffs buttoned? Loose?"

"I don't know," she snapped. "Why does it matter?"

Her exasperation only made the conclusions he was drawing that much harder to face. But he wasn't going to deceive her, or hide what he was thinking. After all she'd done to help his investigation, she deserved his honesty.

"I'm trying to determine what he wanted from you. Hear me out," he added when she turned to interrupt. "If he's been here all this time, he likely heard about Kass Duren's body being ID'd, and he could've been feeling you out, seeing if you would recognize his face, or his voice. Showing you the tattoo when his cuff slipped up could've been nothing.

"But," Kell continued, trying to corral his thinking into words, "if he knew you'd been through the forensic hypnosis, and knew you'd remembered the tattoo, he very well could've been gauging your reaction to seeing it again, and the fact that you didn't react—"

"Is the only reason I'm alive," she said, catching up to his train of thought. "The first scenario would mean he's been around all these years, watching me. And the second…"

Angry enough to spit mortars, Kell finished the sentence for her. "The second means there's a leak in the department, and I dragged you from your safe existence out into the open."

16

JAMIE WOKE TO COMPLETE darkness. Not the darkness she was used to in her bedroom at night, but a darkness so thick, she saw nothing. She knew she was in Kell's SUV, and wherever they'd stopped, they hadn't been here long; the interior was still warm, though missing him.

It had been almost seven before they'd left Weldon. Since Kell hadn't wanted to stop until they reached their destination, he'd asked one of the troopers to pick them up burgers and fries from Juan Cantu's. From the clinic, they'd headed south; from a distance, a cruiser had followed.

Traveling back roads she hadn't known existed, Kell had stopped only once—in a town smaller than Weldon for gas. He'd told her the maneuvers were to guarantee no one but the troopers stuck to their tail, and the troopers were to dissuade anyone stupid enough to try tailing them. If the man with the tattoo was indeed their murder suspect, he'd have no bread crumbs to track to find them.

She needed to use the bathroom. She need to stretch her legs, her back and arms. She was used to moving all day, not sitting, not riding. She needed something besides the melted ice from their to-go order to drink.

But Kell was calling the shots, so she waited. His endless stream of questions before she'd told him she was spent, dried up, out of words, had made her situation perfectly clear. One wrong move—intentional or accidental—could undo all his precautions.

She was aggravated, inconvenienced, irritated, afraid. But she was not stupid. And so she pulled her knees to her chest and curled in on herself, waiting.

Moments later, she heard what sounded like footsteps on planking, and raised her forehead from the cradle of her knees in time to see Kell descending a set of porch steps in front of a small log structure.

Warm yellow light spilled from the doorway, illuminating his way to the front of his SUV. And then she remembered that he'd told her about this place. He fished here, hunted, holed up to get away.

Jamie lowered her feet to the floor and sat forward, waiting as he came around to open her door to the smells of earth and pine and midnight, as he moved into the bright wedge of space there and smiled.

"Sleep well?" he asked.

She nodded. She guessed she had. She'd drifted off before the sun had set, and hadn't even stirred when he'd parked. "What time is it?"

"Ten-thirty or so." He gestured toward the cabin. "I fed the generator and turned on the water. I need to haul in the food from the cooler, but that can wait. I'd rather you get settled first."

She'd been out of sorts earlier, resenting him. Now she could only remember how thoughtful he was, how strong and kind, how cute. She climbed from her seat and stepped into his arms. He groaned and wrapped her up tight.

"Does that mean you forgive me?"

"There's nothing to forgive."

"I know none of this is easy," he said, using the heel of his palm to massage the length of her spine.

She shivered, snuggling even closer. Being in his arms felt so good, so right. "I'm pretty sure life's not supposed to be. At least not all of it."

"Maybe not. But this goes above and beyond what most people face."

"In case you haven't noticed yet, I'm not most people."

He leaned back far enough to see her expression, and stared at her for a long moment, seeming to weigh which thoughts were safe to share, and which were best kept private as he brushed strands of hair away from her eyes.

She wondered about his private thoughts, if they mirrored hers in considering the possibility that they'd been thrown together by fate—and for more personal reasons than solving the Sonora Nites Diner murders.

But he gave nothing away when he said, "I've noticed a lot of things about you. Some of them you may not like."

Uh-oh? "Such as?"

"You snore."

She huffed. "What? I do not."

"You do. And I've got the broken right eardrum to prove it."

He was teasing her, she knew it, trying to keep things light. She appreciated the effort, deciding two could play this game. She pulled away, punched his shoulder, too emotionally spent to be embarrassed over what was more than likely the truth. "I'm sure that was just the hum of all that equipment running there on your dash."

"Trust me. It wasn't a hum."

Okay. Now he was asking for it, she mused, fighting a grin. She could dish back to him as much teasing snark as he delivered. She stomped around him, heading for the porch steps, and calling over her shoulder. "I hope you've got an extra bed because I'll be sleeping alone in yours."

Behind her, he whooped and hollered and cackled like a hyena, and she decided then and there that she loved him.

THEY SLEPT TOGETHER. They didn't have sex. Kell spooned behind her, an arm securing her, and kept her close to his body most of the night. When they'd last been in bed together, he'd told her he wasn't a cuddler and not to take it personally. Now she was left trying to figure out how to interpret that he didn't want to let her go.

With so much on her mind, she woke before he did, and though she lay there soaking him up as long as she could, eventually nature called. As quietly as possible, she slid from the bed. While in the telephone booth of a bathroom, she washed her hands and face, then tiptoed barefoot to the front of the cabin.

Kell had left her backpack on the sofa with his, and brought in the food her mother had gathered at his request. He'd done all that, however, after tucking Jamie into bed wearing her undies. It had been too dark—and too late—to do any looking around, so she found her sandals, a pair of khaki knee shorts, a white camisole tank top, and then she found the back door.

Kell's cabin sat in a valley; she assumed in the Guadalupe Mountains since they'd left the Davis range behind. He'd taken a long and winding circuitous route, and when the sun had set, it had made off with her sense of direction.

From the back porch, she could see the sun teasing the tops of the rocky peaks, and she guessed it was between eight and ten. Either way, she was surprised Kell wasn't up and on the phone. She was also surprised at the sense of absolute peace that enveloped her as she braced a shoulder on a rough-hewn beam and leaned, arms crossed, into the railing.

The day would be miserably hot before it was over, but for now, she welcomed the dry warmth, the air that smelled of piñon and raw earth. She didn't pick up wafts of spicy meats cooking, the way she did when walking to and from work and passed the Cantus'. She didn't catch the scents of exhaust and farm animals that were constants in Weldon. She smelled solitude and comfort and calm.

She breathed deeply, realizing, when she finally heard Kell stirring inside, that her blood was stirring, too, in anticipation. And then she smelled coffee and smiled. Life. The only way it could get any better would be for her not to be in danger of losing hers. She didn't want to lose it. Especially not when she'd just found her place and her man.

Oh, that sounded so good. Her man. She knew she was running on adrenaline, endorphins, and those hormones had a lot to do with her state of mind. The state of her heart was another thing. She hadn't stopped thinking about Kell since meeting him.

Yes, he was working her case and that had brought them into contact. But her thoughts weren't about bloodshed and loss. She thought about the way his eyes crinkled at the corners, the way his mouth did the same when he smiled. She thought about his teeth and his tongue, the pressure of his lips against hers.

She thought about his brothers. Brennan. Terry, whose full name was Terrance, he'd told her. She thought about his mother decorating his house, about his father teaching Kell how to cobble together a computer to cut costs—all stories Kell had shared over their reheated soup and sandwiches before they'd returned from Midland to Weldon.

She thought about his mentor, a family friend, being the lead investigator on the murder case, how Kell was now honoring Warren Sheets by continuing his work. He was an honorable man, her Kell. A good man she was going to fight for. Now that she'd had a taste of the real thing, she couldn't see herself settling comfortably into spinsterhood, even with a daily cup of tea with JB, and a calico cat for company.

Behind her, the door onto the railed and covered porch opened, and Kell came out, two cups of coffee in hand. He had on jeans. Worn jeans. Tight jeans. The lower legs bunched at the tops of his boots. His gray athletic T-shirt hung loose. She didn't know if she was happier to see him or the coffee.

"Good morning. Did I wake you?"

He nodded as he sipped.

"I didn't mean to."

"It's quiet out here. I'm going to wake to any noise.

Especially when I realize that it's you making it." He sipped again. "I like you here with me."

"Because you know I'm safe?"

"That, but mostly because I like you."

She felt her heart beating harder, and she turned away to look at the view. Hope was hard for her. She didn't know what to do with it, how to respond without giving too much of herself away. He might like her, but he might not be ready for the things she was feeling.

And really—she needed to find out first how ready she was herself. "How often do you spend time out here?"

"You like it?"

"What's not to like? I can smell more than vomit and antiseptic. I can hear more than crying babies and excuses from insurance companies for not paying claims."

"I thought you enjoyed your job."

She nodded, cradled her cup in both hands and lifted it to her mouth. "I do. But this is the first time in all the years I've worked there that I've taken a break."

Kell moved to stand beside her, leaning a hip against the porch railing. "You're either extremely dedicated or insane. All work and no play makes Jamie a—"

"A woman who's figured out that staying busy is the best way to live in the moment," she said. "Instead of…"

"Instead of dwelling on the past," he finished for her.

Bringing her history to this idyllic place had not been her intent, but the words had slipped out before she could stop them. "Yes. And I'm sorry for bringing it up."

"We're here because of your past. We're together because of your past."

Were they together? Or were they both just here? She

glanced at him, found him studying her intently, his eyes gravely serious over the rim of his cup. She wanted to look away. She didn't want him to see the things she was thinking. She didn't want to let slip words he wasn't ready to hear.

And so she started to turn, to focus on her coffee and the scrub brush and stunted trees struggling to stay alive beyond Kell's clearing. He reached for her drink, took it from her hand, set her cup and his on the table between the two porch rockers behind them. Then he reached for her.

He moved her to face him, his hands on her waist, and lifted her to sit on the railing. She draped her wrists over his shoulders, hooked her heels around his thighs and held on as he came to stand between her spread legs.

His expression was that of a lover, compassionate, involved, present. His words ones she needed desperately to hear. "I can deal with your past, Jamie. It's not going to scare me away."

Did he know she'd thought that it might? "You're a Texas Ranger, Kell. I think not running away from a crime is part of your job description."

He shook his head. "That's not what I'm talking about. And I'm pretty sure you know it."

She did. That was the thing that scared her. "I'm trying not to read anything into anything. I'd rather rely on what I know is real."

"Then let me show you what's real," he said, and lowered his mouth to hers.

He tasted like coffee. Sugar and cream and beans grown on an Indonesian hillside. And he tasted like

Kell, smelled like Kell. She'd come to know his scent and his taste. He was so familiar already. She knew his movements, too, the insistent thrust of his tongue juxtaposed with the tentative request for entry.

She brought him closer with her heels, her hands, her longing. Beneath the cotton of her camisole, her breasts tightened. Beneath her khaki shorts, her sex grew damp. His kiss did this to her. Made her body ache, weep, want. And kissing him back nearly broke her heart. How would she ever in her lifetime get enough of him?

Needing space, time…sanity, she pulled away, dropped her head onto her shoulders and closed her eyes. Kell was quiet; she knew he was watching her, knew he could see the buttons of her nipples pressing into the fabric of her top. She wanted him to see, wanted him to know. Wanted him to want her, to crave the way she did.

Holding her waist with one hand, he skated his knuckles over her breasts, the peaks, the swells, one side then the other. When she grew dizzy, wobbling, her head spinning, her equilibrium lost in lust, he helped her ease down from the railing. But he was too late.

She'd already fallen for him hard. That's why she wondered if she wasn't hearing things when he told her, "Let's get out of our clothes…and go for a swim."

17

THE WATER in the spring-fed pond on Kell's property measured close to seventy-five degrees Fahrenheit year-round, making it possible to go for a cooling swim in the summer, or a dip to warm up during the months when the air and the ground were freezing outside.

Kell had never been in it with a girl. He'd been here with his brothers, with fellow lawmen. Those swims tended to involve a lot of barbecue, beer and betting on the Super-Bowl or the Final Four. He'd never cannonballed into the center and surfaced, sputtering, to find a woman wearing her underwear waiting on the end of the dock.

Especially one who knew how to swim, but didn't like to, who preferred to dangle her feet in the water from above, to watch it lap at the shoreline. Silly woman. At least he'd finally managed to get her to agree to join him.

"Just so we're clear," Jamie said sternly, her hands on her hips as she stared down, grimacing. "We are not having sex in the water. I don't care how clean you say it is."

Until she'd said it, he hadn't even thought about sex... Okay, he'd sorta thought it, but not seriously... Okay, he'd been serious, but pretty sure she'd say no. Which she had. "Just jump."

"I'm not going to break my neck, am I?"

"Not if you jump in feetfirst. Don't dive. Just jump."

"You're sure I won't die?"

"Only if I come up there and strangle you." The woman was nuts. She killed him, and he didn't know how he'd ever get enough. "Now jump!"

She turned around, took several retreating steps, enough to make him nervous that she might actually leave, then stopped, spun and ran, launching off the end of the dock in a flying leap, screaming, then grabbing her nose to pinch it closed before going under the water.

A huge grin on his face, Kell waited for her to come up. She did nearly immediately, shaking her head, her hair flying, water drops splattering all around her. He swam toward her, chuckling, taking on mouthfuls of water he spit out when he stopped.

"Nice jump," he told her, his legs and arms stroking the water, his face aching from his grin.

"Nice water," she told him, moving similarly, though without the same joyful expression. And then she scrunched up her eyes. "Wait a minute. Are those fish I keep feeling?"

"They are. Mexican tetra. Pupfish. They're harmless." He didn't tell her about the tetras belonging to the piranha family.

Treading water, she looked at him, one dark wet brow arched. "I never thought you would be the one to send me to swim with the fishes."

Kell's laugh echoed around them—until Jamie brought her hand down on the water's surface in a splat that sent a huge splash into his face. He caught his breath, held it, flipped ass over end and dived into the clear pool.

He grabbed her feet and tugged her with him, releasing her before she had time to react, then surfacing right behind her. She turned, the wicked gleam in her eye his only warning. She kicked out and launched forward, her hands on his shoulders pushing him down.

They chased each other from one side of the pond to the other, tussling, attacking, choking when laughing and going under with open mouths. Kell couldn't remember the last time he'd played like a kid, or had this much fun with a woman without being in bed. He was pretty sure he never had, and what a crying shame.

Exhausted after an hour of horseplay fueled by coffee and camaraderie, they wordlessly agreed to a ceasefire, floating lazily to catch their breath before heading for the dock. Kell boosted Jamie up first, then followed. Dripping and spent, he collapsed on his back. She sat on the end, legs dangling.

Eyes scrunched against the sun, he eventually forced himself onto his elbows. They needed to get clothes on before Jamie especially got burned. His T-shirt was here somewhere… "Now are you going to tell me why you don't like swimming?"

She afforded him an over-the-shoulder look. "I almost drowned when I was six. I fell into the deep end of a private pool our church had rented for the summer. Parents dropped off their kids for the afternoon, picked them up before dinner."

He sat up the rest of the way. "That was a long time ago. And you are a very good swimmer."

She shrugged, and he wished he could see her face. "I guess all the years after, I only remembered the fright, not the fun."

Still... "But you did have fun. Today."

"No. I was faking. Like I always do." She glanced back again, winked, returned to facing away. Then, with Kell still looking for the humor in what she'd just said, she sighed with her entire body, braced her palms behind her and leaned back. "I think I could live here. I can't believe that you don't. That you live in suburbia instead."

"Hell of a long commute to Midland," was all he said, curious to see where she was taking this. He was still stuck on her faking it.

"Can you imagine raising a family here?"

This was where he came to unwind, to forget what he came up against the rest of the time. Living here would make it hard to do either. Then again, he'd never thought of living here with her. Or of raising a family... "A bit isolated, don't you think?"

"That's what makes it so perfect." She sat forward again, tucked her crossed legs beneath her, looked all around. "You'd have to clear more of the property. Add on to the cabin at some point. Put in a barn and corral for horses. Section off a spot for a vegetable garden."

The horses he could see. The larger cabin, too. He'd want dogs. Five at least. But a garden? "Have you ever tried to grow anything in what passes for soil out here?"

"Raised beds, then. A greenhouse, even. With a separate area for flowers. God, I could spend hours—" And just like that, she cut herself off, reaching up to press her palm to her forehead as if pushing her thoughts back inside.

Was she embarrassed to be caught dreaming? Or was it that she was dreaming about his place, and he assumed by extension, him? Was there more to her dream than a vegetable greenhouse and horses? He thought back to what she'd said…

Ah, a place to start looking for answers. He moved closer, sitting beside her on the end of the dock, his navy board shorts making puddles that spread toward her. "What about the isolation makes it perfect, Jamie?"

She stared down at the water where Kell could see the tiny tetra schooling. "The quiet. The privacy. Swimming in your underwear and not worrying about an audience."

He smiled at that. "I would think quiet and privacy were both abundant in Weldon."

"Not enough that I can swim in my underwear."

"You don't have a pool," he told her, knowing this wasn't about what she wore swimming at all. "What's going on, Jamie? Tell me what you're thinking."

She blew out a puff of breath, closed her eyes, shook her head. "It's so stupid—"

"It's not stupid."

"You haven't heard it yet."

"Only because you haven't said it. I'm waiting. I'm listening—"

"I'm thinking that if I'd lived someplace like this all these years, he wouldn't have found me."

He could tell by the way she'd blurted it that she was tired of holding it in as much as she was embarrassed by entertaining the thought. But they both knew if the suspect was determined, he would've found her even if she'd been hiding in the desert in Tunisia.

What he needed to do now was make her see that it was okay for her to be scared.

"The home you and your mother made in Weldon? Best thing you could have done. Warren worked his ass off looking for a way to circumvent the rules and regs of witness protection, but there was no pending trial, no suspect for you to testify against…"

Kell shook his head, remembering the mornings he'd come into the office to find that his mentor had never gone home. "Well, he tried. And he was glad to see you and Kate safely settled as the Danbys."

"He helped us a lot. With the red tape of changing our names. I know my mother asked his opinion on the places she was considering before she moved us." She paused a moment, picked a splinter of wood from the edge of the dock, tossed it into the pond. "Now I wonder why we bothered."

"You can't mean that."

"Sure I can. We were never safe. Not if he was living nearby and watching. Even if he wasn't, he had no trouble finding us—"

"He had help. If he knew about the hypnosis through a leak, then that same leak would have told him where to find you." Kell's phone calls this morning while the coffee had brewed were as much about locating the information's source as its destination.

"Like I said." She shrugged, got to her feet. "Never safe."

Kell waited several seconds, then stood, too. He didn't want to burst her bubble, but… "You wouldn't have been any safer here."

"I could have seen him coming."

Because of the wide-open spaces? Maybe if the clearing around the cabin and pond was expanded like she'd suggested he do. As it was, getting close to the cabin without being seen would not be that hard. The thought had Kell lifting his head, looking around. He'd taken every possible precaution on the trip—

Son of a bitch. Son of a bitch! He'd told no one but Norm Greenley where he and Jamie would be. That didn't mean it would take a rocket scientist to think to look here. He talked about his property often. His name was on the deed, and a search of tax records would give anyone looking the exact location.

Shit and double shit. If he'd been using the head on his shoulders instead of introducing Jamie to the one in his pants, he would've realized he could put an end to this thing today. All he had to do was get Greenley to let slip the location where he'd stashed Jamie.

Once the information was out in the open, the leak in the Midland office—assuming that's what had happened—would feed the details to the killer. When the bastard showed up, Kell and his army would be waiting.

He reached for her elbow, turned her toward him. "Hey, we need to get you out of the sun before you crisp. And as much fun as I'm having here, I need to check in with my team."

She pulled away, lifted her hand to shade her eyes. "Did you talk to them earlier?"

He nodded, and started walking in reverse, motioning for her to come with him. "While making coffee, yeah."

"And nothing?" she asked, following. "No sign of the car?"

"Not yet," he said. But all that was about to change.

18

ONCE BACK AT THE CABIN, Jamie left Kell to his laptop and phone—both connected to civilization through satellite links—and headed for the shower. It was the size of a stamp in the telephone-booth bathroom. She bumped her elbows on the enclosure's walls when raising her arms to scrub her hair. If Kell ever added onto the cabin, he'd have to do something about this space…

God, why was she even going there? She couldn't believe she'd talked to him as if they were a couple discussing remodeling plans. She'd even talked about raising a family here. She hadn't mentioned the two of them, but he had to know that's what she'd been thinking.

The worst part was, she didn't know why she'd been thinking about kids when she'd decided long ago having a family was not in her future. No, the worst part was that she did.

Kell would make the most wonderful father. She could see him roughhousing and romping and wrestling with sons and daughters, teaching them right from wrong, helping them with their reading, writing and 'rithmetic.

He was just that kind of guy. He made her think of

home and hearth, of family. Her childhood had been fairly all-American, her parents high-school sweethearts, doting and in love. When her father left, it hadn't been about his relationship with her mother falling apart.

No, he hadn't been strong enough to face what Jamie—Stephanie—had been through. He couldn't deal with what she'd seen, what she'd suffered. The one time in her life she'd needed him more than any other, and he'd walked, incapable of finding the internal strength to be her rock. Pathetic. She hadn't seen him since.

She couldn't imagine Kell doing that. Ever. It was there in everything he did. The responsibility he took. The concern he showed. The way he talked about his brothers with such fondness, about his parents with such respect. His intelligence, his sense of humor, she loved it all.

She loved him.

She sank to her haunches, burying her face in her hands. Water pelted her back, stinging. Yes, she'd known him but a handful of days. Tomorrow would be a week. He'd come to her rescue. But this wasn't that. She swore it wasn't that. She was not infatuated with the man who had saved her.

She was in love with the man who'd walked into the clinic, a gun at his hip and a glint in his eye. The man who was everything she wanted in a partner, one she'd thought her circumstances would deny her. Kell had laid her worries to rest, telling her he wasn't scared, he wasn't running away. And he'd said it as a man, not as a Texas Ranger.

It had to be enough for now. And it was, she thought, making herself leave the enclosure before he came looking to see if she'd dissolved down the drain. She was not going to push him, or pry to see what she could get him to divulge of his feelings. At least not until they were beyond this nightmare and could see the light of day.

Once dressed, she headed for the kitchen that was really just an alcove off the main room and part of the dining area. Kell sat at the table there, his jeans again caught up in the tops of his boots, though he now wore a chambray shirt, the sleeves rolled up his forearms, the khaki setting off the color the sun had left on his skin.

When he realized she had stopped to stare, he looked up. And he smiled, with his mouth, with his eyes, with what looked like his heart. "Ready to eat?"

She nodded, swallowed. Her voice had to be here somewhere. "I'll fix something. You've got work."

"There are staples in the cupboard, and the fresh stuff isn't fancy."

She pulled open the refrigerator door to see what her mother had packed them. Ground beef, sandwich meats, hot dogs, chicken breasts. There was bread and buns and condiments. "Burgers okay?"

"Sure. You want me to light a fire in the grill?" He scooted back his chair, but stayed put. "Or there's an iron skillet if you'd rather brown 'em on the stove."

She'd rather he not make her think about cooking for him for the rest of their lives. Not now. Not yet. "You work. I'll cook. It's the nature of things."

He laughed then, a gusty blast of sound that curled her toes. He'd brought this into her life, too. Laughter that was hale and hearty and male, and made her long to jump into his arms and hug him. Instead, she reached for one of the pounds of ground beef wrapped in butcher paper and tossed it onto the countertop. It landed with a thud.

"Anything new on the case?" she asked, squatting to find the iron skillet in the cabinet next to the stove. It was just dusty enough that she cleaned it before setting it on the gas burner to heat. And in the pantry beside the back door, she found a lazy Susan with spices—salt, pepper, garlic and chili powder for an extra kick.

She unrolled the package of meat, seasoned it, formed one larger and one smaller patty, then set them in the skillet to sizzle. Only when she returned to the fridge for lettuce, onion, mayo, mustard and tomato, did she realize Kell hadn't answered. She glanced over to find him staring, his expression caught between a frown and apprehension.

Uh-oh. "Kell?"

"Neither the car nor the suspect have been located, no." He turned his attention back to his laptop screen, but it was too late. There was something he didn't want her to know and she'd seen it there, the worry, the misgiving.

Double uh-oh. "But?"

Groaning his reluctance, he scrubbed his hands over his face before he pushed to his feet and came toward her, decision made. She found herself backing closer to the stove, bumping the skillet with her elbow.

"Watch it," Kell said, finding a spatula and flipping the meat while Jamie looked on.

What wasn't he telling her? "Kell, tell me."

"After lunch. Okay?"

Her stomach lurched, rattled. "Something's happened. What is it?"

"Nothing's happened. Not yet." He reached for a knife and the onion.

Meaning it was going to. And he knew it was going to. What had he done? And what hadn't he told her? She watched as he sliced the onion, dropping the rings into the grease from the burgers to brown.

Why not? What was a heart attack going to hurt when the killer caught up with her? She breathed deeply, searching for calm, finding a gnawing hunger instead. Her stomach growled. That didn't mean she was waiting till after lunch to find out what he was keeping from her.

"Kell? What do you think is going to happen? And when?"

Kell chuckled as he stirred the onions.

"What's so funny?"

"I am. Thinking you wouldn't want answers now. That you wouldn't figure out I had something up my sleeve."

"So? Talk," she said, using his knife to slice up half of the tomato, finding plastic wrap and storing the rest.

"You said something this morning about being able to see the killer coming—"

"He's coming here, isn't he?" The possibility slammed her so hard she almost doubled over. "To finish what he started ten years ago, right? And I'm not safe here at all."

Kell set down the spatula and placed his hands on her shoulders, then slid them up to cup her face "You're safe. One hundred percent safe. But I'm not so sure I am with the way you're gripping that knife."

What was he saying? A knife? God, oh, yes. God. "Sorry." Her hand shaking, she set it down on the counter. "I guess I was thinking I might need a weapon."

"Yeah. Saw that in your eyes." He let her go then, though reluctantly, as if not quite certain she was steady—she saw that in *his* eyes—then served up the burger patties onto paper towels to drain, and shut off the fire beneath.

She didn't care what he said. She wasn't going to wait until after lunch for the rest of the story. "Is he coming here or not, Kell? Tell me that much at least."

"If he does, we'll be ready for him," he told her staunchly.

That wasn't an answer. And what was this "we" business anyhow? "What are you talking about? How are you and I going to be ready when he took out four of my friends in the blink of an eye?"

And then she got it. By we, Kell wasn't talking about the two of them. "Who's going to be ready? Who else knows where we are? Does he know? Did he find out? Is that what you're not telling me?"

Kell had been loading plates with buns and meat and vegetables, and carrying them along with utensils and the squeeze bottles of mayonnaise and mustard to the table all the while Jamie had stood frozen. Now he took her by the hand and led her to eat.

Once they were seated, Kell continued. "This morning on the dock, you said something about being able to see him coming. It had me going back over all the precautions I'd taken in deciding to bring you here."

They'd driven back roads, a route that had taken twice as long as she assumed the trip normally took. Troopers had followed them to make sure no one else did. Even her mother had no idea where they were. But at least Jamie knew her mom was safe. She had her own set of bodyguards.

Jamie imagined Kell's contact person with the DPS knew; they'd have to stay in touch, after all. Or someone at the ranger station might need to know… Her eyes went wide and her whole chest tightened as she met Kell's gaze over the burger he'd lifted to bite.

"The leak," she said. "If there is a leak in your office, if that's how he found me in Weldon, then the killer knows where we are."

Kell shook his head, set down his burger and headed back to the kitchen for a roll of paper towels. Once he returned, he did his best to set her at ease. "Yes and no. Right now, Norm Greenley is the only one who knows where we are, though obviously, anyone with the capability and access can trace the GPS in my phone or the SUV."

This was not good. "Who has the capability and access?"

"For starters, the techs who monitor the various software programs."

Techs. Oh, God. "Like the one who recorded my hypnosis session?"

Kell nodded, bit into his burger again, chewed. "Megan Holly's only been in the office three years. She transferred in from the Georgia Bureau of Investigation. We're not ruling her out, but she's not the most likely suspect."

There was that royal "we" again. Jamie twisted her hands in her lap. "Who is the most likely? And who is 'we'?"

"Me and Greenley are the we. And as far as suspects,

there's a male tech, Hispanic, who's been in the department since 1995. He was born here, but has family in
Mexico. In particular, a half brother who's been in and
out of jail for petty offenses most of his life."

Oh God. "You found that out today?"

Kell nodded. "I phoned Greenley while you were
showering. He took my theory and ran with it. Did a
background check on Vargas when his jacket turned up
the brother's sheet."

Fast work. "So you did what? Put out a warrant or
APB or whatever on the brother?"

"Not exactly," Kell said, filling his mouth with
another huge bite that made talking impossible. As a
delay tactic, it worked.

Frustrated, Jamie figured she might as well put her
own burger together before the beef and sautéed onions
got too cold to enjoy. If she had it in her to enjoy
anything anymore, which she doubted. Still, she had a
feeling she was going to need her strength.

"Then what exactly did you do?" she asked, using the
last of the tomato slices, skipping the lettuce, and going
light on the mayo and onions. Her stomach grumbled.
The food really did smell good.

"Greenley had Vargas track my SUV," he said, completely matter-of-factly.

Jamie took a bite of her burger. She'd known where
this was going since she'd first mentioned the leak. And
once she'd recovered from the initial shock of fearing
the killer was coming, she'd braced herself for the
worst—that he was.

Of course, it had never occurred to her that Kell

would send him an engraved invitation, which seemed to be what he and Greenley had done. She tried not to sigh. Or scream. "Since the troopers followed us here, wouldn't Greenley's request raise a red flag? I mean, why would Greenley need the location of your SUV from Vargas when he knows where it is?"

"Vargas has no idea about the troopers. No reason he would, unless they told him. Since they're not based in Midland and most likely don't know him, there wouldn't be, so no red flag." Kell pushed away from the table and returned to the kitchen again, this time for two cans of soda.

"That still doesn't explain why Greenley would want your location when he knows exactly where you are," she said as Kell sat and scooted his chair back into place. She reached for her soda and popped the top, knowing she should trust him to do his job. But this was her life. She needed more than a pat on the head. "I can't see how his request wouldn't set off warning bells for Vargas, if he's really the leak."

His burger on his plate, his wrists against the table's edge, Kell leaned forward, his gaze catching hers and holding it tight. "What he's told Vargas is to watch for movement. We have no reason to go anywhere. So if the killer shows up and demands we drive to a more remote location, say, some out-of-the-way place like the spot he took Kass Duren, Vargas will be watching and know something's wrong."

And ostensibly report back to Greenley…or if he wanted to give his brother time to make his escape, maybe not. "What if the killer shows up and just shoots us in the head? Leaves the SUV where it is? Or makes us drive his car?"

"It's a ploy, sweetheart," Kell told her. "That's all. To make sure Vargas gives us up to his brother."

Okay, she was definitely not cut out for this cat-and-mouse stuff. "He won't know that?"

"No reason he should. He'll just think he's doing his job, following Greenley's orders. As long as he's been in the department, he'll understand Greenley's hedging against every move the suspect might make, no matter how far a reach."

It sounded reasonable, she supposed. Except… "You don't know for sure his brother is the killer. Or that Vargas is the leak."

"True," Kell said, sitting back. "That's why Greenley's going to surreptitiously see that word gets out. The fact that I have a cabin in the Guadalupes is common knowledge around the office. If Vargas isn't the leak, the information on our location will hopefully get back to whoever is."

"If there is a leak. If the killer hasn't just been watching me all this time."

He nodded, finishing off his food.

Jamie could only stare at hers. "Either way, we'll never know he's coming. No matter what I said about being able to see if he was."

"That's okay," Kell told her, the smile on his face deliciously, deviously wicked. "Because we're no longer the only ones watching. Greenley and his boys have got our back. There's no way anyone is getting to us without first going through them."

19

WITHOUT LOOKING at a clock, Kell knew it was after midnight. He also knew Jamie was pretending to sleep. The cabin only had one bed, meaning they shared it, or he slept on the couch. Since she hadn't made the suggestion when he'd joined her, he figured she'd come to terms with his plan. A good thing, since he needed her on board.

He never should have told her he'd set up the two of them as bait. Yes, she deserved to know, but it made this whole…thing—was it a relationship?—between them harder to deal with because he'd done it without telling her first.

Overhead, the cane ceiling fan stirred the air, squeaking in a maddening rhythm while drawing the heat from Kell's body. He needed a can of WD-40. He needed a second bedroom, or a longer, more comfortable sofa. He needed a way out of this mess that was guaranteed to save Jamie's life.

He'd done what his experience as a Texas Ranger dictated he do. If it had been anyone but Jamie, he wouldn't be caught up in this circle of second-guessing; every time he told himself he'd done the right thing, he came right back to feeling he'd done wrong by Jamie.

And those feelings were all tangled up with the ones he had for her. The ones making failure impossible. Sleep, too.

"I'm awake, you know."

He closed his eyes, swallowed, opened them again. "I know."

"You can talk to me if you have something on your mind," she said softly.

"I know." He left it at that, mostly because he didn't know what to say. He wasn't going to apologize for doing what he'd done. And if his job cost him her love…

Wow. Yeah. Best he leave it at that.

Jamie sighed, rolling onto her back. "I'm not mad at you."

Anger he could handle. Anger could be worked through. It was hatred he didn't want. Hatred meant she felt strongly, just not the things he wanted her to feel. "You've got to know, I would never put you in more danger. If I thought for a minute that he could get through us to you…"

"I want to be as confident as you are that he can't. That he won't." She pulled the sheet to her chin and held it there. "I'm just not that brave."

Not that brave? Kell found himself frowning, and turned onto his side, keeping the distance he was waiting for her to close. "This guy wasted no time in coming to you after the hypnosis and Duren's body was ID'd. If this goes down, it's going to happen fast. I've got men on every road, footpath, hiking and biking trail that lead to the cabin. He's not going to get to you. It's not going to happen."

"You're assuming he'll use a path or a road or a trail," Jamie countered. "He could be walking in as the crow flies even as we speak."

He could be, but Kell's men had more eyes and ears than their own. They had surveillance equipment. Heat sensors. Motion detectors. Parabolic mics. To avoid apprehension, the killer would have to slip in on a shadow, or like smoke. "He's not going to get to you."

She reached out with one hand and stroked it down the center of his chest. "The good guys don't always win, Kell."

"I will not let him get to you," he told her again, wondering for a moment which of them he was reassuring. He squeezed her fingers, held them over his fast-beating heart.

"I know you'll do your best—"

"No, sweetheart." He was not going to let her lie down and give up. Not after ten years spent in hiding. Not after he'd just found her. "Getting to you is going to require going through me. And I've got a really big gun."

She laughed softly. "That does make me feel better. Even if we're not talking about the same weapon."

His breath caught, his cock thickened. "It's all yours. Anytime, anywhere."

Her nails scratched lightly over his skin. "As long as it's not in my driveway, you mean."

"Next time we're there," he said and sucked back a sharp breath at her touch. "I promise."

"Promise me there will be a next time?" Her fingers were moving now, searching, surrounding. "That we'll get out of here in one piece?"

He would die making sure it happened. But rather than put the emotion overwhelming him into words that would sound too simple, he brought her face close and kissed her, speaking to her in the only way that felt right.

He knew about love. He'd grown up in a home where there was never a question that his parents would make up after fighting. Where actions spoke louder than words, but where the words themselves were never in short supply, and were used wisely, appropriately, used to solve as well as to soothe. Yeah, he knew about love.

He didn't know about this, about Jamie, precious, a gift, making his heart swell, ache, crave, making his body hard, splintering his focus. She was his case, but she was so much more, and he opened his mouth over hers and asked her to be his everything.

Her lips parted, her tongue tasted his. She wedged her body so far beneath him that his only move was to cover her. He did, and she opened her legs, hooking her heels in the small of his back, pressing her hands to his spine. She was supple, pliant, warm like wax, melting into him.

He needed a condom, but he didn't want to turn away. His erection lay pressed between them, pulsing. His mouth hadn't tasted enough of her yet, and he wanted this mating to last until they were both too exhausted to move. If might very well be their last time—a thought he pushed away before it caused him to suffer and soften.

Her fingers massaging up and down his back, Jamie tilted her hips, seeking him. He groaned, freeing himself long enough to hang over the edge of the bed and dig his wallet from the jeans he'd kicked out of last night.

Once he was sheathed, he entered her, no foreplay, no seduction, no romance.

Her sigh as she sank into the mattress was of satisfaction, of a gratitude that humbled him, of love. He had given her something she wanted, a something he was quite certain touched her in places his cock never would, though not for his lack of trying.

He rocked against her, not thrusting, not stroking, but a simple rhythmic motion of his lower body that kept them pressed together from belly to breast, as did his arms scooped beneath her. His head he rested beside hers on her pillow, sharing the air that she breathed.

Neither one of them said a word, they loved gently, slowly, though sounds of pleasure—gasps, moans, whimpers—were impossible to hold back, and punctuated the whir of the cane fan above.

And when neither of them could deny their bodies, they came together, the completion ripping into the core of his soul.

WHEN JAMIE FINALLY WOKE on her first day as killer bait, it was almost noon. Consumed by exhaustion, she'd never even heard Kell get out of bed, or smelled the scent of coffee that still lingered in the air. Neither had she heard him in the main room, walking in the kitchen, talking on his phone, though she was quite certain he had.

She pushed up to her elbows and listened. Then she sat up in the center of the bed. Still not a sound, prompting her to pull on the clothes she'd worn yesterday and left on the floor beside the bed. She'd shower after the mystery was solved. And, middle of nowhere or not, she had no idea whose eyes were prying. She was not going to walk outside in her skin.

Standing in the center of the front porch and shading her eyes, she found Kell sitting sideways in the driver's seat of his SUV, the door opened, his cell phone pressed to his ear. She didn't want to disturb him, but was curious what conversation had sent him outside to talk. They were too deeply involved in this game of catch a killer for secrets.

He saw her movements peripherally, turned toward her and gestured for her to come near. He smiled as he did it, and she relaxed. He didn't tell her to wait. He didn't hurriedly end the call. He welcomed her, and she was glad, even though what she heard told her nothing. He was responding in brief affirmatives, shaking his head as if it made a difference to the person on the other end of the sound waves. That made her smile, and he held out a hand, pulling her to stand between his thighs.

She leaned back against his chest with his arm around her, staring into the distance, wondering where the members of his team were posted, wondering if the killer was on his way. He kept her there until he'd finished, not even a minute, then he turned her and kissed her until she had to pull away to breathe.

"I've been waiting since dawn to do that."

"I seem to remember you doing the same thing not long before. Did you sleep at all?"

"I never sleep when a case is coming down to the wire. I've got too much going on in my mind. It's insomnia's fertile ground."

She wondered if their involvement made his insomnia worse. "Anything new since last night?"

A single nod. "Everyone's in place. Now we wait."

That would have to do. "And you're making your phone calls out here why?"

"Because that's what a prince does for his Sleeping Beauty," he told her, reaching up to tuck her hair behind her ear.

He made her want to laugh. He made her want to cry. He made her want to have his babies…and that was her clue to stop with the wanting. "And what is the prince planning to do about feeding me?"

He canted his head to the side and considered her. "How 'bout a picnic and a swim?"

"Should I paint a target on my back with ketchup?" she asked, considering him in return.

He gave her a look, then hopped down and closed up his SUV. Hooking his arm around her neck, he led her back to the cabin, saying, "I don't want to make you a target. I do want you to relax. That's all."

"In that case, I accept." She'd never had a man pamper her, and as much as she was enjoying Kell doing so, she reminded herself that this was nothing but a detour before she reached the city limits of Singletown where she'd be living the rest of her life. "You want me to do sandwiches?"

"Nope. I want you to change and go." He dropped a kiss on her forehead, then sent her on her way with a slap on her ass. "I'll meet you at the pond in a few."

It was a caveman gesture, and it had her smiling as she found her still-damp underwear and worked them on, then left through the back door, slapping him on his ass as she did. She fairly skipped down the dock to the pond, kicking off her sneakers and leaping into the water.

She surfaced, sputtering, the fright forgotten, the fun all she knew. Kell had done this for her, too. Given her back the parts of her life she'd hidden, out of sight, out of mind. For so long she'd felt she didn't deserve to know joy. That she needed to suffer for the families of the victims. Now she wanted to be happy, and she wanted Kell, forever.

"Stop it. Right now," she ordered herself. She could not keep doing this. Whatever happened, happened. And nothing was going to happen until she knew that for both of them, this relationship was built on more than her case.

"Hey you! Come and get it."

At the sound of Kell's voice, she turned where she was treading water, and swam back to the dock. When she got there, he was waiting, the box of food he'd carried down to the pond sitting next to her shoes. She took his hand when he offered it, tumbling against him when he tugged.

His bare chest was warm, his heart thumping, but her stomach won out. She pushed away and went for the sandwiches he'd stacked in the box between folded paper towels. He'd forgotten to bring drinks, but he had brought a knife—the one she'd gripped so hard in the kitchen yesterday.

She held it up for him to see. "Are you trying to tell me something?"

"Just thought it might make you feel better," he said, grabbing a sandwich and biting a quarter of it away.

She glanced down at the front of his board shorts, unable to help herself. "Because your gun's all out of ammo?"

"If it is, it's all your fault," he said, still chewing.

"I will gladly take the blame. As long as you trot yourself back to the cabin for drinks."

He mock frowned. "Trot? Is that princess for 'please'?"

Really, he was too cute for his own good. Or for hers. "Will you please get the drinks? And sunscreen?"

"As you wish," he said with a wink. "Just watch where you wave that thing. It's called a weapon for a reason."

She dropped to sit on the dock and watched him go, picnicking with herself while she waited for him to return. Oh, but she really could get used to this.

Yes, Weldon was small and quiet, but this…this was peaceful, serene. As if here time meant nothing—a thought that brought a second that was related.

Kell had been gone way too long.

She turned to look at the cabin, saw…nothing. Her sandwich-filled stomach tensed. He could've taken a phone call, but wouldn't he have walked down to the dock while doing so? He should've been back with their drinks by now.

Maybe she was borrowing trouble, overreacting, being plain ridiculous, but she could think of only one reason he wasn't. She got to her feet, slipped on and tied her shoes.

And then she picked up the knife.

20

REMINDING HIMSELF TO GRAB his phone that he'd forgotten to bring with the picnic, Kell frowned into the fridge, trying to remember what it was he wanted. Drinks, right. And, yeah. No matter what he'd told Jamie about his adrenaline-fueled insomnia, he needed sleep.

His sharp edge was dulled, his straight thinking meandering. How else could he explain staring at the cans of cold soda this long? As if they were going to jump into his hands. And now he was hearing things. He really he had to shake off this daze—

Whack!

The refrigerator door slammed him sideways. He stumbled, grabbed the counter for balance, bit off a succinct "What the hell?" and looked up.

Then he bit his tongue and watched the Hispanic man standing there use the hand with the snake tattoo to shut the fridge. His other hand held a gun. Kell did not like being on this end of it.

"The girl," the man—he was gangly, edgy, no more than five foot seven—said in accented English. "Down at the water. Get her to come here. Now."

Think, think, think. Kell remained silent, his sluggish

mind racing, his blood firing in his veins. The man knew where Jamie was, that she was there alone, yet had come after Kell instead. He obviously wanted Kell out of the way before taking care of Jamie. Otherwise, why not shoot her, dump her body in the water and go?

He didn't plan to go. He didn't want a quick kill. That was the only conclusion Kell could come to for the delay. And then he came to another, equally horrifying. Soon enough, this man would figure out that Jamie would eventually return to the cabin on her own. He did not need Kell to get her here. He didn't need Kell for anything.

That meant Kell had to find a reason to become indispensable before the man with the snake tattoo dispensed with him.

"She won't be able to hear me if I yell." It was a lie, of course. With only the whistling wind for noise, Jamie would hear him just fine.

But there was a glassiness to the other man's eyes that made Kell go for it, a stall tactic while he tried to figure out how his team had let this one through. Something was off, wrong. Something big. "And if I'm not back in another minute, she knows to run."

The Hispanic man's gaze sharpened, his thick black brows coming down in a vee. "There is no place for her to go. No one to help her."

Kell weighed how much of the truth to reveal. "I have a man—"

"You had a man. He is not there now."

He'd taken out one of the team. Goddammit. Kell didn't have time to wonder who, what had happened, how serious it was. He only had time for Jamie. "I have more. And once they realize one of their own has gone silent, they'll be coming here to get you."

"Then I will kill the girl, and you will be my hostage." The man raised his gun hand, wiping his sleeve beneath his nose. "Then when I am safely away, I will kill you."

A plan that would keep Kell alive for the moment. Now to work on keeping Jamie the same. He kept his hands where the other man could see them and took him in, the ragged athletic shoes, the worn jeans, dirty with torn hems, the long-sleeved plaid shirt that said hand-me-down charity. The glassy eyes, the runny nose…

"What were you after? At the Sonora Nites Diner? Money to fund your habit?"

He rolled his head on his shoulders, looked around the kitchen, came back on Kell with a wave of the gun. "The girl. Make her come here. Before she runs."

Kell started to tell him to go ahead, pull the trigger, but he wasn't certain that if Jamie heard the gunshot, she wouldn't run toward it instead of away. And with Kell down—or dead—he wouldn't be able to fulfill his promise to Dr. Kate that he'd bring her daughter home. Hell, he'd promised Jamie just last night that they'd get out of here in one piece.

In his line of work, he shouldn't be making promises. *C'mon, Kell, focus, think, focus.* His gun was in the bedroom, his phone on the table, but Jamie had a knife… "I'll have to walk to the dock, wave her up from there."

He was getting nervous, the tattooed man. He couldn't kill Kell and go after Jamie alone; he'd have no hostage should he get caught. And now that he'd revealed himself, he couldn't get to Jamie without going through Kell, and whatever he was on had him just paranoid enough not to go along with Kell's suggestion.

Kell was looking for his next move when he saw a shadow cross the wall behind the killer. He hadn't heard tires on the crushed-shell driveway or the rumble of an engine approaching—meaning the body creeping closer had to be Jamie's.

He kept his gaze trained on the man who held the gun, fought the rising fear that sent his heart to his throat to choke him, wished he had a better weapon than the only thing he'd seen within reach—the iron skillet he'd left on the stove top last night after washing it.

He backed a step closer to the door, closer to the skillet, too, praying that Jamie could hear him and that the killer couldn't hear her. "Is that what you want to do then? Have me wave her up from the dock? I can't say she won't run if she sees you've got a gun. Or sees that you're here, for that matter. Best bet is to let me walk down there alone. You'll still be able to see me, but she won't see you."

He was rambling now, but he wanted Jamie to come near enough without giving herself away, and leave him the knife on the table. That's what he assumed she intended to do, so when she rounded the corner with her arms over her head, all he could do was yell, "No!"

The killer turned. Jamie slammed the rock she held into the side of his skull, sending him spinning. Kell whipped the skillet off the stove and caught the man's flailing gun hand. The weapon skittered toward the back door. He stopped it with his foot, grabbed it up and straddled the man who was on the floor, holding his head in his hands.

"The bedroom. My service weapon," he said without looking at Jamie. She ran off, was back in seconds, still in her underwear and dripping pond water all over the floor. He reached over and released the safety. "Keep it pointed at his head. Shoot him if he moves."

Kell kept one eye on the man while scrounging through the kitchen's supply closet for something…rope, twine, a bungee cord, fishing line… Yes! Duct tape!

Yanking a strip from the roll, he nudged Jamie out of the way and bent at the man's feet to bind them. Next, he pulled his arms behind his back and did the same with his wrists. After that, he took the gun from Jamie and set the two safetied weapons on the table along with the roll of tape.

Finally, he braced his hands on his knees and leaned over to catch his breath. He was halfway through his recovery when he noticed her feet. "Where are your shoes?"

She curled the toes of one foot over those of the other. "Outside the bedroom window."

The window. Of course. He hadn't stopped long enough to think about how she'd gotten in. He straightened, his chest still tight and aching. "I leave you a knife and you come armed with a rock?"

Just as breathless as he was, she looked over her shoulder toward the bedroom, then looked back at him. "I brought the knife. I left it on the windowsill. I figured I stood a better chance against a rock if he turned it on me."

Smart cookie. But just for the record…and because

he wouldn't be able to live with himself if he lost her
while she was trying to save him… "Promise me you'll
never do anything like that again."

"The way it looks, I won't have to," she said softly,
her voice breaking at the end.

He followed the direction of her gaze; when he
looked back, he found her shaking, crying, on the verge
of collapse. Cursing himself for a jerk, he grabbed her
against him so fast he knocked away what breath he'd
managed to catch. He didn't care, not about anything but
taking care of her.

It was over. The terror of her last ten years. No, he
didn't have the answers to explain what had happened
today, or what had happened at the Sonora Nites Diner.
Not yet. But he would have them soon. All of them. That
was his job.

Jamie, she was his life. "No, sweetheart. You won't
have to. Not ever again."

"I LOVE YOU, SWEETIE. And I am so happy to be waking
up from this nightmare. I'll see you when you get here."

"I love you, too, Mom. And so am I. Bye-bye." Jamie
ended the call with her mother, then handed the phone
back to Kell who sat beside her on the top of the cabin's
front steps.

"I'll bet Kate's relieved," he said. He had already
made all the calls he needed to hours ago, checking in
with his team, seeing to the officer who'd been shot,
calling for whoever it was that would take the killer away.

Jamie had waited for all of that to be done before
phoning her mother. She'd wanted to be able to deliver

the good news that the ordeal was now behind them, the killer off the street and out of their lives.

"Yes. Very." Jamie nodded, strangely nervous. She'd finished with her mother, and the members of law enforcement who'd been here were gone.

It was just them now. Her and her Texas Ranger. The two of them alone, safe, the baggage of the last ten years lighter, and less of a stumbling block between them. She was still having trouble breathing, however, not to mention believing the events of the previous eight hours.

Once the suspect had been contained and she'd recovered her composure, dried her skin and her tears, and changed out of her wet clothes, Kell had left her holding his gun long enough to retrieve rope from his SUV's toolbox and reinforce the job he'd done with the duct tape.

Then he'd taken her out to the front porch while he'd contacted Greenley and the rest. She'd been out here ever since, sitting on the steps, or in one of the porch rockers, or for a while on the porch itself. She hadn't gone back into the cabin except once to use the restroom. She'd watched the comings and goings of the authorities from whichever vantage point kept her out of their way.

While she and Kell had waited for them to arrive— a long wait considering his cabin's location—Kell had made more sandwiches, leaving the ones on the dock for the birds who'd discovered the feast not long after Jamie had abandoned it, swimming to the other side of the pond and trekking the long way through the brush to the cabin in search of Kell.

It was when she'd reached the open bedroom window

that she'd decided she didn't trust herself with the knife she'd brought with her. She was scared, feared she'd be too physically shaken to hold on and would lose it in a fight. She'd seen the rock, and been much less intimidated by the thought of using it as a weapon.

She'd hoped she wouldn't need a weapon at all. She'd hoped she'd find Kell had fallen and twisted his ankle, or for some reason was sick on the bathroom floor. What she'd found had been worse than any of her imaginings—the man who had killed her friends, threatening to take her lover's life.

She shuddered now, reminding herself that she'd gotten through that horrible moment—and those that followed—just as she had through the last ten years, though this time she'd had more of a reason to do so, one more valuable than staying alive. She'd had to make sure Kell survived, that he did not sacrifice his life for hers.

Sitting beside her, his forearms on his knees, Kell clutched the phone with both hands, squinting as he stared into the distance, his mouth grim. Jamie loved the crow's feet that stepped from his eyes to his temples.

She did not like the tense set of his jaw, and laid a hand on his thigh to tell him. "It's the end of a case, not the end of the world. You'll get more chances to wear your white hat and be a hero."

He dropped his head forward, a grin teasing at his lips. "After these last few days, I'm pretty much considering taking early retirement."

She knew he was kidding, but she liked a lot the idea of him never again facing the wrong end of a gun. She also liked seeing him smile. It helped with the scary part of not knowing what came next. "And let the bad guys win? I don't think so."

"There are plenty of candidates itching for this job. The bad guys don't stand a chance." He reached for her hand, laced their fingers, squeezed. "But then sometimes the good guys don't either."

"Oh, Kell," she said, pulling free to wrap her arms around him, to pillow her head on his shoulder and hold him close, staring out over his property at the safe world beyond. And it was safe now. She just knew it. "I'm so sorry about your man. But he should be okay, yes?"

"Yeah, as long as he comes through surgery. It's something we all face. That possibility, taking a bullet." He patted her arm where it lay across his chest, tilted his head to rest against hers. "But thank you. For understanding. For being here."

She loved him. "Where else would I be?"

"Yeah. About that." He sighed, made as if to move away, to stand, but only got as far as pulling his feet to the step beneath the one where they sat, remaining in the circle of her arms. "I guess we'd better pack up and get you back to Weldon. Before it gets any later."

She took a deep breath. Here went nothing. Unless it was everything. And if she didn't go for it, she would never know. "Or we could not pack."

He looked over, his expression broadcasting his confusion. "You don't want to pack?"

"I don't want to go back to Weldon." She let her arms fall away from him, and knitted her hands in her lap. Never before had she felt such a need to be brave. "Not yet."

"You want to stay here?" he asked after a short, cautious pause.

She nodded, treading carefully, too. "I'm thinking, it's been ten years. I deserve a true vacation. It would be my first."

Another pause. "And you want to take it here?"

"I do." Deep breath, deep breath. "But it would be nice not to take it alone."

"Me?" It was all he asked, his voice soft, his tone wary as if he were walking a razor's edge of hope.

Hope she could give him. "Of course you. Who else?"

"I don't know." He stretched, but the tension remained, radiating toward her. "I thought maybe your mother."

Now, *that* was funny. "I love my mother. I would never have gotten through the last ten years without her. But I've seen her every day of them. And if I were to take a vacation with her, it would be a cruise, or to a spa. She and I and isolation wouldn't mix."

"But you like being isolated with me."

"I love being isolated with you. And before you run away scared because I used the L word—"

He turned toward her, his eyes flashing, hot and proud and suddenly supremely confident. "Use it again."

Gulp. "What?"

"Use it again," he demanded, pressing, intense. Potent as he growled. "Or else I'm going to."

Oh my. Oh my. This was real. She could barely find her voice. "Then you go first."

"I love you, Jamie," he said, cupping her nape and threading his fingers through her hair. "I know it's been less than a week. I know this has been a wild trial by fire. But I would love you if I'd brought my kid into your clinic for an appointment and met you there."

"You have a kid?" she asked, a question as crazy as what was happening here.

"Not yet. That would be getting ahead of ourselves, don't you think?" he asked, one wicked brow rising. "Unless I'm reading you wrong."

She shook her head, shook it again, kept shaking it until the words and the tears shook free, and her hair began to tumble. "You're not. I love you Kell. It's been fast and furious. A whirlwind. But it would've been just the same if we hadn't spent our first week together catching a killer."

"It'll be the only week we spend doing anything like that," he promised, hefting her up to straddle his thighs.

She looped her arms around his neck, her vision blurred, her heart a swollen mess of emotions. "So we can stay here for a while?"

"What about your job?" he asked.

As if she cared. The only thing she cared about was this. Him. Her Texas Ranger. Her Kell. "Six years of accrued vacation, remember? And then I may just take leave. Or quit."

Half-moon dimples appeared beneath the scruff covering his face. "All these life changes. Maybe you'd also consider moving? Somewhere not too far from your mother?"

"My mother would have no trouble sending me packing if she knew I was happy."

This time his gaze softened, grew dreamy, and just a little bit damp. "Are you happy, Jamie?"

"Exquisitely," she told him before he brought her mouth to his and kissed her with all he had. How could she be anything but in the arms of her one good man?

MILLS & BOON

Blaze

On sale 19th March 2010

(2-IN-1 ANTHOLOGY)
OUT OF CONTROL & HOT UNDER PRESSURE
by Julie Miller & Kathleen O'Reilly

Out of Control

Gorgeous detective Jack is going undercover as a racing driver to reveal a drug trafficking operation. But can he keep his hands off feisty girl mechanic Alex?

Hot Under Pressure

Ashley's delayed flight turns into a molten-hot seduction when she encounters tall, dark business titan David. Yet can their passion survive a long-distance affair?

THE RIGHT STUFF
by Lori Wilde

Glam heiress Taylor is researching her new business project and she needs the help of her ex, red-hot Air Force doctor Daniel. Will their reunion reignite their former spark?

OVERNIGHT SENSATION
by Karen Foley

Actress Ivy has just earned a big role in a movie based on the life of war hero Garrett. Will getting between Garrett's sheets help Ivy get into the part?

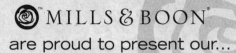

You're invited to three,
beautiful royal weddings!

REBECCA WINTERS
MEREDITH WEBBER
MELISSA JAMES

Royal
ENGAGEMENTS

A Royal Bride of Convenience
by Rebecca Winters

Expecting the Cascaverado Prince's Baby
by Meredith Webber

Too Ordinary for the Duke?
by Melissa James

Available 19th March 2010

M&B

millsandboon.co.uk Community

Join Us!

The Community is the perfect place to meet and chat to kindred spirits who love books and reading as much as you do, but it's also the place to:

- **Get the inside scoop from authors about their latest books**
- **Learn how to write a romance book with advice from our editors**
- **Help us to continue publishing the best in women's fiction**
- **Share your thoughts on the books we publish**
- **Befriend other users**

Forums: Interact with each other as well as authors, editors and a whole host of other users worldwide.

Blogs: Every registered community member has their own blog to tell the world what they're up to and what's on their mind.

Book Challenge: We're aiming to read 5,000 books and have joined forces with The Reading Agency in our inaugural Book Challenge.

Profile Page: Showcase yourself and keep a record of your recent community activity.

Social Networking: We've added buttons at the end of every post to share via digg, Facebook, Google, Yahoo, technorati and de.licio.us.

www.millsandboon.co.uk